A LUMINESCENT DAWN

THE IRIDESCENT SERIES

—

BOOK THREE

BRIANNE WIK

Copyright

This is a work of fiction. All of the characters, organizations, and events portrayed in this novel are either products of the author's imagination or are used fictitiously.

A LUMINESCENT DAWN
Book Three of The Iridescent Series

Copyright © 2022 by Brianne Wik.

All rights reserved.

ISBN: 978-1-955430-04-3 (Ebook)
ISBN: 978-1-955430-05-0 (Paperback)

Editor: Cassidy Clarke - www.cassidyclarkewriting.com
Cover Design: Art by Karri - www.artbykarri.com

To be kept up to date about new releases, please visit BrianneWik.com and sign up for her newsletter.

First Edition: August 2022

Printed in the United States of America

AUTHOR'S NOTE

This book contains descriptions of trauma including, mind manipulation, torture and PTSD. Recommended for ages 16+.

For all the dreamers still waiting on their wings.

CHAPTER 1

Evelyn

A monster slept in my bed.

Deep, steady breathing a mere arms-length away from my face made my insides roil in horror. Apep's cold and brittle hand held mine with an ease that I couldn't match. Wherever our skin touched, mine recoiled.

It was meant as a courtesy, since my touch alone shielded him from his curse. He insisted that he wanted these night hours to be restful and restorative for me, but all I could think about was ripping my hand away and running as fast as I could until I left him and this castle and everything else behind.

Unfortunately, that train of thinking ultimately led me to picture Ryker's curled-up shivering form on that cold, dirty dungeon floor.

Sleep refused to come to me in any sort of fashion. Fitful, restful, it didn't matter; my mind was having none of it. Instead it churned with worry as I stared at the blue-and-gold damask canopy above my head, tracing the gilded patterns with my eyes.

I'd been in this position before, staring aimlessly above me, wishing for sleep and getting none at all.

One warm tear slid silently down my cheek.

Feeling helpless wasn't a new sensation for me, but it was so much worse knowing my helplessness was putting someone else at risk. Someone I cared deeply for. Someone who, if I were more clever, brave, or strong, I might even be able to save. But instead, I lay here wide awake, mind wandering to horrible places, staring up at an unfamiliar view with a betraying hand clutching my unwilling one.

I couldn't remember a time when I'd felt more hopeless than this.

Apep stirred, and I held my breath, waiting for his breathing to level back out again.

"You should be sleeping." Apep's stringent voice was muddied with sleep.

I could respond. I could play the part of the perfect little doting sister he wished I was, but I couldn't bring myself to do it. So I lay there quietly, pretending not to hear him…a small rebellion of sorts, I supposed.

"You know I could help you sleep." He probably thought that was a kind offer, but I only heard a threat.

A quiet half snort blew abruptly through my nose. "I'll never give you access to my mind again."

"If you don't sleep, you won't be able to—"

"What? Shield you from your curse?" I finished for him.

His tone lowered, and even though I couldn't make out his facial expressions in the dark, I suspected his face had pulled into a displeased frown. "I was going to say that you wouldn't be able to visit Ryker." After a long gulf of silence, he continued. "Though, it is fair to remind you that I stay here to give you a reprieve from shielding me. It's important you get true rest to keep up your strength."

His words were spoken like the tender rebuke of a doting father, or in this case, a brother of sorts. But they did not ease my burden like he'd intended—instead, my mind churned with incessant worry and unease.

His hand gently squeezed around my own, and my lungs tightened with dread as I refused to return the gesture. Instead I purposely left it lying there, a lifeless and unwilling partner.

He claimed the reason he stayed here, holding my hand at night, was so that I could shield him without calling on my magic. Because if I wavered in the night, it would allow his curse to take control once more. He would have to rescue Ryker from the dungeon, and he wouldn't be able to continue with his nefarious coup.

But I knew the truth: he remained with me here at night to make sure I stayed in line. He stayed here to remind me that Ryker's life was determined by my actions, and should I falter, he would kill him. He stayed here in order to better control me.

No matter what spin he put on it, that was the undeniable truth.

I pulled my silence around me like a blanket, breathing shallow, quiet breaths so that I barely made a noise at all. I refused to give him the satisfaction of a response or acknowledgement of any kind. What he was doing to me was not a courtesy or a kindness. It was a method of control and dominance.

My eyes traced a fresh damask pattern, attempting to distract my mind from my swirling thoughts.

It had only been a few days since everything had happened, and each day I still greatly struggled to maintain my shield on Apep's constantly moving body. Every time he was far from me, my magic tightened and strained to stay around him. Every movement he made stretched my magic in uncomfortable ways that felt foreign and awkward. Every night I fell into bed, my entire body exhausted, but always far too wired to truly sleep.

And I was already so tired…

He sighed. "I know you're angry with me, Evelyn, but can you not see things from my side?"

I scoffed. "No, I cannot."

"I'm not the enemy, Evelyn. Our people have had enough heartache and condemnation from the humans who imagine themselves our betters. We were once a proud and powerful kingdom, ruled by two of the most powerful fairies known to—"

"I've heard the fairy tales," I interrupted. "I'm not in the mood for a story."

He sucked in an exasperated breath. "They're not just tales, young Evelyn. They're your people's history, passed down through generations."

"And so that excuses your behavior? Your betrayal? Because history didn't last as long as you would have liked?"

Apep shot himself up and out of bed, gripping my hand firmly, as he towered over me. I swallowed thickly staring up into the murky image of Apep's pale face. His features were seething with hostility.

"You want so badly for me to be the villain of this story." His sharp consonants cut through the air. "I am the one who's *saving* you."

The scent of ancient frankincense wafted toward me, making my eyes water. "You asked if I could see your side in all of this, but can you not see mine?"

He stayed there, completely motionless, hovering above me. The grip on my hand was the only indication that his anger remained. "You have lived among the humans too long." His hold loosened, and with his other hand he gently pushed a strand of hair out of my face, trailing his spindly finger down my cheek. "If I have to kill every last human who ever tricked you into loving them in order to make you accept the other half of who you are, then so be it."

I froze, my blood thickening heavily in my veins. I couldn't breathe, couldn't move, couldn't think beyond those horrifying words.

Apep's eyes didn't blink or dart away. There was no hesitation in his withering gaze as he held my own.

Fear washed through me like a raging flood, leaving me panting for breath that wouldn't reach my lungs.

He eased himself back down onto the mattress, facing me and sighing heavily before speaking again. "Let those words linger in your mind for the rest of your sleepless night, but tomorrow morning, be sure to gain fresh energy from Nature. I have plans that take us outside of the palace, and I can't have you fainting due to overexertion."

Rolling his head away from me, he clutched at my hand rigidly until sleep eventually pulled him back under, loosening his grasp.

My heart attempted to beat its way out of my chest, but my tears suddenly felt dried up. My mind raced through every face, every person I knew and loved, and the fear inside me grew steadily. My stomach clenched and convulsed as a thin sheen of sweat dotted my brow. That threat was the furthest thing from idle; he would follow through with it if I faltered.

He knew my mind now. He knew how much I loved, how protective I was. He knew my greatest fear was losing them…losing *anyone* I cared about.

My chin quivered as my nose stung, but the tears still refused to come.

The all-too-familiar deep dark dread slowly uncoiled from deep within my stomach and snaked up my spine, squeezing and stealing my breath as it moved swiftly upward, my heart beating faster and faster until I was panting for air.

I reached up to grip the pendant from Liam that sat just above my breast, tracing the words on the back with my thumb, as had become my habit: *Always you.*

I refused to move an inch further. I refused to let Apep know how much his words affected me. I refused to allow him the satisfaction of witnessing my fearful dread.

Keeping my breaths as silent as possible and my body unmoving, I lay there and endured the overwhelming terror that pulsed through my veins.

Tracing Liam's words again, I took whatever comfort they could offer me, reminding myself that at one point he'd said these words to me, that he'd believed in them enough to have them carved into something I could carry with me forever.

He would come back. For me, for *us*. He was too honorable to stay away once he learned of the events that occurred after his leaving.

Time was cruel. It played tricks on my mind, leaving me questioning when I saw him last and wondering how long all of this had truly been going on. I struggled to count the days. How much time had I lost to despair, to the drain of my magic?

Sweat beaded my brow as my heart rate sped up.

I clutched the pendant in my hand, embedding the words into my flesh. Gratitude swelled in my chest for this tiny proof of his existence. It made room for the dream that he hadn't really left and was instead just down the hall, waiting to see me with that big smile on his face and that shy dimple that seemed reserved for only me.

He will come back.

But he hadn't before. And after how badly I'd hurt him...how badly Ryker and I had *both* hurt him...

I didn't know if honor could outweigh heartbreak.

I wasn't easy to love. I knew that. All my fears, all my worries, all my misgivings and secrets...there wasn't much I could offer him, and maybe he'd figured that out.

But even if he could leave me behind, he would never leave Ryker, of that I was sure. Hurt feelings or not, they were best friends, brothers. Their bond was thicker than their blood.

A pang of jealousy soured my stomach further. We'd once had that kind of unbreakable bond, but it had faded with time and distance.

I missed him more than I thought I could miss a person. I longed to see him again more than I'd ever wished to see anyone, even my own mother, but it was a bittersweet hope. Seeing him again would mean facing that he'd left me, that he'd refused to listen, that he'd broken his promise to me.

It would also mean he was in danger, if Apep found him, and I couldn't bear that.

I gripped his necklace harder as the paralyzing anxiety wrapped around my limbs, chest, and heart. Viscous blood pumped slowly through my veins as my breaths came in hushed and panicked bursts.

I needed an answer. Some kind of solution to this whole mess.

If I couldn't have Liam, I wished I could at least have Jimmy and Cook. Jimmy's kiss to my forehead reassuring me, Cook's chamomile tea to comfort me.

I can't lose them, too.

I wished I wasn't so alone.

My eyes stung angrily. Apep's threat had hit exactly where it hurt the most, and I felt more trapped than ever.

Sleep was nowhere to be found.

CHAPTER 2

Evelyn

The petrifying dread from last night remained in full force as the girls helped me get ready for the day. There was no hiding the dark and puffy discoloration under my eyes. My energy stretched beyond its limits as I placed my shield around Apep, my magic straining uncomfortably as my body ached and trembled with fatigue.

If I gave out today, Apep had no one to blame but himself. Had he not threatened me...

But he wouldn't hear those excuses. If I lost my grip on my magic, Ryker would suffer the consequences.

Apep proudly walked me through the deserted streets of the small town that surrounded the palace, his eyes alight with pleasure as he surveyed the damage. The whole area was filled with ash and lingering fear.

He'd grouped together a sentry of fairies, tasking them to rid the area of humans, and my stomach lodged in my throat. The words he'd spoken to me last night replayed in my mind.

If I have to kill every last human who ever tricked you into loving them in order to make you accept the other half of who you are, then so be it.

I knew better than to hope he would be lenient with any humans they found— I wasn't that naive —but I still hoped that most of them got away.

Most of the homes we passed were kept intact, but several shops, carts, goods, tools, and other various items had been burned or destroyed.

Apep hadn't spoken much to me this morning, but he hadn't needed to. The devastation before me only proved his threat from last night was far from idle.

I pushed down the tremor slowly building in my limbs. I would not let him see me afraid today.

Steeling my voice as much as possible, I asked, "And Hoddleston?"

Apep looked over and down at me as we walked side by side. "Much the same, I believe."

I wanted to cry or gag or scream at him, all the horrific fury building up inside of me needing an outlet, but instead I kept my face steady. "And what of my estate?" I asked, my nerves betraying me as my voice quivered.

He stopped and reached out a pale, bony hand to gently pet my hair and the side of my face. He dipped his finger under my chin and tilted my face up toward him. His face betrayed no emotion, but the action itself was predatory, sending a shiver down my spine. "As long as you do what you're told, I will have no reason to allow your estate to be bothered."

I did my best to hide the true terror that singed my skin at his words, but the small tug at the side of his lips showed I'd betrayed myself in some way. Dropping his hand away from my face, he said, "You have no need to try and hide your true feelings from me. I already know what's in your mind."

With that, he turned and continued walking through what was left of the small town, leaving me behind with yet another lingering threat. I gripped my arms, pulling them in close to my body. I felt nearly certain my legs were going to give out on me at any moment. Between the terror of his threats, the exhaustion from my magic and the lack of sleep I had to force them to move, one foot and then the other, before I caught back up to him walking by his side.

"I know these changes are difficult, but they're necessary for you and the kingdom to embrace your new life and future…with me." Dipping his head in my direction, he placed his hand over his heart, as if that would make him seem more sincere. "I'm your family now." His eyes met mine, and despite the smug satisfaction they held, he *did* look almost vulnerable. *Almost.*

I darted my eyes away and focused on the horrific scene around me. This man was a monster. He'd threatened everyone I loved without blinking an eye. Even if a part of me still longed for the familial relationship he'd promised, the one I'd thought we were building, I knew better than to trust his words now. Or ever again. Every word he spoke was meant to manipulate or control, and I refused to fall prey to his falsehoods once more.

Liam's tanned and beautiful face sprung up in my mind. Though he had never been like a brother to me, he had been my best friend and protector, and I'd *thought* he loved me unconditionally… though I doubted the truth of it now.

Instantly, my eyes stung and watered with longing. Apep's stance relaxed at my side, and his eyes softened at my display of emotion, obviously misinterpreting my internal thoughts. He opened his mouth to speak again, but before he could say another word about it, we were interrupted.

A male fairy, his wings spread out on full display—a light pearlescent green—proudly approached.

"Your Majesty." The fairy quickly offered his deference to Apep. I balked outwardly at the words, but Apep's hand reached out to hold mine and squeezed in warning. The guard turned to me next, bowing slightly less. "Your Highness," he offered.

"Status report?" Apep's words were cold and calculated. This was not the first time he'd spoken them, as the guard had clearly expected it.

"The humans flee," the fairy guard answered. "They're hiding in the forests and running to outside towns. Should we pursue them? Cast them down? Demand they recognize our superiority?"

Before Apep could even hope to answer, a furious cry burst out of me: "*No!*"

Both sets of eyes shot me scathing looks, but I didn't let that stop me.

"How could you?" I asked Apep. "You have no right to treat them like lesser beings, just as they had no right to do it to you. You do realize this makes you no better than they were? Or are you so blinded by your own revenge that you can't even see you've become what you claim to hate?"

My brows furrowed in frustration as I beseeched him. But his gaze remained hard and unforgiving, not even blinking before turning back to the fairy in front of us, disregarding me entirely. "I see no reason we shouldn't lock the humans up in the palace and leave them to rot, just as they did to our people." Before I could protest, he reached out for my hand again, raising it to his mouth in a brief kiss. "However, I do hate to cause my Evelyn undue pain." He turned back to the male fairy. "Leave the humans to fend for themselves and make use of their abandoned homes and items for your comfort. Spread the word that fairies are welcomed to come to this town and take whatever they need to live freely here, without fear of human persecution. All fairies are now under our protection." He squeezed my hand again, but this time it felt like a warning. It didn't take much to decipher that he wanted me to keep quiet.

The male fairy bowed again in deference, his eyes alight. "Consider it done. Thank you, gracious King."

Apep's other hand reached over to pat the one he already held. "Do not despair at the damage, my Evelyn. You forget that fairies will be inhabiting this land from now on. The towns will be restored; in fact, they will be greatly improved from their current and previous state."

I nodded mechanically as Apep took up my arm, lacing it through his own as we continued walking. "We will make this a safe haven for fairies, and you'll see this kingdom flourish under their care. Fairies gifted with earth magic will rebuild, those with growth magic will restore, those with water magic will revive…"

"What about transformation magic?" The second I chanced the question, I knew it was a mistake. Apep's eyes sharpened as they studied my face.

"What do you know of transformation magic?" he bit out.

"I've heard it's very powerful." I tried to sound convincingly innocent. "I hoped there might be a fairy who could transform these ruins."

Apep shook his head. "Just like your gift, that kind of magic is very rare. In fact, I've only known one fairy in my lifetime gifted with transformation." Apep's eyes studied mine again with new scrutiny as he tilted his head for further examination, and a look of awe crossed over his face. "She had eyes just like yours."

Air pressed against the inside of my lungs, straining for release.

"I should've seen it before…" Apep's voice wandered off. He still clutched my arm as he led me through the empty town back toward the castle.

Exhaling slowly so as not to give myself away, I braved the question. "What did you not see before?"

"You have her eyes." He stared at me again with such a deeply intense look, I had to turn away.

"Whose eyes?" I tried to feign innocence, but I feared my wobbly voice might've given me away.

"Her name was Chrysanthemum." Apep said the name with pained reverence, and my stomach clenched with impending dread.

How does he know Chrissy? What had happened between them?

The questions piled up in my mind as we walked back to the palace in silence, but I swallowed them down, allowing him to lead me back inside. I wanted answers, but they'd have to wait for now.

CHAPTER 3

Liam

A soul-crushing sense of loss overwhelmed me, stealing my very breath. The fiery anguish that had been twisting my insides desperately wanted to be released in a furious tirade, but it was as if my body had shut down.

The world around me spun as I sat there, silently leaning against the wooden table, trying to wrap my mind around the words I'd just heard.

Ryker imprisoned. Evy's mind taken over. The kingdom overtaken. *This couldn't be happening.*

Rafe and Becca described what they'd heard—news that had come from Camilla, no less—and I simply sat there in stoic disbelief.

It was as if someone else's story was playing out before my eyes; perhaps they were spinning a grand tale of some fabricated adventure to entertain the group, but surely what they were saying wasn't *real*, it wasn't something that *actually happened*, it wasn't something that had endangered those I loved most in this world.

It felt too impossible, too improbable, too horrifying to be real.

"We have to go back and get them, right now. We can't just sit around here waiting." Becca's voice had a panicked edge to it I'd never heard from her before. She was trying to hide it, but it was obvious she feared the worst.

Everyone's eyes shifted to me, but I could barely move, and I certainly couldn't speak.

I'd seen soldiers in the past who retreated inside themselves due to something that was too shocking to comprehend. Maybe this was what that felt like.

"We need a plan first." Ian replied brusquely.

Chrissy's hand gently squeezed Ian's shoulder. "We can't give Apep much more time to take control. You know how quickly he works. The humans…" Chrissy's beseeching tone made me inwardly cringe. There was familiarity when she spoke of Apep…and fear.

But the numbness inside me didn't retreat. My voice couldn't find its way out.

Everything around me seemed to move slower. I watched as Chrissy and Ian shared a look that I couldn't decipher before Ian rubbed a worn and calloused hand back and forth across his brow.

It was as if the world was slowing down to a pace I could try and keep up with, but it was also distorting everything to the point of dizzying nausea.

"Aye, I know." Ian's defeated tone sent a shiver down my spine. Did he know Apep as well? I couldn't tell for certain.

"If he's taken over the entire palace and guard already, I don't know how we even stand a chance." Rafe's words may have sounded hopeless, but there was a keyed-up edge to his tone that hinted our small numbers alone wouldn't be able to hold him back from trying.

I had always admired his tenacity.

The one thought that kept invading my mind over and over again resurfaced as my attention settled on Camilla.

Did she really betray us like that?

I studied her as she traced the wooden fibers slowly beneath her finger.

Did she know of his plans?

She hadn't said a word since they'd walked into the tavern. She hadn't even looked up since we sat down.

Is this my fault?

Rafe and Becca blamed her. It was hard not to, since she was in the room when Ryker was imprisoned. But *I* was the one who left. I was the one who abandoned them both.

The voices around me warped and distorted into background noise as I watched Camilla seemingly ignore the discussion.

I tried to get my mind to focus on anything else, but the room spun disorienting me as a cold sweat broke out across my brow.

It didn't matter what everyone else was saying, Camilla was my center of focus; she was the one who held the answers I needed.

"Camilla?" My voice broke apart the muffled voices, silencing the table. "A moment?"

It wasn't a question, it was a demand.

I didn't bother waiting for her response. I simply pushed my chair back and stood, walking stiffly toward the tavern door and heading straight into the cold outside.

CHAPTER 4

Camilla

The tavern was dusty and worn. Wood paneled every surface; the floor, the walls, the ceiling, the tables, chairs and stools. I stared intently at the heavily wood-grained pattern on the table our group sat at and traced the grooves with my finger.

It was no wonder this place reeked of stale and rotting ale. There were probably decades of spills stuck between these wooden fibers.

Now that we were all gathered together, everyone seemed to have an opinion on what we should do next, and the voices around me talked one over the other in rapid succession. I kept my mouth shut. There was no need to add to the mess we were in...*because of me*.

Even without looking, I could feel Liam's eyes drilling into me. More than likely he was imagining all the ways he could make me suffer for my betrayal.

I couldn't blame him.

The minute we arrived, Rafe and Becca had told Liam the details of what had happened. He'd remained unnervingly silent as he listened, and I desperately wanted to know what was going on in his head. I wanted to know who he was blaming—more than likely me—but a small part of me hoped that maybe he'd see my side of it all.

He had to know I cared. Maybe not how *much* I cared; I'd kept that as close inside me as possible. I wanted Evy to be happy, I wanted someone to love and cherish her, protect her, after everything she'd been through…

But I also wanted that for myself. What made her more deserving than me?

She never had to try. But I had to be perfect, demure, beguiling, and somehow I *still* wasn't good enough.

I didn't even need to ask why Apep had used me; that one was easy to answer. I was the easy target. The selfish, jealous step-sister always wishing for more.

Rafe's hand twitched anxiously against his thigh under the table, bringing me back from my pity party. He hadn't left my side since we fled the palace, and his constant presence was all the threat I needed to be on my best behavior. I had a sneaking suspicion that hand was ready to lash out at me any moment.

Lost in my own thoughts, I didn't expect to hear Liam's voice cut through the cacophony of tangled voices. But out of nowhere: "Camilla. A moment?"

I closed my eyes, cringing at the thought of having to face him. Although, if I was honest with myself, I'd known this was coming.

He headed toward the front door of the tavern and disappeared around the side. I got up and followed quietly behind him, the table behind me falling silent.

I knew everyone was curious to hear my recounting of what happened, even though I'd already told Rafe and Becca, but this was different. Liam needed more from me. He deserved it. And if my penance was having to relive the moment I last saw Evy and Ryker in order to help him, then so be it.

Once I rounded the corner, I found Liam around the side of the building, one leg braced against the rough and weathered wood siding as he leaned his back into it with his arms crossed.

The minute I stopped in front of him, his voice broke the stillness. "Did you know?"

Pinching my eyes shut, I cringed silently at the quiet promise of violence in that voice.

The day Liam almost died at the tournament, I had deceived

him. I had intentionally led him to believe Evelyn had been keeping secrets from only him and that she had chosen Ryker, despite their engagement. I'd meant to hurt Evelyn with my actions as she'd hurt me with hers. But Liam…

I'd never anticipated having to answer for my actions. I had only thought about my own hurt, my own brokenness and longing to belong somewhere, with *someone*.

Facing Liam now…ached.

A deep and considerable pain punctured through my entire chest, leaving a gaping hole in my center. I didn't want to face this reality. I didn't want to be that person, the selfish, cruel and jealous person who inflicted hurt for her own gain.

But I was.

"Did you *know?*" he asked again, clearly unwilling to let me hold my silence as he'd held his in the tavern.

Sucking in a deep breath, I willed myself to look up, but was unprepared for the torrent of emotion that met my eyes.

My traitorous voice quivered in response. "No, Liam. I didn't know his plans."

His only response was a grunt as he looked down at his crossed arms.

After a long, drawn-out silence, he finally unraveled enough to ask, "Was it my fault?"

His voice was so quiet I barely heard him, but I wished I hadn't. My heart crumbled as the weight of his guilt mixed with my own. It was too much to bear.

Hot tears pricked the back of my eyes as I cleared my throat, steeling myself. I bit the inside of my cheek, finding solace in the self-inflicted pain. "No, Liam. It was mine. I found out about Evy's magic right after my mother's trial. That was when I caught her practicing with Chrissy. It was the reason I was avoiding her…avoiding everyone, really." I paused to take in a quick breath before my next confession. "It was the reason I reported seeing a fairy at the estate."

I could tell he was listening by the erratic tick in his jaw, but he kept his eyes down, absently studying his arms, or the ground—I wasn't sure which.

"She came to see me," I sighed. "It took a while, but when I saw her, I told her that I knew about her and Chrissy. I blamed her and said things…"

"Why are you telling me this?" Liam interrupted.

I looked down at my shoe as I kicked absently at the hard, half-frozen ground. "Because I think I'm part of the reason she never told you about her magic."

That got his attention. Without even looking up from the ground, I could tell he was watching me again, studying me. I lifted my lashes to meet his beautiful, dark, angry eyes.

He was never mine; I knew this already. I knew he and Evy were meant for each other, and I'd wanted to prove my loyalty to her by encouraging them, him…but as soon as I saw her performing magic, betrayal had clouded my heart. I'd thought we were growing closer, repairing what was broken between us, but that sting of deception… it ruined everything. I'd suddenly questioned why *she* should get someone so wonderful, why *she* should have all the prospects, why *she* should get what she wanted.

When *I* didn't.

Selfish.

That was what I was.

Selfish and cruel, and Apep knew it.

He'd brought me into his fold, making me his personal assistant. I'd been struggling to find my place in the palace, and he made me feel like I had a place with him.

He'd asked me things about Evelyn, claiming he cared for her and wanted to help, so I told him about her deepest fears and longings. I shared with him the abuse I had witnessed, even on occasion, participated in.

He'd complimented me, made me feel capable and valued. He'd gently pushed me toward Liam, commenting on how well we fit together and that I deserved a chance at happiness just as much as Evelyn did.

After Liam left, he'd asked me to keep watch in Ryker's room that awful night. Told me that Rafe was otherwise indisposed and he needed the help. I happily obliged.

He'd told me to let the fairies into his room, and when I hesitated, he'd assured me they wouldn't hurt anyone, that they were just there to help.

He'd told me he would be with Evelyn, helping her process Liam's abandonment…

He'd told me so, so, so many things.

And I'd believed them.

I cleared my throat, knowing that I had to tell Liam what I knew about Evelyn. A truth only I knew, because I could relate to it.

"I should've stopped you before you left, but I wanted you to leave her. I wanted her to feel like I felt. Left behind, betrayed, abandoned by the person she cared most about." Liam's entire body stiffened at my hideous confession. "I knew that Ryker didn't know about her magic until you did, she never told him either, I just let you assume…" I paused to take a breath. "She didn't hold back from telling you because she was specifically afraid of *you*, she held back because she'd already been hurt…"

I didn't realize my mistake until Liam's head and shoulders dipped further. "So it is my fault."

I sighed heavily and straightened my shoulders. "Look at the facts, Liam. I've spent more time with her than you have. After you were gone, I was the one who came into her life as a companion, of sorts." At least, for a very short while. I hadn't been a companion to her since we were thirteen and fourteen years old. Being one year older than her meant I'd had to become a "lady" before she did.

"As flawed a companion as I was, she still loved me. No matter what I did to her, or *didn't* do to help her, she still always cared, always tried, always reached back out. And then, at the first opportunity to show her I loved her back, truly loved her back, I rejected her. I made it unsafe for her to share who she is. Between that, her own father, and who knows what all Apep was telling her…" I trailed off again, the image of Evy I'd last seen still fresh in my mind. Her glazed-over eyes struggling to push through, to help *me*.

Run.

Her broken whisper still echoed in my thoughts, both waking and sleeping.

Liam's expression was unreadable as he stared directly into my eyes now. I blinked away the hot stinging tears, trying to force them to stay put.

With a quick clearing of his throat, he asked, "How'd you get away?"

Closing my eyes, I lost the silent battle with my tears as two leaked down my cheeks, my grief drawing my shame out like a gentle caress.

"Evy saved me," I whispered.

He didn't ask for more than that, and I didn't offer. What needed to be said had been said, and I couldn't expect anything more from him. Not now that I was the betrayer, the cruel and selfish step-sister of the girl left behind to deal with the terrible aftermath. I'd have to earn their respect back before I'd be accepted again, but I was all right with that.

It was far more than I deserved, really.

Liam turned away without a word, leaving me to my ragged thoughts and emotions. A part of me wished the frozen ground beneath my feet would open up and swallow me whole. I shivered against the harsh chill from the wind that threatened to freeze my bones as it lazily whistled around the buildings.

Beyond the worn wooden siding of the Tavern, quiet voices murmured as the group tried to make tentative rescue plans. There wasn't much else I could offer beyond what I'd seen.

Apep had never let me know his strategies; he'd only promised that no one would get hurt by my actions, because I was helping protect them and myself. I was doing what I ought to, what my mother had wanted me to do.

My heart twinged with a phantom stab of pain. Apep never even had to use his magic on me. I was the easy mark. The one who could be manipulated by mere words alone. The left-over step-sister desperate for a place to belong after I'd lost everything.

I hadn't realized Apep's nefarious plans until after they'd tied up Ryker and I saw Evy's empty gaze as she stared aimlessly out into the room.

By that point, I'd realized far too late that Liam leaving, or dying, had been key to Apep's plans.

What had Evy felt as her mind was taken over? Was it the same as when Apep had invaded my own mind in his attempt to kill me that night?

His voice still echoed in my nightmares. The memory of pressure building in my head until I thought it would explode wouldn't leave me.

You are of no more use to me.

A violent shudder rocked my body forward, and I had to catch myself against the side of the building, gasping for breath.

Perhaps controlling a mind wasn't as painful as what he'd done to me. I could only hope that was the case, because I didn't know how anyone could live with that kind of agony.

And what would Apep do to Ryker while he was without any protections? The way he'd treated him that night indicated there wasn't a line he wouldn't cross.

Standing here doing nothing wasn't enough.

Evy might've been the strongest person I knew, besides Liam, but that didn't mean she could weather this storm. I didn't know Ryker well enough to know how he would handle this kind of torment, but I suspected no one would survive Apep's wrath easily.

My feet stayed frozen in place, I didn't deserve to sit with the group, and I suspected they didn't want me to either. Standing separately out here in the cold seemed the right thing to do. Staying out of everyone's way.

The group beyond loved Evy dearly; they loved Ryker too. Well, mostly. The fairies seemed a bit undecided on the matter, but overall, our little rebel force wasn't going to back down. Regardless of how impossible the task seemed, I knew they would do whatever it took to save Evy and Ryker.

I just hoped they'd let me help.

CHAPTER 5

Liam

Leaning against the doorframe of the tavern, my chest clenched again, but this time the feeling was colder and more brutal. It was as if the shocking numbness inside of me was finally melting enough to feel sensations again. In less than a heartbeat, I tasted the bitter edge of panic as my heart rate sped up, pumping searing-hot blood painfully through my thawing body.

I watched the table full of tired hopeless faces attempt to debate their way out of this terrifying mess. There was no denying the frayed emotions in the room were taking their toll. We all felt the burden of this new reality.

Tightening my fists hidden behind my arms, I gritted my teeth against the onslaught of internal fury. I'd never wanted to kill someone before, but I *wanted* to kill Apep. I would kill him. I swore it to myself that my blade would run him through before he even had a chance to gasp.

This would be my vow of penance to Ryker and Evy. This would be my burden to carry so no one else had to.

My legs itched to run straight to the palace and leave everyone behind, but the trained soldier in me knew I wouldn't get far on my own. We needed a plan and we needed an army, and right now, I didn't know how to get either.

"I think it best we all wait until we've had some sleep first." Ian's steady brogue helped calm the group as they bobbed their heads in exhausted agreement.

"I'd been tryin' to tell you lot, there's no use debatin' strategy on an empty stomach," Billy chimed in. In my short time here, I'd learned he was always earnest in wanting to help and lightening the mood. And his most devoutly held belief was that food solved nearly everything.

A few tired agreements from the group was enough for Billy to high-tail it back to the kitchen, followed immediately by clanging dishes and metal.

"I know that look." Ian sidled up next to me, crossing his arms in unison with mine.

I quirked an eyebrow in question at him.

"The look that you're about to do something stupid and reckless." He spoke without looking at me, and I followed his eyes to see them steadily watching Chrissy instead.

Shrugging, I looked back down at the floor, but didn't offer a response. My mind was too full of too many things; anger, self-criticism, shame, hate, self-pity, grief…

"She means a great deal to you." Ian spoke quietly enough as to not be heard by the rest of the group.

Turning to face him, I finally met his eyes. "So does my brother."

Recognition lit up his face. "I know that pain well."

I stayed quiet, allowing him the space to share if he so chose.

Ian sighed, bowing his head. "My brother was killed by humans."

Closing my eyes to the heaviness of the statement, I kept listening.

"He was a good male. Had a beautiful young family…" he trailed off. "I found their home after it was over. His body was broken and torn up as if wild dogs had been set to him." He shuttered. "A total massacre. The kids were gone, taken, and his mate was nearly as broken as he was."

When he paused, I looked up to offer a small, "I'm sorry, Ian," But his eyes were focused on Chrissy again, filled with an anguish I couldn't determine.

Billy brought out bowls of stew to Becca and Chrissy, chatting them up, trying to make them laugh. I appreciated his good-humored nature. We needed that right now.

Ian flicked an imaginary piece of lint from his sleeve. "I hated the humans after that. Vowed never to help them again and gathered up as many fairies as I could before the war broke out."

"Did you bring them all here?" I asked.

He dipped his chin. "Aye. After the war we found this place and settled. No humans came to bother us; we weren't on their maps, ye see? And we made a life for ourselves."

I hesitated before I spoke next. "You don't have to help us, you know…"

"It's different for me now, and I'll be there to help. I've never met Evelyn…" He paused, swallowing. "But I'd like to." His eyes lifted back to Chrissy, and his expression fell. "Chrissy has told me a great deal about her."

There was obviously more to the story, but I didn't want to pry. So instead, I observed, "You and Chrissy seem close."

I watched Chrissy smile warmly at Rafe, Becca and Billy as they ate their stew. None of them bothered to invite us over, but it was likely obvious our discussion was of a more serious nature.

"We were," was all he said, not offering anything more. After a long pause, he unraveled his arms and pushed away from the wall. "Best get some food in ye, lad. Won't help to be undernourished before we venture to save yer girl and yer brother." He winked, a forced gesture, before walking away to the kitchen.

I wandered back over to the table and sat down heavily into the wooden chair next to Rafe.

"What are we going to do about her?" Rafe's thumb gestured to Camilla, who was still outside in the cold.

"She can do whatever she wants," I responded tersely.

"What did you talk to her about?"

I sighed, wiping a hand down my face. "Not that it matters, but she confessed her role and how she got away. I just needed to hear it from her personally."

Rafe nodded his head in understanding, taking another bite of stew before lowering his voice further. "When she told us what happened, I almost ran her through in my anger."

Ian sat down beside me and placed a bowl of stew under my bowed head. The savory scent wafted up, making my eager stomach growl loudly.

"That sound means eat up!" Billy chimed in, looking around the table. His long, dark curls swayed around his head. Strangely, his hair fit his personality perfectly, wild and energetic. A concerned look suddenly furrowed his brow. "Where's the other lass?"

I thumbed toward the door. "Still outside."

Billy huffed to himself while standing up from his seat. "Foolish lass, she'll catch her death out there." He muttered quietly to himself as he rose from his seat and made his way outside.

"Don't be too rough on her." Becca's voice was quiet and tired. She stared down at her stew on the other side of Rafe. "Don't get me wrong, I'm as angry as you two are, but she's being plenty rough on herself. She doesn't need much more from us."

I dug into my stew with more force than was generally necessary, my anger rising to the surface again, but the taste of it was like ash on my tongue. As mad as I was at Camilla for her role in all of this, she wasn't truly to blame.

I hadn't had the heart yet to ask Rafe where he'd been throughout all of this. He was Ryker's captain now. He was supposed to be guarding him, always on alert. Where had he been while Ryker was assaulted?

Sitting there in quiet agitation, I didn't bother with idle talk. My mind was too full already. Too overwhelmed with rage and worry.

"Go sit yerself down, lass. I'll bring you some nice hot stew." Billy led Camilla to the table and helped her sit. She trembled furiously from the cold. "And maybe a few blankets," he added, muttering to himself as he left, *fairy-blasted brainless woman.*

I struggled to hide my amusement until my eyes landed back on Camilla's shivering form as she sat sullenly at the table. She looked drawn and worn out. Becca had been right in asking us not be too hard on her, she clearly blamed herself enough.

When Rafe finished his last bites, he pushed away his bowl, giving his elbows room on the table as his hands cupped his head. "I'm sorry, Cap." His voice was anguished and pinched. "I should've been there, I should've…"

"Why *weren't* you?" I questioned, willing my voice to not be so harsh. I quickly lost that battle.

Rafe's face burned crimson as his eyes darted to Becca, who was currently resting her head on a pillow of folded arms.

"Ah." I tried to hide the disappointment from my voice, but Rafe flinched anyway.

"I never meant to. With the Terreno delegation leaving, Ryker had planned a small dinner with Evelyn that night…in my mind, he was safe with Evelyn, and I had this sudden urge to be with Becca." He winced. "I didn't even think twice about it, and then we fell asleep afterward, I…I don't know."

A sudden urge? My eyes whipped back to his face as I studied him. Rafe would never normally shirk his duties so easily. As much as he'd always loved the ladies, they never came before his guard responsibilities. I knew Becca was different for him, but I didn't think it possible for him to have changed quite that much simply because he cared more for Becca than the others. The entire thought process he'd just described was completely out of character.

Then it dawned on me.

How could I not have guessed it sooner? It was so simple. So brilliantly subtle.

I knew Apep could control minds, but I'd always thought of it in terms of big, obvious ways, but couldn't he just as easily use us in such unsuspecting and understated ways? Of course he could. And he'd done it, completely under our noses. How often had it gone by unnoticed?

I shook my head and sighed in frustration as I placed my hand on Rafe's shoulder, giving it a reassuring squeeze. "That sounds like it wasn't your fault, Rafe."

He turned his head in his hands to face me, "How could it not be? I mean," he dropped his hands looking over at Becca's sleepy form, "she's so beautiful." He sighed. "Looking at her, it just…it practically overwhelmed me. It was as if I…"

I gave him a pointed look, interrupting his thoughts and watching as slow recognition registered on his face. His features reluctantly shifted from despair to outrage.

"Dammit!" He slammed his fist down on the table, causing

everyone's cups and bowls to rattle. Becca startled from her awkward sleeping position and blearily blinked up as Rafe stood up from the table and stomped his way outside.

"Stew's up!" Billy set a bowl of stew in front of Camilla, then looked startled at the table. "What did I miss?" Looking back down at Camilla who shivered violently, he cursed under his breath and raced up the stairs to the lodging rooms before coming back down with several blankets in his arms. "Here lass, let's get you warmed properly."

I watched him wrap her up in several blankets, tucking them around her shoulders and legs, and I couldn't help but be grateful that someone was caring for her. I knew it should've been me—it's what Evy would've wanted—but I was struggling too much to see past my own anger and anguish.

Camilla thanked him and awkwardly turned back to eating her stew, the spoon rattling in her grip.

"I think we should go back to Evelyn's estate," Chrissy suddenly spoke up. "We can't do much from here, and I have areas within the forest that could hide us if necessary, but mostly we need information. Perhaps Jimmy and Cook—"

"If they're even still there," Camilla spoke bitterly between her bites.

I leveled my eyes on Camilla. "What do you mean?"

She swallowed slowly, as if it was difficult, and I imagined she hadn't realized she'd spoken out loud, considering her face bloomed a bright crimson under the scrutiny of the group.

Clearing her throat awkwardly, she answered, "Ryker is Apep's insurance that Evy remains under his control. If he loses control of her mind, he'll use the people she loves most against her."

She said it so simply, as if it was common sense that this was his strategy all along.

"You said you didn't know his plan. If that's the case, how could you know this?" I questioned.

Her eyes widened at the pointed accusation in my tone, and she looked taken aback before she collected herself again and answered calmly in return. "I did not lie about never knowing his plan, I'm simply speculating on his strategy." She paused, jaw tensing before she added, "It's what my mother would do."

And with that, I understood what she meant. She'd watched her mother torment and abuse Evelyn ever since they moved in. She'd had a front row seat to the cruelty and control her mother wrought over not only Evelyn, but also herself. She'd been raised on that kind of manipulative control, which would in turn make it easy for her to spot.

I vibrated with an overwhelming fury. Not only was Apep controlling Evy's mind, but the fact that he would use the people she loved to control her…I couldn't bear the thought. There was something so much more sinister about that kind of exploitation.

"It's too dangerous." Rafe chimed in next, storming back inside. "Apep would expect us to go there, he'd have the place surrounded by now."

"But it is a starting point." I countered.

"I'm happy to fly there and see what the status is," Chrissy offered.

"No," Ian stated with a finality that shocked me.

"Ian…" Chrissy grumbled.

"We can't risk you going, and you know it. Visiting Evelyn all this time has been risk enough." Ian's words were gruff and absolute.

"I can go," Billy offered next. "No one there knows me or would recognize me at all."

"It's not a bad idea." I shrugged.

"Jimmy and Cook won't know you either, though." Becca said, clearly awake now that we were strategizing again.

"And with everything going on, I doubt they'll trust you, either." Rafe added.

"I could go with you." I offered, but was cut off by Camilla.

"If Apep found you, he wouldn't hesitate to use you against Evy. Don't put her in that position." She set her jaw in that haughty familiar facade, but it did nothing to take away from her words.

Apep had already used me to gain control of Evy's mind, and I shuddered to think what he would do if he actually had me in the flesh. But it was worth the risk if it got us one step closer to rescuing them.

"I'll go with Billy," Rafe offered, brushing off bits of snow from his jacket. "They both know me and would trust me if I showed up."

He looked to Becca, who obviously wanted to object, but she kept her mouth shut as Rafe continued. "Plus, Apep isn't looking for me specifically. I'm not much of a threat to him or someone he can as easily use against Evelyn or Ryker."

Becca scoffed. Ian sighed heavily. But Chrissy smiled. "I like it. But you boys better not take any risks."

"Are you sure?" I asked Rafe as he walked back over to the table, standing beside Becca.

He dipped his head in acknowledgement. "I'm sure. We need to know more of what's going on, and Evy would want us checking in on Cook and Jimmy anyway."

He was right, and the plan was the best we'd come up with yet.

"All right, then." I said ignoring Becca's very pointed scowl directed toward me. "Billy and Rafe will sneak in to check on Jimmy and Cook first thing tomorrow and then report back here."

"Which means ye lot need to get some shut eye," Ian stated.

"You could say that again." Rafe rubbed circles on Becca's tense back.

"Thank you for dinner, Billy. It was perfect," Becca complimented the fairy, but an angry tone slipped through her cracks as she jerked away from Rafe's comforting hand and stood up from the table.

Billy blushed, and Rafe shot him a warning look before following after Becca.

"Goodnight, everyone." Chrissy waved and floated slowly out the door before taking off into the night. Ian watched her go, his shoulders slightly sinking before he shook off whatever was bothering him.

Billy began to clean up the dishes, and Camilla jumped in to help while Becca and Rafe headed up the stairs.

"Where are you two going?" I questioned.

Rafe raised an eyebrow in confusion. "We're headed to bed."

My panicked eyes darted from Camilla's disappearing form, then back to Becca and Rafe.

Rafe chuckled, his eyes following my path to where Camilla had disappeared inside before smirking back at me. "Just don't kill her."

Becca kept moving determinedly up the stairs before she disappeared into the room they'd be staying in tonight and slammed the door shut behind her. Rafe grimaced before turning around and jogging up the steps behind her.

I threw my head back, groaning heavily as I waited for Camilla to emerge from the kitchen. Still drying her hands, Camilla's eyes collided with mine, and a slight blush bloomed on her face.

"I'll sleep on the floor, you can have the bed." I turned and trudged up the stairs, Camilla following hesitantly behind.

"You don't have to share your room with me," she said as she stood in the doorway.

I cocked an exasperated look at her. "And where will you sleep, then?"

She shrugged.

"It's fine, Camilla." I sighed and ran a hand through my hair. That little piece Evy loved so much flopped immediately into my eye, and I blinked away the sting. Whether it was simply the thought of her or the hair itself, it didn't matter. I wasn't ready to cry. "Tomorrow, you can share with Becca."

Before she could hide it, I noticed a brief sadness cross her face as I opened the door, letting her walk in first. Grabbing an extra pillow and a blanket from the closet, I made my way down to the rough wooden floor.

"Liam, really I don't mind…"

"Goodnight, Camilla." Hopefully the finality of that would be enough to get her to stop talking.

A horribly awkward silence hung heavy in the room until I finally heard Camilla's breathing relax. Still, fear plagued my thoughts, keeping sleep frustratingly far from my grasp. I wanted to be there now, storming the palace, getting Ryker and Evy to safety and cutting down anything and anyone that stood in my way.

It couldn't be done alone. I knew that. But it hurt to not be there. We needed to know what was going on, we needed a plan, but I needed to be *there*, to be with *them*.

I never should've left. I still couldn't believe how easily I'd fallen into Apep's plan.

My mind wandered to gruesome places, picturing Apep controlling Evy and Ryker's minds, using them like puppets for his amusement. The picture churned my stomach.

This was the first step to sliding my sword directly through Apep's sternum. This was the first step to seeing my brother. This was the first step toward forgiveness...

A stillness came over me at that thought. I turned over to watch Camilla's prone form in the bed, her breaths steadily rising and falling.

Maybe we were more alike than I liked to think.

We were both searching for forgiveness from the person, or in my case people, who mattered the most to us. But there was no guarantee. Forgiveness was a choice. And if I couldn't forgive myself, how could I ever expect them to forgive me?

CHAPTER 6

Ryker

*D*rip. Drip. Drip.

There was nothing that could soothe the throbbing ache in my face. Even after sealing and healing it with magic, my newly marred skin smarted day and night, leaving me in a constant cycle of pain.

Day and night. I huffed a laugh to myself. *What a concept.*

I had no way of knowing if it was day or night in this prison. There was no rising and falling sun or moon. There were no regular visits, though Evelyn tried. Not even the sound of the tower clock striking at a given hour sounded down here.

My constant companion was the sharp dripping in some far-off corner, the scraping of tiny nails against stone as rats and mice scurried their way to and from, and the dreaded torch light that Apep kept constantly burning outside of my cell. It was like paint splashed across the wall, an unnerving ruby and orange hue that danced in the shadowed bars of my prison cell.

I refused to touch my face, but I squeezed my eyes closed and clenched my fists, willing away the memory of burning flesh, searing pain, and the orange and red glow that even the back of my eyelids couldn't escape.

Drip. Drip. Drip.

I tried to take a deep breath that wouldn't come. My chest rose and fell in short bursts, and my body bowed in terror.

He'd left that torch to torture me, and he was succeeding.

Forgetting myself, I reached my hands up to wipe down my face—and froze.

The unnaturally smooth and uneven skin felt entirely foreign underneath my palm. I tried to pull my trembling hands away from my face, but they wouldn't work, wouldn't budge. Bile surged up my throat, and I tried to heave off to the side, but I couldn't move. My betraying body wouldn't listen, wouldn't move, wouldn't accept my commands.

I can't do this.

I can't do this.

I can't do this.

I was a trembling, hunched shell of a man. Death seemed preferable to this existence.

Drip.

I pictured Liam's face, his reassuring presence at my side since we were thirteen.

I missed him.

He'll come back. He has to come back. How long has it been? How long have I been in here?

My muscles loosened slightly at the thought of him, but the trembling hadn't ceased. I'd seen Evelyn in this state before, trembling, terrified, frozen. I wondered if she felt the same way I did now.

When was the last time I saw her?

Do I even want to see her again?

I didn't know.

Drip. Drip.

Seeing Evelyn was a painful reminder that this was real. That Liam had left. That Apep had taken over. That Camilla had betrayed us.

Camilla.

Just the thought of her sent fury down my spine.

"You promised not to hurt him…"

I would never forget her words, but the sound of her voice had grown distant and distorted in my mind. Everything mixed together these days, and now the words sounded more like evil incarnate rather than the woman I was once acquainted with.

She'd seemed so genuine when she'd said she wanted a job at the palace; Evelyn had even vouched for her. I had thought her so opposite of her horrible mother. I had given her a chance. But she'd quickly become Apep's personal maid. Too quickly.

Maybe they'd been planning this all along.

She'd been in the room that night. She'd pulled out the chair they sat me in to witness my own demise. Had she provided the rope, too? Just how long had she been in league with Apep? How long had they been planning my downfall?

Just like her treacherous and deceitful mother…

I had believed *him*, too. I had grown closer to him, trusted him with my life, my kingdom, my family.

Drip.

Soft feet whispered on rough stone, and I scrambled to the farthest corner of the cell, pulling my knees up to my chest and praying that it wasn't Apep or one of his goons.

It didn't matter that I knew that soft whispered step now. I still feared that they'd trick me one day, or use her to torture me further.

Did that mean it was morning already?

She liked to come in the mornings.

"Go away, Evelyn," I called out before she even reached my door, hoping to persuade her, or whoever it was, away. If she hated me, she could leave me here, and then hopefully Apep would simply put me out of my misery.

Her shoes stalled, but they didn't turn back.

"Ryker?" Her melodious voice whispered out, hesitant and unsure…perhaps a little broken, even.

My heart broke at the sound. Her beautiful voice both wounded and revived me. I longed and dreaded to hear it, because it meant she was still here. We were still in this mess. She was still being used by a monster, and I was still the leverage.

A strangled, "Please," was all I could get out.

Rustling fabric lowered slowly before my barred door. Dim golden and scarlet light cast half her face in shadows and highlighted the other side in a disturbing amber glow.

Does my face look like that now? One side shadowed and the other a frightening display of reddened flesh?

A pale hand reached through the bars, and I shivered away from it. "I'm here, Ryker. I'm so sorry I wasn't able to visit yesterday. Apep…" She trailed off, worry wrinkling her brow…like she hadn't meant to say his name.

I said nothing; I moved no closer. I couldn't save her from this fate, it was already happening, but I could encourage her to leave. To free herself. It seemed like something Liam would do. Protect what you can. Focus on what you can do.

But that wasn't the only reason I wanted distance from her.

Drip. Drip. Drip.

I had used her. Just like every other woman in my life, I had used her to fill the void in my heart where my mother used to reside. I had clung to her like a lifeline when my father died and had ignored my brother's heart and longing for the sake of my own comfort.

Evelyn had never truly been mine. Even when we grew close, she had always pulled away. Even when I declared my love, she hadn't reciprocated. Even when I promised her everything, she doubted her happiness.

I should've realized it sooner…then Liam wouldn't have left.

Her alabaster hand gripped the bar as she pulled herself even closer to the door, then stretched back out. As if those mere inches would make a difference in reaching me in this far corner. "Please, Ryker, come closer. Let me hold your hand. Let me offer whatever comfort I can."

"No." The words rasped out of my unused and choked-up throat. I feared her seeing my face again, seeing the horrendous state I was in with my dirty and ripped clothing, my trembling body, my dirty hands and feet.

Oh, how the mighty have fallen.

Her dejected hand snaked back through the bars. "I think I may finally be wearing him down to treating you better until I can get you free." She leaned her head against the bars. "I promise I will, Ryker. I will make sure you get out, I will make sure you're free again." Her voice choked on a sob. "I don't care what happens to me, I don't care..."

"I care." My voice was ragged with every unsaid word.

She sighed to cover up her small whimper. "Ryker...what's happening to you...it's unforgivable." Her voice suddenly gained strength, and her warbly voice steadied. "I'm so sorry I couldn't stop it. I'm so sorry I couldn't..." She trailed off. "I won't allow it. I can't. I will figure out a way...some way to get you—"

"Enough." My husky voice echoed against stone, and I quieted before I spoke again. "Evelyn, the thing I want most is for you to leave. Without you, he can't hurt me."

It was a lie. We both knew it was a lie.

If she left, I would die. Maybe not by Apep's hand, but by any other. More than likely he'd simply leave me down here to rot.

"I'll never leave you, Ryker."

Her strangled voice made my head fall onto my pulled-up knees. "I'm no longer meant for this world. He's turned me into a monster."

She hesitated a moment before replying. "We are not our circumstances. You helped teach me that. I could've easily felt the same after what my father and stepmother did to me."

"You were far too bright to be kept in the shadows."

Silence. Then: "So are you, Ryker."

Drip. Drip. Drip.

"You should go," I whispered.

My heart ripped in half, even though it was me asking. She couldn't see me for what I was now. A monster made of fire and darkness. A terrifying creature born of despair. A leech of light and goodness. I had leeched onto her, and she didn't even know it. I wouldn't do that now. I wouldn't use her light to bolster what was left of me. I would accept my fate and do my best to save her in the process.

Soft weeping pulled me back from my dark musings. "I can't keep leaving you here. It's killing me."

Her words broke me, and I found myself scooting forward, hand reaching out to rest gently against her fist gripping the iron bar. "Evelyn."

Her face popped up staring unnervingly back at me, but her eyes didn't focus on mine. They meandered, clearly searching for something distinguishable to latch on to as I hid my face purposely in the shadows created by her own silhouette.

I squeezed her fist. "You should not come visit me anymore. It's too hard for me. It's…it's easier when you're not here."

Panic widened her eyes as she turned to grip my hand with her other. "Ryker, don't talk like that. Please don't push me away. I'm going to get you out of here, I promise you, I'm going to…"

Her words were frantic and panicked, rambling together.

"You need to go. You need to focus on you."

"I can't." She choked on a sob.

"It hurts too much to have you here." I squeezed her fist one last time and forced myself to scoot back into my own little corner. "It hurts to know that I can't protect you. That you are the beauty I will never know again, the love I will never have." I paused my breath choking. "You are the cruelest torture."

Drip.

Her rigid posture didn't move, her lungs didn't expand, her shoulders didn't rise. She held her breath, waiting for me to take it back, but the truth was…that was the truth. Even I hadn't realized it until the words escaped my mouth. The pressure of her gaze weighed heavily upon my chest.

Drip. Drip.

"Leave, Evelyn." I broke the thick silence. "Don't come visit me again."

After another moment, she silently stood and walked quietly out of the dungeon.

It was better this way.

It's better this way.

Drip. Drip. Drip.

CHAPTER 7

Evelyn

A jagged knot filled my throat as I forced myself to take one
more step up the stairs. Leaving Ryker in that horrendous
dungeon cell…it was one of my worst nightmares come true.

I couldn't protect him.

I *hadn't* protected him.

The ache in my chest was a crevice that fractured even further
every time I had to leave Ryker in that dungeon. A flood of guilt
pummeled the crack, wave after wave of accusation threatening to
split it completely open.

What use is shield magic if I can't even keep the people I love most safe?

Clenching my teeth and fists, I waited as a tight tremor wracked
my overly wrought body.

There was a new heaviness that surrounded me now. Between the
pressure of Apep's moving shield, my own unsteady magic, and the
all-consuming guilt of not being able to protect both Camilla and
Ryker…

The memory of my helplessness that night gnawed at me, slowly
chewing away at my confidence in my magic…in myself. I had barely
been able to shield Camilla for those few brief seconds before she ran,

before they could kill her. But Apep's hold over my mind that night had been too strong, too overwhelming, too disorienting.

And I'd failed Ryker in the worst of ways. It was no wonder he didn't want to see me. Still, his words had stung far more than I cared to acknowledge.

Apep had broken him. Having known Ryker's mind all these years, it was no surprise that he knew exactly what to say to inflict the most damage.

I hated him for it.

I hated the delight he took in other people's misery. I hated the control he sought. I hated the way he relished people's fear of him.

Ryker's dejected tone echoed over and over in my mind. *"I'm no longer meant for this world. He's turned me into a monster."*

Reaching the top of the stairs, I clutched at my chest as if I could physically hold everything inside and took a moment to lean against one of the white marble walls.

My breaths were winded, heavy with fatigue. Being further away from Apep took its toll on my magic. The pressure of distance between us felt like trying to lift a tree limb above my head. The exertion left me shaky on unsteady legs, my vision swimming.

Between what Apep had done to Ryker and the magical toll he was putting on me, I wanted to lash out. Shame turned into fiery anguish burning the inside of my ribs. I wanted to sever my shield, grab Ryker, and make a run for it. But with all of Apep's bloodthirsty guards, I knew we wouldn't get far, especially when I was already so tired and Ryker was so beaten down.

I couldn't do this by myself, at least not yet; not until I built up my magical muscles, as Chrissy had called them.

A ragged knot of emotion threatened to spill from my throat as I stared at the marbled tile beneath my feet. I missed her. I missed them all. I missed the life I almost had before Apep ripped it away.

Digging my fingernails into my palms provided a painful sort of relief as I raged silently in that cold and empty hallway. A mere two flights of stairs was all that separated me from Ryker, and yet it felt like an entirely different world up here.

I didn't know what to do now. All my life I had felt alone, but this was different.

This was worse.

My mind flashed back to sitting on the back of the carriage that had carried me away from the home I knew. Fear and despair had come to visit then, too, but I'd had a resolve that day, a *knowing* that I would be in a better situation even if it was new and unknown.

But this? There was no hope in this.

A choked sob escaped my lungs.

I'd let him in. I'd trusted him with my mind, and he'd used it against me. That betrayal somehow hurt far worse than Camilla's. She hadn't been false with me, lulling me into trusting her, but Apep had. He'd presented himself as a brother, a protector, a guide. He'd eased my pain and quieted my thoughts with such tenderness.

And I'd *believed him.*

How could I be so stupid? So naive?

My eyes were swollen, dry and gritty, but my emotions were tangled in a messy weave that allowed the heat of fury to fill my veins. Gritting my teeth, I tightened my resolve, closing my eyes to follow the feel of my magic. It was a strange sensation to have a small part of me in an entirely different section of the palace. Along with the heaviness that weighed on me, feeling the movement of my shield would take some getting used to, especially when I couldn't see it.

As I followed that thread, I walked swiftly down several halls and up another flight of stairs. It distracted me from the heavy fatigue that had settled deep into my bones.

The pull of my magic stopped at the King's office, where Apep sat reading over some documents. His new look still surprised me. His dark robes were gone, replaced with a charcoal gray long-sleeved tunic that wrapped tightly around his body instead of buttoning in the front. I assumed buttons were too *human* for him and that this was a traditional fairy look that was paired with loose fitting pants. Each day saw a new wrap, showcasing his long lean torso, but at least he wore different colors now, even if all of them were still dark hues. Nothing light or bright. A perfect fit for his grim personality.

Without even raising his head, Apep spoke as I entered the room. "The King of Terreno is such a delightfully cowardly man. He cares not that there's been a change in leadership, he only wishes to keep the alliance between our kingdoms intact."

My jaw ached from how hard I clenched my teeth before opening it to speak. "That's a good thing, isn't it?"

Apep's eyes flitted up to meet mine. "Indeed." His upper lip curled into a slight sneer, and his nose flared as he sniffed the air. "You smell of the dungeons. I thought I told you to clean up first before you visited here."

Pursing my lips, I met his gaze straight on and stood a little straighter. "Perhaps it's a good reminder."

The look he leveled at me next made my entire body tense up. He wanted a demure, easy-to-control Evelyn. A submissive, cowering Evelyn.

I'd played that part once before. Never again.

Apep tilted his head before leaning back in the chair, steepling his fingers before his mouth, surveying me with a harsh gaze. Just like my father used to do before doling out his "punishments."

I swallowed thickly. My body slowly folded inward, as if the weight of his stare was too heavy a burden to carry. An instant sheen of sweat beaded on my brow as I tried to calm my breathing.

Not now. Please not now...

My attempt to stay upright was a quickly lost battle. Closing my eyes only made the room spin, so I stared at the chair in front of me. If I needed to, I'd be able to reach and grab it in order to stay upright, or at least catch my fall.

A shadow suddenly hovered next to me, and I tried to get away from it, but my feet were stuck, as if the floor itself had swallowed them up.

I cringed away from Apep as he reached out, waiting for the blow, the pain, the shock.

Instead, he clasped my shoulder. His touch was gentle...kind, even.

"Evelyn?" he asked softly, as if he cared. "What's wrong?"

I didn't want to tremble. I didn't want my body to act of its own volition, but I couldn't help it. My willpower wasn't strong enough, and I was already so tired. My muscles shuddered under his touch, quivering in fear of my own shadows. My past mixing with my present.

"Evelyn..." Concern laced through his voice, and his arm wrapped around me. We were suddenly on the floor as he held me close to him, rocking back and forth. "You're safe. No one will ever hurt you again." I hated it. His gentleness. The fact that I buried my face into his shoulder in spite of that hate, seeking out the only comfort offered to me.

His cold lips kissed my temple as I struggled to breathe. "I promise you, I will keep you safe. No one will ever touch you again. He will never hurt you again."

I remained quiet, willing my body to stop shaking, my heart to stop racing. *Please, please stop. Not now. Not like this.*

I only trembled harder.

Apep's voice was soft in my ear. "I understand more than you know." Hugging my center a little tighter, he rested his head against mine. It was the most broken I'd ever heard him sound. "These memories won't last forever."

I let out a garbled sob into his shoulder. He knew. He knew what was happening in my mind. The flashback to my father sitting behind his desk, his fingers steepled and malice in his eyes. The harsh pain and humiliation that always followed.

"You've already been through the worst of it," he continued. "You survived, and found the strength to keep going, to stand strong, to right these wrongs." He made a soft shushing noise into my hair as he rocked my body back and forth. "He'll never hurt you again, my Evelyn. I promise you, he'll never hurt you again."

My mouth opened and closed several times before words finally came out, though they weren't the words I expected them to be. "But who will protect me from you?"

He jerked back, but didn't let go of his hold on me. "You need no protection from me, young Evelyn."

"And yet, you're the one hurting me."

He pulled back as if I'd physically struck him and stared at me with disbelieving eyes. "I have never, nor will I ever lay a single hand on you in anger."

I scrambled off his lap, gripping at the cold stone floor to pull myself away before I turned to face him. I allowed the silence to slowly unfold as I stared back at him. The deep dark dread still ravaged my insides, but I wouldn't accept even one more ounce of comfort. Not from him. Not when he couldn't understand what he'd done, what he was still doing.

"You don't have to lay a hand on me to hurt me, Apep," I bit out. "What you've done to Ryker is enough."

I watched as his black eyes slowly hardened. His matte black wings extended out behind him, effortlessly lifting him up from the ground until his feet were planted firmly on the floor.

His entire being was a walking contradiction of light and dark. His hair was dark and shiny, hanging just to his shoulders, but his pale skin was light, practically phosphorescent, against his darker features and wrapped tunic. His eyes swirled from dark to white, mixing and swirling in a dizzying spiral.

"And what would you have me do?" He paused, tilting his head to the side thoughtfully. "Would you have me put him back up in his suite? Let him be king again, rounding up innocent fairies like chattel?"

I shook my head, still leaning on the ground. "He's not like that, he's…"

Kneeling before me, he gently brushed his thumb along the soft part of my cheek. "And how would I ever keep you if I let him go?"

"He asked me to stop visiting him," I stated quietly.

Apep's eyes softened. "He's suffering right now."

"Because of *you*." The angry words slipped out before I could pull them back, and I stiffened my muscles, readying for his retaliation.

Apep smiled, dropping his hand. "Yes, because of me." He pulled back and stood back up, offering a hand to help me stand as well.

There was no hiding my shocked expression as I allowed his hand to help me up from the floor.

"Are you truly so cruel?" I whispered.

He tightened his jaw, which slightly pursed his thin, pale lips as he considered his response. "In order to lead, I must show strength. Ryker just happens to be the subject of my ire."

"But what if I promised to stay?" A glimmer of hope ignited in my chest at so simple a promise. If all he wanted was for me to stay, then he could let Ryker go. My freedom for his felt like an easy thing to sacrifice, considering.

He stared down at me thoughtfully, taking in what I was sure was a blotchy mess of a face. Leaning in just slightly, he whispered, "But I could never be certain, could I?"

His eyes gave him away in that moment as I stared into their swirling depths. His magic was just on the surface, dying to reach out, but the shield inside my mind remained strong and unfaltering. He knew I would hope for something like this, a simple solution to save Ryker, even if it was at my own expense.

Am I really so predictable?

I should've known he would never truly consider it. Fresh tears stung behind my already strained eyes. Embarrassment for my own naivety flooded my cheeks.

Apep tsked. "None of that, now." He bent down and kissed the top of my forehead before moving toward a small rolling table that held several decanters.

That was when I noticed his fingers.

Pale light streamed in from the window, illuminating each golden ring perched on his knuckles…rings that used to sit on Ryker's hands.

That same gilded hand now held out a glass to me. "Drink some water."

Absently moving through the motions, I took the glass from his hands and raised it to my mouth before he poured himself an amber-colored drink. Motioning to the seats directly in front of the desk, he moved to sit, obviously expecting me to follow his directive and do the same.

I did not.

Taking a sip of his drink, he set it on the desk and eyed me thoughtfully. "I know it's been a lot to take in, and I know I've lost much of your trust because of my treatment of Ryker."

I sipped at my water, willing the cool liquid to keep my anxiety and nausea down.

"What if I gave you a gift?" His thin lips pulled up slightly at the corner.

"A gift?" I echoed back in confusion.

"Yes. Would you like that?" His eyes were eager, bordering on excitement.

My brow wrinkled uncomfortably as I shook my head. "I don't want a gift."

"You may not think so now, but I think you need this particular gift, and I want to be the one to give it to you."

My stomach sank as the pressure of suspicion built on top of it. He was a master at using his words to hide his true intentions, and I had a feeling this gift, whatever it may be, would be no real gift at all.

Apparently he took my silence for acceptance; he sipped from his drink once more, then stood. "Finish your glass, then go get bathed and changed. I'll move to the office in our suite so your magic doesn't have to work as hard."

The water relieved the tightly knotted sensation in my throat, but it settled uncomfortably in my churning stomach. Apep's smug expression gave away his delight at this whole interaction. Ryker's stolen rings glinted in the sunlight from the window as he slowly finished off his drink.

I hated the way he could manipulate and twist my nerves without using even an ounce of magic to help him. I came in here wanting to give him a piece of my mind. I wanted to yell and scream and throw things at his face just to make him see that he couldn't fully control me, and now I was sitting here, sipping water like I'd been told.

I stared at the figure across from me. The one who'd held and comforted me while I fell apart only moments ago, and then in his next breath manipulated me to his whims. I stared at his smug expression, the slight lines around his dark eyes that didn't properly represent his true age, the part in his dark hair perfectly dividing him in half, his thin lips pulled just barely off to the side in a satisfied smirk.

He may have won this round, but I wasn't going to let him win the war. If it took all of my magic and willpower, then so be it. I would do it. I wouldn't allow someone to use and abuse me again.

Apep had said I was strong, that I'd already survived one horrific reality, and he was right…I was a survivor, and I would do it again. Only this time, I would fight back.

CHAPTER 8

Evelyn

In the days that followed, I ignored Ryker's wishes and visited him every morning. He remained quiet. But I refused to let his silence deter me. I may not have been able to shield him that horrible night, but I would find a way to free him now. And until I figured that out, I would make sure he knew he wasn't alone. At the very least, I hoped that my visits would offer him some kind of routine, a way to know it was a new day.

"My magic is getting stronger… or well, I guess that means I am," I croaked to the darkened cell. "My grandmother said using your magic was like building up a muscle, so I think it means I'm getting better at it. This morning I barely even noticed my shield…departing from me."

I didn't want to use Apep's name in front of Ryker, even though I was sure he knew who I spoke of. There was no point in saying the name of our shared tormentor.

But it was true; it was a little easier to shield Apep every day. The shield I put around my mind came so naturally I didn't even have to think about it anymore; it was just always there. The weight of my moving shield around Apep's body had felt so heavy and burdensome even just a few days ago, and now, it was more like a nuisance than a burden.

Progress was progress. Even if they were small steps, I was grateful for them.

When Ryker held his silence, the guards at the end of the hall snickered.

Turning my head, I shot them all a pointed glare. I knew I wasn't very menacing, but they still quieted down somewhat. However, the damage had already been done; Ryker's shadowed form seemed to shrink even smaller.

I hated this.

I hated *them*.

The horrible lot of them had appeared a few days ago. Apep had introduced us, though I didn't care to remember any of their names, and informed me that they would be my constant shadows, making sure I was always *safe*.

I had scoffed then, just like I wanted to now. We all knew this wasn't about keeping me *safe* as much as it was Apep keeping tabs on me, maintaining as much control as possible.

The whole thing made my skin crawl. I hated the constant sense of being watched. Especially when I'd spent most of my life trying to be small and unnoticed.

"I'm sorry they're here," I whispered as I leaned my head against the bars, picking the dirt out from under my fingernails while I looked down at my hands. "I'm going to figure something out. Some way to get you out of here, I promise."

Silence filled the space between us, and my eyes pricked with building tears that I refused to cry, especially in front of Apep's guards. I knew it was hard, but Ryker and I, we still had each other. Even separated by rough stone walls and iron bars, we were both still alive, still here, which meant we could still have hope.

"Your Highness." One of the new guards approached me, offering only the barest bit of deference with his body language, a subtle slight against my stolen title. They respected and feared Apep, but I saw the looks they flashed my way, making it far too obvious that their respect and fear did not extend to me. "Apep said not to let you linger here. We must be going."

I shot him an angry stare that felt ferocious but probably looked as mild as a mouse to him. His responding condescending smile only confirmed my suspicion.

As it turned out, Apep had chosen his guards well. They were all male fairies who'd mastered their magic, gained their wings, and were loyal only to him. He may have called me a princess in public, but here inside these walls, it was obvious that was only a title. It held no real power beyond him.

"I'll be back tomorrow," I whispered through the bars.

Ryker said nothing at all as I stood from the hard, cold ground and left.

Every time I left him, that crevice in my chest fractured further. Soon it would be a gaping wound I suspected would never truly heal over.

The guards followed me silently up the flights of stairs. Though they didn't speak as we walked through the main palace hallways, I still felt their constant eyes on me, watching my every move, their presence grating my already-shot nerves. Stepping inside the King's suite, I turned and promptly shut the doors on their faces.

Luckily, they weren't allowed in our shared suite. One thing to be grateful to Apep for. He liked his privacy, and I needed a reprieve.

Sighing heavily, I sank down onto the nearest settee inside the sitting room. My entire being felt weary, and my shoulders slumped forward, but it was less from the strain of my magic as much as… well, everything else. Each day was a challenge to get through, to keep trying, to maintain hope.

Plus, it all hurt worse now that Ryker wouldn't speak to me.

Being alone like this wasn't new for me, but this was a different kind of loneliness. There was a hopelessness attached to it that was foreign and unsettling. Even though I was constantly surrounded by people and Apep stayed with me every night, I felt…isolated.

Taking in the room around me, I studied the bedroom's grand double doors to my right. The gilded design was truly ostentatious. Traditional gold, white, and the lighter blue of Alstonia swirled in heavy patterns, embellishing each door in mirrored images.

Those same three colors seemed to stain everything throughout the entire suite, from the blue carpeted floor to the fussy white walls.

There were several settees that surrounded me, all upholstered with velvety blue cushions covered in gold damask designs. Tucked in the corner of the room, a small but ornate wooden writing desk sat vacant of papers or books, simply ready to be occupied at anyone's convenience. Fine tables and chairs were evenly spaced throughout the room, as though it should always be prepared to entertain multiple guests. The painted masterpiece of the ceiling above my head depicted the lush lands of Alstonia, and a currently unlit grand white marbled fireplace completed the room.

The suite was empty, silent.

I was truly alone here.

My mind wandered...no. It worried. I needed to find a way to free Ryker. I promised him I would get him out, and I intended on keeping that promise.

My heart suddenly ached for Grandmother Chrissy. I wished I could see her, or maybe just talk to her for a few stolen moments, something. She'd always had a word of advice, something to help guide me as I...

My mind stuttered as her words repeated in my head.

"Think of your magic the same as using a muscle in your body. It takes practice to build up the strength you need to wield it."

Ever since Liam had left, I'd stopped practicing. But that was the key, wasn't it? If I could build up my magical muscles, I could help Ryker escape.

A giddy laugh bubbled up in my chest. For the first time in what felt like weeks, my heart fluttered with renewed hope. I hadn't received my wings yet, which meant I still had more to learn and discover with my magic. Specifically, to use it in an offensive way, instead of reactive or preventive. I'd done it once before by accident, but that meant I could do it again.

Jumping up from my seat, I looked around the space with fresh eyes.

Not a great place to practice magic, I murmured inside my own mind, until my eyes caught on the door that led to the small dining room. The fact that it was called the *small* dining room still made me scoff in disbelief. It looked more like a small ballroom, if anything.

Pulling the door open, I stepped into the cavernous space, my feet suddenly echoing with each step on the marbled floor. The room was dark except for the large windows providing the only light at the back.

No one was there, but I still walked carefully and quietly across the polished stone floor until my eyes snagged on the small library where Ryker had hosted our intimately sweet dinner. Even though the door was visible, it was still discreetly tucked off in the corner at the back of the room. In this grand and empty space, the little library felt like an inside secret you had to discover for yourself.

Twisting the ring Ryker had given me on my finger, my eyes pricked with tears, remembering how he'd danced with me afterward. That night had been one of my happiest memories with him.

I miss him so much.

It didn't matter that I visited him every day. The fact that he was in the dungeons and not here with me now was the issue. He should've been here. He should've been free.

Turning to face the wide-open space of the dining room again, I surveyed the expansive room before me. The dining table and chairs remained in the middle, near the giant fireplace that was as grand as the room itself, but there were no other obstacles to maneuver around. The ceilings were high, the space was vast, and the long table could be worked around.

I rubbed my hands together in excited anticipation. This seemed as good a place to practice as any, and I needed to take advantage of the time while I was alone. Closing my eyes, I let my mind travel back to the day when my shield exploded outward, keeping Apep actively away from me.

I needed to replicate that moment.

Chrissy and I had tried once during practice, but I'd only managed to singe the leaves that day. I pursed my lips in frustration. I couldn't risk leaving a trace of my magic behind. No one could know I was practicing. If Apep found out, I didn't know what he would do.

Marching myself over to the massive fireplace, I stood directly in front of it. No one would notice singe marks in here.

Imagining Chrissy in my mind, I allowed her words to guide me as I repeated the same actions I'd tried when we'd trained before. Closing my eyes, I felt the magic within me. Focusing on all of my pent up emotions, I slowly brought them to the surface.

The sensation was overwhelming, but not overpowering. I didn't feel fatigued. If anything, I felt energized.

Taking in a deep breath, I pulled all of my emotions into a tight ball of energy and released it into the fireplace as if I were exhaling with a huge woosh of magic.

The flash of light blared bright behind my eyelids, and I quickly opened my eyes to see the stone wall had blackened in the back of the fireplace, as if it had been recently lit and there had been far too much smoke.

But there was no smoke, no remnants of my magic having been there, and—

I checked inward, examining how I felt. Only the slightest bit of fatigue.

It worked!

Biting back a cry of excitement, I allowed myself a quick hop of exultation. This could actually possibly help.

Now all I needed was an object to practice with so that I could see what kind of reaction it had to my magic.

Turning around in place, I searched the room for something I might be able to use. It was obvious I wouldn't be able to do this too many more times—that one burst of magic already felt as though it was draining me. But I had to try at least once more. A little time with nature after this and maybe a good long nap, and I would be fine. Apep would merely assume this was all just too much for me. Poor little Evelyn, so exhausted and afraid.

I smirked to myself. Little did he know…

On the large dining table stood three candelabras. I grabbed the middle one. No one would really notice if just one candelabra was missing…three felt excessive anyway.

Placing it in the center of the fireplace, I opened up my arms, and my magic, but instead of forming a shield, I threw the raw magic at the candelabra. The wax of the candles drooped and slowly melted, making a mess of the fireplace floor. But the metal of the stand remained intact—a little blackened, but nothing more.

Rubbing the back of my neck, my shoulders drooped. The burden of magic was beginning to weigh heavily on my shoulders.

Just one more time, I encouraged myself. I could do this, I knew I could. People were counting on me. I was counting on myself.

This time, instead of keeping my hands wide, I clapped them together at the same time I pushed my magic forward.

A small gasp sounded to my left, followed by the deafening clang of metal hitting stone.

My head shot over to the open door that led to the dining room where Feleen stood, looking both shocked and a bit awed.

Drooping my shoulders forward, my eyes closed and I clutched my chest, taking in a big gulp of breath. Breathing heavily, perspiration dripping from my brow, I reached up with the back of my other hand to wipe away the moisture in both relief and exhaustion.

"I didn't mean to startle you." Feleen's quiet voice barely carried in the cavernous space. "Miss Evelyn, that was…"

I opened my eyes, looking back over at her, but her eyes were glued to the fireplace. Following her line of vision, I gasped when I saw what had happened.

Feleen was by my side an instant as we both stared at the candelabra, which now lay in two pieces instead of one. "I didn't know you could wield magic like that."

"I didn't, either," I whispered. Walking over, I picked up the top half of the candelabra. It was cool to the touch, no heat, no indication that anything had melted through metal. A completely clean break, as though it had been cut in half by the sharpest of blades.

We both turned and stared at each other in disbelief until we heard sounds and movement coming from the sitting room, followed quickly by the all-too-familiar shivering sensation that snaked up my spine.

Scooping up the second half from the fireplace, I instantly searched for someplace I could hide the evidence of my practice. Apep couldn't find out; I needed him completely ignorant of my abilities in order to make use of them without his knowledge.

Feleen seemed to catch on as she grabbed my hand and led me toward the small library. "In here," she whispered.

Underneath all the pillows that lay along the seat inside the window was a small cabinet that housed a few furs and other cozy items to wrap up in. Feleen grabbed the two pieces of the candelabra from me and hid them inside, closing the open cabinet door quickly.

Footsteps echoed in the dining hall as we scrambled to get the pillows back in place. I quickly sat down on the seat, and Feleen ran over to the nearest bookcase, snatching a book from the shelf before handing it to me with haste.

Just as I opened it to the middle somewhere, Apep's head popped inside of the door frame.

"Ah. You are here." He smiled at first, then eyed Feleen with slightly narrowed eyes. "What are you doing in here?"

Feleen straightened, and her mouth bobbed open and closed, though no sound came out.

"She was keeping me company." I slammed the book shut to show my annoyance at his rudeness.

Apep sneered, "She has plenty to do without bothering you." His eyes never left Feleen as he continued, "Go tell the others that Evelyn will need to be ready for a court appearance. I want her looking as queenly as possible."

Feleen curtsied and rushed past him through the door.

"Must you be so rude?" I chided him. "They do so much to help, and you know I care for them. They're my friends."

Apep sighed and lowered himself to sit at the foot of the window seat, forcing me to reel my legs back in order to give him room. He slowly looked out the window, then down to the book in my lap, and finally up into my eyes.

"A little bit of light reading, I see." He quirked a brow, and I looked down at the book in my hands. *The History of Alstonian Agriculture.*

I pursed my lips. "I enjoy gardening, but I've never had the opportunity to study it before." I sighed dramatically. "Now that I'm cooped up in this palace, I've found such *light reading* piques my interest."

Apep ran his pale veined hand, gilded with Ryker's stolen rings, down the sleeve of his tunic as though he was dusting it off. "I do wish you'd talk more with the fairies of our court instead of keeping to yourself."

I shook my head. "I don't particularly feel like meeting new people."

"Fairies," he corrected, annoyance clouding his tone.

I swallowed. "Excuse me. Fairies. I'm not used to it yet."

Letting out an exaggerated sigh, Apep pulled a letter from the folds of his clothing and handed it to me. "Perhaps this will cheer you up. Princess Jada has written you."

I took the letter from his hand, turning it over to see it had already been opened. Confusion crumpled my brow as I looked back up at him.

"It looks as though she was quite taken with you." He smiled, but gave no apology for invading my privacy further, and I struggled to hide my irritation. "Keeping up good relations with Terreno will be essential to the second phase of my fairy liberation plan."

"And what's the second phase?"

He smirked, "All in due time." Tapping the letter in my hands, he rose up from the seat and started perusing the books on the shelves. "Go ahead. Take a moment to read it."

I turned the letter over and huffed out a frustrated breath. The letter had not only been read, it looked as though it had been examined quite thoroughly.

From the side of my eyes, I saw Apep turn his head to look back at me, quirk an eyebrow, then turn back to scan the books before him.

Huffing another notably exasperated breath through my nose, just in case he hadn't gotten the message the first time, I focused on the letter. Jada's writing was just like her; exquisite long lines, elegant script, direct language. She spoke of how much she enjoyed our new friendship and asked me to visit as soon as I was able. She spoke of her desire to see a great bond form between our kingdoms, and that our friendship might be the centerpiece of such a bond. She asked me to write back and update her on all the new developments since she left, and she signed it with a beautiful and life-like hand drawing of a white jasmine flower.

Sighing, I let my hand holding the letter fall into my lap.

"Were you hoping for more?" Apep's voice had moved to the corner of the room.

Shrugging my shoulders, I stared back out the window at the rolling pastures, deadened and browned by the constant frost of winter. "I'm surprised she didn't ask about any of the recent…" I paused, searching for a word that wouldn't incite his anger, "…updates since she left."

"I am as well. That's why I checked it so thoroughly."

I made a non-committal sound in my throat.

"Come, it's time to get you ready." Apep's hand was suddenly in front of me, offering to help me off the bench. "Hopefully after today, you'll start to feel differently and embrace your place amongst our people."

Unease churned low in my gut as I placed my hand in his, still holding Jada's letter in my other, *The History of Alstonian Agriculture* already cast aside. "What's happening today?"

Apep smirked and leaned in as I stood. "The gift I promised you."

My eyes narrowed as my brow furrowed. "And this gift is in the throne room?"

He laughed, delight twinkling mischievously in his eyes. "Always so curious." Offering his arm, he led me back out into the dining room, past the freshly blackened fireplace that he luckily didn't seem to notice at all, and then through the sitting room. "Go allow your maids to get you ready, and I'll see you back out here soon so we may walk in together."

"Not even a clue as to what my gift is?" I tried to ask playfully, keeping him unaware of my rapidly rising anxiety.

Apep chuckled, reaching up to stroke my cheek with his thumb. "No clues." His eyes twinkled as he spoke, and dread filled my stomach. "But you may know that *I* wanted to be the one who gave you this particular gift, and I won't ruin it by spoiling the surprise."

My stomach churned violently at his odd words, and my hand gripped Jada's letter even more tightly. I was grateful her letter had come first; hearing from her was the kind of surprise I needed right now, especially since I had a feeling Apep's idea of a *gift* likely did not match my own.

The only other time I'd seen that purely satisfied expression on his face was the day he towered over Ryker's shivering and broken form in the dungeon.

I just hoped that whatever he had planned wouldn't hurt Ryker further or destroy what little hope I'd managed to cling to.

CHAPTER 9

Evelyn

The girls helped me clean up and ready myself to receive whatever gift Apep wanted to give me. They dressed me in a flowing, airy green gown that had an incredibly low-cut back, which seemed to be the fairy style even though not every fairy had their wings. I took a deep breath, attempting to calm my breathing ,and straightened my shoulders before meeting Apep in the sitting room.

I gasped and reared back as I took in Apep looking up from the small desk in the corner. Ryker's crown was prominently displayed on his head, a shining gold beacon in contrast to his dark hair swept to the side beneath it. He smiled as best he could, but the muscles in his face were stiff and unpracticed.

"You look beautiful, Evelyn." He rounded the desk, slipping his pale fingers under my chin, raising my eyes up to look at him. The cold metal of Ryker's rings seared my skin. "Keep your head high and your chin up. You are royalty now."

With his hand outstretched, he snapped his fingers in impatience, and the girls startled before one of them rushed away and back, handing Apep something that sparkled in the light.

Carefully bringing the item to my head, he tucked it gently

into my curls and I instantly stood up even straighter. The weight sat far too heavily on my head, mixing its burden with the already increasingly heavy weight of my magic. Having Apep nearer to me made it a little easier, but my earlier practice had worn me out more than I'd anticipated.

"That's it, embrace your new status. You're a princess now…*my* princess." Apep stepped away, admiring me with a satisfied expression. "Perfect."

Nausea roiled in my stomach, but I forced a smile.

Offering his arm, he asked, "Ready?"

I swallowed thickly, already dreading whatever was coming next, but reluctantly took his arm and allowed him to lead me away from the safety and comfort of the suite.

The minute we passed through the doors, my shadows guarded closely behind, as did Apep's. Regardless of the truth, we certainly had the appearance of royalty as we walked the halls toward the throne room, even if it was all a farce.

We rounded the corner and steadily strode straight for the double doors of the throne room, which some of his fairy sentries opened upon our arrival. The whole room was packed with fairies in all sorts of dress: formal, informal, flowing, colorful, neutral. Wings of every color, shade and size sparkled in the light from the many windows surrounding the space. Everyone moved aside and bowed low as we made our way to the dais against the farthest curved wall.

Simply stepping foot into the room gripped my stomach in instantaneous dread and twisted. The few times I had been in this room had not been pleasant, the last of which being Katerina's sentencing after she'd threatened to murder Cook, Ryker, and myself.

I didn't want to be in this room.

My grip on Apep's arm tightened, which made him look down at me, his eyes questioning. Knowing he struggled to read my emotions, I did my best to convey my unease and dread through my eyes. He was all I had to latch on to. I knew no other soul in this space and hated how isolated I felt. A small placating pat to my hand was all I received in comfort as he released his hold, helping me sit on the smaller throne.

Every eye in this grand and marbled circular space watched us. The crown that was nestled into my curls grew heavier with each passing moment, as did my fatigue, and I wondered if the crowd present would be able to hear the deafening beat of my heart in my chest. Or maybe they would see the cold sweat breaking out on my brow. I didn't want to fall apart on display for them. Whatever Apep had planned, it certainly wasn't a true gift, not with this many spectators in attendance.

Apep stepped forward, raising his arms and flaring his wings wide so they were perfectly on display. I stared at the wrapped back panels of his tunic and pants. He'd changed his attire to look more regal, more royal: an ornately wrapped black tunic with a longer cut, reaching almost to his knees, with intricate gold stitching that perfectly matched the stolen golden crown on his head, accented by the stolen gilded rings on his hand. The designs had been sewn throughout in beautiful swirling patterns that mimicked wings or perhaps the air itself. If I were in a better state of mind, I might've considered the outfit lovely, or perhaps just a touch too ostentatious for my liking, but I was only focusing on the outfit itself to help my fraying nerves from completely unraveling.

"Thank you for gathering here today and honoring us with your presence." Apep's words were articulate, smooth and lithe, weaving through the crowd with an air of authority. "The time for the Fairies is upon us."

Shouts and hollers rose from the crowd in agreement.

"Today, we celebrate the rightful rulers of this kingdom taking the throne. You now bear witness." Apep's hand gestured out to me. The crowd cheered again and murmured amongst themselves, many stealing both approving and disapproving glances my way. The burden of their stares attempted to topple me as my emotions staggered uncontrollably.

"Princess Evelyn suffered greatly under the usurping humans of this kingdom, and today I shall make amends for that injustice." The crowd cheered again, and my breath caught in my throat. I racked my brain to figure out what he could mean, what he was up to, but before I could—

"Bring out the offenders!"

Those words cut straight into my soul.

No.

He had been saying cryptic things for a while about cutting ties and freeing me from my past. Who did he have? Was it Camilla? Becca?

Liam?

My heart strained under its own rising rhythm, and black edges began to cloud my vision.

Please, no.

And then...there they were.

Not Camilla, not Becca. Not Liam.

Frank and Katerina.

They were brought out in chains and forced to their knees before the dais, and I was thrown straight back into one of the most terrifying moments of my life. My traitorous body began to tremble furiously, refusing to yield to my internal pleas to remain steady. Bile raced up from my stomach just as my throat closed up.

Please, not again. Not again.

My eyes darted everywhere, not knowing where to look. Frank and Katerina's hateful eyes were watching me. I was going to be sick, I was going to...

Apep turned to me and smiled. His eyes gleamed with bloodthirsty delight, clearly pleased with himself and his supposed *gift* for me.

His saccharine tone echoed off the marbled walls. "Princess Evelyn was neglected, abused, tormented, and eventually sold by these wretched humans whom she used to call family."

Horrified gasps and curses resounded throughout the space.

"She was used and mistreated for years." Apep's voice sang over the crowd. "But these *humans*—" he sneered, "—did not care. They did not feel guilt. They did not regret. They did not attempt to amend their wicked ways."

Apep's words and outstretched arms held the attention of every being in the room, and that was when I realized none of this was truly for me. This was all a show, a way for Apep to display his power and invoke justice for a wrong committed he was never able to right. This was for the sister he lost. The one he couldn't save. My father and stepmother were the stand-ins, just as much as I was.

Apep knelt on the ground before their cowering forms, smiling a wide macabre smile, and the crowd grew quiet to listen as though this was a theatre piece instead of the lives of living, breathing people.

"I can read your minds." His slithering words whispered. "I know what thoughts lie inside you. You cannot hide them from me." He paused and stared them both down before he slowly stood back up, raising his voice with his height. "You have felt no remorse, no guilt, no shame for what you have wrought." Apep's head locked directly on my father's shrinking figure beneath him. "Even to your own flesh and blood."

I closed my eyes and tried to breathe. There was no hiding it now; my entire body convulsed quietly as I gasped for air that wouldn't come. My shield around Apep wavered as my ragged emotions welled up inside of me.

Apep was instantly there, gripping my hand as my shield dropped entirely. My chin quivered, and though I tried to keep them in, tears slowly dripped down my face in horror of what I knew was coming. How would he exact his revenge? Would he make me watch? A clammy sweat saturated my skin, slickening my hand in his grip.

His hold tightened as his eyes landed on Katerina. "You weak-minded, wretched woman. You blamed Evelyn for your misfortunes even when they were entirely your own. When I offered a way for revenge, you didn't even hesitate to take it. You allowed me the power over your mind with such willingness, based entirely on the hope that you'd somehow be able to destroy your future sovereign."

He raised my hand then, and Katerina quivered and whimpered as she looked helplessly up at him.

"Look at my Princess!" he demanded, and Katerina's eyes instantly shifted to mine, but instead of the normal haughty and displeased look, I saw the terrified pleading of desperation.

I gripped Apep's hand tighter, needing anything to anchor me in this appalling moment. While I watched, her eyes glued to mine, she began to convulse violently. Her eyes widened to the point of being near-grotesque, unblinking. Her mouth gaped open in a scream that didn't sound.

"That's right. Let them in," Apep spoke quietly, tilting his head ever so slightly to examine her torture. Tears ran in rivulets out of her gaping gaze. "How does it feel?"

She twitched and shook and wept in horrifying silence. There was no way to tell what he was forcing her to see.

The fairies that surrounded the throne slowly moved away from the woman being tortured on the floor. Quiet murmurs matched with a mixture of shocked, delighted, and nervous faces as they took in the scene before them.

As they realized the extent of Apep's power.

Satisfied, Apep straightened himself, releasing a gasping, sobbing Katerina, who collapsed bonelessly to the floor.

Giving my hand a squeeze in some sort of misguided comfort, Apep continued, "You are hereby sentenced to torment until death, just as you tormented Princess Evelyn for nearly eight years of her life." He lowered his voice slightly. "However, I personally don't think you'll last quite as long." He winked at the crowd, who chuckled uncomfortably. "You will not be able to speak or think or move without these torments plaguing your mind until you submit to death."

Katerina writhed from her prone position on the floor as a smooth, sinister smile slowly filled Apep's face in response. The only smile that seemed to fit his face.

"Take her away."

The order fell from his lips with pure pleasure. Guards moved swiftly, pulling on her chains in order to drag her writhing body out through the crowd. Unable to watch, I glanced up at Apep, who viewed the procession with a cruel and terrible light in his eyes.

Once they were out of sight, Apep's hungry eyes latched onto my father.

"Frank Coulter." A cruel smile laced his lips. "Yes, I can hear your thoughts. Your pleas for mercy. Your hope that your daughter will speak for you again."

A choked sob lodged itself in my throat.

"But this is *my* gift to her." Apep cocked his head to the side, studying my father's bowed form. "I gift her with ridding the world of you and your wretched wife." He lowered his voice in a theatrical stage whisper. "I gift her with true justice."

"Apep, please." My voice was strained and thin.

He turned to look back at me. "I do this for your own good."

Raising my clenched hand in his, he gently kissed the back of my knuckles, and since words wouldn't come easily to me, I pulled down my shields, allowing my mind to be heard instead. If Apep refused to listen to me, I'd make him. I knew the risks of letting him in, but I couldn't bear the thought of watching my father die before my eyes. It was too much, too complicated, too horrifying.

Apep turned immediately to me with questioning eyes as he read my mind, as he felt the terror that consumed my thoughts. I pleaded with my mind for him not to do this to me. I begged him to let Frank live out his life in the fields serving fairies, as was his original punishment. That was justice enough for me. That was all I needed.

I remembered the good times with my father, when I was just a girl...when he'd twirl me in his arms, when we had picnics with my mother in the field of wildflowers. I wanted Apep to see that though he'd wronged me, he was still my father, and on some level I still cared for him.

My vision clouded further, and my eyes began to close of their own accord as Apep knelt in front of me.

You will not be free of your humanity until the one who sired you is gone. He spoke the words softly inside of my mind as he stroked my cheek with his knuckle, brushing my tears to the side. *One way or another, you will be free of the monster who hurt you.*

Please, I pleaded in my mind.

"You will thank me in time," he said out loud.

He truly believed that. He truly believed that what he was about to do was a gift to me, a freedom. Watching my father be slaughtered in front of my own eyes.

I shook in horror, allowing the blackening edges of my vision to take over.

Apep's eyes softened as he listened to my thoughts. But still he stood, turning back to my father.

"Cover his face."

A black coverlet went over my father's desperate eyes, effectively shielding me from his expression.

"Kill him," Apep ordered.

My eyes still clenched tight, Apep gently caressed my hand, and a comforting sensation flooded my body, easing my tension. In the back of mind I knew it was a false calm, an artificial composure, but I couldn't stop it from flooding my veins. My body relaxed and my tears dried as one of the guards approached with a long blade in his hand.

No, I screamed, but my tongue wouldn't work. My voice was trapped behind a gag of forced indifference. *No, no, no!*

One minute the shining blade had been on display for everyone in the throne room to see, and the next minute it was inside my father's chest, cutting through his back. A deep red stain bloomed across his dirty and threadbare shirt.

Somewhere inside of me, there were screams. But even those couldn't find their way out.

Apep knelt in front of me again as the guard pulled his sword back out. My father's body listed to the side with a sturdy thud against the stone.

"He is no longer your family," Apep consoled. "The day he sold you, he gave up that right." His eyes searched mine. "*I* am your family now, Evelyn." He gestured out to the audience of fairies still standing before us. "*We* are your family now."

There was no answer to give. Nothing but silent screaming, on and on and on.

Apep gathered me back up to my feet, still holding my hand, and presented me to the crowd. Everyone bowed and moved to the sides of the room, clearing a path for us to walk through.

My feet no longer moved of their own accord, but neither did I feel anything as we walked past my father's unmoving body on the floor. My eyes were up, my head held high, and my steps steady as I faced the doors in front of us.

Apep leaned into me as we rounded the corner toward our suite. "If you can manage to place a shield around me again, I will release your mind and allow you some time to yourself."

I felt his influence lift, and I took the opportunity to place a shield around him again, while also reinforcing my own. It took a few tries, but I finally got them settled in place. The burden of the magic, or perhaps everything that had just happened, folded my shoulders forward in utter exhaustion.

The screams stopped. Only fatigue remained.

A few guards stood off to the side of us, waiting for me to join them.

"Go back to our suite. I'll be there shortly," Apep whispered.

I pulled on his hand just as he was starting to let go. "Take them with you." I motioned to the guards, one of which being the fairy who'd just executed my father.

Apep glanced over my shoulder. Thankfully, he seemed to understand why I had requested it. "Only for tonight. You four, come with me." He promptly left me in the hall without another word, his guards following obediently behind him.

As soon as I could no longer hear their steps, I walked quietly and swiftly down the long hall to a familiar door and carefully opened it to the abandoned space before gently closing it behind me. The fading light of sunset illuminated the tiny space. The bed still wasn't made and random clothes were strewn about, silver armor perfectly on display, shining in the fading light.

The room still smelled like him.

Curling up on the bed, I slowly inhaled the comforting scent of musky cedarwood and sweetgrass. The scent of home. I wrapped the messy bedding around me as tightly as I could, pretending it was Liam's embrace soothing and comforting me.

Gripping his pendant directly over my heart, I buried my face into his pillow and allowed myself to mourn all that had just taken place.

The hardest and most shameful part of it all was that no matter how awful it had been to watch them be sentenced like that, a part of me felt...relieved. I was grateful, so grateful, that it hadn't been Liam or Becca, Cook or Jimmy, Chrissy or even Camilla.

What kind of horrible person did that make me? Maybe I was more like Apep than I wanted to be. Maybe that was why my father didn't want me in the first place. Maybe that was why Camilla had betrayed me. Maybe that was why Liam left...

Maybe it was me.

CHAPTER 10

Liam

The morning Rafe and Billy left for Evy's estate, I woke up early to see them off. Not that I'd truly slept the night before ,anyway, my mind racing with every update, every regret, every possible horror Evy and Ryker could be facing. That night and the nights following, it was hard to tell if I was having actual nightmares or simply imagining the worst.

Four days later, and we were all waiting on pins and needles for Rafe and Billy to return. Chrissy had taken to communing with nature as much as possible. Ian had inferred this was how she spent most of her time, and I noted the way his eyes always seemed to follow her. I hadn't wanted to pry, but it was becoming more and more obvious how he felt about her…Chrissy, on the other hand, was much harder to read.

I slammed my axe down with a heavy thud, followed by a quick slip of metal breaking apart the wooden fibers of the log in front of me. The midday sun did nothing to ease the frozen temperatures, but sweat still dotted my brow from the exertion.

Becca had been making herself useful as she tidied up the tavern and helped Ian serve. I had taken to chopping fresh wood for our fires each day, and surprisingly, Camilla had taken up preparing food in the kitchen. She'd mentioned Cook had taught her a few things, and we were all grateful for it. Ian, unfortunately, was no cook at all...one could only take in so much gruel before their stomach began to revolt. Wiping my brow with my forearm, I continued to chop. Staying active helped, especially my far-too-neglected muscles. I enjoyed the burn of physical activity; it kept me distracted, mostly. The constant ache in my chest was difficult to ignore, and my patience had been wearing thin as we waited for Rafe and Billy to return. Every day I spent away from the palace felt like a new tear in my soul.

A throat cleared right after I swung my axe particularly hard, shooting the freshly split logs off to the sides and lodging it solidly into the wide stump beneath.

"You look like you could use a break." Chrissy's bright green eyes stared at me with such warmth and familiarity, it was hard to look at her without tears smarting the backs of my eyes.

Wiping my brow with my forearm again, I released the handle of my axe. The thing didn't even budge from its wedged position in my chopping stump. "I suppose you're right." I tried to smile, but I knew it fell short.

"Come take a walk with me?" she asked.

I nodded, picking back up the warm coat Ian had offered me while I worked outside and jogging up beside Chrissy.

At first we just walked in silence, seemingly aimlessly through the town and then into a dense evergreen forest. The crisp, rich scent of fir filled my senses. The aroma slowly relaxed my overactive brain as we walked between the ancient trunks. It was surprisingly warmer walking between the tall trees that practically blocked out the sky, as if they helped insulate us from the cold. I sucked in another deep breath through my nose. Chrissy was right—this was exactly what I'd needed.

"I was mated once, you know. Or married, as you humans call it." The sudden sound of Chrissy's voice almost made me jump in comparison to the extreme stillness of the forest.

"I figured." I let a little amusement cloud my voice. "Considering you're Evy's grandmother and all."

She waved her hand casually through the air. "Evy's grandfather is an entirely different story. The story I want to share with you today was from my first love."

I furrowed my brows, deciding it best to just listen and allow Chrissy the freedom to share at her own pace. There was so much I didn't know about her; not even Evy knew many details from her life before, from what I'd gathered, so having her open up to me like this felt like something special, something that couldn't be rushed.

"He was killed by humans who viewed him as…lesser-than." Her words jarred me from my own thoughts.

I took a deep breath in through my nose and exhaled slowly before I spoke. "I'm so sorry, Chrissy, that's…"

"It was the worst moment of my life." Her voice was quiet, pained, like she was reliving the moment all over again. "He was a good male. Nature had gifted him powerful magic, and he was a leader among our kind, doing his best to keep us all together even as the humans wrenched us apart."

My heart sank. My people had done this to her. A fresh wave of new guilt washed over me, but Chrissy reached out to pat my arm. "It's good for you to know the truth of your people's history, but there is no reason to hold onto that guilt yourself. As long as you're willing to learn, accept, and grow from past transgressions, you will be a good leader that ushers in what's needed to heal."

I shook my head. "I'm no leader."

"Ah. But you are." We kept walking forward, weaving our way over crunchy brown pine needles and around large tree trunks and branches. "My mate was a reluctant leader as well. He didn't choose the job; it chose him." She spoke with such fondness in her voice. "I see much of him in you." She smiled, looking up at me then.

"Thank you." Though I couldn't see myself in the same way, I appreciated her words all the same.

"However, he wasn't without his faults." Her wings fluttered gently behind her. "He left us once, right after our son showed his gifted magic for the first time. What should've been the happiest of moments devolved into a fearful retreat. Our son was powerful, even in his sweet toddler years, and we knew that it would cause trouble."

I tried to swallow down the shame bubbling up from my chest, but there was no avoiding the feeling.

"I wanted to hate him, to curse him for leaving us vulnerable and giving into his fear, but the moment he returned…" She paused, staring off into the distance. "None of it mattered. I loved him, he loved me. We were tied together by invisible bonds that couldn't be broken, and he never left my side until the day he was taken from me. He was kind, just, and wiser from his mistakes. He fought for our kind and protected our way of life as best he could." She grew quiet, lost in her thoughts and memories. "I'm still proud that he was mine."

I wanted to reach out and comfort her, to offer something other than my presence and apologies, but she didn't give me the chance.

Turning toward me, she stopped, and I followed her lead as she looked me square in the eyes. The words she spoke next would be forever etched into my soul: "You are a man of great promise." Her hand reached up to touch the center of my chest. "But if you allow shame to take up residence here, you will fail many times over." Pulling her hand away, she continued, "Learn from your mistakes, grieve what's necessary, and then do better."

I stood there and blinked absently at her while her words soaked in.

"I'll see you back at the tavern." She winked and floated away, her pearlescent wings sparkling behind her even amidst the shadowed forest.

I sucked in a deep breath through my nose and watched her float back to the tavern. She'd somehow taken us in a circle through the forest and brought us back to the edge of this small mountain town. I'd been so engrossed in her story that I hadn't even noticed, but as soon as I felt my feet again, I began the short walk back to the tavern.

She was right. Shame wouldn't save anyone. Though my fear still plagued my thoughts, I hoped that Evy and Ryker would forgive me. I hoped for the first time since I'd heard of Apep's takeover that I could make an impact against this wrong. Even if it was small, even if I didn't know what we would do to get them out of there…I had hope.

Do better.

Those final two words echoed in every corner of my mind, and a renewed energy ran through my blood. Yes, I'd made a mistake— many of them, in fact— but now I had the chance to do better, and I was going to take it.

CHAPTER 11

Camilla

No one seemed eager to seek me out for planning or other things, but that was all right. I preferred quietly busying myself, hidden behind the wooden swinging door of the tavern kitchen. I was no Cook, but what little I had learned from her seemed to be working well.

The few patrons that visited the tavern each day for their midday meal and supper were pretty much a regular lot. They were polite, but still distant, though a few of them were warming up to the idea of having humans around quicker than others. Liam and Becca talked with several, getting to know them and making friends. I, on the other hand, was grateful for a door to hide behind.

Becca bustled in as I pulled a roast out of the oven. "Smells good."

I smirked slyly. "Hopefully it tastes good, too."

She didn't quite crack a smile, but it looked like she wanted to. "You've been doing a great job in here the past few days. I can tell it's a huge relief to Ian." She glanced back at me carefully. "May I help you prepare some plates? Ian said he's got fifteen people ordering food already tonight." To my surprised expression, she offered, "It really does smell good out there."

"We may have to be stingy with our portions, then." I handed her a plate, and we silently prepared each plate of food. After a few were ready, she would pick them up, go back through the swinging door to serve those waiting out in the main room, and then come back in to continue helping me.

We kept this up until everyone had been fed.

"Don't forget to eat." Becca handed a plate to me, taking a bite of the roast of her own as we stood in the kitchen. A hum of extreme satisfaction buzzing from her lips. "How'd you learn to cook like this?"

I shrugged. "Cook taught me a few things when I stayed with them after Evy's birthday."

At the mention of Evy, Becca grew extra quiet, and I took the opportunity to bite into the meal I'd taken the entire day to make. Savory juices saturated my tongue, and I almost moaned in pleasure. Not only had I made a delicious roast, but I also realized I hadn't eaten all day.

"See? I told you it was good," Becca teased.

"And no one is poisoned yet?" I questioned playfully.

Becca laughed. "Not yet. We'll see how the night goes."

"Well, here's hoping." I shoveled another piece of roast in my mouth. Poison or not, at least it tasted good.

Becca looked up at me then, eyes serious. "What makes you so jealous of Evy?"

I pursed my lips, chewing slowly, the roast suddenly dry in my mouth. No one had actually asked me that outright before. Swallowing hard, I cleared my throat. "It's not just one thing," I stated plainly. Becca's arched eyebrow looked back at me skeptically. "And...it was never truly Evy."

She took another bite, eyebrows lifted, waiting for me to continue.

"Mother always compared me. Not just against Evy, but every girl, woman, even some men. In her eyes I was supposed to be the brightest, wittiest, prettiest. I was her hope of a better future...and her ultimate disappointment when I didn't meet expectations. If I could snag a well-off husband, I'd be able to provide for her."

"So she tried to use you," Becca said—more of a statement than a question.

I shrugged. "I suppose so. She compared me to Evy constantly, but in the same breath would complain about how wretched and awful she was. It never quite fit, though, because I liked Evy. When we first met, we were fast friends. It wasn't until Mother started pulling me away and saying those things about her that our relationship changed. Evy always had that glow about her, you know? Even the boys noticed her first. She was so lovable, and if that was considered wretched…"

"Ah…" Becca nodded in understanding. "So you believed that if Evy was wretched, even though she was noticed and admired, that it meant you must be extra wretched to not even be able to garner that attention."

Becca's astute words hit surprisingly hard. Shifting uncomfortably, I stared down at my plate. "I don't want to talk about it."

"I'm sorry, I was just…"

"I know what you were trying to do. You were trying to find my motivations for betraying Evelyn." I leveled her with an unflinching stare. "The truth is, I didn't really know I was. I just wanted her to feel as alone and hurt as I did. My goal was only to take Liam from her, not everything else."

Becca's eyes hardened as she stared at me a good long while in utter silence. "Apep never had to convince you, did he?"

Making my face as neutral as possible, I looked her straight in the eye. "I was never under his influence."

Maybe that made me wretched in truth. But lying to Becca now would have made me something worse.

Still, Becca bristled, setting her unfinished plate down before storming out of the kitchen.

The minute the door stopped swinging behind her, my shoulders fell. I knew it made it all so much worse, that I had acted on my own without Apep's outside influence. Becca had been offering an olive branch by talking to me tonight, but I didn't expect forgiveness from her, or anyone really. I couldn't take back what I'd done; I couldn't fix it or make amends. The best I could do was try to make things right. Even if that ultimately meant sacrificing myself in the process, it would be what I deserved.

Loud voices and exclamations sounded out beyond the swinging door, catching my attention. Setting down my plate, I pushed open the door and peeked my head outside. Rafe and Billy stood by the front entrance, hugging their friends, smiling, patting backs in welcome.

A sharp pang of longing pierced my heart at the sight of everyone celebrating their return. I knew I would forever be on the outskirts after what I'd done, but it didn't stop the yearning I felt to be a part of it all.

Rafe and Billy looked tired from the fast-paced journey, but no worse for the wear. Rafe's eyes were heavy when he looked upon Becca, but instead of his usual longing, they were lined with fresh grief.

The group gathered around, ushering the two to a table to sit, eager for an update. I was content to stay out of the way in my own little corner and simply listen.

"The devastation is far worse than I expected it to be. But the good news—" Rafe started.

"The good news," Billy blurted in, "is that the estate is perfectly untouched. No one goes near for fear of Apep's wrath. Apparently he made it clear that the estate was Princess Evelyn's and was to be left alone."

"*Princess* Evelyn?" Becca quirked a brow in question.

Rafe and Billy both awkwardly shifted under her gaze. "Yes, Apep calls her his Princess. All the fairies look at her as official royalty now," Billy said shyly.

"And what of my family?" Becca's hopeful eyes beseeched Rafe's.

His face sank as he reached back to scratch his neck like I'd seen him do a thousand times before when he didn't know what to say. "Becca…I…"

"Did you find them, at least?" A hint of desperation colored her tone.

Rafe shook his head. "We got as close as we could to the shop, but Hoddleston was abandoned. Wrecked. If it wasn't torched, it was claimed by fairies. We saw…" Rafe grimaced.

"Rafe, please. Tell me." Becca's eyes shone with tears, and my heart broke for her.

"We saw what looked like blood outside the door."

Becca gasped, covering her mouth with her hand as her face crumpled.

"There was no way to know if it had anything to do with them, though. With the mayhem surrounding us, it could've come from anywhere," Rafe rushed to say, reaching for her other hand. "There was no sign of a struggle that I could see, but I wasn't able to get close enough to do a thorough examination of the place. A fairy had already taken over the home and shop. I'm so sorry Becca. I tried to find them, I swear it, but there was no sign of them. Nothing to follow."

Becca's head bowed in silent grief, and Chrissy floated over, laying a hand gently on her shoulder. "Not finding them means there's still hope."

Becca nodded, but didn't look up.

"What else can you tell us?" Liam inquired, bringing the attention back to the most important details. His back was to me, muscles twitching with what I assumed was either irritation or impatience; perhaps both. Tension tightened his broad shoulders, making his posture a bit straighter and more rigid.

He hadn't spoken to me since the first day we got here, but I supposed I should've expected that. I really didn't have much hope for that bridge to be repaired.

"Cook and Jimmy were both perfectly fine," Rafe continued. "The entire place was still thriving under their care." He paused. "And there were others."

"What do ye mean, others?" Ian intoned.

"Humans and fairies alike are gathering there. It's become the secret safe haven for those either fleeing Apep's wrath, or standing against it. It couldn't be more perfect." Rafe's eyes beamed with excitement.

"How many?" Liam asked.

"At least fifty," Rafe answered, "but many were injured."

"There were more fairies than I anticipated being there," Billy chimed in again, looking toward Ian. "Considering that Apep has set himself and Evelyn up as the fairy saviors and royalty, it was surprising to see how many weren't buying into the dogma. The humans, however…were a bit worse for the wear." He grimaced at the thought.

Rafe's eyes flashed to Liam. "They're expecting us now. We'll have to travel carefully, but at least it's a relatively safe place for us to gather more information before we make our official plan."

Everyone took in this knowledge with varying levels of excitement or worry.

"We should leave at nightfall," Liam suggested. "Moving at night will help us avoid any fairies who might be patrolling the area during the day."

Ian nodded reluctantly. "Tomorrow night, then. I'll let the others know."

"I'll get some food packed and ready." Several heads all turned to look at me, as if they'd forgotten I was even there. I did my best to keep my face entirely emotionless, as I was always used to doing, but I still wanted to pitch in, to be as helpful as I could be.

"Thank you, Camilla," Ian said as he stood up from the table.

Billy jumped up. "I'll help ye."

I thought he meant to help Ian, but he headed straight for me instead. Surprised and a little shocked, I turned away mechanically, heading back in through the swinging door, Billy fresh on my heels.

"Looks like we got a bit o' cleanin' to do, too." He smiled crookedly at me, but there was no malice or distrust in his eyes. Just genuine willingness.

I filled the basin with water from an inside pump, adding a good amount of soap and starting to clean and dry each plate.

"I couldn't help but notice yer friends don't seem too happy with ye." Billy broke the silence, his gentle brogue easing the uncomfortable topic.

"No, I don't suppose they would be," I replied succinctly.

"And why's that?"

Shifting awkwardly on my feet, I scrubbed a bit too hard at the plate in my hands. "Because I betrayed Evelyn and King Ryker."

He froze, then slowly looked up from the plate he was currently washing. "What do ye mean, ye betrayed 'em?"

I sucked a harsh breath into my lungs. "I was the one who told Apep what Evy needed to hear in order for her to finally trust him." I paused, and he waited, knowing there was more to the story. "I also helped drive Liam away."

He thoughtfully dried the plate in his hands before putting it away in the cabinet. "And why'd ye do those things?"

I slammed the dishes down into the water. "Because I'm an awful person." I looked him in the eye. "Is that what you want to hear?"

He raised a questioning eyebrow. "Is it the truth?"

I sighed, gripping the edges of the basin and dropping my chin. "I caught her practicing magic with Chrissy right after my mother had her mind taken over by a fairy. At the time, I didn't know who'd done it," I offered in my defense. "I guess I still don't know for certain who it was, though the answer seems fairly obvious now. But I'd told Evelyn how much I abhorred magic and fairies, and seeing her practicing magic…" I trailed off. "For a brief time, I thought maybe she'd been the one behind it, though I suspected Chrissy more." I paused, standing up straight, my eyes forward. "My mother *was* horrible to Evy. If I'd experienced that kind of treatment, it was probably something I would've done."

He remained silent still, waiting.

I couldn't look at him. I didn't want to as the confessions poured out of me. Looking back down at my waterlogged hands, I sighed. "She was all I had left." My voice came out reedy and frail. "And suddenly she became the enemy."

"Hmm," was his response. Just, *hmm*. Nothing else, no comment or insult or even an indignant remark. I huffed out an irritated breath. *Infuriating man.*

Who I was currently spilling all my innermost thoughts out to, but still.

"I was raised to believe fairies were evil and wrong, you see?" I paused, deeply regretting this entire conversation. "So when I saw her…" I trailed off.

"Ye felt betrayed yourself," he filled in the gap.

I shrugged as I scooped up and started washing another dish. "I guess. It doesn't excuse what I did, though."

"No, it doesn't."

That was when I noticed Billy wasn't actually hand washing the dishes; he simply placed them in the water, and the water would swish and swirl around the plates, cleaning them entirely without the use of his hands at all.

My eyebrows shot up, and I stared at him in disbelief. "You can control the water?"

Billy smiled slyly over at me. "Just now noticed, did ye?"

Heat blossomed instantly on my cheeks, and I ducked my head back down. "Forgive me, I'm not used to being around fairies."

Billy made a sound of agreement. "I can finish up here. Why don't ye gather a few things for tomorrow and head on up to bed. Ye'll need good sleep before the journey back tomorrow."

I dried off my hands on my apron before hanging it back up. "Sure, thank you."

"Thanks for steppin' in while I was gone." He smiled again. A crooked, rascally type of smile that suited him.

"I was glad to help," I replied softly.

He nodded, and I set off to gather a few items in cloths for easy packing tomorrow. We left it at that, no more explanations or questions. I was grateful.

Outside of the kitchen felt like an entirely new whole world I wasn't ready to face. Liam sat at a table by himself, slowly sipping at an ale. He raised his eyes up from his glass just long enough to say, "You're still staying in Becca's room tonight. Rafe and I have some more planning to do. He'll crash in my room, but you should get some sleep while you can."

I nodded, then made my way up the creaky wooden stairs to the room across from Liam's.

Knocking quietly, I waited a moment, secretly hoping Becca was already asleep, but no such luck. Rafe pulled the door open, brushing past me without saying a word.

Softly latching the door behind me, I stripped down to my chemise and carefully climbed into bed next to Becca. We'd slept like this the past few nights, but now a fresh tension pervaded the small space, making it harder to relax.

After we both laid there for a while, I knew neither of us were asleep yet. Becca's labored breathing alone told me she was either still steaming with anger from our earlier conversation, or was worried about her folks. Probably both.

Slicing open the thick silence, I spoke plainly into the air. "No matter the initial reason, I hate what I did to Evy and Ryker. I hate that I let my anger and jealousy get the best of me at the expense of them. I'll never stop regretting it."

Becca didn't respond, and I simply let the words lay heavy in the silence between us as I slowly allowed an exhausted sleep to take me under.

CHAPTER 12

Liam

The next evening, at the very least, felt like action. Like I was finally getting to do something to save the people I loved. Our small crew had expanded in size as several of Ian's fairies joined the cause. I knew we could use all the help we could get, but I worried a larger group would also bring more attention.

Everyone was bundled and packed. The journey back to Evelyn's estate would take at least two days on foot, which with our larger group we had to do. My horse and one other were used solely as pack horses for the journey and to bring supplies to Jimmy and Cook.

Buckling my sword belt around the coat Ian had given me, I saw the tired but eager faces of our group looking to me. Chrissy's familiar green eyes met mine, and she nodded in encouragement. Her words echoed in my mind: *You're a leader, Liam.*

I cleared my throat and pulled my shoulders back as though I were about to give orders to my guard. Until this moment, I'd almost forgotten that this was what I was good at, what I'd been trained for. I may have technically become a prince, but I was a guard at heart.

"The goal is to travel to the estate unseen. Rafe, Billy, and I will each lead a smaller group should we get separated. If the worst should happen, feigning ignorance is your safest route. Using magic or lethal force should be your last resort."

With that, I turned around, leading my horse down the trail. We'd have to pass distantly by the palace and Hoddleston before we made it to the estate, which meant far too many opportunities for us to be seen or discovered, but that wasn't my focus now.

Just like I had told Ryker the day we rescued Evy, we had to take it one step at a time. I had to focus on each step individually, remembering that they would bring me closer to Evy and Ryker in the end.

***

The macabre scene in front of me was painted orange by the falling sun and framed by the deadened branches and wintery bushes that surrounded our lookout. A few browned and lifeless leaves clung to their branches, waving noisily in the wind, but they drew no attention to our hiding place.

Half-destroyed buildings, surrounded by rubble, was all I could see of the little town that sat just outside the palace grounds. It seemed some of the buildings had remained intact as Rafe and I watched fairies flit by, their outlines shadowed by the fading light.

After traveling fast for two days and sleeping for a few scant hours on the cold and hardened ground, I was grateful we'd made it here so quickly, though exhaustion was swiftly settling into my bones.

We'd stopped here to reorganize and split off into smaller groups now that we were in a more populated area, but being this close to the palace and still not being able to go inside was like ripping myself in two.

"That must be his guard," I murmured to Rafe, pointing out the few fairies who stood out in their stark black tunics and pants. Their clothes were far more uniformed; some even held blades attached to their sides, and all of them had wings.

Rafe's affirmative grunt meant he knew exactly which ones I referred to. "Best to avoid that lot."

I smirked. "Indeed."

"Still think we should split up here?"

I nodded, pointing at two guards walking down the road that led to Hoddleston. "They seem to be patrolling the area. Smaller groups will be less noticeable if we stick to the trees."

Rafe scoffed as the two guards started laughing. "They don't seem to be paying much attention."

"Maybe not, but we still have to get past Hoddleston."

"I'm not convinced you should go last," Rafe said quietly. It wasn't the first time he'd brought it up.

Sighing softly, I swiped a hand through my hair. "I know, but I feel a responsibility to make sure everyone gets there safely. I can't..."

Rafe gripped my shoulder and squeezed. "It's not your fault, Liam. We *all* made mistakes leading up to this."

I nodded, but it didn't change my mind. "Chrissy and Ian will be with me. We'll be fine."

Rafe huffed out a snort in disagreement, but turned to relay the news to the others. Night was almost upon us, and we needed to move now while we still had some light to see, but the cover of darkness was growing thick enough to help distort our moving figures through the trees.

Ian replaced Rafe's position, surveying the smoldering scene in front of us. "I won't lie," he croaked, "it feels good to see my kind flying about freely like that in front of the palace."

"Never at this cost, Ian," Chrissy's soft voice sounded next to him.

Ian's head fell in a heavy nod, and Chrissy gently twined her hand with his as they stared out at the scene together.

Turning away, I watched Billy gather his group deeper inside the trees. He'd quietly taken to caring for Camilla, and I was grateful he had none of our experience or judgement to heap on her. As much as I wanted to keep her safe, at least for Evy's sake, I still couldn't forgive her actions. She'd used me, even after I'd begun to trust her. But she still needed a friend, and someone who could look out for her better than I.

Rafe gave some brief instructions, as showcased by the nodding of heads in his direction, and then Billy was moving further into the woods that lined the road to Hoddleston, followed by Evy's estate.

Rolling my shoulders back, I watched the group disappear as they weaved quietly through the barren branches and brush.

Ian stiffened at my side, and I watched a guard fly closer to our little hideout, looking back and forth before flitting back toward the palace.

"They're very watchful," he muttered.

I grunted in agreement. "Hopefully only because we're so close to the palace. I can't imagine Apep has enough men to be this vigilant around the whole area."

Turning back to look at Rafe, I watched as he readied his group. We hadn't wanted to space them too far apart in case one group needed help. It was still another hour or so to Evy's estate, and a lot could go wrong between now and then.

I scooted away from the bush we'd hidden behind to scout the area and carefully crept over to Rafe and Becca.

"Ready?" I whispered.

Becca shivered a little, and I couldn't tell if it was from nerves or the cold. I knew passing Hoddleston would be difficult for her, but she nodded her head in determination.

Rafe gave me a solid pat on the arm, followed by a little squeeze. "We'll see you back at the estate."

"See you there."

I watched him grab Becca's hand and retreat into the trees with a few fairies following silently behind.

Turning my gaze back to the palace, I silently searched every window, every parapet, every shadow for any sign of them...anything to help ease the tension of being so close and yet so far from the both of them.

A warm, gentle hand landed on my bicep. "They'll be all right," Chrissy whispered, and I sucked in a ragged breath through my nose.

"But this will change both of them," I countered.

Chrissy hummed thoughtfully. "Likely, yes. But it's also changed you."

Gritting my teeth so hard they ground together audibly, I did my best to stave off the stinging tears threatening to drown my eyes.

They were *right there*. Both of them, right inside those high stone walls. A hair's breadth away from me, and yet I couldn't reach them, I couldn't save them, I couldn't even see a glimpse of them or tell them we were coming.

I'd never hated the palace as much as I did in this moment. Not even when I was still a boy, taken from my home, *my Evy*, and brought here to train, to become what I was now. The palace had seemed so large and unforgiving back then; I'd hated what it had stolen from me. But I'd never felt this mixture of rage and despair so potently as I did now, staring down the sturdy stone obstacle that separated me from the people I loved most in this world.

A scream wrenched through the air, and my head whipped back in the direction Rafe and Becca had just gone. Chrissy and Ian waited to follow my lead, ready to run toward the cry, but I hesitated, watching several fairy guards fly toward the sound as well.

We needed to be behind them—the element of surprise was all I really had against magic, and I wouldn't waste it by rushing in too soon. Once the new fairies passed us, I drew my sword from its sheath.

Chrissy grabbed my arm tightly and whispered, "You must be careful. Do not let them know who you are."

I nodded and met Ian's eyes next, who grimaced, but encouraged me forward.

As we grew closer, another muffled cry rang out, and I picked up my speed, stopping short of the scene before us.

Becca had been wrestled to the ground with a fairy guard hovering above her, his hand around her neck and the weight of his body pinning her down. The brutal fairies laughed as Rafe swung his sword wildly toward them, chopping furiously through various vines that kept wrapping around him, impeding his fight.

The fairies who'd been traveling with them lashed out with their magic, distracting several of the guards, but they'd obviously been caught by surprise and were trying to play catch-up in the current skirmish.

My heart raced as I did my best to make a plan before charging directly into the fray, but our time was running out quickly.

"Chrissy?" I turned to face her.

Her eyes narrowed. "I'll transform the vines around Rafe right as you attack from behind. That way, he'll have a fighting chance."

Picking up a stick in front of her, she transformed it into a sword and handed it to Ian, who nodded gratefully.

"Don't overdo it," he whispered before kissing her temple.

Chrissy's eyes remained focused as Ian and I moved silently into position behind the two closest fairy guards. There were only four in total, and if we managed to catch them by surprise, we'd overpower them quickly. I motioned that I'd take the left if he took the right, and we both moved in quiet unison, using the fairy guards laughter to camouflage the sound of our approach.

I focused on my target.

The guard before me wielded his magic against the fairies in our group as if he was playing with some kind of new toy. The incredible conceit these fairies displayed proved that they'd had little to no opposition so far.

But that was about to change, and I was ready to unleash my pent-up fury.

At their next bout of laughter, I charged in behind, running my sword directly through the guard's back. I hated fighting like this—there was no honor in running your opponent through when his back was turned—but there was also no room for courtesy when my friends' lives were on the line.

The fairy before me went immediately limp on my sword just as Rafe's sword cut through the fairy who covered Becca. She violently gasped and coughed for air, shoving weakly at the already tipping body that was still over her.

Ian sliced at the guard next to me, getting only a piece of him as he turned a hair too late, realizing what was going on.

Pulling my sword from the guard's limp body, I pivoted quickly on my toes and swung at the guard engaging Ian. With one swipe of my sword, I cut across his side, leaving a wound that bloomed a deep red and spread while I twisted again and sank my blade in through his neck.

Rafe made quick work of the last remaining guard who'd tried to run, while the other fairies from our group lowered their hands in relief, pale and panting for breath.

I fell to Becca's side and pushed the dead body further away from her before supporting her head so she could breathe a little easier. Rafe was there a moment later, taking over and making sure she was still whole.

Ian knelt with one knee beside us, running his fingers gently over

Becca's neck until the bright red and already purpling blotches slowly receded. As she sucked in a clean and unlabored breath into her lungs, I finally released the breath I'd been holding.

I sat up straighter on my knees, ready to jump up at the slightest sound while I listened and scanned the area for more guards.

Nothing.

Small favors.

The four guards we'd taken down were now lifeless corpses littering the ground around us. Chrissy was already with her fellow fairies, gaining some strength back from the earth just as I'd seen Evy do before, but Ian was quiet, pensive.

Touching Ian's arm, I searched his gaze. "Are you all right?"

"I avoided war for a reason," he said.

I nodded in understanding. He'd picked a side, but now some of his kind were dead by my hand—a human's hand. I didn't know how to comfort him in this moment or what to offer.

"Would you be opposed to hiding the bodies?" I asked softly.

He shook his head, but didn't say another word.

After I cleaned and sheathed my sword, we moved quietly to the closest body, carrying it further into the woods and hiding it behind some brush. Darkness had already descended, making it harder to see, but we got all four bodies moved, covering them with dried leaves and twigs in relative silence.

Chrissy and the other fairies already looked as though they had more color in their cheeks, and Ian moved in to help her stand.

Saying as few words as possible, I motioned for us to continue on. Becca looked beyond startled, unable to keep her tears at bay now that she was safely in Rafe's arms.

Unexpected envy rose up, overwhelming me. I wished that was Evy and I.

Dipping my head so no one could see the harsh emotions displayed on my face, I led our group through the woods, following along the path that led us past Hoddleston and on to Evy's estate.

We moved slowly and steadily through the trees and bushes, trying our best to make as little noise as possible. Being overly cautious, I stopped several times, making the group wait while I listened for any suspicious sounds.

What should have taken barely over an hour took several, and that bout of exhaustion that had been eating at my energy returned with a vengeance. The cruel way the guards played with and jeered at Rafe's group before we arrived, seemed to be commonplace under Apep's rule. I noted how no other fairies had shown up, either to join in or stop it. It was blatantly obvious that Apep's guards also weren't accustomed to opposition.

How can he allow this kind of cruelty, even to his own kind?

The thought only succeeded in angering and frightening me further.

If Apep was allowing this kind of cruelty amongst his own kind, what kind of cruelty was he performing behind the palace walls?

My overly alert and exhaustion-riddled mind finally settled somewhat at the sight of Evy's estate peeking out through the stripped tree branches of winter.

We'd made it…at least for now.

From here, we had to leave the safety of the trees and join up with the main road. But as I listened, there were no sounds of any life beyond us, or the nocturnal insects creating their nightly symphony.

And though I felt farther away physically, it still felt like one step closer to ending this. One step closer to holding Evy in my arms again, if she'd let me. One step closer to groveling on my knees for forgiveness and begging for yet another chance I didn't deserve.

As we rounded the bend of the courtyard and came upon the main house, I couldn't help but smile at the comforting and familiar lines of Jimmy's weathered face as he peeked through a curtain. A few shouted words, later and the door was flung open as several people ran outside to meet us.

Jimmy's worried eyes scanned my coat, still stained with blood from our fight in the woods.

"It isn't mine." I said quickly.

He nodded and patted me gently on the back. "Welcome home, Son."

My eyes and nose instantly smarted at his words, and I sniffed to ease the sting just as a new form exited the home, approaching us carefully.

The last time I'd seen her, I'd been dying on the arena ground.

Aster nodded grimly at me. "It's good to see you again, Liam. We best get you inside and cleaned up. I have news you'll want to hear." When I didn't move, she took in a deep breath. "It's about Evelyn."

CHAPTER 13

Evelyn

A gentle hand circled softly on my back, easing me awake. Diffused light filtered through my closed eyelids as I struggled to crack them open.

Is it morning?

I sucked in a slow breath as I came to, smelling my favorite scent in the world, rich musky cedarwood with a hint of sweetgrass.

Liam?

"Not Liam."

A tremor coursed through me as all thoughts of Liam died inside my mind. Apep's languorous voice was the last one I expected to hear. Instantaneous fear ripped my crusted eyelids open as I threw a hasty shield up around my mind.

Apep stared down at me, his expression cool, but not cruel.

"I couldn't find you," he said.

I slowly pushed myself up into a more seated position as the realization struck.

I was in Liam's room, on his bed, wrapped in his covers.

"I had everyone searching," he continued.

I rubbed at my eyes, attempting to remove the film that skewed my vision. "Forgive me, I must've fallen asleep."

He chuckled, but there was no mirth in the sound. "It would seem so."

"I just…" What could I say? "I needed some time."

Eyeing me thoughtfully, Apep cocked his head to the side. "He's not coming back, Evelyn." Each word stung, opening up the fresh wounds of loss once more and stealing my breath. "Why do you mourn him still?"

Time was no longer my friend. I didn't know what day it was, let alone just how long Liam had been gone. Had it been two weeks or three? Three seemed too long, it couldn't have been that long yet… *right?*

My mind struggled to keep up with everything happening. Inside was a tangled mess of thoughts and emotions I hadn't had time to unravel yet.

I was in Liam's bed because…

Instantaneous dread soured my stomach.

Father. And Katerina.

I tried not to show it as my breaths came in quick pants.

"Is Katerina still alive?" I whispered, carefully, as though she might hear me.

"No." Apep straightened his spine. "She died last night, unable to withstand the tortures in her mind." He examined his hand as if it were far more interesting than the topic at hand before fluttering it off to the side in dismissal. "I had thought her a bit stronger than that, but alas, she is no longer of this world."

When he reached out his hand toward my face, I flinched. His eyes darkened. "She can no longer torment you, my Evelyn."

A wave of dizziness swamped me, daring to tip me over. "But why must *you* torment me?"

His eyes widened in shock. Could he still truly believe that yesterday's executions were a *gift* for me? That by killing my father and stepmother so brutally, he had freed me from the hurt and pain they had caused?

My hand pushed against my aching chest, the red stain that bloomed across my father's shirt played out behind my eyes as though it was happening all over again. I swallowed back the sting that choked my throat.

My father was dead.

Katerina was dead.

And Apep stared at me with an appalled look.

"*Torment* you? You torment yourself," he berated. "I've done nothing but protect you and attempt to raise you higher. Your father and stepmother weighed you down, Liam and Ryker weighed you down…and yet, you choose to blame *me*?" He shook with rage as he stood from the bed, his wings flaring out behind him. "They were all stains on your otherwise flawless canvas."

His voice was low and miserable, spoken mostly to himself. Death was closure to him. It was the power to erase, to right wrongs and live without being weighed down.

But death provided none of those things for me. Death took without mercy, death was unforgiving, death was devastating.

Pacing for a few extended breaths, Apep gathered back his wings, straightening his spine and sliding his face back into an impassive expression.

Sitting back down on the bed next to me, he spoke calmly… too calmly. "It's time for you to let them go."

He reached for my hand, but I pulled it away from him. "That's not your decision to make."

My voice tried to waver, but I was proud that it stayed surprisingly even, despite the fact that my heart was attempting to pound its way out of my chest.

Apep's knuckles turned white as he tangled his fist into Liam's sheets and squeezed. "I know what's best for you, Evelyn. These people from your past do nothing but weigh you down. They take away from your light, they make you *weak*." My eyes met his swirling ones as icy magic circled my head, looking for ways in.

My chin quivered, wiping all my previous bravado away at his statement. I *hated* being seen as weak. Even more than that, I hated *feeling* weak. But I couldn't allow him to trample me with his beliefs. This wasn't his decision, and he couldn't force me into it, no matter how hard he tried.

"There's no point in trying, Apep. I already have my shield up, and I won't be lowering it for you again."

His stare turned dark as he released his fist and stood up, offering me his hand. "Come with me. There's something I must show you."

Reluctantly, I pulled myself out of Liam's bed and stood, pointedly ignoring Apep's offered hand. If he thought me weak already, I wouldn't prove it further by allowing him to help me, even in the smallest of ways.

He bristled, but walked to the shared door that led to Ryker's bedroom, opening it for me to go inside. The blue velvet curtains had been closed around Ryker's bed and the fire remained unlit, but what caught my eyes was the strange excess of mirrors in the room.

"Why are we—" I started, but Apep interrupted me.

"You let your shield drop last night, Evelyn." His elongated voice was grim as he came to stand beside me, taking in the darkened room.

Pure panic solidified in my veins, freezing my entire body in place.

Apep turned, meeting my gaze, and my entire body quivered under his unflinching stare. My eyes darted back and forth between Apep and the closed drapes of Ryker's bed. Was his body lying behind those curtains? Was he dead already?

Please, no.

Apep walked casually over to the bed and carefully pulled back one curtain, revealing an unconscious Ryker sprawled out on the bedspread.

I couldn't move, couldn't breathe, couldn't think.

Please, be alive. Please be alive.

Apep gripped my chin in his cold and brittle fingers, moving so quickly I barely knew it was happening before he lifted my face to look at him. "When your shield lifted from me yesterday, I was forced to bring him out of the dungeon and provide for him. To care for his wounds, hunger, and thirst while everyone else searched for you." He looked at me pointedly, but I already remembered his threat.

My entire body suddenly felt far too heavy to keep upright any longer, but his grip only tightened on my chin as my legs trembled.

"Do you remember the punishment for allowing your shield to part from me?"

My vision blurred with sharp tears. "Please," was all I could croak out. "Please, Apep. I didn't know. I didn't mean to."

I would plead, cry, get on my knees if he wanted. Anything to keep Ryker alive.

His eyes remained cold and hard as he reached his other hand out to caress my face. "Put your shield back around me, Evelyn, and I will let you go to him."

I hesitated.

Darting a look back over to Ryker's serene face, I realized I had a choice. My shield had already fallen from Apep, and right now he was forced to care for Ryker...

"I see your mind, considering." Apep stepped closer to me, forcing me to continue looking up at him, but dropped his hands from my face, clasping them in front of him. "And you are clever to do so." He paused, head tilting to the side like he was examining his prey. "But you should also consider that if you do not do as I ask, I can always go after someone else. One of your maids, perhaps?"

I sucked in a sharp breath, and Ryker stirred in his sleep.

"Or maybe that servant you love like a father. His name is Jimmy, isn't it?"

All life drained from my body as Apep's words landed like physical blows to my chest.

"Or," he continued, "you can do as I have requested, and then I will let you go to Ryker."

I was already exhausted, both magically and mentally. Yesterday's secret practice in the dining room had drained me. Not that I could have anticipated witnessing my father's death only a few hours later, but the combination had obviously killed every last ounce of energy. And without taking any time to recoup in nature...

I could barely maintain my own shield, let alone anyone else's.

Swallowing back my fear, I attempted to place my shield back around Apep, but cried out as sharp pains radiated up my spine.

The weight of it was too much. I wasn't strong enough.

Ryker stirred again, a low groan reverberating in his throat.

How would I be able to shield them both?

Fat tears fell unwillingly down my cheeks as I stared at Ryker's prone form in the bed. He'd already endured so much, *too much*. How could I let that happen to him again?

I tried to shield Apep again, but failed a second time. Sweat drenched my hairline, and my breaths came in heavy pants.

If I didn't do as Apep asked, he might not be able to hurt Ryker, but he could allow his guards to hurt him, and he could hurt others. He'd threatened Jimmy.

Not Jimmy.

A horrified sob slipped out of me then, and I used all the strength I had left to fit my moving shield around Apep.

Apep sighed in relief as I scrambled away from him and up the tall bed to reach Ryker. If I could touch Ryker, I could shield him. Apep couldn't hurt him while I was touching him.

Ryker stirred fitfully, but looked free of any new injuries as I anxiously searched him for any fresh bruises or cuts. It was such a relief to see him cleaned up and dressed in better, warmer clothing. But in the light of the day, his new scars stood out in varying shades of pink to white with craggy shadows tarnishing his perfect skin.

I pulled him close to me, clinging to him as I cried into his shoulder. His arms slowly reached around me in return, gripping me tighter as he neared consciousness.

"Iridescent?" he rasped through his unused and broken throat.

"Ryker. I'm here. I'm here." I pulled away just enough to stare into his pale blue eyes. "I'm sorry, I'm so sorry."

"Why am I..." he started to say, but then the girls were there, opening the remaining drapes surrounding his bed, exposing him to the light of the room.

Gasps rang out, innocent as they were, and Ryker physically flinched with each one. His grip tightened on me ,and his eyes pinched tight as he shrank back, his eyes watering from the glaring brightness.

He pulled away, looking around, but I refused to let go of him. I watched helplessly as his gaze met the horrified glances from the girls, and his eyes hollowed out into shameful pits of despair. I looked on, powerless to stop him as he spied the first mirror, and his hands shook. Reaching one hand up, he traced each scar on his unfamiliar face.

That's when I realized why his entire room had been filled with mirrors.

"You are excused." Apep's voice cut through the excruciating silence as the girls swept out of the room.

Ryker's entire body shook while he stared at his new reflection.

His face was still beautiful, but it now hosted the outward scars of his tormentors.

Silent tears ran down my cheeks as I tried to comfort him, but could only weakly watch the horror wash over his face. Gripping his hand in mine, I refused to let him go.

But I couldn't shield him from this.

"Ryker?" My voice cracked as his eyes whipped to mine. The fury they held rivaled Apep's, but the shame they carried rivaled my own. He whimpered at first, then screamed. Ripping his hand from mine, he turned, reaching for the first solid object he could find and hurling it at the largest mirror set before him.

Apep grabbed my arm and ripped me away from the bed.

"No!" I pulled back at him, but he was far too strong and powerful for me to overcome him. "He needs me!" I yelled out over Ryker's bellows.

"Don't look at me!" Ryker roared back. "Leave!" His face shone with an anger so deep, I shivered in response.

"We must go," Apep said in my ear as he led me toward the bedroom door.

I tried throwing a shield around Ryker, but my body stuttered, black dots clouding my vision. Apep hauled me up and off the ground as he pulled me away, my shield slipping from around him too.

"No!" I fought against Apep's hold.

Ryker's guttural howls were swiftly followed by the crashing of glass raining down on the floor.

Fairy sentries stood just outside the door, locking it soundly behind us.

"Once Ryker has finished with his temper tantrum, deliver him back to his cell," Apep commanded.

I fought against Apep's tightening grip around my waist and wrist. "No! Leave him alone." My free fist pounded his arm, his shoulder, any part of his flesh I could reach. "How could you do this to him?" I cried out.

He didn't set me back on the ground until we reached the hallway outside of Ryker's suite. Gripping my wrist, he pulled me closer to him, his voice a pointed threat. "Disobey me again, and it will be far worse the next time around."

I turned to go straight back into Ryker's suite, but Apep's next malicious words stopped me dead in my tracks:

"Don't forget you have many people you care about, young Evelyn."

All the blood rushed from my inflamed face.

Apep's breath unexpectedly whispered into the back of my neck. "How do you think sweet Feleen would fare under my torment, or perhaps the cook you're so fond of? Hm?" He paused dramatically. "Put my shield back, Evelyn."

I gasped and sobbed at the same time, pulling my hand over my mouth as my shoulders shook furiously. I called my shield back around Apep, allowing my whole body to cave inward.

"If you waste Ryker's life, I have many others I can still use." He released my wrist and walked slowly away. "Stay obedient, follow my instructions, and I promise they will all live."

My heart sank as well as my knees as they landed on the hard stone beneath me.

Ryker's agony was my fault. This punishment was because I'd let my guard down. I hadn't even been thinking, I'd just…

Every crash and yell that sounded from his bedroom ripped through me like stabbing wounds that I doubted would ever heal.

On shaky arms and legs, I pushed up off the ground, stumbling into a run.

Running from the grief and shame doing their best to suffocate me.

Running from the agony of Ryker's shouts and cries.

Running from the helpless and terribly lonely feelings that smothered every breath I took.

How would I save us now? How would I get us out of this horrific mess?

Pressing my stilted legs to keep going, I wrestled with the deep sobs that tried to force their way out of my chest until I reached a door.

The Queen's garden.

Ryker's garden.

Without the key, I knew I wouldn't be able to get in, but I still banged hopelessly on the door, pushing and shoving at it, making it take the brunt of my anguish and desperation.

"Looking for this?" A vaguely familiar voice sounded from the shadows, and I was surprised to see the healer fairy's face appear. The one who'd healed Liam and protected me from notice after Katerina's attack.

Aster.

"How did you…" My voice drifted off, startled at her sudden appearance.

"Best not to talk here." She brushed her thumb gently across my cheek, sweeping away the wetness. "Let's get outside."

Unlocking the door, she ushered me into the secret garden before latching it soundly behind us.

CHAPTER 14

Ryker

The gasps echoed in my ears as my mind tried to catch up to what was happening. Light blinded my eyes as they tried to peek open after so much darkness. Evelyn's soft, tender hands gripped me tightly to her.

But then my eyes caught on a monster. A monster with half my face.

At first I shrank away in terror at the sight, then I screamed in rage.

The mirror shattered, shards of glass colliding together and littering the floor in fragmented reflections. A small moment of relief…only to turn and find another mirror facing me, reflecting back what was left of me, so I shattered that one too.

Evelyn had left at some point. I didn't know when, but I couldn't find her.

Apep had her. Apep, who had done this to me, betrayed me, destroyed me.

I sucked in several shallow breaths, attempting to fill my lungs but failing miserably.

My face…

My kingdom…
My family…
My girl…
No. Not mine. None of it was mine now.

I screamed again at the agony of all my defeats and cringed at the deafening sound.

Even my voice was altered now. Haggard and roughened by my constant screams as they'd melted my flesh.

And it was. Melted.

One side of my face was completely unrecognizable, somehow even worse than I expected it to be. Skin that once was taut and unblemished now drooped and gaped over my eye and down my face. Uneven pockmarks thick enough to shadow in the sunlight defaced my flesh. I was missing an eyebrow. The skin still looked raw, like it had been turned inside out, but it was hardened and glossy to the touch.

I was a monster. A beast. Something to both fear and pity.

The mirrors…the mirrors were everywhere, taunting me, reflecting my ruined soul back to me, showing my failure as a king, a son, a brother, a suitor.

Apep had taken it all. He'd taken everything from me.

No. He couldn't be blamed for all of it—my failures were my own. I'd never taken the role seriously. I'd never wanted to be a fighter like Liam, or a king like my father. After Mother died I'd lost a part of myself that sought the comforting embrace of a woman. It never mattered that the relief was temporary; it was a relief, and that was enough.

Evelyn came close, though.

A strange calm draped over me as I reached for the candlestick at the side of my bed and wielded it like a weapon. I swung at each reflection. Shattering every image of my ravaged face, every hope I'd had for myself, for my future. I raged and shattered and didn't stop until all the mirrors were as battered and broken as I was. And once that was complete, I started in on everything else. The desk, the armoire, the bed, the side tables…anything I could break apart, ripping at them with hands like claws, feet kicking, objects flying.

It wasn't until everything was broken, mangled, shattered or ripped in some way that my fury subsided. My chest heaved in heavy pants as I sat in the middle of a pile of blankets, staring at my blood-coated hands and broken fingernails. A sluggish ache slowly penetrated my consciousness. There was no part of my body that didn't hurt. After so many days of disuse, my body shook from the excessive exertion. A bone-deep exhaustion pulled me toward oblivion.

Shock tore through me as my head sank, staring at my feet. My bare feet, which had stomped over shards of broken mirror. Sharp and horrifying pain hit me the moment my eyes laid eyes on my ravaged soles. Cuts bled freely around pieces of jagged glass. I tried to lose any contents in my stomach then, but was interrupted by the door flying open. Several of Apep's fairy guards strolled in and surveyed the mess with vicious smirks permanently attached to their faces.

"Not so great now, are you?" One of them sneered. "Feeble king."

Their boots crunched over glass, feathers, and wood alike as they hefted me off the ground, their fingers digging into my armpits like dull knives. My clothes were bloodied and ruined. Fresh clothes, I realized far too late.

Apep's wrath knew no bounds. He had known that I would break. He had set up the mirrors to torment, to taunt and torture me. He had brought me up here, giving me false hope that my torture had ended, that my days of darkness were complete. He had clothed me and cared for me, only to provide the perfect stage for me to ruin it all again. He hadn't needed to use his mind magic on me; he just needed to provide the outlet for me to torture myself.

The tops of my feet and ankles were dragged over the jagged entrails of my savagery. The pain and exhaustion were so great, I was dead weight in their hands. Any strength I'd had left me vanished the moment I'd seen what I'd done to myself.

When I showed no sign of a struggle, I was hefted over a shoulder and marched back to my cell. I watched the trail of my blood in splattered drops on the white marble as I bounced in pain back to my own personal darkness, to my slow and pitiful death.

Without a reason to keep my eyes open any longer, I let them shut and allowed the dark oblivion to take over, removing my consciousness from what had become my horrifying reality.

CHAPTER 15

Evelyn

Before we made it too far into the garden I gripped Aster's elbow and whispered, "There's a hidden entrance behind the willow somewhere."

She patted my hand in reassurance. "That's been taken care of. Without use of the garden, he hasn't even realized the door has been sealed shut."

I stared at Aster with a renewed sense of curiosity, narrowing my eyes in question at her. She just chuckled. "There are quite a few of us who don't support Apep's radical ways. We don't wish for fairies to be on top; all we've ever wanted is to be equal."

I swallowed thickly. "How will we get Ryker out?"

"Just Ryker?" she asked back, both eyebrows raised in question.

Just Ryker...

I closed my eyes, fighting the grief that welled in my chest. We had been right here, in this garden, when he'd introduced himself to me as *just Ryker*. A fresh wave of shame washed over my heart, splintering it further.

I couldn't protect him.

"Evelyn?" I jolted back as Aster reached out to touch me.

I shook my head to dislodge my troubled thoughts. "Forgive me." I raised my hand, touching my lips where he'd kissed me.

Would he ever kiss another now, after all of this? Was there a chance he could ever be happy again?

Tears blurred my vision as I tried to look at Aster. "Anna, Feleen, and Brigitta too. I have to get them out, I have to..." My mind tripped over itself, trying to keep up with my thoughts while my body shook uncontrollably. I felt weak. "I just can't let Ryker keep—" I sucked in a ragged breath, "—what he's already had to endure..." I trailed off.

Stilted thoughts and ragged words were all I could offer between the onslaught of emotions and my withering body.

Aster patted my hand and gently led me to the bench where Ryker and I sat. "I know, dear. We all know what has happened to him—"

"It's my fault," I wept, unable to assuage my tears. My hands shook, heavy with guilt and fatigue, as I tried to fit them onto my lap.

Aster held my hands tightly together, facing me. "What's your fault?"

I choked and stuttered through my words. "All those mirrors. He was so horrified, and then he wouldn't stop yelling." My head dropped with a sob, "Apep knew...he always knows." I couldn't stop shaking, I couldn't breathe, I couldn't think.

"Come here, you need some time with the earth." She guided me to the willow tree behind us and helped me dig my hands into the cold, damp soil.

I breathed out a sigh of relief as Nature's renewing energy rushed to fill up my own empty reserves. I hadn't realized just how drained I'd been...I couldn't believe I hadn't passed out like I'd done before.

My watery joints slowly strengthened as Nature filled me back up, warming and comforting my soul from the inside out, my tears slowing and my breaths evening out.

Aster's hand gently cupped my shoulder. "I know something just happened with Ryker, and I have a feeling I'll be called soon..." She hesitated. "To check on him." I glanced over at her, my hands still buried in the soil. "Forgive me, Evelyn. We don't have much time, and there's much I need to tell you."

I nodded, giving her my full attention.

"I've been to your estate," she said.

My eyes widened with hope and joy. "You have?"

"Jimmy and Cook say they are well. No one has bothered them or even stepped foot on the estate's property." She sat back then, dusting off her hands. "They're safe, and they've created a safe haven for both humans and fairies alike to escape Apep's wrath."

I wanted to cry tears of joy instead of sorrow, but I refused to let more tears fall now that I was hearing good news.

She continued. "Liam, Camilla, Rafe, Becca, and Chrissy—plus some new friends of theirs—showed up last night."

My vision blurred for the second time, and my breath lodged in my throat. Overwhelming hope threatened to overload my battered heart.

"Are they all well?" I asked breathlessly.

She offered a small smile, and then pulled two letters out of her dress pocket. "They are."

Tugging my hands quickly from the earth, I hastily brushed them together and down my dress before gingerly accepting the letters from her hands.

Liam's compact and steady script stood out on top, and my heart stuttered, knocking the air from my chest.

He'd written me.

I pressed the letters to my chest, and Aster's hand covered my own, her eyes tightening with worry. "Be sure to read those when you're alone, and burn them immediately afterward."

I nodded again, not trusting my voice to form a proper response.

She pursed her lips and leaned back again, both of us sitting on the ground, facing each other. "We're going to do everything we can to help."

I swallowed thickly at the thought. "I can't have anyone else getting hurt or captured. You already risked so much to see me like this."

"I did," she agreed. "And I'd do it again. There's always a balance you must walk. Knowing when to risk and when to hold back will be your greatest strength." The fierceness in her voice bolstered my own courage. "You received a letter from Princess Jada recently, correct?"

My eyes widened. "I did."

Leaning forward slightly, she dropped her voice. "Read it in front of a fire. *Very* close to the heat."

"Why?" I whispered back; even though there was no one present who could hear us, this felt like the kind of secret you couldn't speak out loud.

"Look for hidden words on the page," she said with a wink. Moving to stand, she dusted off her hands, offering me one of her own to help me up. "I wish I could stay. Read your letters, and should I have news for you, I will find you. Apep must never know of my dual loyalty. He must always think me loyal and grateful to him."

I nodded in understanding.

Aster looked toward the garden door, worry furrowing her brow. "What do you believe will be the nature of Ryker's injuries this time?" she asked in a hushed tone.

I deflated, waves of shame at being unable to protect him battering against my already weary bones as I recalled his pained cries. "I don't know for certain, but there were a good many number of mirrors that he was…well, shattering."

She hummed in response. "I'd better go, then."

I reached out to her, gently grasping her arm. "Thank you. For all of this."

She patted my hand, then pulled the necklace with the key to the garden up and over her head, handing it to me. "Come here if you need to get away from him."

I clutched the key in my hand and slipped the chain over my head. "When did he give this to you?"

Her eyes turned sad, and she briefly looked down at her hands as though they'd somehow betrayed her. "I was the one to help heal him…before." Her words were hollow and regretful. "He handed it to me that night, asking me to keep it safe." She looked back up and patted my cheek. "Stay strong. You aren't alone."

With that, she turned and darted back out the garden door, closing it quietly behind her.

I stayed for a few extra moments, soaking up the serenity of the garden. Due to the colder winter season, most of the plants were in their hibernation stage, but in my mind's eye I saw the rare, nocturnal white blooms basking in the moonlight. The delicate yet strong flora that only needed what the moonlight provided in order to survive the darkness that surrounded it.

Pressure clamped down on my chest, where I still clutched the letters to me. I wanted to be like this garden. Flourishing and blooming even amidst the darkness. If the soft and delicate blooms that normally adorned this garden could bloom with so little light, then so could I.

Feeling renewed, I carefully stuffed the letters in the pocket hidden beneath my dress and headed for the door.

***

Hurrying past the guards stationed in front of our suite door, I slammed it shut before they could even barely look at me. Leaning my body back against the door, I caught my breath and searched the room for any sounds of another soul present.

The letters weighed heavily in my hidden pocket, but I didn't dare reach for them until I knew the suite was clear. Slowly peeling away from the door, I made my way to the bedroom, peeking around every corner, even checking under the bed like I used to as a little girl.

Nothing.

No sound.

No one else was here.

Scrambling for the hidden pocket in my skirts, I nearly ripped the letters in my haste to pull them free.

My heart pounded so loudly in my ears, I feared I wouldn't be able to hear if anyone did come in.

Carefully shutting the doors to the bedroom, I latched and locked them for good measure. My fingers trembled as I unfolded the precise penmanship that instantly blurred my vision with desperate longing.

Dearest Evy,

I'm having to write this in haste, and even without such time constraints, I fear I wouldn't be able to produce the words needed to tell you how immeasurably sorry I am. I offered you my heart, and at the first test of my devotion, I betrayed your trust. I allowed my jealousy and fear to take over, and though it is no excuse, it is the only explanation I can give.

I don't deserve it, and so I will never ask for your forgiveness, but I will give you this hope—I will do whatever it takes to break you and Ryker free from this torment. I am aware that my words may mean very little to you, given my past history of broken promises, so I will not promise with my words, but with my actions.

I love you, Evy.

I love you with my whole heart, my complete soul, my entire being. All of me calls out to you day and night; it always has. The beat of your heart is my own, and no matter what happens next, I will be there for you. I will do whatever it takes to grant you your freedom again.

There is something else I wish I would've said sooner...I wish I would've told you how strong you are. People think I'm the strong one because of my outward appearance, but I let my fear cripple me. You, however, never do. Your strength may be too quiet for many to see, but I've seen it. I see it in the way you approach life with so much love. I see it in the way you adapt to your surroundings. I see it in the way you persevere no matter your circumstances. And even though it's not fair, I ask you to stay strong even now.

We're coming, Evy.
We'll be there to help before you know it.
You're not alone.

Burn this letter. Do not let Apep see that you have it.

Never lose hope. I will see you soon.

All my love,
Liam

Several oversized tears dropped from my cheeks, instantly distorting the letters on the page. Liam's words echoed over and over in my mind. *I love you with my whole heart, my complete soul, my entire being. All of me calls out to you day and night; it always has.*

My heart swelled several sizes too large, pushing against the caged in bones of my chest.

He still loves me.

I gripped my pendant, warmed to the temperature of my skin, and traced the engraved words on the back. *"Always you."*

As much as I wanted to keep this perfect letter, I knew it would be far too dangerous. So instead, I read it again, memorizing every word so I could hold them tightly in my heart. He had no idea what a balm to my battered soul this was, or how much I had needed to hear these words from him specifically. A part of me feared seeing him in person again. Would my heart be able to handle the onslaught of emotions? Would I be able to forgive him as readily as I felt I could right now?

Marching over to the unlit grand fireplace that faced the bed, I put my hand over the dark coals to check for warmth. Nothing. Wiping away the leftover emotion clinging to my face, I grabbed the logs perched on the side of the hearth and placed a few large ones on top of the cold ashes, stuffing small slivers of wood, dried moss, and Liam's letter in between.

Opening the tinderbox, my mind wandered to the first time my father taught me to do this. Striking the steel and flint only three times before sparks caught, I leaned down to gently blow. He'd made me practice building fires over and over again until I could get good sparks in just three tries. From that day onward, it had been my duty to tend all the fireplaces in our home. For a while, he'd nicknamed me his little cinder girl. I'd liked that. The name had felt playful and precious, because he'd said it for me only. But eventually that died away too.

Died.

My breath caught as bright orange and deep red shades spread across the kindling like…

Father's shirt blooming deep red.

The image of his death flashed into my mind, startling me backwards from the flames. As I thunked painfully backward on the hard stone floor, I scrambled to sit back near the fire and blow on the blooming spots where the sparks caught and took root.

As the fire slowly built, I sat back, pulling my knees to my chest. The early flames licked at the fresh logs, charring it with every swipe of its fiery tongue.

Carefully unfolding Becca's letter, my heart stuttered at her very first words.

You're not alone.

I closed my eyes, relishing the words she used to say to me every time she saw me at the market. The reminder she would always tell me when things felt their most bleak. The encouragement she would never let me forget, not even now.

Liam took up most of the time writing his letter, so I'm left with mere seconds to compose my own.

I giggled at the imagined image of her standing over Liam's shoulder, hounding him to hurry up so she could write me, too.

Keep holding on, Evy. We're working on a plan now, even if it's obvious Liam's ready to leave us at any moment and storm the castle all on his own. (Be prepared, I honestly wouldn't put it past him to do something stupid like that.)

Aster has to get back soon, but I want you to know you can trust her. She's been telling us what she can about the situation in the palace; she's on our side.

Remember who you are. Remember that you are my strong, capable, and incredibly clever ~~best friend~~ sister. I love you, Ev.

*P.S. Kick Apep where it hurts. You're just as clever as
he thinks himself to be. Trust who you are.*

Always,
Becca

The giggle that bubbled up inside me caught in my swollen throat.
Sometimes I wondered how I got so incredibly lucky to have Becca
in my life. I often wondered if somehow, from somewhere beyond,
my mother was looking out for me. Some things felt far too perfect to
have been merely chance encounters.

Wadding up the letter, I tossed it into the flames, watching it
shrivel and blacken into nothing but ashes. They had no idea how
much their letters meant to me, especially today. Taking deep breaths,
I buried my head into my knees as I rocked back and forth, allowing
their encouragement and love to seep into my wilted bones. For now,
while I couldn't rely on my own, I would rely on their strength and
the hope of seeing them again.

At the heavy sound of silence, my head popped back up and I
pushed off the ground, heading toward the small table next to the bed
where I'd stashed Jada's letter.

Racing back over to the fire, I got as close to it as I dared with
the letter in my hands, not wanting it to burn before I uncovered
its secrets, but hoping this was close enough for the paper to feel the
heat.

Much to my astonishment, fresh browned words slowly unfurled
on the page, revealing themselves as if somehow burned into the
paper...

Just as the door slammed shut in the sitting room just outside.

My father...

Moving the paper wildly over the flames to make sure every hidden
word was heated, the door to the bedroom shook, and my eyes darted
anxiously to the movement.

"Evelyn? Are you in there?" Apep's muffled voice called through the wooden fibers.

Heart pounding furiously, I looked back down on the page.

...will send help...

He jerked on the door again. "Evelyn?"

My clammy hands gripped at the page I stared at, unwilling to blink should I somehow miss the words.

...if Prince Liam...

"I want to be left alone." I called out, hoping that if Apep at least heard me answer, he might go away.

"Evelyn." His voice turned almost soft, but more placating. "You cannot hide yourself away in there."

Choosing not to respond, I looked back down at the page.

...asks for it.

Running my sweaty palm through my already disheveled hair, I practically cursed. Liam must ask for it? Of course the request must come from Liam; King Jai would never accept my word alone, or that of any woman, I supposed.

Balling up the letter, I threw it in the fireplace just as the door rattled again.

"Open the door now, Evelyn." Apep's frustration leaked through his tone, and I almost smiled at how easy it was for me to vex him.

"No," I said back.

But how would I get word to Liam? Aster told me not to seek her out. It was imperative Apep believe her loyal to his cause.

"You are not a petulant child. Open this door now." I heard a small squeak that sounded distinctly feminine. "Or I will be forced to make you."

My stomach flipped at the threat, realizing the girls must be out there with him, too. Racing to the door, I flung it open, nearly smacking him in the face and seeing a terrified Feleen in his grip.

Channeling Becca's boldness, I reached for the hand that clutched at Feleen and one by one unclamped his fingers from around her bicep without losing eye contact with him.

A pleased grin slowly bloomed across his face. "Good to see you feeling more like yourself again."

I hugged Feleen gently to my side, running my hand up and down the arm he'd gripped too tightly.

"Get cleaned up." He raised a thumb to swipe at something on my cheek. "Why is there soot on your face?"

I shrugged. "I was cold."

Arching a brow at me, he pursed his lips. "Be ready for dinner in half an hour." Without another word, he swept back out of the suite, and the girls all fell toward me in hugs and thanks.

As we all pulled away, a crazy thought entered my mind. "I need you girls to do something for me."

"Anything," Brigitta said sincerely.

I lowered my voice to barely a hushed whisper. "I need you to get a letter to Liam."

Wide eyed gazes met my own, and I sincerely wondered if we would be able to pull this off. But no matter what, we had to try.

CHAPTER 16

Liam

Soft snorting interrupted my thoughts. I turned to the side to see a very hefty Daisy making her way slowly to me as she sniffed every inch of the ground—searching for food, I imagined.

I spoke her name, and her big pink head lifted to look at me before she trotted over happily. I gave her head a pat, followed by several scratches around the ears. "You've gotten so big, girl." Lifting her little pig face to look at me, I gave her a few chin scratches at the same time. "You know, Evy will cry when she sees how big you've grown without her. You should know better," I chided playfully.

Daisy happily settled back into sniffing the ground as she made her rounds around Evy's garden. Most of the plants had been harvested, but there were a few hearty winter vegetables still growing.

My chest clenched again. Seeing Daisy walking around, completely oblivious and happy as ever, made it seem like Evy would walk around the corner at any moment. A jagged knot filled my throat as I found myself staring at the nearly empty garden bed, wishing she was sitting next to me, just as we had done the last time we were both here. Now I was here, but she was gone.

"Liam?" Rafe's voice was rough and dry.

Lifting my head up to face him, my eyes met his troubled and swollen ones.

"Can you…" he started and failed, voice cracking from the strain. "Can you ever forgive me?"

I tightened my arms around my knees, "Forgive you for what?"

I patted the spot on the ground next to me, my eyes swooping back to Evy's garden. It felt like a lifetime ago that we'd sat side by side just like this. I had wanted every day to feel like that; to wake up early with her, work in the garden, talk, eat breakfast with Cook and Jimmy. The longing of it was so intense, it nearly weighed my entire body down.

Rafe lowered slowly to the ground next to me, wrapping his arms around his knees to mimic my position.

"She should be here with you." He lowered his eyes to the ground. "Ryker should be king. We shouldn't even be in this mess."

I knew he blamed himself for not being there for Ryker when he should've been, but we all knew there was more to this story…that someone else had been pulling the strings behind the scenes.

His chin quivered with guilt and grief. "I should've been there…it was my job, and I should've…"

I reached over to grasp his shoulder, giving it a gentle squeeze. "It's not your fault, Rafe. We both feel exactly the same, but neither of us could've stopped this from happening."

He shook his head allowing his floppy curls to bounce around before plopping his face directly onto his arms. "The torture Aster described…"

My eyes closed up tight at the thought. "I know."

"Do you think he'll make it?" Rafe asked.

I grimaced. Ryker had never had to face physical hardships like this before; he was used to a plush and easy life. Even in training, everyone had gone easier on him. The hardest thing he'd had to face was the death of his mother, followed a few years later by his…our father. I honestly didn't know if he'd survive this kind of cruelty, and I worried what kind of mental affliction Apep would use against him. It was no secret that Apep had been roving about our brains for far too many years unchecked.

"He will," I stated. Far more confidently than I truly felt.

Soft footsteps approached us from behind, and Rafe turned his head to look, his eyes instantly softening in that particular way. I smiled, mostly to myself, knowing whose voice I'd be hearing next.

"Ready to come inside, you two?" Becca laid her hand on Rafe's shoulder, and he covered it with his own before pushing off the ground to face her. I pushed up as well, coming to stand next to them. "Chrissy has an idea, but it's a little far-fetched..." She shot me a look, then shrugged. "I still think it could work."

Wiping my dirty hand down my pants, I mumbled, "Right now I'll take anything, as long as we have a plan."

Becca smiled, but it didn't quite reach her eyes. Aster's news of Apep's torture and blackmail had us all reeling and even more anxious to take some kind of action. "I figured you might say something like that."

Linking her fingers with Rafe's, she led us back inside the house, past a busy Cook currently nursing something that smelled beyond delicious on the stove top, and Camilla, who was busy boiling some water.

Climbing up the stone steps into the main house, we passed the people recovering in the dining nook and sitting room. Fairies and humans alike flitted back and forth from person to person to make sure wounds were properly cared for. Soft quiet murmurs and muffled groans blanketed the space as we stepped around the people and down the hall to the study.

Ian's rough brogue ripped through the hushed hum before we even reached the door.

"Nay. I cannot allow it. It's asking too much of ye..."

Upon opening the door, a red-faced Ian stared down a resolute Chrissy, and Billy's eyes volleyed back and forth between the pair.

Jimmy acknowledged us the moment we entered the room, his warm eyes warring between amusement and worry. "Ah, so you found them," he said as cheerfully as he could, his signature wide smile lacking much of its luster. The lines around his face somehow looked even more shadowed, as though they'd grown deeper since I last saw him, and his shoulders slumped forward from the invisible heavy burden of worry I knew he carried. The one we all carried these days. He felt the acuteness of Evy's absence even more than I did; he looked at Evy like a daughter now more than ever, and all I could hope was that our small cavalry would be enough to bring her back to him.

Chrissy tutted, bringing my attention back to them. "Not if I regularly renew my magic."

"And risk Apep discovering ye?" Ian asked, incensed. "It's too dangerous."

We moved further into the room, and I posted up against a wall, crossing my arms in front of me as Camilla appeared next, carrying in a tray of tea and cups. A faint redness in her cheeks made me wonder if she was remembering the first time we met, right here in this room, as she paraded herself about…offering more than just tea.

"Thank you, Camilla." Chrissy said kindly, moving to pour herself a cup.

"Chrissy…" Ian pressed.

"Ian." Chrissy's face hardened as she stared him down, blowing lightly over her tea cup.

"As much fun as this show is, I for one would like to at least *hear* Chrissy's idea," Rafe chimed in.

Ian huffed. "It's not an idea, it's insanity."

Billy snorted through his nose and muttered under his breath, though still loud enough for all of us to hear, "That's the way to win the ladies…"

Rafe nearly spit his tea out, and Becca clapped him on the back, rolling her eyes.

"What's your idea, Chrissy?" I asked. Ian looked ready to object again, but I untucked my hand and held out a hand to him. "You can't deny her sharing with the group. You know she's going to anyway."

Ian grumbled under his breath, and Chrissy handed him a cup of tea. "Sip on that to calm your nerves." Her eyes darted around the group, then landed on mine. "I believe I can get you into the palace."

Crossing my arm back over my chest, I raised a brow skeptically, but it was Rafe who jumped in first. "How are we going to infiltrate a palace full of fairies with who knows what kind of powers, and an evil mastermind running the place who can *literally* read our minds and anticipate our every move?"

Chrissy turned and smiled at him. "I can make you *look* like fairies."

Ian threw his arms up in the air.

"But Rafe brings up a good point. How can we pretend to be fairies when Apep could simply read our minds and find out the truth?" I questioned.

The group fell silent, contemplating our biggest obstacle.

"Apep already saw himself above the palace staff before he took his place as king," Camilla chimed in. "I highly doubt he would bother to vet every staff member. Not to mention, Aster said there are plenty of fairies on our side within the palace walls who would probably help us get in, or at the very least help hide our presence in the palace." Her cheeks flushed as all the eyes in the room fell on her in surprise.

"We could certainly slide into a stablehand position with relative ease," Rafe said, looking at me.

I nodded slowly, considering.

"I could try and pose as a maid," Becca offered to the group.

Rafe opened his mouth with the clear intention of denying her just as Camilla's smoky tone cut through everyone's thoughts again. "I could join the kitchen staff."

"You would want to go back there again?" Becca asked, her brows twisted with worry.

Camilla's face darkened. "After everything he's done..." She paused, clenching her jaw briefly. "I want to help stop him."

Becca stood up a little straighter. "Well, if you're going, I'm going." She gave Camilla a respectful nod, then stared directly at Rafe, raising a high brow that simply dared him to tell her no.

"Chrissy..." Ian's voice was stern, bordering on the edge of angry. "Ye can't keep up that many transformations. It's too much, and ye know it."

"He may have asked you to protect me, Ian..." She reached up and tenderly cupped his jaw. "But you've done enough. This is our best chance to save Evelyn and Ryker."

"But..." Ian's voice cracked as he stared into her eyes, his own rapidly filling up with liquid.

I stared at the two of them as all the words they weren't speaking hung thickly in the air. "What are we missing here?" I asked. "Why would this task be too much for you, Chrissy?"

Ian looked away as Chrissy's gaze landed on me, then observed everyone else's faces, eager to hear more fairy secrets.

"I can't let you do anything that would endanger you," I added. "You know Evy would never forgive me." It was a gamble whether she would forgive me at all, not that I deserved it, but I hoped my letter to her would help soften the blow. Mostly I hoped it gave her some hope until we could get inside and help her through this.

"Wielding magic…" Chrissy began, "takes a physical toll. The body has limits, though magic has none."

"Like when Evelyn faints?" Jimmy's soft voice questioned.

"Exactly like that." Chrissy's tone was grave. Her eyes slipped back to mine, and she swallowed uncomfortably.

"What she's *not* sayin'," Ian jumped in, his face the picture of agony as spoke, "is that her body could die from too much strain." His face swung toward Chrissy, and a slight warmth radiated from his eyes as he paused to take her in. "Chrissy can handle more magic than most, but even she has her limits."

"I thought all fairies were immortal," Becca softly whispered.

"Not immortal." Chrissy smiled reassuringly. "We just age very slowly, giving us far longer lifespans than humans."

Wanting to get to the heart of the matter, I asked the question we seemed to be skirting around. "So using this much magic, to transform the four of us," —I motioned to the familiar faces around the group— "into fairies could essentially kill you?"

Ian's face tightened as he stared at Chrissy.

Chrissy's bright green eyes twinkled with determination, "Some risks are worth it."

CHAPTER 17

Ryker

"How did you like seeing yourself for the first time?"
A ragged breath left me at the sound of the slippery voice that now haunted my dreams.

Aster had only just left from healing me. Why was *he* here now?

Apep paced back and forth in front of my cell, his whispering steps grating painfully against my ears. Without even seeing his face, I could picture the cruel smile pulling at his mouth, the smug expression that he'd once again bested me in a game I never knew we were playing.

"I quite admire the work my friend did with your face. It has an air of poetic justice, I believe." Each word slithered through his mouth sinuously, hitting on every consonant with an emphasis that set my teeth on edge.

"You took so much pride in your appearance. Thinking it made you better than others, entitled to have whatever you wanted, whoever you wanted, whenever you wanted…" He paused. "How will you learn to survive now? Hideous as you are. It seems your outsides finally reflect your insides."

"Go away, Apep." The words were choked and rough, my throat scraped entirely raw. Though Aster had done what she could to repair the damage I'd inflicted on my own vocal chords, they were still tender and raspy. I had a sneaking suspicion this would be my voice for the rest of my life now.

He barked out a laugh. "This palace is mine now, boy. Tell me, Ryker, what will you say to Evelyn when she visits again? Will you be cruel and send her away, or simply remain silent?" He paused as if expecting an answer, knowing full well he wouldn't get one. "How long do you think she'll keep visiting when you treat her so poorly? One can only take so much abuse…wouldn't you agree?"

The question was superfluous, merely one more taunt, one more game to play with me, to toy with me, to break me.

But he'd already won.

Cold tendrils snaked up my spine, making me want to shiver, but I knew this particular cold sensation was false. It was easy to know now when I was under his influence and when I wasn't. This feeling of loathing, hate, and utter irritation toward him disappeared when he infiltrated my mind.

Unnatural in every way.

I still didn't know how he'd fooled me so well. I should've been able to see it so clearly. I'd never looked at Apep as a good or helpful figure. Most of the time he'd been a constant thorn in my side, but there were some days, when I was just a boy, that I'd imagined him to be some kind of truly evil villain using my father against me. Father had always chided me for my disparaging remarks against Apep; little had I known he'd been just as much under Apep's influence as I'd been…*a week ago? A month? Several months?*

Apep's voice pierced through my thoughts far too deliberately for it to have been of my own accord. "I didn't use your father the same way I've used you. I was honest with him, a true advisor. He listened to me, treated me like an equal." Apep stopped pacing and stood before my cell, darkening it even further. "He never had your stubborn streak."

"Why me?" I was as surprised as Apep at the troubled words leaking through my haggard throat.

"Because you were undeserving and simple-minded, like those before you. Always thinking yourself above the rest, thinking you could simply take what you wanted. Even your dear brother Liam was caught up in your tangled web of selfishness."

Hope swelled in my chest at the thought of Liam. Once he found out about what had happened, he would be here. He would come.

Apep huffed a humorless laugh. "Even now you take Liam for granted. Do you really think he'll forgive you? After all you've taken from him? You forget, I saw into his thoughts just as I've seen into yours." A small drip sounded somewhere in the dungeon as Apep paused for dramatic effect. "He loves her more than you can fathom. You've never known this kind of love. All you knew with Evelyn was infatuation and a lust for what was not immediately offered to you."

But, I loved her. I loved them both...

Apep chuckled bitterly again. "Your eagerness to win, to use Evelyn to fill that void in your heart...that's what crushed him. *You* are the one who drove Liam away."

I could tell he was still watching me and I wanted to shudder as I pictured his eyes scanning my shadowy, huddled form.

He tsked. "What a pitiful creature you've turned out to be. So weak-minded. Pathetic, really."

A powerful image shot through my mind's eye of Evelyn's beautiful face. Her long hair hanging down in soft flowing waves along her back, her skin sheathed in only a thin white chemise. One of her shoulders was completely exposed, and the image was intimately satisfying. A figure leaned into her, reaching his arm around her and pulling her closer, the other hand plunging deep into her hair. He lowered his face to hers, and she moaned breathily, "Liam."

That's when I jolted back, slamming against the stone wall behind me, trying desperately to get away from the image.

He laid her down on the bed, tugging the white fibers of cloth up her legs to her thighs. Kissing, grabbing, moaning, their mouths devouring each other in the way I had longed to hold and relish Evelyn in my arms.

"Enough!" I yelled out, my ravaged voice aching at the violent cry.

Another dark chuckle accompanied the realization that Apep had been taunting me with that vision as the cold crept from my head and back down my spine until it disappeared altogether.

"He'll never have her either, rest assured." Apep said.

"*Leave!*" I shouted, pushing through the pain of my tender throat.

Apep tutted. "You've always been so temperamental. Was that vision not to your liking? Shall I try another one?"

A sob burst through my chest. I had no shame left, no hope, no reason to hide. "Please, just leave me alone."

"I suppose you have had enough for a while. Evelyn learned her lesson, which was the entire point in the first place." With a whispering swish of fabric on stone, he moved down the hall and called out behind him, "Rest up, *Your Majesty*. I'll be sure to visit again soon enough."

My entire body trembled with both rage and anguish. Lifting my shaking hands to my face I finally understood why Evelyn often had this reaction. My body was overwhelmed, overwrought, and abused beyond recognition. There was no coming back from any of this. Even if Liam did come, what would be the point? I had nothing left. I was…nothing.

CHAPTER 18

Evelyn

That night, I feigned sleep. Deep, calculated breaths, closed eyelids fluttering discreetly, a slowly loosening grip on Apep's hand. I entertained my mind with ideas of how to get the girls free tonight as I waited for Apep's grip on my hand to relax and his breaths to quiet, becoming more and more even. If I moved too soon, I would only disturb his slumber, so tonight was a game of patience. I had no plan, no true idea of what to do, only the knowledge that it couldn't wait, and I had to try.

Liam needed to get word to King Jai, and I needed to get word to Liam telling him to do exactly that. Freeing the girls from this forced imprisonment was just the icing on the cake. At least by giving them something to do, it might assuage their guilt over leaving me. I'd reassured them a hundred times, but they'd still looked so upset.

The image of Apep gripping Feleen's arm earlier played over in my mind. It wasn't the first time he'd threatened her, but I wouldn't allow him to use her against me again. Not any of them. Not when we had the possibility of getting them out of the palace and somewhere safe, or at least with the others.

Apep's breaths remained slow and steady, his hand loose and

relaxed. I chanced opening my eyes to check on him, turning my head to face him oh-so-slowly.

He remained still, lashes fluttering with only the slightest movement.

Calling my shield over him, there was only the slightest bit of pressure, but it settled quickly. I needed sleep, but my time with Nature earlier had already helped me recoup what I'd lost before. I was ready for this next challenge.

This was going to work. It had to.

There weren't many ways for me to stand against Apep, but this was one of them. This was my way of defying his control without getting anyone else hurt...or at least I *hoped* it wouldn't get anyone else hurt. If I'd learned anything so far, it was that there were no guarantees in this horrifying new reality.

Slipping my hand out from beneath his, I made certain, with painstaking slowness, that my shield was in place around him and he wouldn't miss my touch once it left him. Watching his every breath for any sign that he felt my withdrawing, I pulled free and slipped out of the bed.

Nothing. Not even a stir.

Inwardly, I sighed in relief, creeping on bare feet across the cold stone floor to the double doors that led from this room to the sitting room.

It had to be the very wee hours of the morning by this point, and I hated to send the girls out in the dark on their own, but this was the only time I could help them escape without being suspected of it.

With careful precision, I turned the main doorknob. Every slight slip and grind of the tiny turning gears in the handle seemed to echo across the entire room. My eyes darted to Apep's sleeping form, but he still hadn't stirred, his breathing deep and steady.

Holding my breath fast, I pulled the door slowly open, its well-oiled hinges blissfully silent, and tucked my body through the narrow opening. Closing the door behind me, I didn't dare risk latching it completely, leaving it slightly ajar for my return.

We'd have to be oh-so-quiet for this to work.

Turning around to survey the room, my focus stretched out over the living area illuminated only by the dim embers left burning in the fireplace. I moved past the front doors, careful to not make a sound in case the guards out front heard me and came in to investigate.

This whole crazy scheme was so beyond risky.

But it was worth it.

On silent toes, I slowly made my way across the room until I could see the girls huddled on the ground before the dimming warmth of the fireplace, all sound asleep. Anger blanched my insides as I saw their slight forms shivering on the ground. They'd not even been provided blankets or pillows as a bare minimum of comfort.

I knew Apep hadn't allowed any humans to have servants' quarters; they were required to sleep wherever they served, but to not even provide them basic care, like blankets…that made my blood boil hot in my veins.

My silken nightgown whispered softly against the stone floor as I knelt down next to Feleen and gently brushed her arm in an attempt to wake her. Her eyes fluttered open and grew wide, eyebrows shooting up in surprise. She opened her mouth to speak, but I briskly shook my head and motioned with my finger to my lips to stay quiet, my eyes shooting toward the suite's main double doors. She nodded in silent understanding and moved to help me wake the other two girls. Repeating the process in urgent soundlessness until all three girls were up and alert, I motioned for them to pull on their shoes and ready themselves to leave. They hurried to obey with only the slightest rustles of fabric breaking the silence.

I was so afraid to speak, even to whisper, but I knew we wouldn't be able to simply walk through the front door where Apep's guards stood at the ready.

Huddling us all close, I barely allowed my whisper to break open the hushed air. "Is there a hidden servants' entry?"

"It's been locked." Brigitta's soft reply was barely louder than my own.

I nodded, but looked her straight in the eye. "Show me."

We did our best to walk on the rugs placed about the room, which helped dampen the sounds of our steps as Brigitta led us to a back entrance hidden in the wall, much like the hidden door that led to the Queen's garden…*Ryker's* garden.

Without asking them anything further, I stepped forward to

inspect the hidden door. Pushing on it would normally unlatch it, allowing access to the hidden back halls beyond the gilded walls of the palace, but when I pushed, nothing happened.

The seams between the wall and the door were too fine to be able to tell where the lock was specifically. I knew my magic *could* sever as precisely as that thin crack, but could *I* be that precise? I highly doubted it. Not without more practice. The truth was, even if I ruined the wall, it was a far better outcome than trying to get past the guards standing watchful at the only other exit we knew of. The girls would be free to get my message to Liam, and that was what mattered most of all.

Some risks are worth it.

Turning back to the girls, I reached out to grasp Feleen and Brigitta's hands. Anna sat in the middle of them, trembling like a leaf clinging to its branches.

I wanted to smile, to offer something more than urgency, but urgency was all I could give.

"You can't go through the front door. If Apep's guards see you…" I shuddered, and the girls shuddered with me.

"We know," was Brigitta's solemn reply.

"I'm going to try and open the door with my magic." I nodded toward the hidden servant's entrance, "You must promise me you'll leave and *not* come back." Before they could object, I continued on quickly, "Find Liam. He should still be at my estate."

I knew they'd been there before, but I waited to make sure I could see the recognition in their eyes. They nodded in silent but nervous understanding.

"Tell him that he must send word to Terreno requesting help. Tell him that without his word, they will send none." I squeezed their hands gently to emphasize my point, and all three sets of eyes widened at the news. "Tell him to be safe and that I got his letter. Tell him…" I choked slightly, water instantly stinging my eyes, "Tell him to rescue Ryker first, no matter what."

All three girls looked at me with glistening eyes in return.

"But what about you?" Anna asked.

"Can't you come with us tonight?" Feleen pleaded. "We can't just leave you."

I shook my head, "I have to stay." I paused. "If I leave, he'll kill Ryker."

There was a collective gasp of breath, but each girl nodded their head in understanding.

Pulling them toward me, we hugged as a group in silent farewell. I didn't know if I'd ever get to see them again, but I did know that no matter what, it was worth it to get them out.

"Be safe. Thank you for everything."

Someone in our group sniffled as we pulled apart. I nodded at them, pulling back my shoulders as I turned to face the hidden door. I could do this. I had to.

I looked over at Brigitta, who held the other two girls' hands in her own. "This could be messy and loud. Be ready to run."

They each nodded, but Brigitta added, "Thank you, Evelyn."

All three braced, and the beat of my heart pounded so loudly in my ears that I feared the sound alone would alert the guards.

I stepped up close to the door, gathering a shield in my hands, its iridescent and almost purplish hue illuminated the room in surprising light. A gasp sounded behind me in response, but I ignored it, focusing only on forming my shield into the thinnest straight line I could imagine. Taking a moment to breathe, I reminded myself that this was raw magical energy I was wielding, that it could cut through anything without issue. Steeling myself, I took in another deep breath, holding it tightly in my lungs. My heart hammered in my chest and my palms dampened with anxiety and anticipation.

As if the air itself held its breath, there was the slightest pause in the room before I sent my magic slicing through the narrow fissure in the wall.

A loud crack resonated through the silence, breaking open not only the lock, but seemingly sound itself as the door slowly fell open. I rushed to yank it open further, hurrying the girls through the exit. "Hurry! Go." I pushed Anna in first, then Feleen. "Be safe," I whispered out behind them.

Brigitta charged through last, hurrying the girls into the darkened and abandoned servants halls. I wished I could've sent them with a light or something to help guide their way, but a light would only make them easier targets.

Quickly closing the door behind them, I surveyed the damage and winced.

What had been a door-sized thin break in the wall was now a lengthy gap, about the width of two fingers, reaching all the way up to the ceiling.

Far too obvious.

I suddenly wished I had my grandmother's transformation magic to hide my blunder, but perhaps no one would notice?

Definitely wishful thinking.

With the lock and latch broken, the door swung freely open, and I scrambled to figure out a way to shut it again.

Stopping to listen for any sounds throughout the suite, I heard nothing.

The crack had been loud enough to wake Apep, and I was certain the guards right outside the door would've heard, but there wasn't even the catching of a breath or the mumblings of quiet voices.

Nothing but the quiet stillness of night.

Moving into action again, I frantically scanned the room for something that could help keep the broken door closed. I found a small footstool that sat in front of a settee in the middle of the room. Dashing across the floor on bare toes, I picked up the footstool, racing back and pushing it in front of the gaping doorway. It didn't weigh enough to make the door flush against the wall again, but it had enough hold to make it at least *less* obvious.

Again, wishful thinking.

Sweat clung to my skin as I carefully and quickly made my way back to the bedroom. Still, no sound came from beyond the main double doors, and I suddenly wondered if the guards outside were sleeping on duty. It would figure, considering they weren't truly trained for this line of work. Not like Rafe and Liam.

Dawn had yet to breach the horizon, but the darkness would soon be overcome by the rising light, and I still had to slink back into my spot on the bed without waking Apep.

Pushing the already-ajar bedroom door open, I slid back inside and pushed it closed, turning the handle as gently as possible. The latch of the door still clicked obnoxiously loudly in the silent room, but if Apep hadn't woken up to the sound of my magic blasting through a lock—*and a wall, for that matter*—I highly doubted he'd…

Apep stirred.

My heartbeat pounded violently in my chest as I approached the bed. Sweat saturated my nightgown, making it cling uncomfortably to my skin. Carefully lowering myself back onto the mattress, I pulled the covers over me. My hand haltingly slid back underneath Apep's cupped palm. I made certain our skin touched before I cautiously peeled my shield away from his form.

He stirred again, and I rapidly closed my eyes, feigning a bad dream, which had become a regular occurrence since his takeover of the palace anyway.

"Evelyn." The back of Apep's hand brushed gently across my cheek. "Evelyn, it's okay. You're safe. No one will ever hurt you again." He shushed me quietly, and I willed myself to calm down, blinking my eyes open slowly. He faced me, his eyes the picture of sincerity. "It's okay, just a bad dream. I'm here, you can go back to sleep."

I nodded reluctantly and closed my eyes again, listening to him shift on the bed into a more comfortable position. He gripped my hand tighter briefly, and I let out a ragged sigh.

What would he do when he discovered the girls had escaped? Would he suspect me? Would he hurt Ryker?

There would be no sleep this night as I hoped and prayed the girls made it safely to the estate.

No matter what happened next, I prayed my message would reach Liam and we could get the help we so desperately needed to take Apep down from this false throne and restore Ryker to his rightful place.

Apep thought to make me cower, make me submit to his control, but he'd forgotten that had already happened to me…and I would never let it happen again.

CHAPTER 19

Liam

The faintest hint of a lightning sky caused the shadows across the ceiling to gradually grow. Tension crept into my shoulders, slowly tightening every muscle. The relief of sleep eluded me entirely. I was much too eager for the day to begin.

Today, we would make our way to the palace.

Our small crew had taken over the office, moving furniture aside so we could all find a spot to lay on the floor for sleep. Jimmy and Cook had offered whatever blankets were left, but I opted out. There was no need when I couldn't sleep anyway.

Acid gathered in the back of my throat as I went over and over Aster's recount of Ryker's torture. I swallowed thickly, my tongue feeling far too wide for my mouth and my throat suddenly dry.

I'd left him to this fate.

Soft breathing surrounded me, interrupted only by the occasional snore every now and then.

Was Evy awake right now? Did she struggle to sleep too? Was she staring at the ceiling like I was?

The simple notion that we were both awake, staring at nothing together, brought me the smallest measure of solace. I could only hope Ryker slept as much as possible, avoiding his torment whenever the senseless bliss of sleep would allow it.

Small feminine whimpers pulled me out of my pensive thoughts, and I turned my head to the side to see Becca tossing and turning in agitation. She bore her bravery well, but I knew she worried for everyone. Her folks, Evy, Ryker, the girls she'd grown close to at the palace, the people from her town. There was far too much left unknown, too much that felt too big, too beyond us.

Our plan to pretend to be fairies to infiltrate the palace might get us inside, but it was a fool's errand. The probability of being discovered was...*high*, to say the least.

A tight tremor of anticipation rolled through me. If anyone was caught, I hoped it would be me.

Such a grim thought.

But, if I could somehow take the attention and torment away from Ryker, it would be worth it. Not to mention, my ego was convinced that if I was able to get that close, it gave me that much more of a chance to take down my opponent.

None of it was true, but my exhausted and delusional mind apparently wouldn't be deterred from dreaming of saving the day. The truth was, the entire situation was stacked against us. Our chances of success were slim to none.

Apep had been planning this coup for years, generations.

We'd given ourselves less than a week.

I wanted to groan, but I swallowed it back. The temptation to simply get up just so I could pace about outside was incredibly tempting. My mind was obviously far too restless; I'd need to find a way to sleep at some point soon, or else I'd be of no help to anyone.

The smallest knocking sound broke the silence of sleep currently coated the house.

Woodpecker? I wondered.

The knocking grew louder and more insistent. Fast, light taps that increased in urgency.

Not a woodpecker.

I shot out of bed, grabbing my sword before moving to the front door. Jimmy appeared on the stairwell behind me, and I nodded, waiting for his silent approval before opening the door.

Unlatching it, I swept the door open to three surprised and anxious faces.

"Brigitta? Anna? Feleen?" I ushered them in quickly. "Come inside." They scurried in and rubbed their arms up and down to chase away the cold. "What are you three..."

"We bring you a message from Evelyn," Brigitta jumped in immediately.

My heart stopped. The useless thing sat there heavy in my chest, not daring to beat another pulse until it heard her message.

"Well, let's get you girls warmed up first." Jimmy's comforting voice broke through my frozen status as he bundled his arms around the girls, leading them down toward the kitchens where the fires were always burning. "How long were you out there without a coat among you..."

Brigitta interrupted his care to face me. "This cannot wait. I believe we were followed."

My body stiffened on alert. "What do you mean, followed?"

"We suspect one of Apep's guards may have seen us escape. We tried to be quiet, of course, but they know our faces. And since we are Princess Evelyn's maids, that makes us even more recognizable, at least to some. So we practically ran all the way here—" Anna jumped excitedly in.

"Anna, enough." Brigitta shot her a look, before turning to me again. "I don't know if they would pursue us all the way here, but you must know what Evelyn said before..."

"What's all the commotion about?" A sleepy Rafe slouched in the doorway, yawning lazily.

"They might've been followed." I shot Rafe a stern look. "Be at the ready and wake as many as you can."

Rafe blinked a few times and then moved immediately into action, arming himself as he woke the others.

"Jimmy, grab extra blankets where you can." I turned back to Brigitta. "Tell me your message swiftly."

She nodded and took in a deep breath. "The King of Terreno stands with you and Ryker as the rightful rulers of Alstonia, but he will not send support unless he receives word from *you* specifically."

I sucked in a ragged breath. "So he knows of what's happened here?"

"That's what I gathered, though there wasn't much time to discuss it."

Rubbing the bristling coarse hair on my jaw, I took in all that was being shared. We needed the help— we likely wouldn't defeat or overthrow Apep without it, but how would I get a letter to King Jai without...

"Incoming." Rafe's voice broke through my whirling thoughts.

"Where?" I asked.

"Just coming up the drive."

I scanned the room of people. "How many do we have ready?"

Ian, Billy and Rafe stood in the hallway.

"More will be ready soon," Ian responded. "Becca and Camilla have taken on the task."

"Are you armed?" I looked over the two fairies.

Billy wiggled his fingers. "Always."

Ian drew a sizable dagger from his side.

It wasn't much, but it was what we had at the moment.

"Get away from the windows," I told the girls. "Help the others move away as well. We'll hold them off as long as we can."

Frightened eyes stared back at me, but all three girls bobbed their heads in understanding.

I looked back at the men. "Go around back, gather who you can. Billy, you're with me."

Opening the front door, I walked outside, watching the growing figures move in between the shadows. Billy followed right behind, standing guard beside me.

"This home is protected," I called out. "Who goes there?" Facing them head-on was the best defense we had at the moment.

A low voice called out from the shadows. "Protected by whom, *false prince*? You?" A dark chuckle sounded, followed by several others. "The King has indicated only an old man and woman live here, but I do believe he'll be pleased to know of your...arrival."

"I prefer to see the face of whom I am speaking with. Show yourself," I called out.

Several shadows moved to our sides as a main one slowly sauntered into view. At the very least, our distraction seemed to be working, but there was far more opposition than I'd anticipated.

The fairy who'd been speaking appeared from the shadows. His face was split down the middle, one half cast in shadow, one illuminated by the slowly rising sun. "I don't take orders from false princes who don't know their place," he sneered. "We're looking for three human girls who may have stopped here. They're servants of the crown, and their defection must be answered."

I kept my face stoic and unmoving. "I have seen no such girls here at this impudent hour, as I was attempting to sleep."

"Your knowledge of our arrival suggests otherwise," he contradicted.

"Or perhaps it was yer foul stench that alerted us." Billy mockingly sniffed at the air. "I could smell ye a mile from here easily." He wrinkled his nose in disgust, and I nearly lost my composure.

"You dare side with this human filth?" The shadowed male hissed. "Have you any idea what he and his brother did to our kind?"

Billy shrugged. "At least he don't stink." He gave me an exaggerated inhale for good measure. "Smells rather nice actually. A little woodsy, but clean nonetheless."

"Enough!" the fairy yelled. "Bring us the girls, or face the consequences."

As I pulled my sword from my sheath, the fairies all around me snickered. "You think your metal can match our magic? Foolish human."

"I think you've gone far enough." My voice was like steel cutting through the air, the threat clear.

I'd given our people plenty of time to get into position, but we were out of it now. I personally couldn't wait to take my anger out on these goons for as long as I was able.

Waiting patiently, I gave no warning, moving my muscles at the very last second, before going directly for the shadow closest to me on the left.

The hiss of metal sung through the air as my blade met its target, followed by a pained grunt. Before he could recover, I swiped back down, cutting through skin and bone alike, severing whatever I could. Thick, warm liquid hit my face and torso in slick streaks before I moved on to my next mark.

Evelyn's courtyard transformed into violent chaos. Water circled several heads as Rafe and Ian ran their metal through distracted backs. The fairy who'd been speaking faced me, his expression twisting into something like delight as rocks flew directly into my face, body and limbs. My sword deflected very few of the hurled stones, but I covered my head with my other arm as best as I could and trudged forward. My sword swiped at empty air, attempting to reach its intended goal but missing it completely.

Grunting through the pain, I was pelted from every side. Heavy branches and what I assumed were large rocks smashed into every piece of available flesh I had. The chaos of flying objects was too much to see through as something particularly heavy punched into my stomach, and I fell to one knee.

Malicious laughter echoed out in front of me. "Typical human, bringing a sword to a magic fight. How little you must know of our kind."

The torrent of objects flying at me prevented any reply I might've liked to offer up, but the moment I was able to see, I felt my expression widen in surprise as one incredibly large tree limb whipped toward me at a speed I couldn't dodge. I braced for impact, but I couldn't truly prepare for such a blow as I was leveled heavily to the ground.

My eyes blacked out, and I gasped for air. My hand clutched at my sword, unwilling to let it go just yet. The blow had certainly injured my ribs—shooting pains shot through my lungs with each gulp of air.

The fairy knelt in front of me, a smug expression covering his face. "Lost your voice, did you, *false prince?*"

I coughed, and something hot and metallic bubbled in my throat. *That isn't a good sign.*

"Lost your platoon," I panted, "*false guard?*" The pithy remark wasted precious breath, but the look on his face was well worth it. Surprise and disgust at first, followed by deep, unbelieving fear as he looked around him and realized that everyone else had fallen.

He turned to run, but was caught up by a fellow fairy whose roots snagged and held him down long enough for Rafe to finish him off.

The silence of death surrounded the courtyard. It was my first true battle—the first for all of us here. In the past I'd had to fend off marauders or the occasional thief, but never anything like this. We'd waged a small war on the steps of Evy's estate, and now the air held its breath in solemn recognition.

I tried to suck in another breath, but it felt watery and impossible. The bulky tree limb sat heavily on my chest as I panted and puffed, taking in whatever small amounts of air I could.

"Liam!" A shout from somewhere… my right? Or was it my left? Black dots clouded my vision again as the panic for air overtook all my thoughts.

"I've got ye, lad." Ian's easy voice blanketed me. "Help me get this off him."

I blinked several times, but I couldn't see Ian's face. I tried to speak, but the words wouldn't come. Soft hands circled my head, raising it up a little higher, and then Chrissy's face flooded my clouded vision. Her mouth moved, but I couldn't comprehend the words as I struggled and fought for any available air to flood my lungs.

A warm sensation, much like when the sun touches your bare skin, gently flowed through my body. Blessed breath finally filled my chest. I panted furiously, greedily sucking in as much air as I could manage before my breaths finally steadied into longer inhales.

A searing fire suddenly seized my lungs, taking my breath from me again in a silent cry of pain. But the scorching agony was over and done before I could even sound an alarm. Air flowed eagerly back into my lungs as I inhaled deep, desperate breaths. The aches and pains all over my body blazed similarly for only brief seconds before relaxing into a warm embrace.

Ian's motions came into view as my vision cleared. His hands roved over my body, never touching, but every place they hovered flared to life and then simmered into a warm acceptance.

He was healing me. Ian was a healer.

I looked at him with a renewed sense of awe as he lowered his arms, wiping one over his brow first.

"Thank you, Ian." My voice was still breathless.

He nodded, "Let's get you up then, lad." He turned to Chrissy, who I realized held my head in her lap. "Help get him inside?"

She helped raise my head as I shakily pushed off the ground, placing my arm around her shoulders once we were both standing. "I think a good cup of tea might be in order," she teased.

I chuckled. "That feels like an understatement."

She smiled sadly back, and I watched Ian check the pulse of every fallen fairy, noting none of them were ours.

"Was anyone else hurt?" I asked.

"Only scrapes and a couple of bruises." Rafe nudged my still tender ribs with his elbow, making me hiss in discomfort as he slipped my other arm over his shoulders. "You just *love* barreling into danger, don't ya Cap? Serves you right to have your—"

"Rafe…" Becca's scolding tone silenced him instantly, causing me to snigger under my breath. "Everyone is fine, Liam. Thank you for what you did out there."

"Are the girls…?" I started, but didn't finish the full thought.

She nodded. "They're fine. Camilla's getting them warmed up, and Cook is feeding them as we speak."

Good. I needed to find out everything they knew, and then we had to figure out a way to get word to King Jai.

CHAPTER 20

Evelyn

"**W**here are they?"

Startled, I flinched as Apep's low and sinister voice darkened the shining morning that had brightened the room. I must've fallen asleep after I came back to bed.

"Apep?" I attempted a curious and confused tone. "What's wrong?"

He gave my hand a squeeze. "Forgive me, Evelyn. It feels late, and those lazy maids of yours have yet to make an appearance."

I blinked my eyes open in a grogginess that wasn't feigned as my eyes grated against my eyelids. "Are they sick?"

"If they are, they'll wish they weren't," Apep grumbled.

Taking in a deep breath through my nose to calm my nerves, I squeezed his hand. "I care for them, Apep. If they're sick, I'll want them taken care of."

He sat up without answering or looking my way. "I need a shield, Evelyn."

My entire body ached as I reached for my magic to command a shield over him, pulling my hand from his the minute it was done.

Immediately he stormed toward the doors, yanking them both open in obvious annoyance. I wanted to race behind him, but my movements were sluggish and reluctant. Carefully grabbing my robe, I slipped one arm at a time through each sleeve, wincing as Apep's voice carried throughout the entire suite.

"Where *are* they?" He so rarely raised his voice that the grating sound made my hairs stand up on end.

Would he suspect me right away? Would he suspect me at all?

The guards posted at the front door reported no one leaving or coming in. They also reported they'd heard nothing last night, and I laughed inwardly—it seemed they *had* been sleeping on the job. Apep slammed the door in their faces and whipped around, scanning the room.

I squashed down the urge to smirk in victory as Apep's fists tightened by his side.

"No…" he whispered, nearly to himself. "It can't be."

I shivered despite myself and stepped toward him. "Apep, you're starting to scare me. Did something happen to them?"

He turned his furious glare toward me and studied my face. I did my best to keep the worried and concerned look attached to my face, hoping that a slightly fearful expression clouded my features so he wouldn't suspect I knew anything.

"Guards!"

My whole body jumped at his call. Realizing how nervous I was, he came over and gently rubbed my upper back, but the movements were stilted and stiff.

The two guards from outside the main door carefully peeked their heads inside. "Your Majesty?"

Apep motioned around the room. "Princess Evelyn's maids are missing."

They stumbled over their words, defending themselves until Apep cut them off. "I want them found."

He moved away from me toward the servants door, his brows furrowing as he stared at the wall, his head tilting back while he followed the perfectly cut rift running up the wall.

"And bring me a new maid for the Princess," he called out. "I'll want her vetted."

My heart sped up as he continued studying the wall, dismissing the guards with a wave of his hand, leaving us alone again. Apep's expression changed from one of annoyance to something more like awe as his eyes swept up and down the wall. He kicked the stool aside, allowing the hidden door to fall open.

Doing my best to keep my facade up, I made a little gasping sound. "How many hidden doors are within this palace?"

Apep smiled in response, "Many more than you know, I assure you." His hands touched the metal latch on the inside of the door. "Clean through," he muttered under his breath.

I swallowed down my nerves, trying to figure out ways to distract him. "You could tell them not to bother with a maid. I'm perfectly capable of dressing myself. I have for many years."

Apep backed away from the door, drifting toward me with practiced ease. "You're always far too gracious, young Evelyn. But those days are behind you now, I'll not have my Princess dressing herself like a commoner." Apep reached out and gently cupped my cheek, staring intently into my eyes. "I need your honesty, Evelyn. Do you know where they are?"

My eyes widened in sudden horror, and I shook my head emphatically. "No. Of course not." He eyed me skeptically, but I steeled myself against his sharp gaze. "Of course, I'd be lying if I said I wasn't happy they escaped."

He smiled at that, but it was a knowing smile that shot shivers down my spine. "You are assuming them not being here means they got away."

A sharp gasp cut through my lungs, and I looked down.

They got away. I knew they got away.

"Your heart is too big," Apep taunted.

I stood up a little taller, facing him head on. "And yours is too small."

His eyes lit up with amusement, and he laughed out loud. "Oh how I've missed your fire." He chuckled again. "Tell me, young Evelyn, how is my heart too small?"

Sucking in a deep breath, I clenched my fists until I could feel my own fingernails digging into my flesh. "You have become what you supposedly fight against. Treating humans like they're less than dirt."

"They did far worse to us," he retorted.

"But these humans, the ones from *this* time, they did nothing to you."

"Nothing?" His voice raised. "Did you not see what Ryker put our kind through?"

I shot up an eyebrow at him. "We both know he was being... *influenced.*" Apep scoffed, but I continued, "It's the opposite now, Apep. *You* terrorize *them.* You're so stuck in the past you can't even see that these humans have long been removed from that ugly war. They don't all hold the same prejudices."

"That ugly war was for a just cause," Apep seethed.

"But it isn't anymore!" I sucked in a harsh breath. "Every day I'm watching you hurt people I care about, watching you hurt Ryker... you think I won't—"

"Won't what, Evelyn?" A cruel shadow of a smirk played at his features. "Won't stand for it? Won't let me?" He walked closer to me again, circling around me. "You're barely in charge of your magic—"

"I can do more now," I seethed.

"Can you?"

And there I realized my mistake.

He'd been staring at the wall far too thoughtfully. My only assumption was that he knew it was me—he just needed me to say it.

As he circled back in front of me, my eyes met his in defiance. "I have more control over my shields now. They come easier each time, and I get tired less often. I know it takes time," I jutted out my chin, "but every day I'm getting better."

His eyes glinted with something I couldn't read. "I see great improvement in you indeed."

I sighed and turned away from him, walking back into the bedroom. "I'm going to change now."

"For your sake, I hope the girls did escape." Apep's hushed voice murmured behind me. "Neither you nor they will appreciate my response should I find them."

His words sent a charge of fear down my spine, but I refused to look back or acknowledge his threat, pretending to show only confidence instead. Closing the bedroom door behind me, I leaned against the insignificant barrier between us. My hand pressed firmly against my chest, willing my beating heart to slow just as my legs folded beneath me, taking my body to the floor. Between the debilitating mixture of fear and exhaustion, it was going to be a long day.

All I could hope for now was that they made it safely to Liam, and Apep never found them.

***

After dressing myself for the day, I left the bedroom only to find guards lounging in the sitting room. My eyes widened as I took in their casual demeanor.

"What's the meaning of this?" I demanded.

The two guards immediately jumped up, straightening their black tunics before bowing haphazardly. "Apep said the only room you are allowed privacy in is the bedroom, now, ma'am. I mean, miss." The second guard elbowed him in the ribs. "I mean, Your Highness."

I sucked in a harsh breath through my nose as I ground my teeth, staring at the two interlopers. Finally, I released my breath. "Well, I suppose there's nothing to be done about that, then."

Not offering to talk any further, I opened the door to the hallway, only to see two more guards posted outside. I paused, sucking in another breath but not offering them any words before I charged down the hallway.

Apep wasn't being subtle with his new warning. He couldn't prove I'd helped the girls escape, but he was certainly trying to make sure I wouldn't try anything else.

My feet led me straight to the stables. I found myself coming here more often than the rose garden these days. The familiar and comforting scent reminded me of Jimmy, and I needed his comfort now more than ever. Stopping to stroke a few velvety noses, I walked through the stable, my eyes instantly smarting at the comforting aroma of hay and horse.

The horses were more anxious than normal, stomping hooves and snorting. I realized my frustrating guard retinue was making them uneasy. I didn't blame them; I felt exactly the same way. Even if I couldn't remove my irritation, I could certainly remove theirs.

I headed behind the stables, where a thick copse of trees helped warm the ground slightly, keeping the soil slightly softer. With these cold winter months bringing in their icy chill, the ground was harder to dig my hands into, but as my fingers sank beneath the dirt, relief and renewed energy flooded my very essence. Ignoring my guards, who spoke quietly amongst themselves, I wondered how I might get rid of them before visiting Ryker.

Gaining my fill from Nature, I brushed my hands on my skirt, not caring one bit for decorum and finery as I walked straight to the kitchen. Without my girls bringing me breakfast, I was starving, but I also wanted to bring Ryker something. I didn't know when he got fed, but I figured it was part of Apep's torture to not feed him properly, and I couldn't let that stand.

One of the kitchen girls gave me some buttered bread and a meat pie with a glass of water. I thanked her before taking my small bounty to the dungeon with me. Nerves battled violently in my stomach. I hoped Ryker wouldn't refuse to talk to me today; selfishly, I needed his comfort as much as I wished to offer my own.

Turning to my guards before I walked to the darkest corner, where Ryker sat day in and day out, I said, "You know exactly where I am, and obviously there is no way to escape." I shot a pointed look back at the corner. "I request some privacy while I visit with my friend."

"Your *friend* is a traitor to our people, he doesn't deserve…"

"But *I* am your Princess." The words felt wrong and forced on my tongue, but the response shut him down quickly enough.

Bowing his head, he said, "Forgive me, my Lady. We'll grant you…"

"No. She's not allowed private time with the prisoner," another guard broke in. His face was familiar, all cruel edges and sharp eyes. He was one of Apep's closest guards. "And what is that you have there?"

I unveiled the meat pie I'd swiped from the kitchen. "Breakfast."

Snatching up my small bundle, the guard shoved his dirty fingers into the meat pie and milled them about until the pie was completely mutilated, then he tore apart the bread and stared at me as he stuck his fingers in the obviously clear water as well to wash them off.

He smirked, chuckling maliciously at my scathing look as he handed the mess back to me. "It's clear."

I took a moment to gather myself before I spoke, simply staring at the male in pointed silence.

"I did not specify *whose* breakfast this was." I paused, making sure he heard the accusation. His eyes widened, but only by a fraction. "Considering that *I* haven't eaten yet today, I will not thank you for now ruining my perfectly good breakfast with your disgusting fingers."

I stepped closer into him as he puffed his chest out slightly. All the other guards stepped away in an attempt to distance themselves from this incident. It wasn't until then, but his eyes finally started to look troubled. Allowing my anger to boil over, I spoke quietly, narrowing my gaze. "If you ever stick your fingers into my food again, it will be the last time you make use of them."

My nerves trembled, but I held my body still, not breaking eye contact with the horrid male. Little did he know I could truly make good on my threat now that I knew how to wield my magic like a blade. Though my accuracy still needed improvement. He could just as likely lose far more than his fingers if I ever truly tried. The thought made me smile inwardly, and I felt the side of my lip raise in response.

His eyes widened at me, and I relished the power, however fleeting. It felt good to stand up to these abusers. I found I quite liked it.

"Now, leave us. I want a moment alone." I shot a pointed look at the arrogant guard. "And fetch me more breakfast that your fingers haven't tarnished."

"I'm not a blasted servant," the guard fired back.

I shrugged. "Suit yourself. I'm sure Apep would be delighted to know that you not only shoved your fingers into my food, but that you proceeded to disrespect and insult me, including disobeying a direct order from your Princess."

The guard looked as though he wanted to argue, but he backed off, dipping his head in a barely-there bow as he turned, heading back up the stairs to what I hoped was the kitchen. The remaining guards had the decency to look at least a little ashamed as they stood firmly stationed next to the old stone doorway, allowing me some privacy to visit with Ryker in peace.

My shoes clapped softly against the rough stone floor as I walked down to Ryker's dim corner. The moment I reached his cell, a raspy voice sounded from the shadows. "I've never heard you threaten someone before. That was..." He paused thoughtfully. "Remarkably terrifying."

My eyes shot to the back corner, where Ryker's huddled mass sat. I hummed a mirthless laugh. "Who knows? You might even hear another threat from me in the very near future when I bring you another breakfast treat tomorrow." I scolded myself inwardly as I lowered my body to the ground, leaning sideways against the bars. "I should've known and brought you a second one today."

"It's not in you to constantly assume the worst of others."

It wasn't, but I was beginning to learn.

"Ryker..."

"Don't say my name."

My whole face crumbled at the despairing sound of his voice. "But that is who you are, and I don't want you to forget it."

"That is who I *was*. What I am now is nothing more than some lowly creature."

"Please, Ryker—"

"Stop," he croaked. His bent over form shifting in the shadows as he sighed heavily. "I don't want to see you."

"I can't stop—"

"I don't want to see you anymore," he reiterated.

"Ryker, please..."

"Leave me be, Evelyn." With that, he turned back over, and the space grew so silent I wondered if he still breathed.

My breath caught as a knot of emotion lodged itself in my chest. I sat there with my head resting against the rusty bars, tears burning the inside of my lids but refusing to fall. There was a growing numbness that seemed to be expanding inside of my heart a little more each day.

I didn't know what to do. It broke my heart into a thousand shattered pieces all over again, and I began to wonder if my coming to see him really did bring more pain than hope.

A throat cleared behind me. "Princess Evelyn?"

I turned to try and see who was there, but the darkness of the dungeon was too overpowering.

"I asked for privacy," I snapped.

The figure shifted on the stones uncomfortably, "Apep requested to see you, my lady."

My head dropped. I hated leaving Ryker. Every time I left him, it felt harder and harder. Like little bits and pieces were being ripped from us each time. I pushed the water, ripped bread, and miniature meat pie through the bars, leaving them for Ryker when he was ready.

Staring up at the lock, I gripped it, allowing it to help me stand as my hand hovered over the metal.

A sudden idea shot through my mind. The risk of it was enormous, but so was the return.

If I could pull it off.

I swallowed thickly as I surveyed Ryker's cell. He was still in the farthest corner from the door.

I turned to the guard in front of me, motioning with my other hand. "Fine, lead the way."

The minute he turned around, I pulled a shield into my hand, shaping it into a small circle, and then pressed my palm against the lock.

I hope this works.

Driving my shield forward, just like I'd done with the door last night, I pushed my magic through the lock. The flash was over and done in barely a breath, but Ryker gasped anyway. I quickly pulled my hand away, walking behind the guard as he turned around to look at me suspiciously. "What was that?"

I hiked a brow up at him in feigned confusion. "What was what?"

"That bright light?" He glanced around the dark corner, sniffing. "It smells like magic in here."

I shook my head. "I have no idea what you're talking about. I saw no bright light, nor do I smell any magic."

He narrowed his eyes studying me.

I shrugged. "But I am half human, I suppose."

A muscle ticked in his jaw as his eyes searched Ryker's cell behind me.

"Didn't you say Apep requested to see me?" I asked. "I don't know about you, but I don't like keeping him waiting."

That threat seemed to do the trick as the guard sucked in a harsh breath through his nose, turning around briskly. "Let's go."

Without saying goodbye, I left Ryker behind. My chest clenched and my hands trembled, hoping that it had worked, that I might've just given Ryker the opportunity he needed to escape. I could only hope that he took it.

A slow-moving fatigue leisurely settled into my bones. The weariness was already less than I expected, just enough to make me move a little slower, but not enough to wear me out completely.

I glanced back at the darkened cell, with the lonely torch flickering in the shadows. This was a risk, but it was also a chance, and I hoped Ryker realized that before it was too late.

Please try, Ryker. Please try.

CHAPTER 21

Ryker

A bright flash illuminated my dismal hole, bringing to light how truly filthy, dank, and dark my current existence was. She didn't say goodbye as she left, but she'd seen it, the blinding flare. She'd denied it to that guard, but she'd seen it.

Because she created it.

I'd studied my cell for hours, days on end, and there in the center of the lock of my cell was a fresh hole. A perfect circle. Small enough to hide, but large enough to let orange flickers from the single torch through.

How had she done it?

I scooted closer to the door, dragging my knees cautiously across the stone floor toward the leftover food and water. Drinking first and then gobbling up the delicious meat pie and bread, my stomach revolted against the sudden onslaught of food, but I refused to let it come back up. Swallowing down my discomfort, I tested the barred door, pushing just barely on the bars with a single finger.

It moved.

My heart seized in my chest, and a horrible dread weighed down my lungs. I couldn't breathe.

My finger pushed again at the door, and it opened further without a sound. My entire hand could've fit through the gap the door had left open. Shoving my face into the cleft between metal and stone, I peered down the hall to the single guard standing watch in the far doorway that led to the stairs.

My exit.

The guard faced away from me, his body leaning lazily against the wall. If I could quietly sneak out, I could take him by surprise.

Freedom was just up those stairs…

In less than a second, I tasted the bitter panic of fear. It knocked me backward, stealing the air from my lungs.

I had been given an opportunity. An opportunity to attempt leaving. I could leave this place.

But what would *he* do if he caught me? What would happen if people saw me like this? Where could I go for help?

Horrific thoughts ran through my head in a barrage of gruesome images: my body being burned piece by piece, the gasps and shocked expressions of men and women as they beheld my new hideous face, a crowd laughing and jeering at me as they tied me up and threatened to kill me.

My hands shook in terror as I pulled the door closed on silent hinges.

I couldn't risk it. I couldn't…I couldn't endure more.

No more.

It was safer here. Safer if I just stayed in place. Safer inside. Safer in my dark little corner.

Where had this debilitating fear come from? How had I become this creature of terror and dread?

I didn't even recognize myself anymore.

I scooted my backside slowly away from the door, one hand helping me hobble my way back into the corner. That small cut in the metal wasn't enough to save me.

There was no saving me.

My breaths came in fast pants as black dots clouded my vision. I settled my back against the rough stone, clutching my knees to my chest, my entire body shaking.

Rocking back and forth, tears I hadn't shed before dampened my eyes. My mind warred with itself. Maybe what everyone said about me was true. Maybe I was too weak, too fragile, too easily broken. I had been given a way out, but I couldn't take it.

What kind of man didn't try?

Someone who is no longer a man.

I could hear my father's rebuke in my mind. His warm voice that used to chide me when I messed up. Stern, but always gentle.

He'd be so disappointed in me now.

But Father wasn't here anymore. He'd trusted the wrong man and left me behind to deal with the vengeance. He'd abandoned me to this shameful existence.

What had I become?

Camilla's face flashed behind my eyes. *You said you wouldn't hurt him.* Her distorted voice echoed against my brain. She had no idea the damage she'd wrought.

White hot fury flashed through my veins before my body shivered again as I stared at that fresh hole. So indistinct, yet so perfect. I wondered if anyone would even notice.

Was I truly this broken? Was I really just going to sit in here and cower away from my freedom?

Yes.

I shook my head, trying to rid it of my own vicious voice.

You don't deserve to leave. You're a spineless, broken beast who belongs in a cage. No one loves you, they never did. You're all alone.

Fiery tears rained down my cheeks.

You're all alone.

You're…

A sob jumped out of my throat, summoning a dark chuckle from down the hall that made me clutch my legs in even tighter.

Alone…

CHAPTER 22

Camilla

Liam stood on the stairs leading to the kitchen, but didn't come an inch further as Cook tutted at him.

"Wash up first, kitchen second," she scolded.

"I need to speak with the…"

She clicked her tongue at him again. "*Not* until you're cleaned up."

Smatterings of blood covered him as well as dirt and, well, who knew what else. The man was a filthy, terrifying mess. His face was pale, and his eyes held a faraway look that carried both rage and distinct fear.

The girls sat in front of me, staring at him like he was a walking nightmare come to life.

"Drink up now," I encouraged them, attempting to distract them from Liam's…mess.

He finally noticed what I was sure were five horrified expressions before turning around abruptly and heading back up the stairs.

Anna spoke up first. "I hope he killed them all."

"Anna!" Brigitta scolded.

She shrugged her shoulders. "What? The whole lot of them were awful to us."

"They're still living beings," Feleen offered quietly.

Anna's shoulders slumped forward. "I know, but they were cruel."

I took a sip of my tea, "How bad has it been since…" I couldn't bring myself to say anything next. What would I even offer? *Since I betrayed everyone and Apep took over?*

Brigitta sighed. "It's been…difficult."

"Best save this conversation for when Liam returns," Cook chided from her position, stirring over the stove.

Becca came barreling down the stairs, giving the girls only a moment to set their tea cups down on the center island before she slammed her full body into all of them at once. "I'm so glad you girls are safe. How'd you get free?"

"The exact question I want answered." Liam's deep tone rumbled against the stone walls of the small stairwell. Jimmy, Rafe, Billy, Ian and Chrissy were close on his heels.

"If the lot of you are going to stay in my kitchen, I'm going to put you to work," Cook warned, stirring with one hand and bracing the other on her hip.

Jimmy chuckled and walked over to give her a kiss on the cheek. "We'll do whatever you ask of us."

Cook blushed and playfully pushed him away. "Make yourself useful. Fresh water is boiling over the fire. I think everyone in this room needs a cup of tea."

A ghost of a smile pulled at my lips as I prepped the tea pot with fresh chamomile dried flowers. In Cook's world, a cup of tea covered a multitude of strife. Jimmy brought over the kettle and carefully poured the hot water in.

"So how'd you get away from the palace?" Becca asked, bringing the attention back to the task at hand and the question all of us wanted an answer to.

"Evelyn freed us, with a special message for Liam," Brigitta answered.

"It seems we might have more help than we originally planned," Liam jumped in. "Terreno stands with Ryker and I as Alstonia's leaders, but he requires word from one of us before sending aid."

"Getting a letter to him is…" Rafe's voice died off as he got lost in his own thoughts.

"We would need to somehow ensure its delivery," Ian said.

Liam nodded. "Exactly."

"How did Evy get you out, exactly?" Becca asked again, her eyes shrewd, as I poured the freshly brewed tea into several tea cups. Billy came to stand next to me and helped pass them out to everyone. I smiled politely with a grateful nod to him.

He'd been so kind to me ever since we'd had that talk in the kitchen. Even after all the horrible things I'd said against myself and fairies, he hadn't blinked an eye.

Was it out of pity? Was it something else?

Even if it was pity, I wasn't sure I deserved his consideration. I chanced another glance his way and he winked playfully at me through his messy dark curls before handing Feleen her teacup.

"It was incredible!" Anna exclaimed, pulling me out of my thoughts and back to the task at hand. She waved her tea cup animatedly around. I hoped it was empty. "Miss Evelyn used her magic, but instead of using it like a shield, she wielded it like the sharpest sword."

"A sword?" Liam's brow folded in the middle, and a smile pulled gently at one side of my lips. I loved how perplexed he looked at the idea of Evy wielding a sword with her magic.

"We discovered her magic could be projected with an intense speed, but we hadn't been able to practice much," Chrissy offered, filling in the gaps for all of us non-magical people. "Was she able to control its form and where it went?"

"I think so," Brigitta answered, "It all happened so quickly that it was hard to know for sure, but I didn't notice any significant damage."

"This is good news." Chrissy looked expectantly over at Liam.

He nodded at her and sipped his tea, his face still looked a little pale after the fight and I wondered if he might need to rest a bit before we left for the palace this evening. "If she's able to wield her magic offensively, that changes the game."

"It only changes the game if Apep's unaware she can wield her magic in this way," I said, and the group quieted at my raised concern.

Liam regarded me coolly, but inclined his head in respect, and my heart tried to leap into my throat. It was the first true acknowledgement of approval I'd received from him since we'd found him, and I chided myself inwardly for relishing his reaction.

Turning his attention back to the girls, he asked, "How close of a watch does Apep keep on her?"

"At least a pair of guards, sometimes four of them. They follow her everywhere," Brigitta offered.

"The only place she has any freedom from them is the suite," Anna added.

"That's where she was practicing, I think," Feleen spoke up. "I caught her once. She sliced a silver candelabra clean in two. But she was frantic to keep the evidence from Apep, so I don't think he knows."

Awe radiated through her tone as she spoke about Evy's magic, and a twinge of jealousy pricked at my heart. I was slowly starting to feel the same about her magic, but that bitterness from discovering Evy had been lying to me about it still lingered. It was like a stain I couldn't remove.

"And what of the staff?" Ian interjected. "Where does the majority of people's loyalty lie now?"

"I would say it's split in half. Half the servants are human, the other half are fairies. The human half, at least, are against Apep and his cruel guards, but…" Brigitta paused. "There is so much fear."

"Understandably so," Jimmy spoke softly. "And our girl? How is she, truly?"

I stiffened at his question, flooded with unspeakable amounts of guilt by the horribly worried look in his eye. I had put that look on his face. It had been my fault, my betrayal, my jealousy that pushed Liam away and Evy straight into Apep's grasp.

The girls went quiet. Too quiet.

"She is doing her best." Feleen smiled softly in encouragement. "She blames herself mostly for what's happened to Ryker. But she's strong, and so very brave." Her eyes glazed over with a fresh sheen of tears. "She risked so much to save us, after Ryker…" Her voice cracked, and Anna immediately swept her arms around her, pulling Feleen into her embrace.

"What happened with Ryker?" Liam asked. His knuckles were so white I feared he'd break the dainty tea cup clutched in his hand any minute.

Anna and Feleen both sniffled, stifling their cries, and my head sank in shame as I stared down at my empty tea cup. I both wanted and didn't want to hear what else had happened to poor Ryker. He didn't deserve anything that was happening to him. I had been such a fool for believing that Apep wouldn't hurt anyone.

"After Apep killed her parents—" Brigitta began.

"What?" I gasped out, shock racing down my spine as my head shot up to stare at them. "What did you just say?"

Brigitta swallowed. "Frank and Katerina. Apep had them killed."

I did my best to school my features, but after he'd already used my mother so severely, I just hadn't expected him to…

"I'm so sorry, Camilla." Brigitta's face fell. "I wasn't thinking."

Billy was there in an instant. "You're as pale as a sheet, lass." Taking the tea cup gently from my shaking hands, he helped me sit in a chair that I hadn't realized was there before my legs gave out completely from underneath me.

"Where was Evy during this?" Liam questioned, his eyes darting between me and the girls.

Brigitta's features contorted in anger—the sharpest emotion I'd seen from these girls yet. "In the throne room. Apep said it was a *gift* for her."

Horror washed over me.

A gift? Apep called my mother's death a gift?

Becca scoffed and sobbed at the same time, and I watched as her face fell apart while she stared at Liam. "She had to face them *again*. Alone this time."

I hadn't even thought…

Covering my mouth with a shaking hand to keep my sob inside, my stomach sank to my toes. For as hard as it was to hear about my mother's death, I could only imagine what Evy had been forced to witness. I knew she was glad to be free of them, but she had never wanted them to die. It wasn't in her nature to even think that way.

One small muscle ticked in Liam's temple. The obvious tell that he was about to explode.

"Let me just take that…" Rafe reached over and gently took the tea cup from Liam's rigid grasp, setting it down on the kitchen island. "There. Now you can clench those fists." He tapped him lightly on the back, and Liam immediately clenched his fists in response.

"And what happened with Ryker?" Liam asked.

"After Apep killed them, we couldn't find Evelyn anywhere. He had us searching the entire palace all night long. Her shield around him apparently disappeared…" Brigitta swallowed again. "He ordered Ryker be brought up to his old rooms and every spare mirror be placed in there with him. That's when he found Evelyn…"

"She was asleep in your bed," Feleen whispered, looking up at Liam with her sorrowful round eyes.

Wiping a hand down his face, already far-too-pale face, Liam's eyes reddened and glazed over.

"He found her there, and her punishment was watching Ryker see himself for the first time since…" Brigitta shook her head. "It was awful."

Liam pinched his eyes closed with his fingers as his entire body drooped forward into a soul-crushing sob. I'd never seen him break down before, and it seemed the whole room was a little stunned by his emotional reaction. Nobody moved until Chrissy crossed over. She slipped Liam's arm over her shoulder and leaned her whole body into him. He clutched at her like a lifeline as tears spilled down his face.

Rafe placed his hand on Liam's shoulder, giving it a squeeze, and Jimmy approached from the other side, offering the same.

"But she fought back," I said, my own eyes aching as I zeroed in on Liam's bloodshot ones. He blinked, looking back at me in confusion. "She fought back and freed the girls." I motioned to them. "She got you the message you need in order to call in reinforcements and take back this kingdom. Evy is doing what she always does. She's persevering."

I looked around to see the whole group staring at me with varying surprised expressions.

"So we have to do the same." I pressed, speaking to the group as a whole. They all nodded in response, expressions hardening in determination.

Liam needed his moment to break down. It was no small thing, hearing about how your brother and the love of your life were being tortured. It was hard enough hearing about my mother's murder, even though I wasn't sure how to truly feel about it. But right now, the group needed to focus on what mattered.

"Evy's giving us the example we need in order to defeat Apep," I reminded them. "She's showing us that no matter what Apep throws our way, we have to persevere, just like she is."

Liam nodded and wiped underneath his eyes with his thumbs, clearing his throat. "She's right. I say we still move in tonight." The whole group murmured their agreements in response. "I'll write a message to King Jai, but who can we trust to deliver it?"

Brigitta instantly spoke up, "After what she did for us, I would gladly take on this task."

"I agree," Feleen said.

"And me!" Anna added.

A deep voice sounded from the back doorway of the kitchen that led outside. "I would like to help as well."

The whole lot of us whipped around our heads to face the new voice.

He blushed slightly, dipping his head inside. His wings seemed to flutter nervously behind him. "I apologize for listening in, but we're all curious as to what's happening and want to help. I have family in Terreno and know the way. I would be honored to help escort the women." He bowed slightly with his arm over his heart.

"What's yer name, lad?" Ian asked.

"I am Fadel."

Jimmy walked over the Fadel, clapping him on the shoulder. "He's been a great help to us here at the estate. I wouldn't hesitate to trust him with such a task."

Liam's lips barely pulled to the side. "With an endorsement like that, consider yourself recruited." He gave Chrissy another gentle squeeze under his arm. "Do you feel ready to help us transform tonight?"

She nodded. "I'll be ready."

The lines around Ian's eyes seemed to deepen by the minute as his lips thinned into a straight line of disapproval.

"All right everyone, prepare what you need. Get some rest, eat some food, and be ready to leave here by sundown." Liam turned and walked up the stairs, presumably to write his letter while Jimmy introduced the girls to Fadel and two other fairies that came over to the back kitchen door.

Billy walked back over to the kitchen island and poured a fresh cup of tea before coming back to my side and handing it to me. "Ye ready for this, lass?"

"I'm not sure I'll ever feel ready to face this." I stared down into my cup.

"I s'pose that's the truth of it." I looked back up at him as he scratched the side of his cheek, but didn't continue or ask more questions.

I sipped my tea, watching everyone disperse. Ian followed Chrissy outside, and Cook took some bread out of the oven, which Rafe promptly burned his fingers on by touching it far too soon. Between Cook's scolding and Becca's laughter, it almost felt like all the things we'd just discussed were no big deal…and yet, my stomach twisted in painful knots.

My mother and Frank were dead, I'd be seeing Evy again soon, and I'd have to enter the palace again under the threat of Apep, who wouldn't hesitate to kill me if he knew I was there.

"I'm sorry about yer mother," Billy offered quietly, his hand softly resting on my shoulder.

Swallowing down my confused emotions, I thanked him and then mentioned needing some alone time, which he smiled sadly at, but nodded in understanding. Taking my now-empty tea cup, as well as everyone else's, he proceeded to wash them all using his magic, much to Cook and Rafe's delight.

I walked up the stone kitchen stairs to the main level of the home and headed straight out the front door. It seemed unreal that a small battle had just taken place in this courtyard. The sun was fully up in the sky now, and there were no bodies to be found. But tree limbs were scattered everywhere, seemingly ripped straight from their trunks, and smatterings of dark red stained stone and grass.

I walked past it all out to Evy's field. The tall dead grass of winter surrounded me, and I tried to feel emotional over my mother and Frank's death, but I just felt…numb. Disconnected.

There was nothing tying me to anyone now, except Evy. I was officially an orphan, and I somehow didn't care. Instead, a deep, grim anxiousness settled heavily in my bones.

Tonight I would be back in the palace, and I would do whatever it took to help free Evy and Ryker from this nightmare. They might never forgive me, but that was all right. Even if I had to take their place, I would do it in a heartbeat now.

What else was there for me to lose, anyway?

It was a strange feeling, being completely alone in the world, but there was something hauntingly freeing about it. No expectations, no roles to play, no one to miss you if you were gone. It was like a rebirth of sorts. And this Camilla…

I brushed down the skirt of my dress as if wiping away my past self. This Camilla got to decide who she wanted to be…and I wanted to be someone I could be proud of.

CHAPTER 23

Liam

As I handed my letter to Brigitta, I couldn't help but worry about the journey they were about to embark on. All three women were so brave, but they were also innocent and naive, sheltered by palace life for far too long. Three fairies had offered to go with them. Jimmy assured me that all of them were the upstanding sort, *a good lot* he said he'd trust his own life with. I couldn't distrust that, he was even more protective than me often times.

I sighed, meeting Brigitta, Anna and Feleen's eyes. "You don't have to do this, there's still time to…"

"We want to." Demure Feleen surprised me with her determined voice.

"We'll be fine." Brigitta said, but her eyes betrayed their worry no matter how well she hid it.

I looked at the fairies behind them, "Do you have everything you need?"

They nodded, raising various bags of goods. The girls had their bags as well, packed with essentials that Cook, Jimmy and Ian had helped them gather.

I couldn't protect them, or do much of anything really except write these letters. Three in total, one for each of them should they get lost or separated at any point.

"We'll do our part, so you can do yours." Brigitta offered.

I swallowed thickly, thanking them all. "You'd better get going before more of Apep's guards come snooping around here."

As they exited the office I pulled Fadel aside, "I know we don't know each other and Jimmy's word holds greater value to me than most, but," I squared my jaw looking him directly in the eye, "if anything happens to those girls, I will personally hunt all three of you down and—"

Fadel smiled, "I would expect nothing less from you." He patted me on the shoulder, and then held his hand there, "I promise you we shall make haste and do everything in our power to protect this precious crew. You have my word." He bowed deeply then, removing his hand from my shoulder and placing it over his heart instead.

The gesture was humbling and I knew it would have to be enough. We didn't have time for strategic planning or the manpower to send an entire company with them for protection. All we had was haste and surprise on our side, that, and the brave souls willing to face the unknown.

We did what we could to see the six of them off, but once they disappeared down the path, they were on their own. All we could do now was hope that they made it in time and that King Jai would be true to his word.

Rafe walked with me back to the estate after we'd made sure the area was clear. "Cook told me to make sure you eat something before we go tonight."

I laughed at the modest care of that phrase. There was something so normal about Cook making sure we were fed before leaving the house.

We walked around to the back of the home rather than going through the inside so we didn't track more dirt into the house. Several people and fairies all mingled together, enjoying a bowl of whatever delicious stew Cook had made. Becca, Camilla and Billy were all busy filling and passing out bowls to everyone.

I stopped to take in the moment before me. To witness the estate brimming with activity...laughter, talking, sharing...

Evy would've loved this.

The deep stab of regret pressed its way between my ribs as Rafe walked over to grab us both bowls, and the stark realization hit me that I could be seeing her soon. Tonight, even. Though that was unlikely, it was possible.

Dread coated my stomach like a thick viscous layer, churning from side to side.

Would she even want to see me? Could she ever forgive me?

I knew I didn't deserve a second chance, but I longed for one with every fiber of my being. I needed to see her. I needed to make her safe.

And Ryker, too.

My eyes stung, burning with guilt and shame. I had left him, too. Left him to face this alone and fend for himself. I hadn't left his side in eight years, not since we discovered each other at the ripe age of just thirteen. He'd always been my brother in spirit, and now he was my brother in blood…and I had left him behind.

I didn't know how I could face either of them. Give me an enemy to fight any day or night and I was up to the challenge, but confronting the two people I had injured most with my cowardly choices? That thought made me want to crawl beneath the surface of the earth and stay there, hidden away.

I didn't even hear Chrissy's approach until she was standing next to me. Her wild grey and white hair blew lazily in the breeze as she surveyed the crowd enjoying their meal with me.

Her voice was soft and filled with understanding as she spoke. "Forgiveness is a hard thing to face."

"And what if you don't deserve it?" I grumbled.

She tsked. "*You* are not in charge of that decision. It is something freely given and chosen by others. You don't get a choice in the matter. All you can do is learn to forgive yourself."

I huffed out humorlessly. "And how does one learn that?"

Chrissy sighed. "You made a choice Liam. It was a choice that hurt others, but it's not unforgivable."

"I was a coward," I confessed.

"You were. But everyone has been a coward at one point or another."

We both grew silent, and I noticed Rafe hanging back to talk with

Becca a little longer. I was grateful for his discernment.

"Do you really think this will work?" The words barely made it out.

"I can only hope that it does. I'll be right there with you to help along the way."

I turned to face her. "And will *you* be okay?"

She met my eyes and nodded. Her bright green eyes were so similar to Evy's that looking at her made my heart twist almost to the point of physical pain.

"I'll do everything I can, you know." I whispered.

She reached up and squeezed my arm in acknowledgement. "I know you will."

I looked back over to Rafe, signaling that we were done.

He stuck a bowl in my hand, smiling. "Per Cook's orders."

I smiled back. "Thank you."

"Eat fast. The crew is eager to get this show on the road." Rafe winked at Chrissy, making her titter at his shenanigans.

"Becca's most certainly got her hands full with you," she laughed.

I ate in a hurry as I saw our group starting to gather and sucked in a deep breath. Rafe patted me on the back. "Cook said to *eat* the food, not inhale it."

I choked on my last bite, and he patted my back as though that would help.

I shot him a look. "Har, har."

A slight flutter of wings was my only warning before Billy snatched the bowl out of my hands the minute I put my utensil down. He flitted back toward the kitchen, disappearing inside as Becca and Camilla made their way over.

Chrissy nudged me with her elbow, her wings fluttering playfully behind her. "I think it's time."

I looked all my friends in the face, taking in a slow deep breath through my nose as I rolled my shoulders back a few times, loosening up the tension.

Rafe waggled his eyebrows at me. "Ready to go save the kingdom?"

I shot him an exasperated look, and he smiled wide in return.

Chrissy faced the four of us, beaming with pride. "Let's make you into fairies, shall we?"

CHAPTER 24

Evelyn

As the guard led me back up the stairs toward Apep's office, fresh fatigue coated my entire body like a heavy shroud. I already needed more time with Nature. In my haste, I had thrown too much power into breaking Ryker's lock, and without proper sleep or food, I was paying the price.

When I stumbled over my feet trying to climb up the stairs, the guard turned around to grab me.

"Your Highness, are you all right?" He actually sounded genuinely worried.

I tried to assure him I was fine, but all that came out was a breathy groan. Sweat slowly dotted my brow as the floor tipped from underneath me. The guard tightened his grasp on my arm.

"I'm fine." I tried to brush him away. "I'm fine."

"The King doesn't like to be kept waiting." He hoisted me back to an upright position, looking nervously over his shoulder. "Lean on me if you must, but we need to continue on."

Frustration clouded my already worried mind at the lack of regard these guards held for seemingly everything but Apep's wishes. Still, I sighed and leaned against him. I couldn't let Apep see me like this; I couldn't confirm his suspicions that I'd been using more magic than normal. It was too soon. Too obvious.

Fear, fatigue, and worry swirled throughout me in dizzying circles until I struggled to figure out what was up and what was down.

"I need a moment." Letting go of his arm, I reached for the wall, allowing it to help me slide down to the ground in a very ungraceful plop to the floor.

"Your Highness, I must insist…"

I leveled a glare at where I assumed his head was; everything was a bit too blurry to know for sure. "Bring me a glass of water and something to eat."

He huffed. "I'm not a servant. Get up."

I slumped over further, clinging to consciousness in case my shield around Apep disappeared again. I couldn't handle those disastrous results right now.

"What is going on here?" A new masculine voice sounded nearby. I didn't recognize it, but I knew this didn't look good. "What are you…Your Highness? Is this Princess Evelyn?"

The guard huffed again. "Yes, my Lord, she's being rather difficult at the—"

"Water," I whispered out, closing my eyes to ward off the dizziness. Faces and forms were entirely blurry at this point anyway; there was no reason to strain myself further by trying to see.

"Fetch her some water!" the stranger demanded. "What are you even thinking?"

"Apep is expecting—"

"He's expecting me as well," the stranger interrupted him sharply, "and he will continue to expect us as long as it takes for her to recover. Fetch her some water, and we shall both be on our way."

The smallest shuffle of feet followed by a flittering silence was all I needed to know the guard had gone off to do as I had originally asked.

"Thank you for—" I started to say.

A cold hand landed gently on my brow. "You're burning up." His voice was gentler now that guard was gone, but it still held a haughty tone. "When's the last time you communed with Nature?"

Deciding a lie was better than the truth, I offered, "Last night."

"After you get that water, I'd best take you outside," he insisted.

I nodded, opting not to respond.

"What on earth has you so fatigued?" he asked, the slightest bit of worried shock filtered in through his voice.

I sighed, leaning my head back against the cold stone wall. "Apep requires a constant shield from me. I haven't slept well, nor have I eaten or drank anything in a while."

"You must take better care of yourself." The haughty tone was back, but the underlying worry still remained. "Ah, here we are."

A cold cup gently touched my lips, and I opened as the stranger poured water into my mouth, helping me drink. The refreshing essence of the water alone was enough to revive my senses.

"Here's a little bread, as well." The fluffy morsel lightly pressed against my lips next, and I gladly accepted it.

"Thank you for your kindness and help." Maybe it was foolish to trust a stranger in this way, but it was the better alternative to Apep seeing me like this…or even worse, passing out and losing my shield around him again.

He cleared his throat quietly as I opened my eyes, testing their blurriness. Warm hazel eyes met mine as I blinked toward clarity. He held out the cup of water to me, and I gratefully took it with my slightly shaking hands, gulping down as much as I could before finishing off the bread he handed to me next.

"Looking better already." He smiled encouragingly as I lifted my head a bit. His features were handsome, chiseled and strong. He wore his sandy blonde hair in a similar style to the one Ryker preferred, longer on top and swept to the side. His skin looked sunkissed, but not tanned.

"I really must insist we…" the impatient guard started.

The stranger turned to him, glowering with one eyebrow lifted. "You dare to boss your own Princess around? I'm sure Apep would not be pleased to hear that."

"Forgive me, my Lord, I just—" the guard sputtered.

I moved to stand. "It's fine," I interrupted him. "Allow me to catch my bearings, and we'll be on our way."

The stranger gripped my forearm, helping to steady me. "Your Highness, are you sure you're alright?"

I waved him off with the hand that held my now-empty cup of

water. "Yes, I'm fine. Just a little dizzy spell, is all." I handed my cup out to the guard, who shot me an indignant look before taking it.

Choosing to ignore him entirely, I faced the stranger, taking in his luxurious attire. His wings were tucked behind him, but instead of sporting the loose-fitting and wrapped clothing most fairies preferred, he wore tailored human clothes, designed specially to fit his wings. He was handsome to say the least, the green of his gold-buttoned overcoat accenting the hazel tone of his eyes. Looking up strained my neck further than I was used to, so I assumed he was a little taller than Liam.

"You said you were headed to see Apep as well?" I asked.

"Yes, Your Highness." His smile was pompous, but the emotion behind his eyes still seemed wary.

I looped my arm through his. "Then we shall go together, Lord…"

"Silas." He tipped his head to me.

"Thank you for your help, Lord Silas," I said sincerely. A stone of worry sat heavily in my stomach as he escorted me to Apep's office. If Apep wanted to see Silas as well as myself, it couldn't be for anything good.

We walked in silence after that, led by the huffing, overly irritated guard down the halls to Apep's office.

Silas squeezed my arm slightly, leaning in. "He seems quite put out by us, doesn't he?"

I couldn't help but smirk in return. "I'm not certain. It seems the cup may be the biggest offender in this case, considering the way he's holding it just so."

Silas looked down at the guard's hand. He barely held the cup, the rim pinched between his two while all the rest of his fingers were sprawled outward, as though the surface area held all manner of filth.

Silas let out a loud cackle, making the guard turn around and glare at us, which of course only caused even more snickers.

Apep's office door was already open, and the guard moved to say something, possibly even to apologize by the way his brow furrowed in distress, but Apep cut him off. "There you are. I was beginning to…" His eyes landed on Silas next to me, and his tone immediately brightened. "Oh, wonderful! The two of you have already met."

We looked at each other, and Silas bowed his head in respect before answering, "Yes, Your Majesty. I had the pleasure of helping the Princess regain—"

"My footing," I inserted. "I tripped just as he was walking by."

Silas eyed me from the side, but did nothing to contradict my story. Neither did the put-out guard, who was promptly dismissed by Apep without another thought.

"Come inside, both of you, and have a seat." Apep waved us in as Silas politely pulled out my seat, helping me sit first before he followed. The seemingly consummate gentleman.

Apep's nose wrinkled, and he gave me a pointed up and down look. "This is precisely why I called you both here." He turned to Silas, smiling in that way which didn't suit him at all before looking back at me. "Silas and his father are the Lords of Lochronstandt. Silas here is a…" Apep trailed off, searching for the right words, "… connector of fairies. He's been looking out for our kind for a very long time now."

"I was a member of the human court before Apep's reign." His haughty tone only increased in Apep's presence. "A hidden fairy, if you will."

I angled my head to look back at Silas, who was the picture of ease except for the slight tick in his jaw. I nodded politely, "It's a pleasure to properly make your acquaintance, then."

He smiled, dipping his chin, "Likewise, Your Highness."

"Evelyn," Apep said my name in that certain way that was both chiding and affectionate, pulling my attention back to him. "You shall spend time with Silas over the next few weeks and allow him to introduce you to your fellow fairy kind."

I straightened my spine, not liking where this meeting was going. Apep was planning to restrict my time even further by essentially giving me a babysitter.

"There will be a celebratory ball at the end of this month, and guests will be arriving at varying times over the next couple of weeks. That gives you plenty of time to make new friends and meet new fairies."

I bristled slightly and narrowed my eyes. "I don't need—"

"I told you this was a new beginning, Evelyn, a fresh start for you to get to know your own kind." I ground my teeth as I attempted to keep my expression stoic, but I had a feeling I looked far more sullen than I would've liked. "Silas is well-connected, and he will make sure you are well-connected, too. He will meet you each morning," I opened my mouth to speak, but Apep continued, "as you will no longer be allowed to visit the dungeon."

I sucked in a harsh breath. "You can't..."

Apep cut me off. "I can, and I am. You will instead use your time to get to know your people." He looked down his nose at me, like my father used to when he was disappointed. "You are a princess now. Act like it."

Scolded like a child, my eyes burned with anger and unshed tears as I stared him down. Silas adjusted awkwardly in his seat before speaking up. "I will make sure she is well-connected. You know I only consort with the best of fairies."

Apep's smile looked more like a sneer as he complimented Silas, "Indeed you do, which is why I've tasked you to help your Princess... *adjust* to her new role." Apep's gaze slid back to me, studying me quietly for what felt like several minutes. "Are you quite well, Evelyn? You look a bit peaked."

"I'm fine," I said quietly, and Apep smirked.

"Well, then, I'll let you two get better acquainted." He stood in clear dismissal of us. "I'll see you both at dinner tonight."

Silas stood immediately, bowing to Apep before walking around his seat toward the door. I, however, sat in my chair, glaring at Apep.

He smirked knowingly. "Is there something else, dear?"

I ground my teeth to the point of pain. "You won't be able to keep me from seeing him."

"Ah, but is it not *him* who does not wish to see *you*?"

I sucked in a heavy breath, my eyes instantly smarting again.

Apep's barely-there grin surfaced. He was enjoying this. He said he'd missed my fire, and I wondered now if it was because he delighted in provoking me. I wondered suddenly if this was his cruel and misguided way of squabbling with me like we were true siblings. Had he treated his actual sister this way?

"I could use a turn about the garden," Silas announced, breaking the silent tension. "Would you care to join me, Your Highness?"

I blinked several times, attempting to calm my frantic nerves before standing. The pleased look on Apep's face infuriated me to no end, but there was nothing more I could say at the moment, and he knew it.

"See you tonight." He smiled as I turned around and marched out of the office in front of Silas.

He jogged to catch up to me as I stomped down the hall. "Well, the two of you have an…interesting relationship."

I shot him a glare, daring him to continue that line of thought, but he raised his hands in surrender.

"It seems a bit of time outside could do us both some good." He raised a brow, and I said nothing as we both walked outside to the front courtyard garden. I didn't come here much as I found the perfectly shaped shrubs far too boring, but I wasn't ready to walk my favorite places with a fairy Apep preferred.

I should've known better than to let him see me in such a weak state.

"I won't tell him you know," he whispered at my side.

I paused. "Tell him what, exactly?" I shot back.

He didn't have to tell Apep a thing. If Apep truly wanted to know anything, he could get it. But if he *did* tell Apep about my little dizzy spell, it would give Apep even more reason to be suspicious of me, and that was exactly what I was trying to avoid.

He shrugged, grinning knowingly. "Nothing, of course." He winked, and I rolled my eyes. Spending time with him was going to be an unexpected challenge. One that I wasn't looking forward to.

CHAPTER 25

Liam

With freshly transformed wings in tow, no one bothered us as we made our way to the palace.

Chrissy had worked miracles, converting twig and leaf harnesses into shimmering, fine fairy wings of all colors and shades. She'd also distorted our faces *just* enough to be unrecognizable should Apep briefly see us, but upon intense study, we would easily be found out. It was a calculated risk, but one we had to take if we wanted inside the palace.

Several of Apep's new guards had been surprisingly welcoming to us, even going as far as to guide us to the palace, thinking our group fresh out of hiding. It was surreal seeing so many fairies out in the open. Though it was a mixture of those who had wings and those who didn't, I noticed most of the fairies still preferred loose clothing in varying colors. Much like Chrissy always wore.

A very real shame weighed down my shoulders as I realized how prejudiced I'd been, how blind. To have missed all the fairies that secretly lived in our kingdom and dismissed them because I'd been taught that they were somehow bad or evil. That magic was the root of all turmoil. How would I have felt if I'd had to constantly hide who and what I was? None of it sat well with me, and though I couldn't change the past, I could change the future.

Once we removed Apep as a threat, things would be different. I would make sure they were different. There was no way any of us would be able to go back to the way things were, not after what we'd now seen and witnessed.

Our group approached the small town just outside the palace, and both of the girls gasped at the sheer devastation that surrounded us. Homes and the tavern were all that remained as spots of smoke still snaked their way up from hidden fires in the rubble, adding to the growing shadows contrasted by the setting sun.

Two guards stood in front of the palace's side doors that led to the town. Though it wasn't the main entrance, it was still the most widely used. Even the guards in Hoddleston had directed us here instead of the main gate.

Taking the lead, I walked forward with confidence, bowing my head in slight deference. "We're here for some jobs."

When the guards simply looked us over without responding, I added, "We came from the North when we heard about the fairy liberation and made the journey all the way here in hopes of working for the King who helped give our kind this new freedom."

For a fraction of a second, I wondered if their silence meant that one of them had mind reading magic like Apep, but they both looked none the wiser of our true plans as one of them asked, "What kind of work can you provide?"

Rafe jumped in next. "We're good with horses, both gifted with the language of animals."

Chrissy, Ian and Billy had coached us all on how to speak about magic. Billy had known a young girl one time who could talk to animals. The gift was rare, but most importantly…hard to prove. Which made it perfect for us.

"That's a very rare gift indeed." The guard raised an impressed—and skeptical--eyebrow. "And you both have it?"

Rafe shifted his thumb between the two of us. "Brothers," was the only explanation he provided.

The guard looked past Rafe. "All three of you? Your older brother there, what's his gift?"

Billy chimed in then. "Water gift. Used to workin' as a washer in the kitchens. Miss Cami here is quite the cook herself. Makes a delicious roast. I claim it's the best ye ever had."

The guard quirked an eyebrow as he eyed Camilla up and down with an undisguised lecherous gaze. She was beautiful to be sure, but that look made me want to carve his eyes out for her sake. The other guard regarded Becca much the same, causing Rafe to bristle a little too visually. "And the last one? What's she do?"

Becca surprised us all by playing the role of timidity. Batting her lashes, biting her lip. A part of me was certain she did it just to mess with Rafe, and unfortunately, it was working a little too well. I elbowed him hard as she spoke up. "My gift is growth magic, but I've had work as a maid for quite some time now. I do best with cleaning and the like."

The guards looked to each other. "We'll check for you," said one. He stayed as the other went inside, and we waited, making idle chit chat until a sturdy and severe woman strode out the door and eyed our ragtag group with a penetrating gaze.

She had no wings, and I immediately wondered whether or not she was a fairy. By the harshly authoritative look of her, I imagined she must be a fairy, especially if she was in charge of anything here in the palace.

"I'm the head housekeeper. King Apep entrusts me with the upkeep of the palace, and all palace hires must go through me first." She regarded our group with narrowed eyes. "The animal language gift is rare and welcomed; you boys can work in the stables. King Apep will be proud to have such a rare gift under his roof." She eyed Rafe and I carefully. "Especially if you have your wings already."

Flicking her gaze over to Camilla, Billy and Becca, she studied each one in turn. "Who's left? Kitchens and a maid?"

Billy flashed her grin. "Yes, ma'am. I wash," he wrapped his arm around Camilla, tugging her awkwardly into his side, "she cooks."

"And I clean, ma'am," Becca inserted.

"Kitchen can always use more washers. You two will do fine." She inspected Camilla's face as she spoke. "If the chef wants someone else cooking, she'll tell you. Otherwise, you may not get the chance. That alright with you?"

Camilla dipped her head. "Yes, ma'am."

"Fine then. You girl," she pointed to Becca, "come closer and let me have a look at you."

Becca approached demurely, making Rafe have to cover up a snort, pretending it was a cough. The head housekeeper shot him a look of pure annoyance before turning back to Becca. "Have you any knowledge of dressing a lady? Preparing meals, fires, that sort of thing?"

"Yes, ma'am. I…I worked for a human lady, for a time."

Stuttering, stammering and reserved…Becca was out-acting us all by far. The slight distortion on her face made her appear more innocent and youthful, lending itself easily to her new demeanor.

"You seem respectful enough, obedient," the housekeeper observed, and Rafe snorted again. I slapped his back as he coughed exaggeratedly.

"It's been a long journey," I offered, "and he hasn't had much to drink."

With a look of pure exasperation, she waved us inside. "Fine, fine. All of you, follow me."

She led us inside the palace and down the side hall, which then branched off to several areas. Turning to Billy and Camilla, she directed them down to the kitchens, telling them to make themselves known to the chef immediately and not to dawdle or wander. Then she turned to Rafe and I. "The stables are out back. You will report to the stable master immediately." She studied Rafe with narrowed eyes. "If I hear of any funny business, I won't hesitate to throw you out. Rare gift or no, King Apep may be benevolent, but you will not receive any second chances here."

We nodded and turned in the direction she dictated, stepping quietly so we could listen to what she said to Becca.

"The Princess is in need of a new lady's maid."

Becca offered a small gasp that I imagined was not forced or fake at all.

"King Apep would prefer the role be filled by a fairy. Do you feel up to the task of serving her Royal Highness, Princess Evelyn?"

Becca softened her voice. "It would be my distinct honor."

"Excellent. I will take you there immediately. Apep will need to approve of you before you meet the Princess herself."

No. No, no, no, no. Fear latched onto my heart, squeezing it like an iron vice, just as I gripped Rafe's arm before he darted back out into the hallway without thinking.

Becca's distorted features were there, but they were subtle. Upon further study, she'd be discovered. We couldn't let her meet with Apep, or everything would blow up before it even began.

Rafe turned to me, panic etching at his eyes. I knew he wouldn't be able to let her walk away like this, straight into Apep's clutches. "Liam…I can't let this—"

"Oh! Your Highness. Lord Silas," the fairy female exclaimed in surprise.

Rafe and I both stilled before quietly peeking back around the corner just in time to see…

Evy.

Her hair was down and free with her natural waves curling it at the ends. Her dress was flowing around her in a way that I knew she would love, and backless, giving her the freedom of wearing a dress without the restrictions of too many ties. She turned to look at someone who walked up beside her and smiled. From here, it looked like a genuine smile, full of warmth and affection.

She was somehow even more beautiful now than when last I saw her.

But my jaw clenched and my sight turned red at the image of a male fairy stepping up next to Evy, his sparkling wings far too close to her bare back.

My fists strained as I curled them in tight. Perhaps it wouldn't be the *worst* plan to charge directly in and rip those wings straight out of his back, rescuing the girls in the process.

Who was he? Why were they together? And why was he standing so close to her?

I could tell the moment Evy saw Becca as I watched her whole body freeze in place. I couldn't see her face, but I hoped she didn't betray her emotions now. Evy's expressions were usually completely transparent. She wore her emotions just as plainly as she wore her clothing. I'd never seen her impassive or straight-faced, but hopefully that was a skill she'd recently picked up.

"I was just bringing by a new lady's maid for Apep's approval," the staunch housekeeper replied to Evy.

Becca bowed and raised her head, still perfectly playing her role, though her chin may have quivered just slightly.

"How," Evy choked, coughing softly to try and cover up the misstep. "Ahem, what perfect timing then. There's no need to get Apep involved. I can approve of her right now."

"Forgive me, my lady, but Apep was insistent that he must approve anyone who is to be near you."

I watched Evy's jaw tick to the side, her hands grasped tightly in front of her. "Then I shall accompany you."

The fairy male standing next to Evy reached out for her hand, bringing it slowly to his lips. "I will take my leave, then. See you at dinner, Your Highness."

She dipped her head as they both met gazes, sharing some kind of secret message between the two of them.

The look was familiar…too familiar. That wretched male was far too close with Evy, and a vicious, angry part of me wanted to physically rip his arms off so he might never touch her again.

"Calm down there, Cap," Rafe whispered in my ear. "She's got a role to play here too, don't forget."

With a sullen grunt, I watched as Evy walked next to Becca and the fairy woman down the hall before disappearing around a corner. Four guards followed closely behind, and I realized those were the ones the girls had mentioned. Her shadows.

I turned and stormed away, ready to punch anything I could get my hands on. Unease brewed quickly in my stomach. We'd made it inside, but had already hit a huge snag. If Evy hadn't shown up when she did, Becca would've given us all away; she still might.

Pacing back and forth, my mind raced. What if he recognized her? What if he hurt her?

Rafe wasn't faring much better, considering it was Becca on the line now, too. "Do we just let them go?" he asked, his eyes wide with a panicked anger.

I stopped, closing my eyes to suck in a deep breath. We had to think about this logically, not emotionally.

Shaking my head, I ran my fingers through my hair. "If we charge in now, we'll give ourselves away for sure, and them." I paused, looking at him. "Evy won't let anything happen to her. You and I both know she'd sacrifice herself before she ever let harm come to Becca."

Rafe nodded reluctantly, but didn't look comforted before he spoke again, resignation clouding his tone. "So we wait."

I sucked in a ragged breath before nodding. "We wait."

CHAPTER 26

Evelyn

My breaths were too tight, too constricted by my narrowing lungs. *Becca.* Becca was here, walking next to me…straight to Apep's office.

My hand lightly brushed against Becca's as we walked silently side by side down the empty halls, and her pinky intertwined with mine. I couldn't believe she was here, that she was actually next to me, and that in the very next moment she could be ripped away.

Her disguise was good; subtle, but present enough to hopefully hide her from brief inspection. Her wings looked beautiful, a light pearlescent pink shade that contrasted in a stunning effect against her darker skin. Her features had been exaggerated, making her look younger, more innocent and wide-eyed.

But I would know her anywhere. She was my chosen sister, not from birth, but born of the deepest friendship.

The slightest tremble echoed through her pinky, and I gave her a reassuring squeeze. I wouldn't let anyone hurt her; I couldn't.

Maybe we'd get a distraction. Maybe, if everything worked out as it should, Ryker would have quietly found his way out of his cell so there would be no serious repercussions if I had to defend her. It was the least I could hope for if she were found out.

My stomach dropped as we rounded the corner towards Apep's office.

The main housekeeper of the palace walked in front of us, and my guards followed behind. I needed to get a shield around Becca before he could read her mind. I wouldn't be able to hold her finger in front of him; she'd have to stand on her own.

Each step forward brought us closer to Apep's office, and my heartbeat sped up.

I stopped dead in my tracks in the middle of the hall, pulling Becca to stop with me. "Before we get inside, I'd like to hear from you why you want this position. Apep may conduct his interview, but I'd like to conduct one of my own."

Becca's eyes widened a hair at my abrupt action. She dipped into a brief bow. "I-I would like to work for the fairy who helped free us and who protects us still. It would be my honor to serve you."

I smiled and nodded. "Thank you for the compliment. And have you witnessed my magic before?"

Becca's eyes narrowed infinitesimally, as if she were trying to figure out my game, but played along anyway. "No Your Highness, I've never had the honor of witnessing your magic in person."

I nodded, pulling my hands together and creating a shield in its center. All the fairies seemed to be looking on, so I instructed the shield to go around Becca's form visually, allowing it to linger in visual form long enough for it to be considered a "display" of magic before allowing it to seemingly disappear.

I hoped this worked.

My magic now clung to Becca's form by practically adhering to her skin. The weight of her moving shield combined with Apep's was heavy, but not overpowering. Especially since I'd just communed with Nature while on my walk with Silas.

Becca clapped her hands like an innocent child lost in wonder, and I was surprised to see the head housekeeper join her, a look of awe on her face.

"Marvelous, Your Highness. Simply miraculous."

I dipped my chin. "Thank you both." Turning to Becca, I continued, "Thank you for your kind words, but I am in no need of a lady's maid. Forgive me, but I shall ask Apep to reassign you somewhere else."

"But, Your Highness…" the head housekeeper started.

I shot her a look. "I'm perfectly capable of taking care of myself."

And with that, I left everyone in the hallway, marching straight into Apep's office. I knew Becca wouldn't know what I was doing, but as of now, all I could hope for was that Apep would agree with me and assign her elsewhere. It was her best chance at remaining safe and out from under Apep's keen eye.

Her disguise was good, but even now I feared it would not be good enough to fool Apep. He'd already seen her once before and taken the liberty of rummaging around in her mind, while also using her as a threat against me. I'd vowed then, just as I vowed now, that I would never let him hurt her or use her again.

If she kept her head down and her remarks short and sweet, we just might get through this. But if she were to become my maid, he would have far too much access to her. I couldn't allow that. I couldn't put her in that position.

Charging straight into his office, I schooled my features to look irritated instead of worried. I wasn't very good at this game, so I had no idea what my face truly looked like, but I hoped it didn't betray my worry.

Apep looked up, his confused eyes meeting mine. "Evelyn? What are…" His gaze glided over to the door, his expression shifting to one of amusement as the head housekeeper kept her chin held high and her gait rigid while she entered Apep's office, obviously wanting to make a good impression. I struggled to not roll my eyes as she bowed awkwardly. "Your Majesty. Forgive the interruption, but I do believe I have found a new lady's maid for Princess Evelyn."

I shot her a look of disdain, but she did her best to ignore me as Becca entered the room. She shivered slightly, betraying her true nerves, which luckily fit the scene perfectly. Her head was bowed, and her hands clasped tightly in front of her.

"Ah." Apep sat back in his chair and steepled his long spindly fingers in front of him. "Come closer, female, let me have a look at you."

I huffed out an irritated breath. "I don't want another lady's maid,

Apep."

He waved his hand at me in disregard, and I tried not to stiffen as Becca stepped hesitantly closer to the desk.

"What's your experience?" he asked.

"I-I helped a few human women and a lady, be-before the liberation, Your Majesty."

Oh, she was good. I wanted to giggle at her obvious performance, but I didn't dare let even an ounce of amusement cloud my features. Becca was still standing in front of Apep, her chin practically hitting her sternum. Though I knew he couldn't hurt her or invade her mind because of my shield around her, he could still discover her secret, and that was by far the bigger threat.

Apep hummed with an amused expression alighting his face. "And what's your name?"

"Becky, Your Majesty."

"Becky." Apep repeated as a smirk slithered up the side of his face.

Did he recognize her? Did he find the very similar name amusing in some way? I studied his face, looking as indignant and put out as possible.

Apep looked to me then. "She seems a good fit, would you not agree, Evelyn?"

I stared back at him. "I think she would be best reassigned elsewhere. I'm fine on my own."

"Ah. But I insist you have a...companion." A wide, saccharine smile curled out across his face. He faced Becca again. "I'm sure the Princess will warm up to you in no time." Then he turned to the main housekeeper. "Thank you for bringing them by. You're all dismissed."

It wasn't right to laugh, but the overly animated devastation on the housekeeper's face threatened to shatter my control as giggles bubbled up in my chest. Or maybe it was the relief that he hadn't recognized Becca. Or maybe it was just simply the fact that Becca was here. With me. Now.

"I'll see you at dinner, Evelyn." Apep's eyes shined with satisfaction.

Between my own bubbling emotions caught somewhere between giddiness and terror, I simply dipped my head and turned out of the office, practically stomping away. The head housekeeper hurried behind me.

I didn't pause to stop or breathe out in relief. My only goal now was to get Becca back to my suite as quickly as possible. I wanted to wrap my arms around her so tightly that she couldn't move or be hurt or be found out.

As I rounded the corner to my suite, I charged inside, barreling straight for the bedroom.

Becca continued to follow until she was snagged outside of the suite by the head housekeeper. "You will listen and do as you're told. Once you've prepared Her Highness for dinner, you will come find me in the kitchens. There I will set you up with your lodging, instructions, and a tour of the palace."

Becca agreed and walked past the two guards stationed at the doorway, and the other two who were now helping themselves to the sitting room. She kept her head bowed, not daring to look any of them in the eye, which was a smart move considering their short tempers and wandering eyes.

I waved her inside the bedroom and addressed the guards. "This is my new lady's maid that Apep just approved." I tried to put as much disapproval in my voice as possible to make it believable.

A few of the guards cracked cruel smiles that they tried their best to cover, but I knew better. They loved it when Apep put me in my place.

Slamming the door behind us, I didn't even exhale until my arms were around my best friend, gripping her as closely to me as possible. A surprising onslaught of silent and heavy tears rolled down my cheeks as I held her tightly. Her body trembled and shook quietly under my arms, both of us breaking down the moment we were able to.

With the guards right outside, neither of us dared to speak very loudly.

"What are you doing here? How did you get in?" I whispered into her tight ,dark curls.

She scoffed sadly. "Like I would ever leave you here to fend for yourself." We each took a deep breath before reluctantly separating our embrace. "Do you think he recognized me?"

I shook my head. "He wouldn't have let you be my lady's maid if he knew who you were. He's been doing his best to distance me from my *past life,* as he puts it." I rolled my eyes as I wiped my fingers underneath them to remove the excess moisture there.

"Well, he's in for a treat then." Becca smiled before wiping her sleeve across her eyes and nose.

I swallowed thickly. "Is he…" I couldn't get the words out suddenly. "Is *he* here?"

Becca shot me a sassy side-eye. "I'm not sure *who* you could possibly mean…" I groaned in muffled exasperation, and she just smiled. "Of course he's here."

Of course he's here.

I found myself sitting on the bed, Becca's arm suddenly slung around me. The sudden sobs surprised even me, but somehow just knowing he was here had broken the dam in my chest wide open. The outpouring of all my emotions was too overwhelming, too confusing, too hopeful.

He'd come back. He'd finally come back.

"Oh, Ev." Becca tucked me in close to her side.

"He came back."

"Yes," she said softly, stroking my hair. "He loves you and Ryker more than anyone else in this world."

"He's here." I pulled back to look at her, tears distorting my vision. I didn't know whether to laugh or cry or panic. "He's here, and you're here, and if Apep ever finds out…if he—"

Becca shushed me, picking my face up in her hands. "We knew the risks, and you are worth them. You both are."

I blinked back the dampness in my eyes. "But you don't know what Apep's done, what he's…"

"We know," she disagreed, dropping her hands from my face.

I nodded, pausing to take everything in and wipe my eyes for a second time. This time Becca handed me a handkerchief. "Where is he?"

"He and Rafe are stationed in the stables."

My eyes darted to the window and then to the closet as I patted the handkerchief under my eyes before blowing my nose. "I'd better get ready."

Becca was up and looking through my closet immediately. "What should we dress you in?"

"I think there's a purple one in there that will work for tonight."

I started to untie the sash around the waist of my dress when Becca came over to help.

"I'll have to keep my shield around you like I do Apep, since you'll be in such close proximity to him. Even if he didn't recognize you earlier, he could choose to hear your thoughts any time, even from the next room without my shield to hide them from him."

Becca's fingers paused. "Is there one around me now?"

"Yes."

She freed the dress, and I helped it fall to the floor as she pulled the purple dress over, fitting it over my head. "You've gotten better at your magic then. Quicker."

Pulling the dress over my body, I hummed in confirmation.

"I didn't even notice or feel it." She mused. "I thought it was gone once the light died away."

I smiled sadly as she buttoned the few lower buttons on the dress before tying a fresh sash around my waist. "I've had a lot of practice."

As soon as she was done tying, I turned around and grabbed her hands in mine. "I promise that I will do whatever I can to protect you, but please don't go taking risks. Please, stay away from Apep as much as you can, don't ever let anyone know who you are." I sucked in a ragged breath. "Keep your head down, don't let him see your face clearly. Don't—"

"I promise," Becca said, tightening her grip around my own. "Evy, you have enough burdens as of now. I promise I will do my best to stay safe and unseen as long as possible, but I need you to remember that I'm here for *you*." She unclasped one hand to touch my cheek. "You're not alone anymore. I can help carry some of your burden now, okay?"

I stared at her a second longer before reluctantly nodding, and she lowered her hand from my face. "And did the girls make it to you?" I questioned quietly.

Becca's fingers tensed for a moment before she answered. "Yes, they made it. They're on their way to delivering Liam's message now."

"*They're* delivering it?" My voice rose slightly, and I chided myself for being so careless. "They can't do that alone. They'll need—"

"Three fairies went with them, one who still has family in Terreno. They'll be all right." Becca reassured, patting my hand.

"I can't lose more…" I sucked in a long breath through my nose, calming my emotions. "Good. That's good."

Becca moved to my side, tapping my back gently, directing me to walk over to the mirrored vanity. "Sit down, and I'll brush out your hair." As I obeyed, she filled me in that Rafe, Billy, and Camilla were all here too.

"Who's Billy?" I asked, looking at her through the mirror.

She smiled. "Long story."

"But Camilla's here?"

Becca's smile faded a little, but she nodded solemnly. "Camilla is more determined than I've ever seen her. I can tell she feels guilt unlike anything I've ever known."

My whole body deflated at the news. "She shouldn't have come back here, Apep already tried…"

"She wanted to. She wouldn't have taken no for an answer." Becca continued brushing my hair. "She cares deeply for you, and she knows how badly she mucked up. Frankly, I think she felt worse about Ryker, once she heard what happened to him."

I stiffened, ignoring the fresh sting in the back of my throat as I looked at her through the mirror again, stilling her hand as it brushed down my hair. "You have to get him out first. If he's not gone already…" I trailed off. "Tell the others. Apep can't hurt me the way he can hurt Ryker. Someone has to get him out, even if you have to leave me behind."

Becca's eyes widened, her hands immediately going to her hips. "There is absolutely no way we'd ever leave you…" Her brow puzzled in the reflected mirror, and she held up a hand. "Wait, what do you mean if he's not already gone?"

I sighed. "I tried to free him today, but I haven't heard anything. I don't think…" I trailed off, not wanting to admit what I already knew was true. Ryker hadn't left. Even with freedom staring him in the face, he chose to stay. "You might have heard what he's been through, but you don't truly know. He can't stay here." My words were quiet and broken. "You have to get him out."

Becca stared at me through the mirror, her exaggerated eyes widening in horror.

"I'm not sure he'll ever recover." My words were so quiet even I barely heard them, but Becca heard them too, and her whole face collapsed.

A knock sounded on the door outside.

"That'll be my call to dinner," I whispered.

Becca's face shot to the closed bedroom doors, which a guard knocked on now. "Apep just sent word that dinner is ready, my lady."

"Coming," I called back.

I slowly stood as Becca's face transformed into a sneer. "They're really awful, aren't they?"

"Who?"

"Your horrid guards."

My eyes flashed to hers. "Stay away from them, Becca. Don't go near them, *ever*. Don't show your sass or even look them in the eye…"

Becca grabbed my hand. "I'll be okay, Evy. I promise."

Fresh tears swelled in my eyes again, but I blinked away the burn. I couldn't lose her. I *wouldn't* lose her. She had my shield, and those guards couldn't hurt her, nor could Apep hear or control her mind. She'd be safe, relatively speaking.

I straightened my shoulders and moved to the door, nodding at her once just before I reached for the handle and headed out into the sitting room.

The two guards moved to follow me out of the room, but one lingered a little too long, staring at Becca until he saw my look of disapproval and straightened his spine, moving quickly in behind me.

As I walked the short distance from the sitting room to the small dining room in our suite, my emotions warred with each other. On one side, I was completely overjoyed that they were all here, but on the other side I was desperately terrified. If anything happened to any of them, I didn't think I'd ever be able to forgive myself.

The minute I stepped inside the dining room, both males stood, and I scanned the area, searching for *him*. I knew *he* wouldn't be here, but I had to look anyway because *he* was here, somewhere. *He* was on these grounds or inside these palace walls right now, and I was no longer alone. *He* was back, he'd kept his promise, and now I wanted nothing more than to see his face. To see *him* again.

And then get him as far away from this awful place as physically possible.

CHAPTER 27

Camilla

A ll of the servants' apartments were empty, sans the ones we and the other worker fairies were in. It made me wonder where the humans were allowed to sleep. I wasn't sure I wanted to find out.

After the head housekeeper showed us to our quarters, we'd waited until just before midnight to gather out in the hall and make our way to Chrissy, as was planned originally.

Chrissy had warned us several times that her magic would need to be renewed daily, maybe even more, and there was no guarantee that the transformations would last a full twenty-four hours, but so far we all still had our wings in place. That was a good start.

"It's time to go," Billy whispered next to me.

I gave him a quick nod of acknowledgement as we followed the sounds of whispers down the hall to the others.

"Kind of creepy, if you ask me," Rafe commented as we walked up. "Where are all the humans?"

My thoughts exactly, though I didn't say them out loud.

"Let's go," Liam spoke softly. "Keep your eyes open for any patrolling guards."

"I don't think he has enough to spare for constant patrolling," Rafe remarked.

"Especially if we keep killin' 'em off," Billy chimed in.

"He has them all watching Evy, and himself," Becca added. "When I left, there were two inside the dining room and two more guarding the suite."

Liam shot her a look of confusion. "Why so many when she's a shield herself?"

"Sounds like he's wary." All eyes darted to me in various levels of surprise as I simply shrugged. "If you think about it, she's the only thing he can't truly control, because he doesn't have access to her mind unless she grants it. She's not afraid of what he can do to her. That's why he uses others to keep her in line."

Everyone stared at me as though I had grown two heads, but in reality I'd realized he thought much like my mother did—like she *used to*.

My chest wanted to ache and my eyes wanted to burn, but neither reaction happened. My mother was gone, and I still felt entirely too conflicted about it. Sad, but not sad. Relieved, but not relieved. Angry, but not angry.

"I think you're right," Liam said as my eyes darted to his, and he bobbed his head to the side before addressing everyone else. "Stay close. We can't leave Chrissy and Ian waiting."

The halls were empty. No patrols, no whispers, just the echo of our steps filling the vacant space. It was as if the walls themselves stood silently by in fearful anticipation.

Our whispered strides followed Liam's as he led us out behind the stables to the forest just beyond the sweeping meadow dedicated to the palace horses. The trees were denser here, harder to see through, easier to hide ourselves.

Chrissy and Ian popped out from the shadows the moment they saw us. Bruised half-moons darkened the area underneath Chrissy's eyes, her usually vibrant green irises looking a little duller in this dim lighting.

"Looks like you all made it safely inside," Ian remarked.

Rafe scoffed. "Mostly. Becca gave us a good scare."

Becca rolled her eyes as we all naturally moved into a small circle.

"I'm fine, everything was fine. Apep didn't recognize me."

Chrissy's eyes grew wide. "Apep saw you?"

Becca nodded.

"Has he seen you before?" I questioned.

"Yes, one time, when Evy and I were walking through the rose garden." Chrissy looked ready to panic, but Becca continued, "Evy was with me tonight. She shielded my mind from Apep, and he didn't recognize me. He actually made me Evy's lady's maid."

Chrissy looked skeptical still. "I'll do my best to keep your disguise up, then. We'll need to keep your face well-hidden from him."

"I'm not so sure…" Ian started.

Chrissy waved him away. "She's in direct contact with him. She needs more protection than the rest."

"If it's too much of a strain on you…" Liam started.

"Now, don't you start in too. I'll be fine," she insisted. "You two men are worse than mother hens." She smiled and patted Liam on the face before looking at the rest of us. "We'll need to meet like this every night. My magic won't last a full day. I can already sense it waning."

We all agreed, but before she could renew the magic for us, Liam moved into Captain mode. I could always tell because he stood a little straighter, his warm dark eyes focused a bit more, and he tucked his jaw in just a hair.

"So what do we know so far?" Liam turned to Becca. "You have the most direct line to Evy. Did she tell you anything? Give us any information?"

We all knew the question he was really asking, the one we all wanted to know the answer to: *is she okay?*

Becca smiled, but it wasn't her usual warm smile. There was a deep sadness behind it that made my insides churn with dread. "She's fine. She's a survivor, and that's exactly what she's doing right now." Becca let out a humorless laugh. "She didn't hesitate to scold me…well, all of us…for coming back here." She paused, taking in a deep breath. "She's terrified of what will happen to us if we're found out, and she warned us to stay away from the guards."

"They do seem to have a cruel streak," Rafe added.

"Obviously," Liam said.

"She did mention that she tried to free Ryker. Have any of you heard anything about that? Did he get out?" Becca asked.

"Haven't heard a thing," Billy chimed in as he side-eyed me. "But then again, we were stuck on dish washin' duty all night."

"Fun times," Rafe quipped.

She tried to free Ryker? How? Why didn't he make it out? Even stuck washing dishes, we would've heard the gossip from the kitchen staff. But no one had said a word.

"If he didn't get away, shouldn't there have been talk about someone trying to free him at least?" I questioned out loud.

The group fell silent as fresh waves of guilt swept one over the other while I imagined Ryker getting caught and hurt all over again.

"No talk of an escape reached us either," Liam noted.

We all knew what that meant…Ryker was still here.

"I'm sure we'll discover more tomorrow after a full day of being here," Billy chimed in.

Liam nodded before he spoke again, his voice raspy with pent-up emotion. "Let's get the rest we can tonight. We'll gather back up again tomorrow."

Chrissy called each one of us up individually, but spoke to the group as a whole. "If you start to see the magic waning, come find me immediately."

We all agreed, and she renewed her magic over each one of us.

"Be careful," Chrissy whispered in parting. "Apep is more clever than you think."

***

The next day, Becca's cheery face popped into my vision, and I quirked a questioning eyebrow at her.

"Princess Evelyn is in need of sustenance." She dipped her head. "I'm her new lady's maid, Becky."

The head cook behind me hurried me to action. "You heard her, make up a lunch tray for the Princess."

"Yes, ma'am." I quickly moved and began preparing a tray for Evelyn. Somehow, just knowing it was for her made me feel like I was truly helping and not just hiding away in the kitchen.

"She's extra hungry today," Becca said with a slight glint in her eye.

I rolled my eyes and tried not to smirk, placing two of everything on the tray and then covering it with white linen. Having Becca as Evy's maid was a stroke of luck none of us wanted to question. Getting updates from her each day would help ease all of our minds, especially Liam and Chrissy's.

Handing the tray over to Becca, I nodded. It was all I could do with the minimal kitchen staff busying themselves all around us. Not to mention the head cook had her eyes on us "new ones," as she kept calling us. Especially poor Billy, whom she'd given permanent dishwashing duty due to his water gift.

Becca took the tray from my hands and offered a small dip of her head in thanks before she turned to leave, and I went back to my previous duties of chopping everything in sight.

A kitchen this big required many hands, and a lot of work that lasted all day. My eyes briefly darted over Billy's lazily lounging form as he picked carelessly at his fingernails while his magic scrubbed the dishes spotless.

Apparently Apep had requested a large, extravagant dinner this evening. There were far too many special dishes to prepare and barely enough time to get everything done. I chopped and mixed and kneaded and peeled until dinner was being served. Luckily, since I was new, I wasn't allowed to serve the King and his Princess.

Small mercies.

Wiping my brow with the back of my forearm, I joined the rest of the kitchen staff as they began to fill their own bellies with a simple stew, taking a much-needed break.

Billy sidled up next to me with a bowl in his hands. "Ain't bad. Nothin' like mine, though." He winked.

I smiled. "Nothing beats your stew, Billy." I reached out to poke his belly, but he jumped back before I could reach him. The smirk on his face was seemingly carefree, but I knew he was just as on edge as I was as he sat down to enjoy his meal.

Several fairies gathered around the stove top, and I listened in for any word on Ryker or an escape attempt.

"Did you hear? That Lord from Lochronstandt has been sniffing around the Princess."

"Apparently King Apep has been encouraging the friendship."

188 • Brianne Wik

"Friendship," one of them scoffed. "With that face of his?"

All the ladies laughed as one of them lowered her voice even more. "The Princess didn't visit the human this morning."

"Well, that's new."

"I heard Apep forbade it."

"Has he even been fed today?" one of them asked.

"That's not our business," another one hushed her upon seeing me. Had Ryker not been fed? Was Evy bringing his meals?

Panic seized my chest, tightening my sternum in a crushing grip, but I kept my hands perfectly steady as I poured a bowl of stew from the stove top. Slicing off half a loaf of bread, I set it on the edge of a plate before walking right past Billy and heading for the main hallway outside. Billy jumped up and snagged my arm.

"And where d'ye think yer headed?" His voice was low, but there was an urgent edge to it.

"To the dungeons, of course." I spoke quietly but confidently, in case someone overheard.

He shook his head. "I can't let ye try it." His words were barely a whisper. "Ye'd be walkin' straight into danger, lass."

Leaning my head toward his, I whispered, "There's no better time. Everyone is distracted, eating, and I can be *very* convincing." I allowed my lashes to flutter up as I peered into his eyes. "Let me try." When his posture still didn't move, I added, "What if it works?"

He grunted and released my arm, muttering something about dangerous humans. I couldn't tell if he meant it, or if he was just trying to put on a show for the eyes currently watching our little interlude, but he dipped his head and turned back to his table and stew.

Walking briskly away from the kitchen and out into the hall, the same tense quiet from late last night blanketed the walls again. Very few guards patrolled, and those who did paid no true attention to me, beyond the appreciative stares that I'd grown far too used to seeing throughout my life.

I made my way down the cold stone steps, my breath beginning to smoke in front of me. As winter set in, it was colder down here than when I'd last visited. Spiraling down to the darkest part of the dungeon, a young fairy stood guard at the main entrance.

"Halt!" his reedy voice rang out. "What are you doing down here?" I stopped and dropped into a low curtsy in front of him. I made sure to raise my head very slowly, fluttering my lashes just so. "Forgive me." The words came out throaty, and I saw the widening of his eyes as soon as he registered me. "I was told to bring the prisoner his evening meal."

He briefly glanced at the meal before his eyes darted back up to mine. "He's a lucky prisoner to have a beauty like you delivering his meal to him."

I looked down, feigning a bashful demeanor as I spoke softly. "You are quite the charmer."

He puffed out his chest a little, and I continued before he could even think to object of my being there. Inching my way closer to him, I tilted my head to the side. "I don't think I've seen you around before."

He cleared his throat. "I just got approved to be on King Apep's guard."

"Ah. That explains it." I allowed a private smirk to pull on the side of my lips.

His brows furrowed in question.

I lowered my voice a hair, allowing it to sound distinctly more intimate. "You're quite the handsome male," I continued, hoping the slight blush I was aiming for dusted my cheeks. Allowing my eyes to dart ever so briefly down to his lips and back up again, I took a seemingly reluctant step backward and headed through the stone doorway. "I suppose I should…" I shrugged softly and raised the tray in explanation.

He shifted his stance just enough to give me the impression that my tactics were working wonders on him. "Go on in." His voice was lowered, growing the littlest bit scratchy. Perfect. "Last cell at the end." He leaned forward to mock-whisper, "But watch out, he's got a mouth on him."

I wanted to shove the half loaf of bread directly down his throat for that comment alone, but instead I dipped my chin. "I do enjoy a good mouth now and then."

Looking back up, I was satisfied to see his face had turned a deliciously bright shade of apple red. I smirked before turning away.

"Maybe don't let him see you either," he called out behind me. "'Tis more of a gift than he deserves."

Looking over my shoulder, I smiled my fake bemused smile. I'd had this particular one perfected by the time I was fourteen. "You flatter me."

Before allowing him a chance to respond again, I walked straight down the darkened hallway to the last cell, where a lone torch illuminated the dismal space.

The further I walked in, the shadows nearly tripled, lengthening and hiding every cold, dirty stone that made up the place. My limbs shivered violently, threatening to spill both the tray and the stew before I even reached the last cell.

I wondered if my shivers were just from the cold, or the fear of facing him for the first time since…

Would he recognize me? My voice? Would he know who I was?

The lone torch lit the horrifyingly dark area, while every other cell I passed was completely empty. The isolation of this place curdled my stomach.

Reaching the last cell, I peered in, trying to see Ryker on the inside, but there was nothing. None of the darkened shadows moved. The silence surrounding me was palpable, except for one piercing drip of water hidden somewhere in the middle.

I barely dared to breathe as I took in the horror.

I'd done this to him. I'd forced him to be in this position, isolated from everything, everyone, even light itself.

I cleared my throat, trying to make my voice work. Sound finally broke through the silence: "I've brought your dinner."

My voice was unrecognizable. Whispered and shaky.

I swallowed back the acid racing up my throat as I heard the slightest brush of fabric, the only warning before a voice sounded from the darkest corner. "You're not the one who usually dumps my meal in here."

"They dump it?" My voice croaked on the question. The ever-present guilt flayed my insides.

He didn't respond.

"I will not dump it," I whispered low, sinking carefully to the ground and passing each item through the bars.

The bowl of stew was too thick to pass through the bars, so I poured it onto the wooden plate, slipping a spoon underneath the now-lukewarm meat and sliding it under the door before squeezing the half loaf of bread through the bars.

"Please, come eat." I did my best to sound encouraging, friendly, even as my body trembled and shook from the anxiety that pressed in on me from all sides. "I tried to make sure you had enough."

"Who are you?"

His voice was cold, angry. I'd never heard him like this before… never even imagined he *could* sound like this.

"A friend," was all I offered.

"Did Evelyn send you?"

"Not exactly." I hedged.

The rustling of fabric told me he had moved closer, but I still couldn't see anything. Just a shadowed lump moving toward the food.

"Leave."

The command gave me the slightest bit of hope. This was the Ryker I'd heard before. Commanding, demanding, always ready with a quip.

"Not until I know you've eaten," I replied. "I can't leave anything behind."

The spoon tapped harshly against the wooden plate as I heard him shoveling the stew into his mouth.

"Don't eat too quickly and make yourself sick," I chided.

"What do you care?" he challenged.

"I care."

My words hung in the air, suspended in silence as my brain screamed at me for putting him through this. He was a king, not a criminal. He didn't deserve to be here, to be treated so abhorrently. Frankly, no one deserved this torment. It was beyond cruel.

He dove back into eating, a little slower this time, and I whispered into the darkness, "I'm going to help you get out of here."

Could he hear the emotion in my voice? The guilt clouding every syllable? Would he suspect who I was?

Ryker said nothing in return. Not even a grunt of acknowledgement as he steadily kept eating his meal, ripping off pieces of bread to stuff in his mouth.

I didn't want to bring attention to his feral state or ask too many questions. I had a feeling that would scare him off, and this moment felt far too fragile as it was.

He choked, his breath catching, and I reached my hand through, holding out a cup of water. "Here."

As if afraid to grab the cup or maybe even touch me, he scooted away from the offered cup of water. Shame gripped my heart in its firm grasp, and I nearly doubled over from the sheer pain of it.

Setting his cup down on the rough stone floor, I pulled my hand carefully back between the bars, both of us waiting. He took a few more seconds before he grabbed the cup and drank the whole thing down.

"You shouldn't be kind to me."

His raspy, unused voice broke me out of my swirling thoughts as I swallowed down the choking guilt.

"And why not?" I questioned.

"He'll find out."

I almost smiled at his concern and decided to answer a little more playfully. "Not if we don't tell him."

"But you're a fairy." I looked over my shoulder to see my false wings glimmering in the firelight. The torch behind me brought out the faint red hue, and I wondered how much more of me he could see.

"Not all fairies agree with him," I whispered back.

He didn't respond as he silently finished his meal. Awkwardly shuffling back to his dark corner of the cell, I thought I heard a quiet, "Thank you."

This was so much worse than I imagined. This isolated, burning darkness had been his every waking hour since I'd watched Apep have him tied and bound to a chair in his room.

I wanted to give him comfort, to give him hope, but if I told him who I was, I knew he would not trust me. He *shouldn't* trust me. I barely trusted myself.

But I needed him to trust me now. I needed him to gain back some of the hope I helped steal away.

"I'll be back again tomorrow night," I promised.

Gathering up his dishes through the bars, I pulled myself back up to standing before leaning back down to pick up my tray.

That was when I saw it.

A hole in the lock of his iron barred door.

Evy's attempt to free him.

My eyes darted to the corner of his cell where I knew he'd retreated, but he made no sound, offered no explanation or acknowledgment. Silence carried thick and heavy through the bars that separated us. "I'm going to help you leave, Ryker. This is not where you belong." He didn't respond. I didn't expect him to. But I wouldn't let him stay here either, not while I had the chance to free him. Not when there was so much more that needed to be said.

CHAPTER 28

Ryker

In the darkness, I could make out the shape of wings behind the strange woman's back, but not the distinctions of her face.

Who is she?

She'd smelled of smoky spices. Whether it came naturally to her or it was because she'd clearly come from the kitchen, I couldn't tell. But it had been comforting. Settling, even. Something familiar.

Why would she help me? If she truly was a fairy, why would she bother with me, the supposed enemy?

She'd said she wasn't sent by Evelyn—not *specifically*, whatever that meant—so why did she care?

At least it wasn't Evelyn herself. I felt guilty for even thinking such a thought, but it was true. Shame instantly flooded my veins every time she came to visit and saw me like this. She had no reason to come visit anymore.

My constant companion, that infernal drip of water, continued to patter sporadically. I still hadn't found the source and had to assume it wasn't located in my particular cell.

Cell.

I was like a caged animal in here.

You could leave if you wanted to.

My chest clenched again, and I tasted the bitter panic at the thought of leaving. What would the world do with someone like me now? Half man, half deformed monster. A dethroned king too weak to protect his kingdom.

I stared at the glowing hole in my cage. Why had Evelyn given me one more torture to endure? What would happen the next time Apep's guards came down to look upon the pathetic human king? That was what I'd become now: a creature worth mocking.

Tiny skittering claws echoed across the stone floor. The rats stopped bothering me after they realized I had nothing to offer them. Now they rarely visited, but I could still hear them making their way over the cold slabs of rock.

I miss Liam. He'd never taken on as formidable a foe as Apep, but I'd come to rely on him to always save the day.

With all this time to think, I'd now realized that hadn't been fair.

I'd relied on Liam too much, I'd become lazy and careless with my actions. Liam had always been the one to clean up my messes and save me from my own selfish stupidity. And yet I still found myself hoping, still found myself relying on his strength to be my own, even when he wasn't here. Even when he might not ever come.

My eyes ached, but I couldn't cry. In the last eight years, this was the first time I'd had to face the world without him.

Drip.

Staring at the perfect hole in the lock, a ragged gasp caught in my throat. I hadn't realized until now, hadn't ever truly thought about it before, but this was how Evelyn had felt. When Liam was forced to leave by our father so he could come be with us, be closer to the palace, be closer to me…he'd had to leave Evelyn.

A choked sob wrestled its way out of my lungs and I pulled my knees up to my chest, burying my head between them.

She'd felt like this. She'd been alone for the last eight years, waiting for him to return.

But he'd been with me.

Drip.

All this time I'd thought it had been about Evelyn, but really she was just one more thing that tied me to the person I'd never wanted to lose. Learning he was my brother had been one of the worst days of my life, but had been the greatest gift my father could've given me. My best friend was my true brother, the last of my family, and he'd loved Evelyn…so I'd loved Evelyn.

But it was never the same. They were linked by something far greater than lust and desire, even love. They were two pieces of a whole, and I'd tried to stop that. I'd tried to bottle it up and make it my own.

My throat ached as I buried my face into my arms. No tears came. My body was too physically dried up to offer any more water, I had to preserve every last drop these days.

I wanted them to be happy.

It was strange to realize that I meant it. Evelyn and I were never meant to be; I'd known that from the moment I'd first seen Liam with her. He'd only ever asked for one thing, and even that I couldn't give…I really was a selfish bastard.

Well, technically, I wasn't the bastard at all.

I rolled my eyes at my own exasperating brain.

Drip. Drip.

All I could hope for now was that Liam would still come and I could make amends. If I never got that chance, at least I'd learned the truth about myself.

.
.
.

The silence down here was as thick as the shadows, providing far too much time for one to think. That fairy girl had said she'd brought me dinner, which meant it was evening.

I tried to keep up with a normal daily routine, but I'd lost track far too long ago to know what day it was or how long I'd been here. Time neither existed nor let up in my darkened corner of the world.

I moved to lay down curled up on my side with my arm as a pillow, favoring the good side of my face as I stared outside of my bars.

The fairy girl's throaty voice echoed through my mind: *"I'm going to help you leave, Ryker. This is not where you belong."*

Her voice…

She had sounded so familiar. But I couldn't place it. I wondered suddenly if we had met before. I'd never paid that close attention to the staff, another thing for me to note about myself. Maybe Apep had been right about me all along.

Drip.

My torn-up mind struggled not to spin constantly, searching for answers and purpose. Tense muscles trembled in anticipation as I played her husky voice over and over again in my mind.

This is not where you belong.

This is not where you belong.

This is not where you belong.

A calming reprieve to the chaos that surrounded me.

Who was she? Why had she cared?

Everlasting darkness closed in around me, thick and heavy, as her voice played over in my mind.

I'm going to help you leave, Ryker.

I tried to imagine a face that would go with such a voice. She had to be beautiful, there was no doubt.

Would she really help me escape?

Did I even want to?

My eyes drifted closed as my hope swelled.

I hope she visits again tomorrow.

CHAPTER 29

Evelyn

Becca helped me dress in a long-sleeved, cornflower-colored gown for dinner. The garment was composed of fine blue tulle overlay with golden embroidery lining the edges and bodice. The neckline swooped down a little lower than I would've normally preferred, and my heart clenched at the thought that Ryker had commissioned this gown specifically for me. It was beautiful, feminine, regal...and *very* human.

Which was precisely the look I was going for tonight.

That small spark of rebellion inside of me had officially ignited, and I embraced its heat with a renewed sense of resolve. Apep had *said* he missed my fire, so I planned on giving it to him. He'd sought to control me by using others, and though I couldn't outrightly defy him, I would happily use every small opportunity I could to show him he couldn't control it all.

"You're awfully quiet," Becca murmured as she buttoned up the back of the gown slowly. "Worried about tonight?"

I shook my head. "Not worried so much as annoyed."

"Atta girl." I could hear the smile in her voice and curled the corner of my mouth up in response.

A muffled knock reverberated through the entrance door to the King's private dining room. As Becca finished buttoning, she tapped my shoulder and whispered, "Just remember, we're right here Evy. You're not alone anymore."

Voices sounded from the dining hall, muffled by the sitting room and bedroom doors in between as I wondered who else would be in attendance at this dinner tonight. My hand immediately went to the pendant around my neck as I mindlessly rubbed the back inscription before tucking it back into my bodice.

"All finished." Becca turned me around to face her, eyes shining in the dim candlelight. "He wants you to be royalty? Give him a queen." She winked.

I sucked in a slow, empowering breath as I squared my shoulders and picked up my chin, heading for the closed bedroom doors. Before I left, I turned to look back at Becca. "Thank you…" I paused, smirking just slightly. "Becky."

She bit her bottom lip to hold back her laugh as I opened the doors, barreling right past the guards—who were caught unawares, lounging in the sitting room like they lived there—and straight into the dining hall.

The room was already filled with a small group of fairies, all of them floating about, talking and laughing quietly. Candlelight filled the space with a beautiful warm glow that made everyone's wings shimmer with each flutter.

My guards rushed in behind me, followed by the rustling sounds of adjusting garments that made me physically roll my eyes. I stood there waiting as the room quieted, and Apep glided through the small crowd of glittering fairies toward me.

His gaze darted behind me first, looking less than amused, then slid back to me as he surveyed my outfit, pursing his lips in clear disapproval. His near-translucent skin glowed eerily in the firelight, making him look more like a spirit between his wavy dark black hair and his long-sleeved, flowing dark grey tunic and pants. The golden edge of his stolen rings glimmered brightly against the dark grey fabric, giving him a freshly gilded eminence to his once somber and subdued tone.

He'd taken to making himself King with far too great an ease.

Commanding a room with his mere presence, rather than lurking in the shadows and around corners like he once did.

I was glad to offer him small thorns that pricked at his control, and one side of my mouth lifted into a half-smirk as I looked away from him to the small crowd surrounding us.

No one bowed or made an effort to approach and introduce themselves; they all just simply gawked at me.

Give him a queen.

Becca's voice echoed in my mind as I stood a little straighter. Apep sidled up next to me, his mouth opening to say something, but Silas approached before he was able, bowing low and reaching for my hand to give it a chaste kiss.

"Princess." He stood tall, his sandy-colored hair carefully brushed back, highlighting his elegant features and high cheekbones. The warm firelight seemed to gravitate toward him, illuminating every perfectly-placed strand. Releasing my hand, he offered a smug smile. "You look beautiful this evening."

"Thank you, Lord Silas." I didn't bother to say it in return; he knew he looked good in his perfectly tailored wine-colored suit.

The man was far better dressed than most of the men I had ever encountered before—besides Ryker, of course. Even though Silas preferred a more human style compared to the loose fairy fashion I was used to seeing, no one admired him less for it. On the contrary, he only seemed to garner even more attention, which meant he needed absolutely no additional notice from me.

The other fairies followed suit, quickly bowing their heads as Apep stretched out his arms. "Dinner is ready. Let us all take our seats."

He held out his hand to me, and I took it dutifully, grimacing at the feeling of cold metal touching my skin. Cold metal that didn't belong there.

Leading me toward the front of the table, Apep spoke quietly in my ear. "You're not wearing one of the dresses I had made for you." There was a sharp inflection and clear disapproval to his tone that made me want to rebelliously rejoice. If everything with him was meant to be a battle, then I had won this round.

I looked down at the beautiful cornflower gown, smiling to myself. "No, I'm not."

He sucked a deep, exasperated breath through his nose. "What did I tell you about…"

"I'm a grown woman who can make her own decisions about what I wear," I interrupted him. "You may control many things in my life, but I'd prefer to at least choose what I wear." I paused, looking up at him in feigned thoughtfulness. "Or would you prefer to be even more like my father, dictating what I wear every day?"

Apep blanched. It was subtle, but still there as he looked down at my dress again before sighing. "I suppose you could wear anything and still look lovely."

I dipped my chin before taking my seat. "Thank you."

Looking only the littlest bit shaken, Apep took his own seat, then encouraged everyone else to sit as well. Raising his already full chalice of wine, he announced, "Thank you so much for joining us this evening. It is an honor to sit at this table with you all, celebrating our victory over the humans."

Polite clapping followed as the servants set down the first course in front of each occupied seat.

Still holding up his chalice, he continued, "In order to celebrate further, I've chosen to host a celebratory ball at the end of this month. Be sure to spread the word far and wide that all fairies are invited, no matter their status. This should be a night for all of us to remember."

Everyone raised a glass in return. "Here, here!"

Before drinking, I set my glass down, not willing to truly participate.

Apep took a drink of his wine and continued, "I know many of you have not yet met my Evelyn, but I do hope you take the time soon to introduce yourself. You'll find our Princess is benevolent and kind, regardless of her upbringing." He said *upbringing* like he had a bad taste in his mouth. "She is an asset and protector of our kind."

I looked around the table, smiling kindly as something became startlingly clear. Every gaze that met my own was full of suspicion and mistrust.

The fairies in this room looked at me like the enemy.

I was not their Princess, nor was I fully their adversary. It was obvious looking in their faces now that they were unsure about me. Questioning looks were clearly displayed across their brows, wondering if I was loyal to them or doubting my dedication to this cause.

It was as if they saw right through me.

I wasn't loyal to Apep, I did doubt this cause, and I couldn't stand by while humans were treated the same way the fairies had been.

Apep reached over and squeezed my hand, giving me a knowing look before pulling away and taking the first bite, giving silent permission for everyone else to do the same.

I stared down at the small green salad that stared back at me, the fork in my hand unmoving as I willed it not to tremble. This was why Apep had set me up with Silas as my companion and guide; this was why he'd commissioned gowns for me in the fairy fashion and why he was subsequently angry with me tonight. This was why he'd been insisting that I not visit Ryker or fight with him in front of the guards.

It made them all question me.

Quiet conversations sounded up and down the table as I lifted my gaze from my plate, only to meet with Silas's silent study of me across the table. He raised a brow, and my cheeks heated at his knowing stare.

"Is the salad not to your liking, Your Highness?" the fairy woman sitting next to me asked, nearly startling me out of my thoughts.

"I fear I haven't had much of an appetite as of late." I smiled politely, raising my fork to taste the salad.

She smiled in return, taking a bite of her own salad. "As I hear it, you've had quite a lot going on. Aster is a dear friend of mine and keeps me abreast to all the latest gossip."

My lashes flashed up, gaze meeting hers as I searched her unreadable expression. Did she know about Aster helping me? That she was against Apep's rule? If so, why would she be so blatantly obvious right in front of him where he could hear her thoughts? Maybe she didn't know and was just trying to talk about someone we had in common. I truly couldn't tell.

"Aster would know more than most," I said thoughtfully. "I hear being a healer takes a listening ear just as much as Nature's gift."

She beamed back at me, inclining her head. "Indeed, she is a true treasure and friend. We are both lucky to know her."

After several more courses and some stilted conversation with the group, I realized quickly that several fairies in attendance were just as wary of my relationship with Apep as the rest were with my relationship to fairy kind. Aster had mentioned a balance, and I think I was finally starting to understand what she'd meant by that. On one hand, I had to convince the fairies I was on their side, that I cared for them and was one myself, even though I'd been raised human. On the other hand, I had to show what I wouldn't stand for and all the ways I disagreed with Apep.

After dinner ended, Apep thanked the group for coming, and I dipped my head in a polite goodbye as everyone dispersed except for Silas, who lingered near the table.

"Your Highness, I was wondering if you might like to take a short walk with me this evening?" Silas's eyes darted to Apep's. "That is, if that's alright with you, Your Majesty." He bowed his head in deference.

Apep looked down at me, uncertainty sharpening his features. "I don't want her out for long this late. Make it quick."

Silas straightened, offering his arm to me. "Of course, my King."

I looped my hand around his elbow as he led me out of the dining room. "I figured you might need a quick breather after that."

"And what makes you assume that?" I questioned suspiciously.

His deep chuckle vibrated his ribs against my arm. "Perhaps it was the deer-caught-unawares look, or maybe the slight tremor in your hand. Or perchance it was that lovely pink sheen that dusted your cheeks every time you met the gaze of a fairy who made their distrust of you obviously known."

I sighed, "Was I truly that obvious?"

"You wear your emotions very plainly. And I'm beginning to believe I was put into your life for the simple reason alone that I need to teach you how to have a game face."

"A game face?" My brows puckered in the middle.

"You know, when you're playing a competitive game?"

I looked up at him, quirking an eyebrow.

"It's part of the strategy," he continued. "You must never show your opponent what you're feeling. Your game face is often how you win the game. It messes with your opposition's mind."

I hummed in understanding. "I have a perfectly good *game face* when I want to."

"Do you now?" he mused. "Go on then, show me."

We stopped by the doorway that led to the stables, and I gave him my best blank stare. I imagined all the emotions draining from my face, leaving a blank canvas underneath. Silas stood back, observing the look, when my eyes snagged on movement behind him.

My entire being tensed as a shudder rolled its way through me. Warm, dark eyes met mine, making my heart stumble and trip over its own beat. Everything came to a complete standstill as I saw *him* standing there.

His throat worked on a swallow, and my eyes darted to the stilted movement in his neck.

"If that's your game face, it's the absolute worst I've ever…" Silas's words slowly faded as he turned.

I wanted to throw up a shield to protect him from Silas's stare. To somehow hide him from the scrutiny that would surely out him.

"Ah," was Silas's knowing response. I didn't know how he would react, what he would do or say…who he would tell. He didn't know me, and I didn't know him; there was no loyalty between us beyond what Apep had asked him to do for me. "I see."

Turning back to me, he watched the guards standing a decent distance back to give us some semblance of privacy. Silas leaned in closer, and I could've sworn I heard a growl or grunt of some kind behind him. "Worst game face ever," he whispered. He stood back again, surveying me. "I have a feeling we're about to become dear friends, Princess Evelyn." He winked. "I will happily distract the loons behind you so you can have a moment to…yourself. But I don't imagine it will buy you very much time." His brows were raised in a knowing look that said this would become a bigger discussion shortly, but for now, he walked behind me, saying something that made all the guards laugh and move further away.

The breath inside my lungs solidified. No breath came in or out as my gaze moved back to *him*.

He clutched at something that forced his knuckles to whiten in his palm, but that was nothing compared to the grip of his expression, as if his eyes alone could pull me into him. The usual stubble around his face was darker now, fuller, giving him a more rugged look that somehow suited him.

He was so achingly handsome it stung my eyes.

We stood there for several additional heartbeats before his name bubbled up from the depths of my soul, and burned over my lips as I whispered: "Liam?"

I didn't know who moved first in that moment, if it was me or him, or maybe we'd somehow synchronized our movements. Only a heartbeat passed before the shock to my system registered. I *felt* him. His warm skin was beneath my hands, his arms were wrapped around me in the tightest embrace, his solid chest flush against my softer one.

He was here. He was holding me. He'd come back.

He'd *come back.*

Grasping his cheeks, I marveled at the sensation of the wiry growth underneath my fingertips as my palms slowly slid behind his neck, tangling into the longer strands of his dark hair that curled up softly at the edges. My throat clogged with unexplainable emotions as I looked up into his solemn deep brown eyes.

His hand dragged slowly up my spine, intertwining with my hair at the base of my head.

"Evy."

That voice.

His voice.

The one I heard in my dreams and begged to hear in my waking hours. That rich, deep, somber tone lodged itself directly into my lungs, causing my breath to hitch and break apart.

He held me so tightly, as if he could somehow shield me from the world with just his body alone.

"I'm so sorry." His voice choked and shuttered.

I should've been mad, or at least shown my hurt. I should've screamed and cried and yelled and showed him what he put me through while he was away, but all I could do was blink back the dampness behind my eyes and savor the feel of his warmth and nearness.

None of the rest of it mattered now. It didn't matter that he'd been gone, it didn't matter that he'd left in anger without allowing me time to explain, it didn't matter that we'd both been hurt. Because right now, we were together again.

That was all that mattered.

My nose stung as my eyes blinked away the growing moisture there. "You came back."

He held me aloft, but I couldn't hold back any longer. My lips sealed themselves against his, pressing all my love, joy and relief into a kiss that could hopefully convey how I felt when words failed me so completely.

He kissed me back, his full lips soft and pliant against mine but laced with an agonized desperation. His mouth pinned my own, aggressively taking and savoring every inch I gave him.

I didn't think anything would ever be able to match this kiss, and no words could ever explain the emotions that poured out from us. A reuniting of souls partially severed, but fusing back together with every caress.

With one hand tangled in my hair and the other wrapped around my waist, he moved his arm slowly upward until he cupped my cheek. I was entirely lost to his every movement, wishing I'd never had to know what it felt like to be without this. Hoping that I'd never have to know that kind of pain and longing again.

A clearing throat was all it took to break apart the fragile moment, giving us time to pull apart just as Silas came back around the corner, my guards filing dutifully in behind him. Thankfully, they were all chatting and laughing, too distracted to truly note Liam yet.

Liam's eyes flared with a rage I'd rarely seen in him before as he studied the fairy behind me. Before Silas could introduce himself or make any remarks, Liam gave me a stilted bow, whispering, "I will find you again soon." Then he stiffly turned back to the outside doorway that led back to the stables.

I tried hard to blink back my tears, but a few still spilled over my eyes as I watched him disappear.

Silas's hand gently latched onto my arm, guiding me away from the scene. My heart beat so heavily in my chest, I could barely hear his words over the booming pulse in my ears.

"I see why you are often irritated with your guards," Silas murmured. "That male was quite handsome, in a rugged, dashing sort of way." He smiled down at me ,and I balked at his careless attitude to the situation even as I reminded myself he didn't know who Liam was and was entirely clueless as to what had just occurred.

I cleared my throat awkwardly, swiping my fingers under my eyes.

"I understand needing to hide who you love," he spoke softly in my ear.

I looked up at him through teary lashes that stuck together. "I'm sorry to hear that."

He shrugged, giving me a few additional moments to compose myself before leading me back to my room.

"Was that a reunion of sorts?" he questioned quietly.

I nodded, but offered no additional details.

"I thought as much," he mused. "And I'm assuming Apep doesn't approve of the match now that you're his Princess?"

I nodded again in confirmation, allowing him to draw his own conclusions.

Silas stopped, turning me toward him, both hands on my shoulders. "I know we're still just getting to know each other, but I hold love in the highest of esteem. I swear to you that your heart is safe with me."

Blinking back my emotions, I studied his expression for any signs of deceit.

He squeezed my shoulders before pulling back and turning to walk again, tucking my arm back into his. "I told you we were about to become dear friends." His voice lowered even further. "I've been denied love simply because the one I loved didn't fit expectations. I swore on that day that I would never allow someone else to be denied love if I had anything to do with it."

I recognized it then. The words of a survivor, just like me, but in a different way. His confession was solemn and earnest, but lined with a deep despair that I easily recognized and understood.

"I'm sorry you had to experience that," I replied softly.

Silas looked down at me, patting my hand just as we reached the suite Apep and I occupied. "As am I, dear Evelyn. I'll see you again tomorrow." Releasing my arm, he dipped into a shallow bow. "Sweet dreams, Princess."

I dipped my head in thanks, "Goodnight, Lord Silas."

He left down the hall while the guards took up their usual posts. Maybe Silas wasn't as bad as he seemed? Or maybe it was simply because he didn't know who Liam was? Regardless, his reaction and confession just now had been so genuine, I believed him. My heart ached for whatever story had left that shattered look in his eye.

I still didn't know if I could trust Silas, or what his ultimate goal was. But I hoped he was truly on my side.

CHAPTER 30

Liam

Chrissy had looked even more rundown last night than the night before, and I worried we wouldn't have long before we'd need to make some drastic moves.

"Do you think we'll make it until this *ball* Apep is throwing?" Rafe asked as he brushed the horse down in the stall next to mine. Becca had informed us last night that she'd learned from Evy about an upcoming ball at the end of this month, some grand soiree to celebrate his takeover.

Brushing down my own steed, I kept my voice low and quiet. "It's definitely our best opportunity, but I won't risk Chrissy more than what's necessary."

Rafe and I both quietly focused on our work, doing our best to not draw attention to ourselves and keep the horses happy so no one asked us to use our gifts.

"What about this fairy guy sniffing around Evelyn?" Rafe whispered, loudly. I rolled my eyes, cringing inwardly.

Giving my horse a little extra nose rub, I put the winter blanket over him before letting myself out of the stall. Latching the door closed behind me, I leaned against the stall Rafe was in. "You know, if you whisper any louder, the stable master might hear you."

He shot me an overexaggerated grin. "Well, these are important questions that need answers."

I shrugged. "I suppose I need to find out more about him first. But he did give us a moment last night. That seemingly bodes well. Though it doesn't make me like all that much more."

Rafe laughed. "Wouldn't expect anything less."

I tossed the brush I'd been using in the sack between stalls and clapped my hands together in an attempt to dislodge the extra dust clinging to them. Rafe patted his horse's cheek, giving the mare a little extra love before covering her and letting himself out of the stall, tossing his brush into the sack with mine. Our next task was to muck out the livery stable, making sure it was spotless in case any "nobles" came to see the horses, but Rafe leaned his back against the wall between stables, staring at me with a notably impish look.

I crossed my arms. "What?"

Rafe raised a hand, pretending to look at his nails. "Oh, nothing. Just wondering why I haven't heard any details yet about your *moment* last night with Evelyn."

"Because you don't *need* any details."

He shrugged. "Maybe not, but it doesn't stop me from wanting them."

I snorted. "Well, tough luck with that, because you're cleaning out the stable while I'm gone."

"What?" Rafe's mouth fell open in clear protest. "And where are you going?"

I smirked and shot him a little wink. "To have another *moment*."

Rafe laughed and shook his head before unraveling his body from the wall and stalking toward me, his face turning serious. "Don't get reckless just because she's seen you. I know she needs you, but so do we all." He looked me straight in the eye, his expression darkening. "We're still a long ways away from winning this battle."

I grabbed his shoulder and shook it a bit. "I know, Rafe. I'll be as safe as I can, but I promised I'd find her today, and we didn't get much time to, uh…talk yesterday."

He grinned, elbowing me in the side. "That's my Cap." But his grin faded as he looked out toward the palace. "Just be careful."

Turning away, he grabbed the nearest shovel and set himself to cleaning the empty stalls as I darted off, going the long way around the palace. Heading straight toward the rose garden, I hoped it was still one of Evy's more frequented haunts. She'd loved walking among the blooms before Apep's coup.

Voices met me as I rounded the corner. I stopped to listen: all masculine tones, not feminine, which made my hopes sink just the smallest bit. I turned to quietly head back into the palace until I heard, "…with the Lords and Ladies being in place soon, we should be able to extract the remaining hidden humans."

"And you have kept this knowledge from Princess Evelyn?"

Apep's slippery voice was unmistakable, and I was far too close for comfort to their position just on the edge of the garden. Staying hidden wouldn't ensure my safety from Apep's wandering magic, but strategically thinking, this seemed too important a conversation to miss.

Especially if he wanted it hidden from Evy.

"Of course, my King."

"Good. Keep working on her sympathies with the fairies before you try to change her mind about humans all together. She's far too sentimental."

"I understand."

A long, uncomfortable silence had me questioning if Apep could tell someone was there, that *I* was there. Sweat beaded on my brow and slowly dripped down the side of my face as I waited for the conversation to either continue, or for them to uncover me from my hiding spot behind a rather bushy shrub. I didn't dare breathe until I heard Apep speak again.

"You still have more to prove if you want to be considered as my eventual successor, but I will admit, you've impressed me at how quickly you've earned some of Evelyn's trust." He paused. "She does not trust easily."

"Well, then, that is high praise indeed."

"Indeed. Don't mess this up."

The rustling of fabric and fluttering of wings was all I heard to indicate that the two had left. I stayed put a while longer, not trusting to give away my hiding spot quite yet.

When no other sounds took place, I finally allowed myself to back track, not daring to follow behind where Apep and his conspirator had gone. Sneaking into the palace through a separate side entrance that was rarely used, I hoped to go unnoticed as I stalked through the hallways, keeping to the shadowed corners as much as possible.

As I moved quietly, I mulled over what I'd just overheard.

Apep using another fairy to gain Evy's trust, and thus manipulate her, was not surprising. He'd been using us all as pawns long before we had any idea it was happening.

But that voice had sounded familiar.

If this other fairy had gained some of her trust already, would she believe he was under Apep's thumb? Or would she give him the benefit of doubt? I shuddered at the idea of her not only being used, but also the idea of her trusting and bonding with another male.

Call me a selfish and jealous brute, but that's exactly what I felt imagining this fairy developing a bond with her. A *false* bond at that. I hated him already.

Stewing in my worried thoughts, I rounded the hall, heading toward the royal wing when I heard voices coming my way.

Quickly scanning the area, I grabbed the nearest door handle and ducked into what I hoped would be an empty servants' closet. One of the many lining this hall, each with its own purpose, in order to care for the royal wing specifically.

The voices walked slowly by, and I recognized Evy's instantly, followed slowly by the recognition of the male I'd heard only moments ago in the garden with Apep.

"What's your fancy this afternoon, Princess?"

"Does he force you to call me that?" Evy's voice chimed sweet and soft, ringing across the marble stones like the prettiest bell.

I had missed that voice so desperately. Even now, with her mere feet away from me, I still missed it.

The male laughed, and my blood boiled. "I use it as a sign of respect."

"Well, I wish you'd stop. I am no Princess."

"My lady, you are the—"

"I am nothing now. Not a lady, not a princess, not a peasant." I hated the sadness that infused her tone. The utter despair that seeped through each word.

The group stopped as the fairy turned to face her. His eye immediately caught mine, and I ducked further behind the door, heart pounding. "I know you are quite overwhelmed at all the changes that have occurred, but you are no less a princess simply because you do not feel like one." He paused. "Princess Evelyn needs a moment to herself." The door to the linen closet slowly pulled open, and I scrambled for a place to hide. Opting for the floor, I snagged a sheet to cover me as I crouched down.

Of all the stupid, reckless things…Rafe would never let me live this down.

If I make it out of here alive, that is.

"Yes, I know you are to constantly watch her, but what harm could happen to her inside a linen closet?" The fairy male argued for a moment with the guards before the door swung wide open, allowing all the light from the hall to fill the tiny space. "Take a moment, Princess. Ah—no, I insist. Go on."

With a puff of air and the scuffling of feet, the door closed again.

An exasperated feminine sigh was all the hope I needed to pull away the sheet and reveal myself.

"It's me, don't scream," I whispered as quietly as possible.

A gasp, and then faint iridescent light gently glowed from Evy's cupped palm. Her eyes, even in this darkness, were wide and bright like softly glimmering emeralds. "How did you…" she trailed off.

I stood and closed the gap between us, circling my arm around her small waist. "I was trying to come find you."

She shook her head, still staring at me in complete awe. "You can't, I'm constantly guarded there's never a moment—"

"To yourself?"

"Not anymore." Her eyes glistened in the faint light as they frantically searched mine. "You shouldn't be here, you can't be discovered like this. This is too dangerous."

"Rafe told me not to be reckless, and yet…" I pulled her closer to my body, relishing the quiet gulp of air that made her chest flush against mine, "I find myself wanting to risk every reckless moment just to hold you in my arms again."

Tears gathered at the edges of her wide and fearful eyes. The next words she spoke were whispered so softly I barely heard them. "Do you truly forgive me for not telling you about my fairy heritage? Can you really—"

I pushed my forehead against hers and laced my fingers into her soft chestnut hair at the base of her skull, pulling her closer to me. "Evy, the way I behaved…what I said and did…" I paused, choking back my own emotions, which we didn't have time for, "I was so wrong. At the first sign of you putting your trust in me again, I betrayed it because of fear, petty jealousy, and my own self-loathing." One lone tear escaped down her cheek, and I reached up with my other thumb to catch it. "I don't deserve your forgiveness for how I behaved."

"Yes, you do," she whispered. Her air became my air, her breaths my breaths. I soaked in her sweet jasmine and vanilla scent, silently begging for more. She smelled like home.

"I love you, Evy. I have loved you ever since I first laid eyes on you, and I have never stopped. I am…" The words caught in my throat. There was so much I wanted to say, so much I wanted to atone for. I wanted to lay everything at her feet and never stop groveling. But our time was too short, too uncertain. Allowing those final words to choke out felt like a relief and a burden still. "I'm so sorry."

"I love you, Liam." She lifted her hand to her bodice, then just above. I looked down between us and watched as she pulled the chain and then the pendant from the depths of her bosom. The slow movement had me aching in ways I hadn't felt since I left.

I reached for the pendant warmed by her skin and flipped it over, rubbing my thumb over the inscription.

"I forgive you, Liam. Can you forgive me?" she whispered, and all semblance of thought left my brain.

Looking up, my eyes landed on hers before they darted down to her lips, and suddenly my mouth was there, begging her to open for me to give me a taste of what I'd been missing. I may not have deserved it, but I craved it with every fiber of my being.

As she opened her mouth to me, I slid inside and tamped down the groan that lodged itself in my throat. Moving my hand so slowly, so gently down her back, I encircled her waist, tugging her even closer while my other still clutched at her pendant. The back of my hand resting on her chest sent desire flaring with a pulsing twist of heat that curled low the muscles beneath my stomach.

I relished every brush of her tongue against mine, her sweet flavor and scent encompassing every part of me. Carefully tucking the pendant back into her bodice, I gently touched the tops of her breasts. Leaving my palm there, I devoured her soft moan and delighted in the fact that my touch alone brought her that kind of pleasure. That even in the midst of this horrible situation, I could bring her this moment of bliss, this escape.

Her heart beat frantically against my palm as I rested it protectively over her chest. A silent promise that I would never again injure her heart. That it was safe in my hands. That she was safe in my arms.

Voices sounded outside the door again, and I kicked myself for not talking to her more about our plans and what I'd just heard in the garden before finding her. She needed to know that this fairy male couldn't be trusted, but I'd run out of time.

She pulled away, fear shadowing her gaze as she looked up at me. "Come to the stables as soon as you can. Take a ride," I spoke so softly in her ear, I could barely hear myself. "And don't let that male too close. He's—"

"Are you jealous?" The slightest hint of teasing entered her tone.

"No." *Yes.* "Evy, you need to—"

"Princess?" A sharp knock on the door. "Feeling any better?"

"Don't worry about me," she whispered, pushing me back into the corner and throwing the sheet over me right as the door opened.

"I've convinced your guards to give you a little more breathing room." The male voice sounded in the doorway. His tone dripped with confidence and self-satisfaction that made me want to knock the imagined grin right off his face.

"Thank you, Silas." Evy's voice was already turned away from me.

He chuckled low and quiet. "My dear Princess, you look quite thoroughly kissed."

She gasped, and every muscle in my body went on alert, ready to jump and strike out however I must should the occasion arise...or maybe just because I felt like it.

"I suppose we should take a walk outside now and give you some air." He paused. The next time he spoke, his voice was closer, lower: "Your hiding spot is terrible, by the way. You're lucky I'm the one who caught you." His tone turned serious. "Don't come down here again unless you're looking to be caught. They do not take their eyes off her."

With that, the door shut, and I was left to the darkness of the linen closet again. Evy's sweet scent permeated the space, leaving behind a dizzying and very unsatisfied effect on my body that I wasn't eager to showcase outside of these tiny enclosed walls.

My head sank into my hands as my body slowly—unbearably slowly—relaxed.

That male's voice had been the same one I'd heard in the garden with Apep. So why was he helping us see each other if he was just…

My thoughts wandered off as a realization hit me.

This was how he was gaining her trust so quickly. It was because of *me*.

For all I knew, he had already told Apep about our passionate reunion, and would inform him of this moment too. It could all be part of the scheme he and Apep were cooking up to get Evy under Apep's thumb.

But whether or not he'd told Apep wasn't the point. He clearly didn't know *who* I was; he only saw the opportunity to gain her trust in one of the easiest ways possible.

A shared secret.

That bastard.

Removing the sheet again, I slowly stood before moving to the door. Pressing my ear against the wood, I listened for any sounds outside in the hall. No footsteps echoed on the marble pathways, no voices bounced off the stone walls; the coast seemed clear.

Rafe was right; this had been too reckless. I'd allowed my desperation to see her cloud my judgement, and I'd given that fairy male a chance to gain more of Evy's trust in the process.

She'd forgiven me. I knew I didn't deserve it, but I also knew I would spend the rest of our lives proving to her she'd made the right decision in giving me a second chance. Part of that proof would be helping protect her from this false friend.

Carefully opening my exit on silent hinges, I peeked up and down the halls. Quiet and empty. Good.

Making my way down the hall of the royal wing, I carefully snuck into my old room that connected to Ryker's. It was exactly how I'd left it. Crumpled sheets on the bed, Rafe's cot in the corner, my golden armor on its stand—now with a giant hole in the side—and my various extra weapons tucked in the corner. It was shocking to me that this room had been left untouched, and that made me curious about Ryker's room.

The girls had described his latest ordeal, but I wondered if the room had been cleaned since then, or …

Turning the handle of our shared door, I carefully peeked inside, listening for any sounds, but the room was dead silent. The horror that faced me was nothing short of a terrible nightmare come to life. Shattered mirrors filled the entire space, splattered blood dark and dried covering the jagged edges. The bed had been ripped apart, feathers and fabric and wood littering the area.

Nothing had been left unmaimed.

My knees suddenly felt weak as I imagined what horrors Ryker had to face in order to create this kind of carnage, and I finally understood Evy's plea to get Ryker out first, leaving her behind if we must. Though it killed me to be so pragmatic about it, it was clear that Apep was taking care of her basic needs. She wasn't physically harmed or left wanting, but this mess made me realize I couldn't say the same for Ryker.

I had to get him out. Even if that meant leaving Evy behind for a time, we had to save him from this.

CHAPTER 31

Evelyn

After several days of trying to either sneak down to the dungeons or out to the stables, I'd been foiled every time. Today, it was because Apep had arranged a dress fitting for me.

The seamstress pulled a beautiful turquoise gown from behind her, holding it up to me. "Apep requested this style and color specifically for you, Your Highness."

I gave her a polite smile. "It's beautiful." It really was, but the idea that he had commissioned it naturally tainted its appeal.

Becca helped the seamstress slip the gown over my head and let it fall to the floor. It was a bit too long, so she started on the hem first.

Pale, dark, and vibrant turquoise shades mixed together in waves of fabric that sparkled and draped over my body in cascading loose lengths. A plunging neckline and back cinched at the waist without truly showing anything, much to my relief. Gauzy silk flowed down my hips and legs in liquid fabric.

The shape of the gown itself was barely there, but somehow it still showed off my curves in a very subtle way. Elegant but free. The sleeves alone were long and flowing, catching every breeze as if they were constantly floating in water.

In a word, the dress was stunning.

"Do you like it?" The seamstress looked up at my astounded face with a hopeful but hesitant look.

I brushed my hands gently down the fabric, "It's..."

"Absolutely gorgeous, is what it is," Becca chimed in, totally forgetting her demure persona. "This is way better than those stuffy dresses you used to..."

I shot her a look, and she trailed off, adding, "Human styles don't suit you, Princess. This looks far more natural on you." She winked in the mirror at me while the seamstress was busy pinning.

A knock at the door had Becca going over to answer it as Aster popped her head in. "I heard there was a dress fitting today."

The seamstress looked up and smiled fondly at Aster as Becca let her into the room.

"You look breathtaking, Your Highness," she remarked in admiration.

"Thank you, Aster." I inclined my head to her. "It's so lovely to see you again."

I kept my voice buoyant and friendly, trying not to give away the fact that Aster said she'd seek me out if she ever had news to share.

She dipped her head in response. "Likewise. I didn't want to interrupt; I just thought I might join you and bring you this." She held up a small book that looked quite old and worn from use.

The seamstress scoffed. "You just wanted to sneak a peek of my creation before everyone else saw it."

Aster and Becca both chuckled. "Guilty as charged," Aster said with a flash of her palms.

The three of them began chatting amongst themselves, and I found myself drifting away from the conversation. What a strange thing to be standing here admiring myself in the mirror, being fitted for a dress, while at the same time my kingdom was falling apart, Ryker was imprisoned, the girls were risking their lives traveling to a foreign kingdom, and my friends and family were risking their lives to try and help defeat Apep by sneaking into the palace.

Was it wrong to enjoy small moments like this? To wish for some normalcy amidst the chaos? Could I even let myself enjoy it?

"Evelyn?"

I pulled out of my daze to three sets of worried eyes trained on me. "I'm so sorry. I was lost in thought. Did you ask me something?"

Aster jumped in first. "We were just wondering if any fairy male had caught your eye recently?"

I stiffened at the question, but she smiled knowingly.

"Not necessarily," I said, "but I have noticed many handsome males about."

"Too true," the seamstress agreed. "Have you seen the new stable boys? They're delicious."

Aster smirked while Becca and I startled. "You should definitely make your way to the stables sometime soon to meet them, girls," she teased.

It was then that I realized the bedroom doors had been left slightly open, and my guards waited outside. Was Aster trying to prep them for me? I turned from the mirror and smirked at her.

"I *was* hoping to go for a ride soon." I mused.

All four of us giggled just as the seamstress said, "Done! I'll get these changes made and have the gown ready for you in time for the ball."

"Thank you."

Becca closed the door as the seamstress and Aster helped me carefully remove the gown, pins and all, for the seamstress to take with her. She slipped out the door, closing it firmly behind her while Becca prepared some warm riding clothes for me.

"Any news?" I whispered to Aster, who now sat on the bed.

She shook her head, responding quietly in return, "I've been listening for any word from Terreno, but I haven't heard any updates yet."

My shoulders and head sagged.

"But I did want to bring you this." Aster picked up the worn book from the bed and handed it to me.

Flipping gently through the pages, I said, "This looks like one of the fairy tales that *Becky* likes to read."

I emphasized her name, and she sprung up from her spot in front of the wardrobe. "Ooh! Let me see," she said as she looked over my shoulder.

Aster laughed quietly. "It's a tale about the first kingdoms, before

Alstonia existed."

"Oh, I know the one!" Becca jumped in. "Married by Dusk is about the Princess and Prince from rival kingdoms who had to marry in order to unite the fairy race before the war and—"

"That's the one." Aster said, but her eyes grew dark. "But it's more than a simple fairy tale. That was what the humans labeled it in order to hide and diminish our history." She gave me a somber look that made me stand up at attention. "You will have a very hard uphill battle to bring our current kingdoms together."

My brow puzzled in the center as I looked at her in question.

"The kingdom of the Humans and the Fae. That was what we used to be called," she added after a moment. "Take some time to read it and better understand our past. There are many of us who still remember. A few who even experienced it." Her voice grew low. "And there are many more who will stand with you, in hopes of a better future."

After Aster left, Becca helped me bundle up in riding slacks and a layered tunic, including a warm cape with gloves and extra fabric wrapped around my neck. Each day had been growing colder, and riding would only make the chill in the air even worse.

Setting out for the stables, my guards following dutifully behind, I was grateful there were no signs of Silas. It had been nice in a way to have a companion each day. Between his company and Becca's consistent presence, I was starting to feel less alone here. But regardless of the partial confession he'd shared about being denied the love he longed for, he hadn't opened up again. Instead, he'd been my constant shadow these past few days, mostly gossiping about other fairies I'd never heard of, and I was growing weary of his constant presence.

Even though he'd helped Liam and I have a private moment or two, he seemed insistent on accompanying me everywhere I went. Just as much of an obnoxious guard as the ones I already had. I suspected he reported daily to Apep, or else I doubted Apep would've allowed him so much time with me. Perhaps that was where he was even now.

With the ball taking place in just under two weeks, the excitement around the palace was growing. I loved seeing the halls more lively as I walked to the stables, but it made me realize that fairies had never been granted the chance to attend past balls. Instead, they'd been forced to hide who and what they truly were in order to survive in a land and kingdom that had outlawed them.

For all the bad Apep had done and was still doing, this truly seemed like a good thing. Something to bring hope and promise to the fairies. It unfortunately also solidified his reign even further.

We'll cross that bridge when we get to it, I told myself determinedly.

Reaching for the door of the palace that led out to the stables, I marched my way straight there. Nothing was going to stop me today, and hopefully I'd be able to persuade my guards to let Liam ride alongside me, preferably while they stayed a good distance back. It might not be a private moment, but at least we might be able to have *something.*

Just the thought alone that I was freely, at least mostly, walking up to Liam...that he was *here*, within reach...brought a sharp sting to my nose and throat. It had been so long since I'd had this.

I walked right up to the stables, approaching the back of a very recognizable curly flop of dark brown hair.

"Excuse me, but I'd like you to saddle me a horse, please," I said in a feigned haughty tone that I knew he would get a kick out of.

I couldn't help but grin at Rafe's surprised face as he turned around. At first he stumbled about awkwardly, not knowing what to do as his eyes darted behind me to see my retinue of guards. He gave me a hasty bow, clearly caught between wanting to hug me and trying desperately not to blow his cover. I held back my laugh by pulling my lips inward and biting down.

"Of course. Right away, Ev...Your Highness, Lady, ma'am."

Unable to help it, a breathy laugh escaped me, forming a brief cloud of fog in the cold air. "Is the other stable boy nearby? I was told I needed to meet him."

Rafe shook his head in amusement. "I'm sure he'll be here any min...ah, there he is now."

Sure enough, Liam was racing down the hall of the long stable, nearly stumbling before he quickly checked himself and slowed his approach.

"Princess." The way the words rolled off his tongue in that low timbre had my insides pulsing in a twisting warmth. He bowed low and slowly stood, allowing his eyes to run over every inch of me.

"How may I be of service?"

I swallowed, words escaping my brain entirely until Rafe's chortle had me grasping for an answer. "I want to go riding."

Liam cocked an eyebrow up.

"With you."

My guards moved closer in. "Your Highness, Apep hasn't approved…"

I spun with Becca's words echoing in my mind: *Give him a queen.*

"I am your Princess, just as Apep is your King. Do not attempt to dictate what I can and cannot do." I gestured to Liam. "This male has a rare gift, and I'd like to learn more about it. Two of you may accompany us. The other two will remain here, waiting for our return."

"But Your Highness, I must…"

I held up my hand and turned back to both Rafe and Liam. "Saddle up three more horses, please." Turning to Liam again, I noted the look of sheer awe and surprise on his face. His eyes glimmered with pride, and I wanted to revel in that look. "That is, if you'd be willing to share your story with me?"

He dipped his head, grinning slightly. "It would be my greatest pleasure."

The guards behind moped and groaned, but they didn't attempt to stop me again. That reaction itself boosted my confidence more than mere words ever could.

Perhaps I *could* step into this role, just as Aster had suggested.

I waited silently while Rafe and Liam readied horses for us, ignoring my guards entirely as I watched Liam's back muscles shift and contract while he went about his work. Sucking in a steadying breath, I exhaled slowly, fighting the need to either fan myself or remove my warm cape.

"The horses are ready, Your Highness." Rafe bowed and offered me the reins of the bridled mare.

"Thank you." I took the reins as he gave me a boost up and swung my leg around, seating myself firmly in the saddle. My guards huffed some more, but none of them said a word.

Liam had already mounted and walked his horse up beside mine. "Shall we?"

I couldn't help but grin at him. This moment wasn't quite free, but it was the most free I had felt since Apep's coup.

His eyes met mine, and my heart leapt into my throat at the sight of him next to me: his broad shoulders standing tall, his slightly mussed dark brown hair pushed back as though he'd just run his hands through it, that little lock of hair that, much to his exasperation, always fell into his eyes, the new beard around his face. He was so achingly handsome, it practically hurt to look at him; and when he turned to look at me, that shy dimple made an appearance, and my heart felt as though it swelled to the point of physical pain.

I loved him so much.

"Let's…" I began playfully, darting my eyes backward to see my guards waiting on Rafe, who was only just now starting on saddling their horses. "Go!" I yelled.

And we were off. Racing our way out of the stables, my guards were left behind, yelling for us to halt.

I couldn't help the laugh that bubbled up out of me, Liam echoing the sound with his own.

"We might be able to lose them in the trees!" he called to me.

A spark of mischief tightened my chest as I directed my mare to follow behind his lead.

We quickly disappeared into the trees, the guards forgoing saddles entirely, using only bridles to race behind us and try to catch up. We had to slow down significantly as we wound our way inside the thick copse of trees, hoping to lose our interlopers.

Somewhere behind us, twigs snapped and brush shuddered. Liam led our horses behind a thick tree, probably older than Alstonia itself by the sheer size of it, and hopped down, tying his steed to a low branch. I followed suit.

A strong arm latched around my waist, twisting me around until we were face-to-face and Liam's lips crashed into mine. Bark dug into my back as Liam pressed me against the tree, his muscular thigh pushing between my legs.

This kiss was fiery but short as he pulled away, panting heavily. His breath left behind smoky tendrils in the air.

"As much as I want to kiss you right now," his voice was breathy and low, "I need to talk to you even more."

I glanced down at his body still leaning in toward mine. One arm still wrapped around me, and the other braced on the tree next to my head. "They'll probably be here any second," I warned.

"True." He lowered his head, nuzzling behind my ear. "And we'll tell them I was showing you how I talk to the animals." He smirked against my skin, leaving a feathered kiss there before continuing to whisper, "You can't trust Silas."

My eyes widened in surprise, as he pulled back slowly. I was not expecting him to say *that* of all things.

"I caught him and Apep talking one day, and he's completely in Apep's pocket. His entire goal is to *lead you in the right direction.*"

I huffed out a cloudy sigh. "And he knows about you." I worried my bottom lip. "Not who you are truly, but what you mean to me."

"He seems to find our sneaking around amusing. Perhaps he hasn't told Apep yet?" Liam wondered aloud.

Pushing up on my tiptoes, I kissed him gently again. "I wish I had answers," I whispered.

He leaned back in, stealing a peck under my jaw before raising his forehead to press against mine. "I hate being parted from you. Even when you're so close, you're still out of my reach." He sank into me a little deeper. "It's absolute torture."

A dangerously low heat threatened to ignite in the pit of my stomach, every thought leaving my mind except the feel of his body against mine.

"We're planning to free Ryker during the ball," he muttered softly.

"Th-the ball?" I stuttered, attempting to make my mind work again.

"It's the perfect distraction," Liam whispered, his breath hot against the side of my neck.

I cleared my throat. "I am the one currently distracted."

A deep chuckle vibrated through his body, causing mine to shiver, but the thought of him getting caught or being recognized at the ball was like throwing ice directly into my face.

My eyebrows caved inward with worry. "Just, please be careful."

"Save me a dance still?"

I glanced up seeing the sincerity and emotion brimming in his eyes. "I'll give you all of my dances," I whispered.

He breathed out an agonized sigh just as we heard a twig snap behind our tree. Liam pushed away from the tree, allowing me to step free as well as he turned to pet his horse's snout. "And that's how we speak with them."

"Your Highness!" one of the oafs bellowed loudly from directly behind the tree.

"I'm right here, you two," I said calmly.

One of the guards came around the tree, his face red from either the cold or his anger—maybe both. "What were you thinking? We thought we'd lost you."

"Forgive us." I smiled sweetly. "We saw a squirrel and tried chasing after it so he could show me how to talk to the animals." Liam kept petting the horse's snout, and the guard flashed me an incredulous look.

"They liked the run," Liam added, while still looking at the horse. "It gets their hearts pumping. They're far too cooped up in the winter time."

The guard scoffed and called over to the other one while Liam helped me mount my horse again. "I suppose that means we should run them some more, then?" I asked, feigning innocence.

He leaned in, pretending to listen to the horse's answer. "They emphatically agree."

We both smiled and wound back through the forest, my guards keeping right up with us this time.

***

"Who was that young male you spent your time riding with today?"

Apep was waiting on the bed when I entered the bedroom, sitting with his arms crossed. My gaze flashed from him to Becca, who was mindlessly tidying, doing anything to look busy and evade his gaze.

I swallowed down my fear and pulled off my gloves slowly. "One of the stable boys." I answered. "He said the horses needed to go for a run, and I wanted some fun." I shot him a pointed look. "One can only walk in the cold gardens so many times a day."

Becca covered up a snort she accidentally let out, and I thanked Nature that my shield was still solidly intact around her.

Apep shot her a suspicious gaze, his eyes narrowing with far too much interest for my liking. I plopped down on the bed next to him, surprising him entirely as I asked, "You say I am a princess now, but I noticed that I'm not part of any of the decision making around here."

He wants a princess? Give him a queen. I repeated the phrase in my mind, gathering whatever strength I could from the words.

Apep opened his mouth to speak, but I continued, "I have never been good at being bored. I need more to do."

"Perhaps you need to be spending more time getting to know our new nobles rather than gallivanting with some stablehand." He glowered.

"Yes, I'm sure you're right." He startled again, and I relished the confusion that marred his brow. "As Princess, I should be spending more time getting to know your newly appointed court, but I still feel as though I have no purpose here. Even my guards don't respect me the way they respect you."

He pursed his lips at that, his face entirely unreadable.

"And," I added, "You've never looked down at a fairy before, regardless of his or her station. Has becoming king truly made you so snobbish?" I quirked an eyebrow up at him.

Apep blinked very slowly and leaned in closer to me. "You've made your point Evelyn." Reaching for my palm, he gently rubbed his thumb along the back of my hand. "I will consider giving you more responsibility if you promise to do your part in getting to know our new court. Many fairies need reassurance you're on their side."

I nodded, "I picked up on that recently."

"Good." He squeezed my hand, "Everything I do, every decision I make, is to help and protect you, Evelyn." His eyes locked onto mine as he reached up and pushed a piece of hair back behind my ear. "The day is coming when I will rid you of your past entirely, and you will be free to move on into the new world I'm creating for you."

I watched in horror as his eyes slowly left mine and landed on Becca, whose back was currently turned to us. His eyes remained fastened on her figure. "I know you test your boundaries, as every young fairy should, but eventually I will make you into the fairy queen you were meant to be, and then you will be ready to lead our kind." His eyes slowly trailed back, boring into mine. "Until then, I will be watching very closely to see that you…behave."

With that, he stood up from the bed and glided toward the door. I swallowed hard, sickness flooding my stomach.

"Oh, and Evelyn?"

I shuddered at the way he stretched out my name with his slippery vowels. My heart hammered uncomfortably against my ribs. Turning my body to face him, I braced for what he would say next.

"I expect you to be on your best behavior tonight at dinner. You will greet and talk with all the fairies present, and you will be *on time*." Silence hung between us for a brief moment; so he'd noticed that small rebellion, after all. "You now know what's at stake." His eyes darted to Becca before bouncing back to me. "Don't disappoint me."

CHAPTER 32

Camilla

The cold air attempted to freeze my lungs the minute Billy and I stepped outside, taking a much needed break during the middle of the day. He needed to replenish his fairy magic, and I needed some fresh air that didn't smell like bacon grease or onions.

I shivered immediately, second-guessing if it was worth it to be out here now that I was facing the frigid temperatures head on.

It had been a couple of weeks since I started visiting Ryker, and though he was still taking a while to warm up to me, I looked forward to my visits with him. However, experiencing him so quiet and reserved was beyond eerie. He was nothing like the self-confident and poised king I knew before. But I still had hope.

Every night he seemed to linger a little longer with me, come a little closer, talk a little more. Maybe that was just my imagination, but I hoped not.

Luckily, the grand ball Apep was throwing was just around the corner, only one week away. *Mere days*, I kept telling myself. I was getting far too antsy for this nightmare to be over; we all were. But they weren't the ones seeing Ryker each day. They couldn't begin to understand how hard it was watching him drag his broken form across the darkness of his cell to eat his one and only meal a day. A meal I wasn't sure would even be provided if I wasn't the one bringing it.

I knew we had a plan, and that plan required using the ball as a distraction so we could get them *both* out. But if it had been up to me, I would've pulled Ryker out the minute we arrived.

When I'd suggested it, Liam had hesitated, but Rafe was quick to point out the obvious…if we pulled Ryker out right away, it would give us away, and we wouldn't even get a chance at Evy.

I knew he was right, but I worried at how much longer Ryker would last in this extended torture. I would've gone mad by now, and I truly didn't know how he was keeping it together as well as he was.

Secretly, I hoped I was a part of what was holding him together, even though I had no right to wish for such a thing.

As evidenced on the ground, the lightest dusting of snow had started falling late last night while Chrissy renewed her transformations for us. I hated seeing her look so exhausted and sick. Every time we all came together, she looked a little worse for the wear, but she kept insisting she was fine. Ian's face, however, told an entirely different story.

The freezing temperature hadn't warmed up enough for the light snowfall to melt away, and I imagined that meant it was here to stay, meaning winter was officially upon us.

I hated winter.

I hated the cold.

I shivered and rubbed my hands together in quick succession as Billy knelt, placing his hands steadily on top of the earth.

"How can you stand the cold like that?" My teeth chattered as I spoke, and I brought my hands up to warm them with my breath as I bounced my knees in place behind him.

Billy chuckled, not even shivering as he hunched over on the ground. "When ye've been doin' this as long as I have, lass, the cold barely bothers ye anymore."

I eyed him skeptically. "You make me glad I'm not a fairy."

He barked out another laugh before falling silent at the sounds of voices not too far off. Turning back to me, he motioned with his hands. "Come sit next to me, it'll make ye look more authentic."

Sucking in a long breath through my nose, I eyed him angrily while pursing my lips. His answering smile was full of mischief and entirely unhelpful as my shaking legs precariously lowered me to the ground next to him.

"Is this payback for all my *risk-taking*?" My voice shook with cold as I placed my hands on the frozen earth. Billy hated that I put myself in danger to see Ryker each night, but he understood it was an opportunity we couldn't afford to lose.

The snow underneath my palms melted away slowly, leaving only the cold hard ground behind.

I glared at Billy, who smirked back at me in silent triumph before his features sobered. "All I want is fer ye to stay safe, lass."

I sighed. "I know. It means a great deal to me that you see me in such a way."

Billy straightened up to a sitting position on his knees as the voices entered our clearing. "Ye need someone lookin' out fer ye, and I'm happy to do it."

A ghost of a smile brushed across my lips just as—

"Oh! Forgive us, we didn't see you there…"

The soft intake of air froze my body in place. Completely forgetting the cold, I suddenly felt hot all over.

"Come, Princess, we can give them a few more moments with the earth."

"N-no," Evelyn stuttered slightly, then cleared her throat. "Forgive me, I just meant that I know this woman."

"Female," the fairy with her corrected. "When we're speaking of a fairy, we say male or female."

Evy bristled. "Yes, of course. I forgot myself for a moment." She cleared her throat. "But I'd like to take this opportunity to catch up with my old friend."

Looking up at her then, Billy stood next to me, brushing off his hands on his pants before bowing to Evelyn. "It's a pleasure to meet ye, Your Highness."

"Evelyn will do just fine, thank you." Evy smiled at Billy kindly.

"He shall address you as such because it is appropriate, Princess," the handsome fairy male next to her chided with a haughty tone that could've rivaled mine once.

Evy's lips pursed as she blinked her eyes slowly—very slowly—

before looking back at Billy. "And your name?"

"Name's Billy." He bowed again before turning to offer his hand to me. I felt bad when he winced from my tight grip as I stood up, offering a polite curtsy.

Evy's face brightened at hearing his name. I assumed Becca had mentioned him then. "It's a pleasure, Billy." She turned to me next, "Will you two gentlemen—I mean males, give us females a moment please?"

The fairy escorting her huffed out a cold, breathy laugh. "We shall happily stroll behind while you two catch up."

She smiled, but it was rehearsed, polite, fake. Catching that small moment alone made me want to smile at her. She was holding her own here and learning quickly what it took to navigate this proud world of nobility. Apparently even Apep wanted to keep up these pretenses, which didn't surprise me in the least, considering how much he loved flaunting himself above others.

Evy offered me her arm, and I jerkily took it, my shivering limbs robbing me of all possible grace.

We walked ahead of the men, or males as it were, in utter silence. I hadn't the heart to look over at her, not after what I did...and what she did to help me. If my shivers hadn't already been caused by the cold temperature outside, I would've been trembling out of fear alone. Facing Evy again, after what I did...

"I've wanted to come see you, but I'm being—"

"Watched like a hawk?" I provided.

She huffed out a sad laugh. "Indeed." She took a moment before adding, "I wish you hadn't come."

I dropped my head. Of course she would wish that; I would too. I was surprised she was even walking with me now instead of ignoring my presence entirely.

Leaning into my arm, she whispered gently, "I can't have you be caught again."

I sucked in a harsh breath, trying to tamp down the building tension in my chest. "And I couldn't leave you and Ryker here. None of us could."

She gently rubbed my arm up and down, her wool gloves easing away some of the cold biting at my skin.

"Evy, I…" my voice croaked, both from the cold and my own guilt, as I stumbled over what I wanted to say. Where could I even start? How would I ever make amends for what I'd done?

"You're still my family." Her voice came out slightly strangled, as if she was fighting back her own emotions. "Have you been informed about—"

"About my mother and Frank?" I finished for her.

"So you know."

I nodded. "I do."

Evy hummed softly, her voice clipping with emotion. "I can't lose you too."

I raised my other hand and gripped her hand that was rubbing absently up and down my arm, pausing its motion. "We're all being as careful as we can." *Mostly.* "I'm visiting Ryker in the evenings, bringing him his nightly meal. Billy and I work in the kitchens together."

Chancing a look over at her, I caught Evy's chin quivering, her eyes reddening around the edges as she blinked rapidly. "He needs that. He needs help. He can't keep…"

"We're going to get him out of there, Evy. I promise you he won't be there for much longer." I spoke as softly as I could, leaning into her both for warmth and privacy. "At the ball—"

"You plan to make your move," she supplied for me. "Liam told me." She sniffed and sucked in a deep breath. "It's just, what he's been through…" She trailed off.

"I know."

"Please be careful." She swallowed and cleared her throat. "You need to get back inside, you're freezing out here." She gave me a shallow smile. "I think I like Billy."

I snorted out a small laugh. "He's definitely a character. He and Ian—"

"Ian?" Evy quirked an eyebrow in question.

"Chrissy knows them both, he gave Liam a place to stay while he was…" I sucked in a startled breath, realizing my error. Liam had left because of me, because of my betrayal, and here I was talking about his absence with her like it was old news.

She swallowed while nodding her head absently. I didn't even think she realized she was doing it, so lost in her own thoughts. I hated seeing the pain that drifted across her distracted gaze.

Turning to face me, I realized we were back at the palace entrance when she surprised me by saying, "Once this is all over, you and I are spending some time together. I know there is much for us to discuss." She tugged me into a tight embrace, and I wound my arms around her in return. "For what it's worth, I still love you, but I am equally hurt by your actions." Her words sank into my bones, weighing them down in equal parts shame and hope. "And please, tell Ryker I'm sorry I haven't been there. I've been trying…"

"I will," I promised.

Pulling away, she clasped my hands in hers, speaking at a normal volume. "Thank you for the walk, It was lovely to catch up. Hopefully, I will see you again soon."

I curtsied politely as she walked back inside, her fairy escort right on her heels.

"He's an interesting lad," Billy said as he sidled up to me, his eyes on Evelyn's escort.

I quirked an eyebrow up at him. "Interesting how?"

"He's got two faces."

Billy led me back inside and down into the kitchens as my brows furrowed in the middle. "What do you mean, two faces?"

"Double-faced is what he is. Always playin' at two sides."

"Well, that can't be good." I murmured as I rubbed my palms together and then held them out to the always burning fire in the kitchens main stove.

He shrugged. "Doesn't mean it's bad, either."

***

As it turned out, confidence—and a good amount of flirting—could get you just about anywhere. I hummed in amused pride as I walked right down the hall to Ryker's cell with only the dip of a chin and a far too obvious perusal of my body as I passed tonight's guard.

He hadn't even tried to look at my tray of food, which was good, considering I'd brought Ryker all sorts of things this evening. Broth, bread, meat pies, extra water and fruit he could save for later, even a small dessert for an added treat.

For the past couple of weeks, each night I would sit down in front of his cell and pass the prepared items through his bars. While I did so, I'd talk about what I brought him and something dull like the weather turning colder or the first snowfall. Each night he spoke a little more in return and eventually started sitting against the wall I leaned against as he ate his evening meal.

I'd selfishly come to love these moments with him, stolen as they were, since he had no idea who I truly was.

"I've brought you quite the array of options this evening," I said. "A few fruits you can munch on throughout the day tomorrow, if you choose to save them."

The scuffling of Ryker's clothes against the stone was the only indication he'd heard me until a hand appeared near the bars. I handed him the broth first, followed by a meat pie; he ate silently while I waited to see if he'd stay anything tonight.

Just as I was about to fill the silence with mindless jabber, his quiet voice rasped against the stone walls. "She hasn't visited me."

I could pretend I didn't know who *she* was, but he was talking, sharing something with me, and I didn't want to feign ignorance to that.

"She told me she keeps trying to," I replied, "But Apep is doing everything he can to keep her away."

"Is he..." He trailed off. "Does he hurt her?"

I shook my head, pushing back the cuticles of my nails absently. "No," I whispered. "He doesn't hurt her, he just does whatever he can to control her. Right now he's got guards on her nearly every waking hour and a new fairy male who's *showing her the ropes.*" Obvious irritation filtered through my voice. "He wants her to forget all about you and Liam and her past." I paused. "He's a fool if he thinks she'll ever forget or let any of you go."

"Liam." He choked on whatever he was chewing. "Liam is my brother, you know."

I smiled sadly at that. "I know."

"I miss him."

The ache in Ryker's voice cracked my chest wide open.

All this time I'd thought about how I'd taken Liam from Evy, but I'd never stopped to realize I'd taken Liam from Ryker as well. They were brothers in truth and the closest of friends; even if a wedge had been driven between them, it would've never been enough to sever their bond.

"He's here, Ryker." My own voice broke at the confession. "He's trying to get you out, we're…working together."

"Liam? Liam's here?" Ryker's voice was urgent, desperate and full of so much hope for the first time since I'd started visiting. "Is he all right? Has he been hurt?"

"He's all right. We have a plan to get you out of here soon. I hope you'll trust us to get you free."

Heavy silence suffocated the air around us. I wanted to know what he was thinking, what he needed to hear to be reassured, what he might need to know in order to trust us and finally leave this awful place.

"He misses you desperately," I continued. "If he were able, he'd have already marched you straight out of this nightmare."

He choked on his own words as they seemed to overflow from his mouth. "I wasn't fair to him. I was never fair to him. Not really. I should never have pursued Evelyn after I knew who she was to him. I should've *listened* to him. Shown him how much I value him. You know?"

"You can't blame yourself for your own feelings, Ryker," I gently chided.

He paused. "But I *knew*." His whispered words fell out like a confession. "I knew it would hurt him. I knew it wasn't right, not really."

I allowed his words and my guilty silence to linger, before I spoke again. "I've hurt a lot of people, too."

Ryker scoffed, and that disbelief alone drew a small smile from my lips. That he could think so highly of me already, when he had no idea who I truly was.

I shook my head again. If he understood who he was talking to, then he wouldn't have seen me like that. He wouldn't have opened up to me like he did just now or trusted me.

No, he would've been angry.

This was my moment to be honest. To tell him who I really was.

But I didn't want to.

I wanted to give him hope, and if he knew who I was, he wouldn't feel hope; he'd just feel hate. Hate I definitely deserved, but hate wouldn't help him right now.

"I speak the truth." I paused, taking in a breath through my nose. "I hurt my own sister. I knew she loved a boy, and I did my best to sabotage it because he didn't look at me that same way. I hurt my friends when I listened to someone who would abuse and use them, instead of warning them."

"Why would you do that?" His question held no malice. It was thoughtful instead of condemning, which made it easier to answer.

"I'm not sure. I think I let my own petty jealousy control my actions for a while. I was scared and alone and tired of being overlooked. I know it doesn't excuse anything I've done…"

Ryker huffed out a humorless laugh. "I've never been overlooked, until now." His voice was suddenly muffled, like his hands were over his mouth. "The punishment befitting the crime, I guess."

"You didn't do anything wrong, Ryker."

"I imprisoned innocent beings. I pursued my best friend and my brother's only love. I took liberties my whole life because I felt I was due them. I never heard the word no, never even expected it. My whole life I've been spoiled, selfish and unkind. I don't deserve…" He trailed off.

"Ryker…" I tried to gently coax him.

"Liam is selfless and just. He's the loyal one, the protector, the noble one. He should've been King, you know? Not me. Never me. I was always the selfish bastard."

"That's enough," I scolded. "Liam has his own selfish tendencies, and you well know it. He left both you and Evelyn. He drank when he couldn't deal with the change and the pressure. He lied when he should've told you the truth. He let his anger get the best of him when he didn't know what to do." I was giving far too much away, but I didn't care. I needed to get Ryker out of these destructive thoughts that wouldn't do him any good but help him sulk further into the gloom that was his world right now. "Don't make him out to be some sort of saint. You both have your issues."

"I told her to stop coming to see me." His words were quiet again, forlorn. It was as though now that he'd opened up, the floodgates could no longer hold back his confessions.

"That's not the reason she hasn't been here," I gently offered. "Apep threatens to hurt you further if she doesn't obey him."

A long silence hung heavy in the cold damp air that surrounded us. "How do you know so much about all of this?"

My mind raced for an adequate answer. "Well, I do work in the kitchen…" I bit my lip to keep from saying anything else.

He chuckled softly. "The kitchen staff does always seem to know everything that goes on in the palace." He paused before adding. "Thank you for being so kind to me."

"You deserve it," I whispered.

"I don't."

"Well, I think you do."

Now the silence that settled between us was comfortable, companionable. I waited to see if he'd want to talk more or dismiss me. Either way, I wouldn't leave until I absolutely had to. He needed this…we both did.

"I look forward to your visits." His raspy words were gentle, vulnerable.

I smiled again.

"And I don't just mean because of the food," he rushed to say. "It's your company…it brings me hope."

My breath caught in my lungs.

I had no right to bring him hope, and yet, that was all I wanted to do.

"What's your name?" Ryker asked quietly.

I took a deep breath, gently wrapping my hand around one of the bars. "I-I can't…I can't tell you that."

Ryker's hand slowly closed over the top of mine, and I let out a shuddering sigh. His hand was lukewarm, despite the cold permeating every inch of this dismal place. The skin on his palm felt cracked and worn, roughed from the coarse stone in his cell. But his touch was a comfort. A solace when I didn't deserve it.

"Do you fear telling me?" he asked.

"Yes," I confessed in a barely-there whisper.

"I'm sorry." He started to pull his hand away, but I placed my other hand on top of his, desperately trying to keep our connection.

His breath hitched, and a tremor echoed through his arm.

"It's not because of you or anything you've done, Ryker." My body shivered at the confession. "It's because of me. Because of who I am. Because of what I've done."

"It couldn't be worse than what I've done." His tender but scratchy voice was like a vise around ribs, slowly choking the breath out of my lungs. "Thank you for being here with me."

A lone tear rolled down my cheek. "We're getting you out of here." My voice was strained and choked. "I won't let you stay in here."

He didn't respond, so I tightened my hands around his, but he carefully pulled his hand away and sank back into his darkened corner.

"I'll be back tomorrow," I sighed heavily.

"I look forward to it," was his only response.

CHAPTER 33

Liam

"Apep's been snooping around."

I flashed a concerned look at Rafe, "Where'd you see him?"

He jerked his head toward the meadows, "He was standing out there watching the horses."

"Just watching?" I puzzled.

Rafe shrugged. "None of the horses would come near him. He seemed pretty deep in thought, but I made sure not to get too close." He grunted as he hefted a saddle up in the tack shed to be stored after cleaning and oiling the leather. "I think that little joy ride you and Evy took is what's made him especially... *curious*."

"That's not good." I stated.

Rafe shot me an exasperated look before putting all the supplies away, brushing his hands together to remove any excess dust.

It'd been almost a full week since Evy and I had our last stolen moment together, just barely over three weeks since we'd arrived, but it already felt like a lifetime ago. We'd made the plan, and it was our best bet, but waiting...that was the hardest part. Especially when the people I loved were still suffering while we waited.

This stupid ball couldn't get here quick enough.

The horses began to stir in their stalls as a creeping cold sensation slithered up my spine. Something about it felt familiar. I'd remembered feeling this a few times in the palace when Ryker...

My breath caught in my lungs. "We have to go," I grabbed Rafe by the arm, hauling him outside behind me. "Now."

I'd left my sword up in my room, but the dagger I'd collected from my old quarters was concealed under my tunic. It wouldn't do much against magic, but it could still do damage if the timing was right.

Harsh laughter echoed inside the stable just as I pulled Rafe through the entrance. We skirted around the side of the building doing our best to avoid several of Apep's guards who stood at attention, surrounding the entire stable.

We were sitting ducks out here in the open, surrounded only by open meadows and the giant stable with its small bordering outbuildings.

I motioned to the trees, and Rafe nodded. Making a run for them would make us incredibly obvious, but it was also our only relative line of safety. I started a countdown as I watched one of the guards disappearing behind the building, but then I heard the stablemaster's voice.

"They were here just a moment ago, sire."

"Hm. Perhaps they're hiding." Apep's low, slithering tone grated my insides. Rafe pulled on my arm, indicating with his head that we should run.

"That wouldn't make sense..." The poor stablemaster had no clue of the small battle currently taking place, but his words died off as Rafe and I made a dash for the trees. Cold tendrils snaked up my spine as I pushed Rafe to go faster.

Rafe's face went suddenly white as he stumbled, and then—

A calloused hand gently tapped my face. "Were you two just sleeping out here?"

I blinked my eyes open, confusion clouding my brain.

"Get up, lads. The king was just here, and you both missed him." The stablemaster's blurry face slowly came into focus. "You're lucky I don't tell him you lot were lazin' about out here."

I slowly pushed myself into a seated position, dazedly looking over at Rafe, who I was sure mirrored my confused expression as he scratched his head in bewilderment.

Looking out beyond the stablemaster, I saw that we were in the open field that lay between the stable and the surrounding wood, exactly where Rafe had tripped.

We didn't make it?

But Apep hadn't caught us…

I couldn't understand it. I pressed a palm to my temple.

Why were we just laying here? What happened?

Rafe's startled gaze met mine again, and his entire face went pale, which startled up my last memory before now.

I turned away again, blinking up at the stablemaster. "Is the King still here?"

"No," he said, "and you're lucky he already left. If he'd found you two out here wastin' the day away, he'd probably dismiss the both of ya." He motioned with his hands. "Up, up, up. We still have plenty of work to do before the sun goes down."

Slowly pushing to my feet, I rubbed my hand over my eyes. I couldn't remember anything past Rafe tripping as all the color drained from his face.

Nothing.

Not how we got there, not why we were unconscious, just… *nothing.*

The stablemaster strode away leaving us to trail behind.

"I can't remember what just happened," Rafe said.

I shook my head. "I can't either."

"Do you think he…" Rafe trailed off as he shivered, "Do you think he got to us? Messed with our minds somehow?"

My face and resolve hardened, even as my insides quaked, and I nodded in confirmation. It was the only explanation I could figure out, especially after I'd felt that slippery cold just before…nothing.

"We have to warn the others tonight and lay low," I said quietly. "Apep obviously knows it's us, but he also left us here unharmed and unshackled."

"Do you think that could be because of Evy?" Rafe's hopeful question stabbed right through my stomach.

I shook my head, rubbing a hand down my face again. I just

couldn't get my bearings.

"I highly doubt it." Swiping both hands through my hair, we entered the stables as if nothing had even happened. "He's obviously got a plan."

"And now we're a part of it," Rafe concluded.

I nodded and ran my hands through my hair multiple times, trying to ground myself in the moment and not let the panic of what just happened overwhelm me while Rafe grabbed some shovels nearby.

"Get to work, you two!" the stablemaster called out behind him as he stomped out of the stable.

Rafe handed me a shovel, and we looked at each other wearily as a dark, foreboding dread shadowed both our features.

We had no answers, only questions and the knowledge that we'd just somehow become Apep's pawns, but we had no idea what game we were playing or what his next move might be.

***

"So ye're tellin' us that Apep knows about ye and he did something that messed with yer minds?" Ian asked.

"It seems the most likely assumption at this point," I answered.

He swore under his breath, pulling Chrissy a little tighter to his body. She looked as if she'd fall over if Ian wasn't holding her upright. Her skin had grown brittle and pale, and the bruises under her eyes were far more pronounced than they'd been even just last night. The wrinkles on her face deepened as she frowned at us, her bright green eyes growing dim. I hated what was happening to her, but we only had two more days to get through. Two more days until the night of the ball. Two more days until this nightmare was over.

At least, hopefully.

The moon hung bright in the sky almost directly overhead, indicating it was technically the next day already and the ball was officially tomorrow.

I took in a deep breath. "Chrissy, we can't have you wasting..."

She waved me off. "I'll be fine."

"Ye will not," Ian growled. "Ye're *dying*, and ye know it. This is all too much." I recognized it then, the despairing pain in Ian's voice. He knew he was losing Chrissy, but he also knew it was her choice.

"Ian…" Chrissy's brittle voice whispered quietly.

"I swore to protect ye," he whispered back.

She raised a hand to Ian's face. "And you have. Now it's my turn to protect you." She turned to the group. "All of you."

"Chrissy," I croaked, "We can figure something else out."

"I'm not convinced any of this is worth it." Ian's stern voice sounded. "Ye haven't heard a word from Terreno, yer extraction plan for Ryker and Evelyn is risky at best, and ye're hopin' to just run out of the palace with both of them in tow? You and I both know he'll follow ye to the ends of the earth for her. He'll never let ye just simply walk away with her and hide." He threw me an accusing glare before turning to Chrissy again, pleading. "This isn't worth dyin' over."

"Ryker's cell is already opened, and Billy can easily take out one guard." Camilla looked to Billy, who nodded. "You have to let us at least save him. Evy has asked that of us on multiple occasions."

Ian's head dropped down, and Chrissy placed a hand in the middle of his chest, leaning her head against him.

"Compromise," I said. "Rafe and I will make do without wings. If he already knows about us, there's hardly a point anyway."

Rafe nodded, and Becca flashed me a glare of equal if not more ferocity than Ian had.

"We'll be fine," Rafe told her, and she looked down, but that scowl didn't fade.

"I can cover up my would-be wings as well," Camilla added. "Everyone knows I hate the cold."

Billy laughed a bit too loudly for the quiet, still night that surrounded our group. "Nothin' truer than that statement, lass. The whole palace knows about yer freezin' from the way ye bellyache about it nonstop."

She humphed, but a small smile tugged at her lips. I loved that the two of them had grown close. Billy treated her like a little sister and watched over her like a big brother. I found I wasn't nearly as angry with her as I used to be, especially since she'd been risking everything to help Ryker.

"That just leaves Becca," I said. Rafe shot me a look, and I shook my head. "She's in too close proximity with Apep regularly to not have wings and a mask of sorts."

Ian nodded, looking down at Chrissy, his eyes glistening with unshed tears. "I can agree to just Becca."

Chrissy scrunched her nose at him. "Good, because you don't really get a choice."

The group chuckled, but it was half-hearted. Chrissy was pushing herself too far, and we all knew it, but we were too far in it now to completely abandon our plans.

Becca stepped forward slightly, shifting from side to side. "I think..." She paused, shooting Rafe a regretful look. "I think Apep might know who I am, too."

All of our heads turned to her.

"What do you mean, he might know who you are?" Rafe's voice was laced with a fine fury.

She shrugged. "I can't prove it. It's just been little looks here and there. Passing comments. Certain ways that he talks to Evy." She bit her bottom lip. "I haven't wanted to tell Evy, or any of you. I didn't want anyone to worry."

"Is her shield still around you?" I asked.

"Every day, even when she sleeps now. The first few nights she lost it, but she's been maintaining it easily lately, no matter where I go in the palace."

"Incredible," Chrissy commented.

"Do ye think that means she'll come into her full magic soon?" Ian asked Chrissy quietly, awe coating his voice.

Chrissy looked up at him, matching his expression. "I don't know, but her improvements have been swift and consistent. It's absolutely incredible how fast she's learning and growing."

I rubbed the back of my neck, attempting to release some of the pressure there. "And I don't even think she knows it," I added.

"You can't go back." Rafe walked up to grip Becca's shoulders, turning her to face him fully. "If he got a hold of you..." Rafe didn't finish, but instead pulled her flush to his chest. Becca protested, pushing against him, but he didn't let up an inch as he clutched her fully against his chest.

Camilla spoke up next. "He'll use you against Evy." Her eyes took on a haunted look. "You don't know what it's like..."

"I'll be fine." Becca's muffled response, a pointed echo of his words. "After the ball, hopefully all of this will be done anyway."

I shot her a side-eye. "That's a pretty big gamble."

She finally pulled free of Rafe's embrace. "We're all gambling on this chance."

And we were. We had to.

CHAPTER 34

Evelyn

"**A**re you ready for tomorrow?" Becca asked, breaking the silence as I mindlessly stared out the window.

Frost seemed to cover everything lately, including my troubled mind. I worried that the dungeon was too cold for Ryker. I worried that Becca would be found out, that all of them would be discovered. I worried that the small amount of time I'd had to practice my magic wouldn't be enough…but with all the additional supervision, including Silas, I'd had no time, no space, no opportunity to try.

I didn't bother turning to face her as I answered. "As ready as I'll ever be, I suppose." I sighed and stared out at the meadows and the surrounding thick woods, just hoping for a glance of Liam. I hadn't seen him in just over a week.

Even a week feels like an eternity these days.

Becca's warm presence stood gently next to mine. "Hopefully, after tomorrow, this will all be different. We'll be far away from here, Ryker won't be imprisoned anymore, and you'll…"

I reached down and squeezed her hand next to me, cutting her words short. "I'll most likely not be with you." I turned to her then and gave her a sad smile. "But you never know."

"Ev…" She trailed off. We both knew that nothing was guaranteed, and the most important thing tomorrow was getting Ryker out.

I knew Liam had a plan to get me out as well, but it still felt impossible.

All of this felt impossible, unlikely, doomed.

I kept looking at her intently before I added, "If they're able to get Ryker, you need to go with them."

She shook her beautiful black curls at me. "Nuh-uh, no way. If you're staying, then I'm stay—"

"I think Apep knows it's you," I interjected, followed by a deep exhale as my chin sank to my chest.

I hadn't realized I'd been holding my breath. Probably because I didn't want to have this conversation; I'd only just gotten her and Liam back, and I wasn't ready to let them go again. But my hopes of escaping with them tomorrow felt overzealous and unrealistic.

Apep would hunt me down, and I feared how many people he'd hurt in the process. Including Becca.

She sighed and squeezed my hand back. "I think he might know it's me, as well. I didn't want to worry you, but I can't disagree."

"Does he suspect any of the others?" I asked carefully, closing my eyes tightly before opening them again to look at her.

She nodded slowly…so slowly that my heart fell into my stomach. They had to leave. All of them.

"Rafe and Liam mentioned they had a strange encounter yesterday." My heart pounded in my ears as Becca spoke. "Apep made a surprise visit to the stables, and when they tried to run, they suddenly woke up in the middle of the grass right before they would have reached the forest."

Dread thickened in my veins, my blood moving through my body at far too slow a pace.

What had he done to them? What had happened while they were unconscious?

Before I let my fears overwhelm me, I steadied my voice and asked Becca, "Do they have any idea what happened?"

Becca let go of my hand and moved closer to my side, wrapping her arm around my waist. I followed her lead, doing the same as we both stared out the window. "They both think he controlled their minds somehow. But nothing's come up yet." She paused before adding, "I'm worried. Whatever Apep has up his sleeve, we both know it's not good."

I choked on my frustration. "I feel like he's always a step ahead of me, and I can never catch up."

She gave my side a squeeze and leaned her temple against mine. Just having her near like this to support me felt almost too overwhelming. I wanted to crumble underneath her touch, to fall apart and let all of this bottled-up emotion out. But it wasn't the time. Maybe it would never be the time again. Everything felt so different now. So final.

"The girls said you cut open a wall, and Camilla mentioned you blew a hole clean through an iron lock. That's incredible, Evy." Her voice filled with awe. "And Chrissy just last night was talking about how quickly you're improving. She looked so proud of your progress."

I looked down at my hand, turning it over. "But if I can't stop Apep, what's the point?"

"Who said you can't?" Becca asked me pointedly, pulling her head away from mine before looking over at me. "What if you're the one who *can* beat him?"

I scoffed.

"No, really," she insisted. "Maybe he hasn't fully recognized it yet, or he deludes himself into thinking you're weaker than you are. But deep down, I think he knows you're the one that can stop him."

"But what does *stopping him* truly mean?" I gave her a sad look before pulling away, crossing my arms over my chest and walking toward the bed. "You say that like it's an easy thing, but what we're really talking about is killing him." I shook my head. "I don't think I can do that. I don't know why…"

Becca raced over, crouching in front of me, pulling my arms apart so she could hold my hands in hers while looking up at me. "Evy, I don't think anyone could look at you and think *cold-blooded killer*. But you could remove your shield from around him."

I shuddered at the thought, remembering what he did to Ryker the last time I removed my shield from him, even if accidentally.

Becca continued, "If the shield isn't there, he's far more vulnerable. The curse still remains on him which means he can't hurt Ryker or Liam." Her eyes searched mine as she practically pleaded. "Tomorrow night, at the ball, when everyone makes their move. Remove your shield from him. Just that action alone might be enough for this to work." She gripped my hands tighter. "You're not alone this time. We'll be with you."

"That's what I'm afraid of."

Becca pursed her lips, but didn't push. Even though it terrified me, I knew what she was saying made sense. But Apep seemed to defy logic, and my fear most definitely didn't want anything to do with logic.

"I'll do it," I said.

"If I could, I'd make all of this magically disappear." She smiled, but it didn't quite reach her eyes. "In fact, if I were a fairy, I'd want that to be my gift."

"What?" I arched a brow, smirking slightly. "Making things disappear?"

"Well, that would be pretty great, but no. I'd right wrongs, like this one. Maybe I could reverse time or something."

I shook my head, smiling now—a real one. "I don't think Nature gifts that kind of magic."

She shrugged, still crouched in front of me. "You never know."

A loud knock sounded on the bedroom door, and we both startled apart as Becca got up to open it.

"I'm sorry to bother your rest, Your Highness." The seamstress stood in the doorway, gently bowing her head as she clutched my ballgown in her arms. "I was just delivering your dress for tomorrow night. May I bring this in?"

"Yes, of course." I stood up from the bed as she moved through the room, hanging the beautiful turquoise gown on an open door of my armoire.

She turned to me and winked. "Is it to your liking?"

Smiling softly, I admired the gown. It was extremely exquisite work. "It's perfect, thank you."

She dipped into a curtsy and let herself back out of the room, attempting to close the doors behind her when one of the guards popped his head inside. "The King requests an audience." His eyes darted to Becca before he turned away, clearly expecting me to follow.

Sucking in a deep breath I sighed heavily and shot Becca an

exasperated look before following behind the guard out of the suite.

They led me silently to Apep's office. I cringed inwardly, chastising myself that I already referred to it as his instead of Ryker's.

This was Ryker's office.

He was the one that was supposed to be sitting behind that desk.

Not Apep.

"Ah. Excellent timing." Apep's voice sounded as I stepped through the office door. "Come in, come in. Have a seat." He turned to the guards then, "Stand guard." They dipped their heads in acknowledgment of the command and took up their stance in front of the door. Apep shut it behind them and glided his way back to the desk.

Holding up a few papers, he informed me, "King Jai and Princess Jada have written again."

My entire being went on alert. I didn't know what had been included in these letters, and I didn't want to seem too eager, or not eager enough. I was grateful he couldn't read my thoughts right now as I eyed the letters in his hands.

"I'm glad you've built such a good relationship with Her Highness. She seems to equally value your friendship." He looked down at the top letter in his hand. "It says here she wishes you could come visit, especially during these colder months, for even though it is their winter season, the daily temperatures are still quite warm. Enjoyable, really." He looked up at me then, smiling in the way he smiled, which was barely a smile at all. "She continues to say she's thinking of you and hopes that you're adjusting to your new fairy status with ease. Lovely girl."

He paused then and held the letter over the lit candle in front of him.

All of the blood froze inside of my body. I watched in horror as the secret words bloomed on the page. *We're coming. Look for my symbol.*

Apep tilted his head, looking at me with enraged eyes. "It seems you've been keeping secrets from me, Evelyn."

My breath stuttered in my chest, and my entire body began to shake.

Apep's eyes narrowed. "I don't like seeing this reaction. You know I won't hurt you."

I shook my head as warm tears fell onto my clenched hands. "No." I tried to speak as strongly as possible. "I don't know that."

His eyes widened as he set the papers down slowly in front of him. "I have never hurt you. You know this. But this," he gestured to the letter, "this hurts *me* deeply, Evelyn. I thought you understood what I was doing here. I thought you were with me."

I steeled my shoulders, pushing them back as my dampened lashes flicked up to stare him straight in the eye. "I have never been with you, and you know it. It's why you used Ryker against me, to keep me in line. You think you haven't hurt me, but *that* hurts me." My voice rose a little louder, and I pushed a finger onto the desk in front of me. "Him still being in that horrifying dungeon cell? That *hurts* me." I raised my hand to my chest to emphasize my point, my voice rising until I was nearly shouting. "The fact that you blame your twisted cruelty on *my actions?* That *hurts me!*"

He sat there quietly for far too long, simply staring back at me. His hands folded on top of the desk, calmly assessing my reaction as though I were some sort of side show.

"I'm sorry you see it that way." He stood from his desk and moved smoothly toward the door, opening it briefly. "Bring her in."

My heart attempted to leap out of my chest, but somehow lodged inside of my throat instead. Dread permeated my every pore, and my breaths came in too quickly.

One of my cruel guards drew Becca in through the door behind him, and Apep shut it behind her with a force that made the walls shake.

"I warned you, Evelyn."

My whole body shook as Apep carefully turned my chair around so I was facing the guard gripping Becca. The grasp didn't truly touch her arm, not since my shield was like a second skin on her, but she looked terrified nonetheless.

Apep crouched down in front of me, much like Becca had just a moment ago in our room. But this felt entirely different. My heart raced, and I could feel sweat coalescing at my brow. My chin trembled even though I held my jaw firmly locked in place.

"I told you what would happen if you got out of line again." He looked down at my hands mindlessly ripping and picking at my fingertips and laid his hand gently over them to stop the nervous motions. "But you're right; I think Ryker has had enough punishment for a while."

I couldn't speak. I couldn't breathe. My heart wouldn't stop speeding up. At some point you'd think I would reach a limit, but my heart didn't seem to know it.

Keeping his hand resting over my clenched fists, he turned to look over at Becca, narrowing his eyes. I watched as they swirled, light and dark mixing together in a nauseating spiral. When nothing happened, he tried again. Then, much to my astonishment, he laughed delightedly. The sound was still sinister, but he looked so pleased.

"So you've been managing to keep up three different shields," he mused, looking back at me as he stood slowly. "Impressive."

I shook my head absently from side to side. "I don't know what you're…"

"I may not be able to read your mind, young Evelyn, but I'm no fool. You've shielded your maid. Expecting me to do something like this, no doubt." He shook his head. "Brilliant, really." Then he looked back down at me, his right hand stroking his chin. "But did you truly think I wouldn't know who she was?"

Becca stood her ground in the face of being outed, but I saw her legs quiver.

"Perhaps some time in the dungeon would be a good enough punishment." He turned to look at Becca now while still talking to me. "Or would it be best for her to remain with you, simply knowing what I know?" He shook his head as he walked behind her. "Excellent work on your wings, Miss Becca. I wonder, who made this creation for you? Perhaps if you tell me, I'll be more lenient with you then I was with Ryker."

I stood up, seething. "You won't lay a finger on her, *ever*." My body rippled with pent-up energy, my magic rising to the surface, ready to be called at a moment's notice. It had never done that before, but I would do whatever it took to save her, to get her out of this mess.

I'd known it was a risk to get word to King Jai, but it was worth it. I had to protect the people I loved.

Apep turned to me, a saccharine smile firmly planted on his face. "You think you'll be able to keep up this shield? That you won't ever falter?" He walked toward me, his height towering over my own. "You are but a child learning her magic for the first time." He sneered. "And you've already faltered once before, did you not?" Still facing me, he commanded, "Take her to the dungeon. Tell the staff no food, no water, no warmth."

"*No!*" I yelled just as my magic flared to life, shoving Apep and the guard back with a blinding light that made them stumble away, shielding their eyes. Becca was untouched, but blinking wildly at the sudden brightness. I rushed forward, grabbing her hand and flinging the door to the office open, racing outside.

The guards were ready for us, though. They pulled Becca out of my hand, instantly severing our connection; though their grip couldn't hurt her, they could still control her body and movements.

I reached inside my power, ready to flare again, even though I had no idea how much energy I'd wasted. But before I could, a cold hand shocked me when it slammed heavily down on my shoulder.

"I don't think so," Apep whispered in my ear, followed by a sharp pinch on the side of my neck.

Everything went black.

CHAPTER 35

Evelyn

Iridescent silk cascaded around me in enchanting waves of fabric as an acute giddiness bubbled up in my chest. Twirling over and over again, just like I did with Mama, I could swear the smile on my face was permanent.

Becca smiled in return as I turned to face her, and we both giggled furiously.

"See? I told you fairy princesses exist." She winked.

Pushing her playfully, overflowing laughter bubbled up and out of my lungs. Becca's giggles made me even more giddy, and I snatched up her hands, making her twirl around the room with me.

"Do you think Liam will find me a good dance partner?" I asked dreamily.

Becca's laughter was boisterous and all-encompassing. I loved her laugh. She had such a great laugh. "I think no matter how terrible of a dancer you are, he'll never even notice."

I mimicked a clumsy dance move, faltering my steps on purpose before bending over and giving her the belly laugh she was aiming for.

Standing up straight again, I declared, "I love him!"

She smiled sweetly, putting her hands on her hips. "Oh, we *all* know that. And we all know he loves you back."

I grinned. "He does, doesn't he?" *Twirl.* "He's mad about me."
Twirl. "He wants to marry me." *Twirl.*

Sweet little Daisy tangled between my legs and twirling skirts,
snorting and trying to jump. I loved her pink little face so much. For
some reason, seeing it now made my eyes water again. I loved her so
much. My sweet pet. My perfect gift from Liam.

I stopped and swooped down, scooping the little piglet in my arms
and nuzzling her tough but soft pink skin.

"So marry the boy already!" Becca called out behind me. "Put
down the pig and put him out of his misery."

I feigned mock outrage. "This is not a *pig*. This is Daisy, and she
comes with me." Though I did set her down, because of course, she
would follow anyway. "Okay, let's go."

She scoffed, grinning at me while she knelt down to pet Daisy, and
Grandmother Chrissy suddenly appeared before us.

"So beautiful," she whispered. "Just like your mother."

Tears stung my eyes again. Grandmother Chrissy always knew the
right things to say.

"I miss her," I confessed.

Chrissy leaned in to give me a tight squeeze, and I buried my head
between her neck and shoulder.

"She's right here. She's always with you. Just as I will be." As she
pulled away, her form began to ripple and fade.

"Chrissy?" I tilted my head as alarm bells went off in my mind.
"Grandmother?"

Her form kept disintegrating right before my very eyes.

"Where are you going?" I asked, panic stretching my voice thin as
I reached out for her, but there was nothing to hold on to. She smiled
softly and waved goodbye. "Don't leave me! I just found you!" I cried
out, trying desperately to hold onto anything, but she was only made
of vapor now, nothing tangible.

"Becca!" I tried to enlist her help, but Becca's startled gaze met
mine.

"Evy? Evy! What's happening?" Becca held a squirming Daisy in
her arms, and her panicked squeals cut me to the core. The pain was
so acute I looked down to see if my torso was bleeding.

"Evy!" Becca's cry snapped my attention back up, and I was met with her fading image.

"No!" I cried out. My face felt hot as I reached and reached and met only air. "You can't have her! You can't have her!"

"I didn't want to take her, but you gave me no choice." Those deep, slithering vowels shook me to my core. The familiar icy tendrils raced up my spine.

No.

I squeezed my eyes closed tight and brought forth my shield. I promised I would never give him access again, and I meant it. His chill receded, and I breathed in deeply.

"I'll leave her unharmed, and even let her go, if you do as you're told tonight."

Opening my eyes, I found Apep's head above mine. His eyes were worried at the corners, and his body tilted over mine.

My breaths came fast and short, and my eyes darted in a panic around the room. Becca, Chrissy, and Daisy weren't here. My hand flew up to my chest and felt the soft velvet of my dressing robe. I wasn't wearing the iridescent gown Chrissy had made me for me.

None of that was real.

I clenched my eyes closed again.

It was just a dream, I told myself.

Not real.

"Evelyn, are you listening to me?" Apep's patronizing tone seized my attention again.

Details were catching up to me slowly, but I was still distracted by Becca's terrified and disappearing face in my dream.

"Where is she?"

"She's somewhere safe," he answered calmly. Far too calmly. "I decided it would be in your best interest if I made sure she was unharmed...for now."

"Where is she?" I asked again.

He smiled a simpering smile, full of condescension as he brushed a strand of hair away from my face. "Of course I can't tell you where she is. That would defeat the purpose."

I tried to sit up, and as Apep helped me, I noticed his other hand was tucked around mine.

Terror seized my insides, slowly compressing every organ as I stared at our joined hands.

Had I failed her so easily?

My breath lodged painfully in my lungs.

Apep must've seen the horror on my face as he squeezed my hand gently. "Your magic fell away the moment you were unconscious."

Unconscious? How...

He continued, not minding at all that I was barely hanging on by a thread. "You were out for longer than I expected, and I still have many things to do in preparation for tonight. I've asked the healer and seamstress to come help you get ready this evening."

Get ready?

My mind was trying to put all the pieces back together as quickly as possible.

"The ball?" I questioned out loud.

Apep leveled me with an exasperated look that soured my insides. "Yes, Evelyn. The ball is tonight, and we both need to get ready."

The deep dark dread that I'd been keeping at bay for so long was squeezing its way through my organs and slowly clawing up my chest.

In less than a breath, the dread had taken over. My body convulsed softly at first, but picked up speed quickly.

I couldn't handle this now.

I'm going to be sick.

Tears stung my nose. Perspiration gathered on my upper lip, forehead and neck.

Where was Becca? Had he hurt Ryker? What had he done to Rafe and Liam? How had I lost so much time?

... *Thump* ... *thump thump* ... *thump* .. *thump thump* ... ... *thump*

"Now tell me," Apep's polished smooth voice brought my attention back to him again. Was he still trying to get into my mind? My shield felt strong, but my strength in general was waning.

When had I last gone outside?

Apep brushed a hand over my sweaty forehead, pushing my hair to the side. "It's okay, Evelyn. Everything is going to be okay, but I need you to tell me what Jada's symbol is."

I blinked my eyes rapidly, willing my brain to catch up and the panic to go down. "H-her s-s-symbol?" I stuttered.

I need to think!

"She told you her symbol," he pressed. "What is it?"

I shook my wobbly head. "She told me nothing of a symbol."

"You are *lying!*" Apep yelled.

My eyes widened in fear, and he saw it. He couldn't miss it. It was the first time he'd truly yelled at me.

My trembling body shook even harder, harsh and hot tears burned my eyes, my chin quivered in terror.

His face fell. "I'm not like your father, Evelyn. I won't hurt—"

"Do-on't even s-say it," I whispered harshly. My breath wavered out in trembling ripples. "S-stop trying to convince yourself you're doing—that—that you're doing the right thing."

"I know you're frightened—"

"Of *you!*" I screamed, trying to wrench my hand away from his.

It felt good to do that. To scream out my horror and rage. It took the dread away. For one brief second in time, I was able to take in a solid breath of air, and my trembling paused.

Suddenly, instead of being afraid, I was angry.

Very angry.

Apep had the decency to look affronted, but he still gripped my hand, unwilling to let me go any further.

"Now, Evelyn," he chided, but it was gentle, careful. "I'm the one who should be angry with you, you know." He reached up with his other hand to turn my head back toward him. "You're the one who has been plotting against me with Terreno."

I scoffed, and he lifted an eyebrow in silent response. "Perhaps Terreno is simply plotting against you."

"Because I'm a dark fairy?" he questioned. "And you would support this supposed benevolent king who discriminates against his own subjects?"

"He puts fairies up in a place of respect," I argued.

"Light fairies," Apep said, a smoldering anger breaking through his recently recollected facade. "Not dark fairies."

"At least he does something," I shot back. "And Jada will be—"

Apep guffawed, cutting me off. "He would sooner have me hanged for my dark fairy heritage than let me live, and you brought him to my doorstep."

"*Our* doorstep," I corrected with a glare of my own.

Apep's smile was sinister and cruel. "Yes, *our* doorstep." He paused, narrowing his eyes at me. "You know, your magic is unique. I haven't met another who has a gift like yours. It hasn't shown itself to be of light or dark descent yet." His eyes glinted spitefully. "I wonder if your precious Princess Jada would look as kindly toward you if she suspected dark heritage in your blood line."

I clenched my jaw, attempting to ignore him. Maybe he didn't know that Jada didn't care one bit about light or dark heritage, or maybe he thought I didn't know that this was a point she and her father heavily disagreed about.

But Apep's words echoed off the walls of my mind, and I wondered if he somehow knew *my* heritage.

"You suspect I'm a dark fairy?" I asked, curiosity getting the better of me.

He shrugged condescendingly. "I only have my theories."

I jutted out my chin. "I see no dissimilarity between dark and light fairies. Why should it make a difference what you are? What I will be?"

A shadow crossed over Apep's eyes. "The humans took great offense against the dark fairies. Even though our kingdoms had combined and we no longer inwardly fought, the humans felt themselves superior, especially over the kind they deemed evil."

"The dark fairies," I filled in.

Apep nodded. "You've read the fairy tales."

The book Aster gave me popped into my mind.

"The humans called them such," he continued, "but to our kind, it's simply called history."

I swallowed, but held my tongue. Every word felt like it could incite his anger, and now that he held not only Ryker, but Becca, I couldn't risk it.

"My sister was stubborn like you," he suddenly spoke softly, thoughtfully. "She was willful and curious, but never outrightly so." His dark and light eyes bored into mine. "It was a hidden fire within her soul. One you had to be lucky enough to see, should she have ever given that honor." He sat back slightly, his eyes staring at our clasped hands. "You have that same fire, Evelyn. And somehow it hasn't been snuffed out of you." He paused before adding, "I don't want to be the one who does that to you."

I sucked in a harsh and shaky breath.

Silence. Dreadful, heavy silence sat between us. This time when he looked up, I saw him again, the Apep he hid from everyone else. The one shadowed by unrelenting pain.

My eyes and nose stung as he held my gaze before standing up, still holding my hand.

"Give me your shield, Evelyn."

I sucked in a breath and pushed my shield over him like a second skin. As he let go of my hand, he placed it gently back down on the bed.

"You will be given no time with Nature," he said without looking at me. "Should you feel your shield faltering, it's your responsibility to find me immediately." His contrasting eyes darted back down to mine. "Or else, you know what will happen." Walking toward the door, he added, "Tonight you will behave like the Princess you are, greeting and caring for her people, a true hostess." He paused at the door, his hand resting on the doorknob, waiting to open it. "Do not test me tonight, Evelyn. I was gracious and forgiving before, but that will not be the case again. If you move against me...I *will* kill them both."

With those parting words, he opened the door and swept out of the room, firmly closing the door behind him. The telling click of a metal key locking into place was the only sound that broke the deep hush left behind.

My chin quivered again, and my body froze to the bed.

Just like that, he'd taken Becca from me.

I'd promised I would never let her be hurt, and I'd failed so pathetically.

My head sank back into the pillows and my eyes clenched tight, pushing out all the tears that had been building up.

Just like in my dream, I felt as though all the hope I'd had was slowly fading right before my eyes, and I desperately feared what would come next.

CHAPTER 36

Liam

"We have to find her, Liam. Something's happened. She would've been there last night if something hadn't happened to her. She wouldn't miss it, not for anything. She—"

I clapped a grounding hand on Rafe's shoulder, while Billy and Camilla watched us with matching worried expressions.

"We're going to find her and get her out of here, but first we have to stick to the plan," I reassured.

He nodded, but his eyes were blank and troubled. I had a feeling he wasn't listening to me at all.

I wiped a hand down my face, then looked back up at Billy and Camilla. "You two know what to do." I jerked my chin off to the side. "Stick to the plan. Get him out, and then we'll go from there."

They both acknowledged me with nods, turning to leave and head back down to the kitchens, but I grabbed Billy and whispered quickly, "Don't let Apep get a hold of Camilla. If things go wrong, get her out."

Billy looked me in the eye and dipped his head once in confirmation before dashing off to follow behind Camilla. I knew he cared for her and would do everything in his power to protect her, which was a huge relief. One less thing I had to worry about tonight.

Now came the hard part. Especially since Rafe was already distracted and he and I had also become a liability. We didn't know what Apep had done to us; all we could do was hope that whatever he had planned wouldn't be tonight, or that we would figure it out before it was too late.

It was easy to assume he wouldn't want to wreck his own party, but when it came to Apep, I trusted nothing. The man had years upon years of scheming and strategizing and perfecting his plan. We both knew he could outmaneuver me with just a single thought…but still, all we could do now was press on and try to get the two people I loved most in this world to safety and out of Apep's grasp.

Rafe and I finished dressing for the ball. We each wore long tunics with wool overcoats for the winter cold, a style we stole from some of the fairies in the village just outside the palace. The style was simple, like that of a commoner, but it was the best option we had that would also conceal our lack of wings.

I looked over Rafe's outfit from head to toe and covered my mouth to hide the smile threatening to burst out from behind it. We'd had to find something quickly, and we weren't tailors…

I snorted, clearing my throat in order to hide my obvious amusement. Pursing my lips to keep from laughing, my eyes darted down to his comically short pants again. The length of them was so short it showcased all of his ankle with a hint of his calf. "We should've grabbed you some boots.

Rafe looked down, grimacing at his exposed hairy ankles. "That would make me look ridiculous."

For a brief moment, both of our eyes collided before we both exploded into a fit of laughter. It might've seemed wrong to laugh with so much on the line and so many worries to think about, but Rafe had taught me a lesson long ago: *when things are hard, find the humor in it.* He'd said that once when we were still working our way up through the ranks and both of us busted into laughter one day during an extra tough training session, much to our previous Captain's chagrin. Rafe believed that laughter was a tool that was never used often enough. When you could laugh in the face of hard things, it gave you a moment of reprieve and perspective. As wrong as it felt, laughter was exactly what we needed right now.

Sucking in a nice long breath, I put my arm around his shoulders. "We would never leave Becca behind. We will find her."

"I know," Rafe acknowledged with a heavy sigh. "But if I find out he's hurt her in any way, I'll kill him."

I shot him a look. "Get in line."

"Okay. I'm first, you're second."

I shoved his head down playfully before walking down the hall. "We'll see who gets there first."

***

The grand ballroom was packed. The expansive white marble room was gilded from head to toe with golden accents and mirrors reflecting the glittering scene back into the room. Warm glowing candlelight surrounded us, from the impressive chandeliers that were currently lit to the candelabras lining the ornate walls.

The last time I'd been here, Evy had stood on this balcony, surveying the crowd, looking like a dream come to life.

Rafe and I split apart, each taking one staircase to walk down before we were on opposite sides of the room. I knew Evy didn't believe we'd be able to get her out, but there was no way I was going to leave here without trying.

The overwhelming scent of sweet treats, champagne, and wine permeated the crowded space as I weaved my way through the crowd. I made sure to keep my head low and did my best to blend into the sea of faces and colors.

Posting up near the sidewall, I chose to stand next to several fairies who were dressed much like I was and carefully scanned the array of faces for the one I was looking for.

My breath caught as my gaze landed on the resplendent figure in flowing turquoise. She was magnificent. Her hair was down and long, curling lightly at the ends. Every movement made the fabric of her gown look as though it was dancing underwater. With each turn, the crowd made a wider and wider circle, allowing her to be seen by all.

Slowly dragging my eyes away from her, I grimaced at her current partner. Silas was tall and lean, showing off perfect posture and coiffed dusty hair. His clean-shaven face and Alstonian blue attire, complete with glittering wings on full display, made him look nearly as regal as she did.

I hated him.

Unfortunately, not for what I *should* hate about him, but jealousy was fickle like that. I should've hated him for his discussion with Apep about deceiving Evy and gaining her trust, but right now I simply hated him because he was dancing with *her*.

Pulling my gaze from the couple, I landed on Apep next. He sat upon the throne high up on the dais, watching the festivities happen with a gleam in his eye. His black hair was wavy and long, making his pale skin stand out even more starkly. It was strange seeing him in something other than those long robes he used to wear, but his flowing tunic was still black. The cut of it was straight and sharp; gold embroidery gleamed in the candlelight, as did his stolen golden crown. I watched closely as Apep lifted his hand to his chin…

All my thoughts stopped.

Sucking in a harsh breath to keep from reacting foolishly, I stared at the rings.

Ryker's rings.

The fury that had been festering in me since the day I left flared to life, flaying my insides with a righteous anger I'd never felt until this moment.

He turned his wrist and they flared in the light, a flashing golden beacon begging me to charge up there and rip them off his spindly fingers.

I sucked in another hard breath through my nose and forced my eyes to study his face some more. He hadn't taken his eyes off the dancing couple, but I could tell by the click of his jaw that he was taking this opportunity to listen in on thoughts that weren't his. His expression was too focused, too keen, too careful.

As the song began to slow, I made my way closer to the center, just wanting to be near her.

A fresh song started, and she motioned for the crowd to join in the fun. Silas followed her lead. Her smile was welcoming and kind, but a dark shadow hid behind her eyes. She looked tired, already worn out before the night had truly begun.

"I need to take a moment," I heard her say to Silas.

"Of course, Princess," Silas bowed and then offered his arm. "Allow me to escort you off the floor."

Following in their wake, I waited until they were almost to the edge of the crowd before I gently reached for her hand. "May I, Your Highness?"

She twisted around, her bright green eyes flaring with recognition at my touch alone. Silas shot me a knowing grin, relinquishing her arm with ease. "I shall fetch you some wine." He inclined his head before supposedly heading off to do just that.

I bent down slowly, bringing my lips to the back of her hand. "You are breathtaking," I whispered against her skin before kissing it gently.

"And you are going to get us caught," she chided, nervously glancing around the room.

I offered out my hand to her, bowing slightly. "Princess?"

She smiled sweetly, but it was laced with trepidation as I pulled her toward me, mimicking the hold of the couple next to us. Fairy dances were quite different, and I most definitely didn't know a single step, but we bumbled our way through them to start.

"Liam, if he sees you..." she huffed under her breath.

For the briefest moment when her hand touched my shoulder I saw a flare of magic. A light tickle danced down my body as the slightest weight—more like a film—settled against my skin.

I looked back up at her, completely in awe, "Did you just..." Worry flared in my mind at the sight of sweat beading on her brow. "Evy," I whispered hoarsely into her ear. "What's wrong?"

She shook her head. "He has Becca." Somehow she kept her head high and her face blank as she spoke the words. "He's using her to make sure I stay in line tonight." Her pointed stare bore into my own. "I can't go with you. You need to leave without me."

One thing at a time, I told myself. "Where is he keeping her?"

"I don't know." Her voice broke as she whispered. "He said something about the dungeon, but he could have said it to trick me."

I wanted to ease her burden, give her the space to feel what she needed to, but we didn't have that luxury right now.

"I know it's hard, but we'll find her." I did my best to reassure her, squeezing her hand in encouragement, but she didn't look convinced.

Watching the dancers around us, I bounced and twirled and moved with them steadily through the crowd until I'd made it to the side hidden door that led to the Queen's moonlight garden. We stopped dancing as though we needed a breather and I carefully unlatched the door, tugging both of us through before closing it soundly behind us.

A voice in the back of my mind was yelling at me. *This was too dangerous. I shouldn't be trying to steal a moment away with her right now.*

But when I took note of the empty corridor, I felt the overwhelming sense that I had to be with her, now. I had to hold her in my arms. Kiss her. Make her see that she needed to come with us tonight.

I wouldn't leave without her, that was for certain.

The muffled sounds of the ball going on just outside the door made this moment feel even more intimate. Before she could try to dissuade me, I turned back to her and pinned her up against the door we'd just come through. Her back hit the unforgiving wall, but I couldn't help myself; being close just wasn't enough. I needed more, I needed to take it, to taste her, to wrap my body around hers.

That little voice inside of my mind chided me. *You shouldn't be doing this, this isn't part of the plan. You're being too reckless.*

Mmm. Yes. *Reckless.*

In a desperate kiss, my mouth was against hers. Tasting, seeking, reveling in her small but lusciously soft lips. Her supple body fit perfectly against my harder one. I wanted to push in, to make her my everything; my every breath, my every heartbeat, my every movement.

I was unraveling. Lost to anything but the feel of Evy.

Evy.

I groaned, and she gasped slightly, allowing me to take full advantage of her open mouth, deepening my kiss as my tongue tenderly caressed hers. The soft moan she rewarded me with was like oil to my fire, making me press my body even further into hers.

Not close enough. Never close enough.

My hand on her neck, the other around her waist. She fit me perfectly. The way she softened into my embrace. The way her small body fit into mine, like a missing puzzle piece. The way she tilted her head back to accommodate my height. I was consumed by her.

This is wrong.

I shook my head, disregarding the thought. How could this be wrong? There was nothing wrong or bad about Evy and I. In fact, we were right. We were as right as ...

Stop.

Pulling away, Evy struggled to catch her breath. Her cheeks were pink, her chest rose and fell in quick bursts, her eyes were wide with awe and a little confusion, and her perfect lips were faintly swollen.

Standing before her, I couldn't help but smile. I raised her hand up to my heart. "You have my whole heart, Evy."

"And you have mine," she whispered breathlessly as she tried pulling away again. "But you are officially being heedless and ..."

"I couldn't help myself." I admitted, smirking.

Her eyes softened as they fell briefly to my lips. "I will be missed."

"You already are."

She rolled her eyes, and I sighed. "I'll be okay." Kissing the top of her head, I unwound myself from her body and reached down for her hand. "Ready to get out of here?"

"I'm ready for *you* to get out of here. I can't let him…"

I leaned in, kissing her again. "I know." Looking fixedly at her, I added, "You must promise you'll leave if you're able."

She shook her head. "You know full well I cannot and will not make that promise."

I couldn't help but smile at the steel in her tone. "Stubborn girl."

Carefully opening back up the hidden door, I checked to make sure no one was watching before I pulled her out behind me.

We skirted our way behind the still-dancing and exuberant crowd, making our way to the ballroom stairs and up, up, up.

Still holding her hand, I gave it a little squeeze, looking back at her. And for those two seconds, everything was perfect. Evy was with me. I was getting her out. Ryker was being saved, and this nightmare would finally end. I didn't know what we'd do next, but I knew if we were out from under Apep's thumb, we'd at least have a chance.

At the top of the stairs, I turned looking out at the crowd below from the vantage point of the balcony.

Still no sign of Apep. No one seemed to even notice we were leaving the party as the revelers danced and cheered, laughing and drinking to their heart's content. An anticipatory hope expanded in my lungs as I stepped through the double door ballroom entrance at the top of the stairs.

"Going somewhere?"

No.

No. No. No.

My grip tightened on Evy's hand, unwilling to let her go.

"I'm disappointed, Evelyn," Apep's snake-like voice tsked as a bevy of guards fanned out from behind him with their wings flared wide in defiance. That swine Silas included.

Evy's hand trembled, and I couldn't help the wash of failure that doused all my previous faith.

Swallowing down my fear, I raised my gaze to meet Apep's, but his eyes weren't on me. They were glued to the woman I stood protectively in front of.

"Did you think I wouldn't notice?" He raised a sardonic brow.

Evy's shallow breaths came in fast and hard behind me, like she couldn't get a full breath of air in.

Apep took a step toward me, and Evy stepped forward, angling herself in front me as if to shield me with her own body. My heart stuttered at her indomitable strength. If anyone mistook her trembling and tears as signs of weakness, they were sorely mistaken and would soon regret underestimating her. She'd experienced darkness and refused to let it extinguish her light.

To stand with no fear was easy. To stand in spite of fear? That was strength immeasurable.

"You can't have him, Apep." Her chest rose and fell in fast bursts, but her voice was low and threatening. Pride warmed my chest. Loyal to a fault, and just as protective as Becca, only more quiet about it.

Apep smiled cruelly in return. "I was hoping it wouldn't come to this."

He raised a hand, never losing eye contact with Evy, ignoring me entirely.

Several guards pulled forward a squirming and struggling Becca.

"Becca, stand still." Evy's command was clear, surprising even Becca into shocked stillness, and the guards hauling her in actually lost their grip for a moment in their shock.

Evy's magic flared so quickly I would have missed it if I'd blinked, settling around Becca before disappearing.

"You've been practicing, young Evelyn. It's very impressive. Three moving shields all at once," Apep mused.

No sooner had Apep said the words than Evy faltered, her legs practically giving out beneath her.

I snatched my arm around her and pulled her back toward me before she could hit the ground.

Apep stepped closer, a looming presence even if he wasn't any taller than I was.

"That's close enough, Apep," I warned. Even though we both knew I wouldn't be able to do a thing to him, I would still fight him to the very bitter and quick end if I had to.

Bending at the waist, he tilted his head to look at Evy, who was panting and sweating. "How long do you think you'll last? Hmm?" Apep's taunting question seemed to do the trick as Evy shuddered and trembled harder in my embrace. "When you take on too much, magic begins to eat at the wielder, and I do not wish to see you perish, my young Princess. Shall I apply my pressure point again?"

Evy jutted out her jaw, shaking her head.

"Drop it, Evy!" Becca's voice sang out from behind Apep. "Drop it now!"

Becca's words seemed to bolster Evy's strength as she straightened her spine and pulled away from me.

A shadow flashed through Apep's eyes, but he ignored Becca, keeping his focus on Evy. She stood tall before him, tilting her head thoughtfully to the side, just like he'd done to her, and he froze.

"Evelyn…" he said in warning. "If you do this, I *will* kill one of them."

She drew in a deep breath, still relying on my strength to keep her upright, but keeping her spine unswerving entirely on her own. "Not if they're both gone."

Apep laughed then. "Think wisely now Evelyn." His eyes darted to someone off to the side of me. "You have more to lose than you think."

Becca cried out as familiar curly locks rounded my peripheral vision.

No.

Evy bristled, finally seeing who Becca and I knew already as Rafe walked forward, silent, unblinking, unseeing.

The minute he stood in front of Apep, he started convulsing uncontrollably.

Evy begged Apep to stop; pulling away from me, she dropped to her knees in an attempt to touch Rafe, but Silas swooped in and hauled her away, muttering fiercely in her ear.

That was my last straw.

I didn't have my sword, but I had Evy's protection, and my fist could be good enough for the time being. I charged straight at Apep, aiming my swing at Apep's face, but was suddenly cut off by arms holding me back.

"You know what I am capable of, young Evelyn." Apep's eyes swirled, glowing softly as they hardened.

I twisted forcefully, hitting one of my assailants in the stomach before turning to take a swipe at the other's jaw.

"Stop it!" Evy's voice mixed with Becca's cries. "I won't, I won't take it down. Please, just don't kill him."

I hated the sound of her acquiescence, but I understood it. She would never allow innocent people or fairies to suffer, especially for her actions.

My fists clenched, and I took another swing at another one of Apep's guards as he flew toward me. Three against one were never good odds, but Evy's shield was doing what it did best and shielding me from any of their blows and Apep's mind control.

"Make your choice, Evelyn." Apep's words filtered through the grunts and thuds against flesh or shield.

Her breath hitched in her throat. "What?"

"I'll give you the choice." Apep's seedy voice sneered.

Evy cried out, and that was when I realized my fighting wouldn't help her now. It was an impossible choice, one that both Apep and I knew she could never actually make.

In the meantime, Rafe's body convulsed uncontrollably.

"Choose," Apep taunted.

"You pale, pathetic monster!" Becca spat out. "Are you so weak that you must always prey upon the vulnerable in order to get your way?" The guards tried to silence her, but her shield remained intact.

"You're nothing but a scared and spineless snake slithering around on your belly, always looking up at what you can't truly have."

"Stop, Apep." I stopped fighting and pushed my way through his guards to face him head-on.

I couldn't protect them all the way I wanted to, but I could give them this.

"I will go with you willingly," I croaked. "Leave them be."

"Excellent."

Rafe's torture abruptly stopped, leaving him collapsed and unconscious on the floor.

"Liam, no." Evy's breathy plea overwhelmed my ears.

"Take him," Apep ordered.

The guards holding Becca flung her toward Evy and took me instead, gathering Rafe up behind me and dragging him along the floor. Becca's sobs were only interrupted by her threats in between. I loved her fire. I loved how she inspired Evy to show her fire as well. At least he had freed her, giving Evy someone to hold on to. An obvious manipulation tactic, but one I was still grateful for.

Instantly Apep was in front of Evy, gripping her chin while Silas still held her upright. "Do not attempt to threaten me again, my Evelyn, or I won't be as gracious."

Tears streamed down her face as several hands pulled me away from the scene. It was strange being tugged along when you couldn't feel the hands pulling at you, only the pressure to move.

Evy's devastated face watched me the whole way. I knew she felt at fault, like she should've done more. I mouthed, "It's okay," one more time before we rounded the corner of the hallway.

What would happen when she slept? When she got too tired to maintain my shield? Exhaustion looked like it would take her at any moment.

All I could do now was pray that Camilla and Billy had succeeded in getting Ryker out.

As we made our way downstairs, I finally realized my feet weren't on the ground, but instead I was being flown straight to my cell. The sensation was jarring, considering I couldn't feel their hands either.

In an attempt to injure me, I'm sure, they threw me into the second to last cell in the darkest, deepest part of the dungeon. With

Evy's shield around me, I felt nothing but the thud of landing on stone.

The fairy guards all sniggered. "You finally have some companions, *Your Majesty*," they called out.

My heart sank.

The guards walked away, leaving us in the dark.

Hungry silence gobbled up every sound, leaving an empty hollowness in its wake.

"Ryker? Rafe?" I called out carefully.

Silence.

"Ryk? Are you there?"

The faintest shifting of fabric shuffling against stone sounded in the next cell over.

"Liam?" His voice was a rasping whisper of pain, which made me choke inside my own throat.

"It's me, Ryk. I'm here. I'm here." Suddenly out of breath, I crawled over to our shared wall, placing my hand on the cold, uneven stone. "We're going to get out of here. I'm going to get you out of here."

Groaning sounded from the cell next to me...or maybe across from me? These darkened cages were far smaller than I had ever thought them to be. The roof was tall enough that I could stand if I tilted my head just so. It was definitely far easier to sit.

"Rafe?" I asked again.

No response.

"Are you really here?" Ryker's defeated voice echoed across the cavernous space, making it sound even more forlorn somehow. He'd suffered so much, he'd been in here so long...

"We are. We're really here. I'm so sorry, Ryker. I'm so sorry I—" The words died in my throat at the sound of another pained groan nearby.

"Rafe! Wake up," I called into the darkness. "Let me know you're okay."

"Rafe's here, too?" Ryker asked.

I rubbed the back of my neck. "Yeah."

"What are you doing here?"

Closing my eyes, I cringed at my next words. "We're here to rescue you."

He huffed out a humorless laugh. "It doesn't sound like you've done a great job at that."

"Well, circumstances could be better," I admitted with a hefty side of sarcasm.

After a long pause, Ryker finally spoke again. "You should've stayed away."

"I could never truly leave you…either of you. It was a horrible mistake…I never should have—"

"We both know she was never for me." Ryker's confession cut me off. The shock of it rushed through me like an arrow hitting its target. He'd stated it so plainly. So coolly. Without a hint of emotion. "I should never have pursued her once I knew who she was to you."

"Ryker, it doesn't matter now, it's in the past. What matters now is—"

Voices sounded down the corridor, many feet marching at once as I cut off.

"Whatever happens next," I whispered, "do *not* give up, Ryker. Don't you dare give up."

CHAPTER 37

Evelyn

Apep released my chin, his hand reaching out instead to touch my face, but I flinched away.

The arms around me squeezed tight in warning.

"Remember, my young Evelyn." Apep's hand flared out as if stung, before he lowered it to his side. "I gave you back your friend. You may keep Becca if you wish, because I know she brings you comfort." His eyes darted off to the side of me, where Becca now stood, and then slowly looked beyond me to the ballroom at large. "Keep our guests entertained while I pay a little visit to our latest prisoners."

He turned and jutted his chin toward the hallway as he walked through the grand ballroom double doors, his guards following suit. Calling out over his shoulder, he eyed Silas behind me. "Stay with her, help smooth things over." Then his eyes fell back on me. "Should your shield slip from me due to your exhaustion, you know what will happen. Do not test me again, Evelyn. I already gave you a second chance."

With that, he turned and was gone, the double doors slamming behind him.

"Can you stand on your own?" Silas asked from behind me, his

276 • Brianne Wik

hold loosening the slightest bit around my waist to test my steadiness. I nodded. "Yes."

The moment I was free, I immediately turned to check on Becca. Her eyes were wide with worry and anger, but she was otherwise unharmed, much to my relief.

Becca's eyes darted to Silas over my shoulder, and her gaze narrowed. "Why did he leave you here? Who are you to that monster?"

I was happy to let her unleash her wrath on the two-faced jerk. Nature knew I barely had the energy, or else I'd do it myself.

Liam had warned me. He'd told me Silas was in Apep's pocket. But after spending so many days with him, so many hours talking... *about nothing,* my mind reminded me. He had never shared anything important, except for the vague confession around loving someone he couldn't, but what if that had been a lie? A way to gain my trust through sympathy? If he was anything like Apep, it was a likely theory.

"Apep trusts me to help keep the peace," he paused, putting on that haughty tone I hated, "through *non-violent* means."

I turned around, unsteady on my feet, but Becca's reassuring presence was right there. Her hand pressed against my back to help keep me steady as I straightened my spine. "Did you tell him about Liam?"

Silas's eyes flashed—either with hurt or worry, I couldn't tell which—before he responded, "I did not." He cleared his throat, "I don't know how he knew, but I can assure you..."

"Assure someone else," Becca snapped. "No one up here believes you."

Silas's eyes darted back and forth as if trying to look behind him without turning. "Ladies, please, we have an audience."

My eyes moved to the crowd below, and my brain finally caught up enough to help me realize that the ballroom was dead silent. No music played. No one spoke. No one dared move a muscle.

We were still on top of the grand staircase. A high stage for a dramatic performance that no one was meant to see...or perhaps, knowing Apep, one they were absolutely meant to see.

Always one step ahead.

Silas leaned in again, whispering softly as I stood there frozen in place, just like I had been the first time I stood here looking out at the ballroom scene beneath me. How long ago that felt now. "I truly am sorry, Evelyn. I never meant nor wanted to hurt you. But you know I can't—"

"Not now," I scolded. I couldn't fall apart yet; I still had to figure out what to do next, how to save them all, and how to keep myself from fainting.

The crowd in front of me waited on pins and needles to see what I would say next. This moment felt like some strange nightmare, but also an awkward gift. For the first time since Apep took over, *I* had the floor. He was too consumed with his own revenge vendetta to have truly even noticed, or maybe he thought I couldn't rise to the occasion. Either way, this was an opportunity I wouldn't squander.

Scanning the faces, I noticed angry expressions, anxious expressions, everywhere from entitled to excited, but the overall tone was utter confusion.

I'd never spoken to a crowd of people, let alone a mixture of minds that would either agree with me or vehemently disagree. I never anticipated I would ever be in a position like this.

Aster had mentioned there were more supporters than I realized… and if I could give them enough courage to stand up with me, maybe they'd help us and rise against Apep.

I pictured Liam, Rafe, and Ryker in the dungeons. Apep had left me behind, expecting me to play the dutiful Princess he was trying to create.

His mistake.

Stepping up to the balustrade, my hands trembled furiously, but I placed them on the marble railing, gripping it like it was a lifeline.

Taking in a deep breath…

Stay brave and strong. Never lose hope.

I repeated my mother's words over and over…

Give them a queen.

And Becca's.

I wouldn't allow myself to be cowed ever again, and this was my chance to do something about it.

Clearing my throat, the anticipative crowd below looked up, and I spoke like how I imagined a queen would speak. What I was about to say was not for everyone in this crowd…it was specifically for those who wanted peace.

I was about to make a lot of fairies angry.

"I know for some of you, the scene you just witnessed was confusing. And for others, you delighted in that display of violence." I allowed my voice to carry across the cavernous space. "Violence I do not condone, nor will I stand for it." I paused and turned to Becca, who gave me an encouraging smile and then immediately turned to hold off a creeping forward Silas.

"Today you have witnessed the actions of a coward." My voice rang out strong and true. It was as intimidating as it was liberating. And while many faces in the crowd didn't like my words, there were just as many who seemed to agree with me. "Apep is a usurper of the crown. He touts ideologies that sound good in theory, but in reality he rules solely by fear."

I took a pointed pause. "And that's no way to rule a kingdom. It is no coincidence that this is the first time you are hearing me speak. Apep has attempted to silence me, to force me to heel at his side and ignore my own convictions for his personal vendetta. But today, I stand before you, not as a false princess, but as a fellow fairy who's been downtrodden far too often in her life." I sucked in a gasping breath, willing my racing heart to somehow slow down.

There were so many eyes on me...

"We cannot let this behavior stand. I refuse to be controlled by a dictator and fearmonger simply because I did not have the strength enough to stand up to him. Today was meant to be a celebration, but what were we ever truly celebrating? That we are now acting as the humans always acted toward us? I refuse to behave like my abusers before me, and with this brief moment I've been given, I will now ask you to rise up with me. Do not make the same mistakes of your forefathers, stand with me for what is right. Humans and fairies should live together."

Boos and hisses echo loudly across the ballroom. Guards—a couple of my familiar shadows—had begun to make their way toward me, sharp anger in their eyes.

"I am proof that we can live in harmony, that we can..."

"Evelyn!"

Silas's body crashed into mine, pulling me to the ground as an unnaturally speedy glass of champagne shattered directly behind me.

In less than a second, Becca was right there with us as angry voices rose to the surface. Shouts and flashes of bright magic quickly filled the space. I looked out through the balusters and saw the crowd below arguing, some already fighting with each other.

"What have you done?" Silas muttered over me.

"We need to get her out of here before she becomes the target." Becca tugged at my arm, helping to pull me away from the chaos unfolding on the ballroom floor.

Turning to her, my eyes flashed with worry. "We need to find Camilla and Billy."

She pursed her lips and dipped her chin with resolve. "And we need to get rid of this one." She thumbed toward Silas, who had the gall to look affronted.

"I just saved your life," he protested.

"From flying champagne?" Becca scoffed. "She would've been fine."

"You're no match for—"

"Silas," I said, irritation rippling through every letter.

He turned to look at me, which gave Becca just enough time to lift the artfully displayed vase of wintry branches next to her and smash it on the back of his head.

Silas collapsed instantly back onto the floor.

Becca's proud smile lit up her whole face. "That oughta shut him up for a while. C'mon, let's go." She held out her hand and I took it, allowing her to help me up from the balcony floor.

Still strong as ever, Becca threw open one of the grand ballroom doors, allowing us to race outside into the hallway. We moved as quickly as I was able down several servants' hallways and flights of stairs until we reached the kitchens. My eyes scanned every face, begging for Camilla to be safe. *Please let nothing have happened to her. Please let her be okay. Please, please, please...*

"Evy?" The familiar smoky tone had me swaying with relief... or maybe that was the exhaustion. "Evy, what's wrong? What's happened?"

My eyes were sagging of their own accord. I'd reached the last of my apparent reserves. "I need...Nature." Panic shot up my spine.

I couldn't pass out. I couldn't let my magic go. I couldn't drop my shields. Liam, Ryker and Rafe all needed me. "Hurry, please."

Strong arms gathered me up, slinging my arm over a shoulder as the other wrapped around my waist.

"I've got ye, lass. Brace yerself now, we're headed outside."

CHAPTER 38

Ryker

"Ah. The two brothers of the conquering Penvarden line, exactly where they belong," Apep's voice sneered. "I think it's only fair to say the two of you have been separated for far too long. It seems a reunion is in order, don't you think?" Jutting out his jaw in my direction, the cronies behind him headed straight for my cell. "You still haven't had a chance to see my new *artwork,* Liam."

I didn't want Liam to see my face. I didn't want him to know what had been done to me, I didn't want him to see the monster I'd become.

Hiding in my little corner as though this spot could somehow protect me, I clenched my eyes shut, unwilling to witness Liam's face when he would see me for the first time since…

"My King, you may want to…" The guard's voice trailed off as he went to unlock my cell.

I knew what he saw. What my mysterious fairy saw the first time she visited and every time thereafter. The reason she reminded me so often that I wouldn't be here forever.

I cringed inwardly at the thought of Liam knowing my shame. Not only would he have to witness my ruined face, but now he'd know this shame, too.

A shallow groan echoed a few cells down, but this time Liam didn't call out Rafe's name. In those brief moments before Apep came down here, Liam's voice had been frantically trying to wake Rafe, trying to reassure me.

Do not give up, Ryker. Don't you dare give up.

His words echoed throughout my mind like someone calling into an abyss that never ended.

How disappointed was he going to be when he realized I already had. That I was already broken. That there was no fixing me now.

I'd chosen to stay, even when presented with a way out. And in a matter of seconds, Apep would know it too.

Apep's face appeared on the opposite side of my bars. "What is it?" His eyes scanned my cell, searching me, searching the darkened area, searching for the...

There.

They snagged on the hole in my lock.

The ominous orange light illuminated one side of his face, showcasing his delight as if it were dancing with the macabre shadows from the flame on the wall.

A sinister laugh, deep from within his belly, wound its way up and out of his lungs. He knocked his head back, roaring with amusement, adding yet one more nail to my nearly sealed coffin.

Swinging the door open, Apep stepped inside and crouched in front of me, his eyes swirling as he read my mind. I'd figured out his tell now.

"Such a sad little king, can't even leave his cage." He tsked. "Time to show your long-lost brother my handiwork." He turned, walking back out, motioning for his guards to pick me up. I was glad he wouldn't touch me himself, happy he felt I was too far beneath him for that.

Hands swooped under my armpits, but I refused to move with them, giving them my dead weight to lug out. If they wanted to torture me, they'd have to work for it.

"And I want that lock fixed," Apep sneered, "regardless of the fact the little king refuses to leave."

Liam sucked in a harsh breath. I knew it was him. I knew he'd be disappointed in me. I hated that he would be disappointed in me.

I missed him so much.

I'd imagined him rescuing me from this torment too many times…
But never like this.

Never with my shame so perfectly on display.

Before I was put on parade outside of Liam's cell, two more guards rushed into the area.

"Your Majesty!" The urgent and slightly dismayed voice echoed against the rough stone walls. "We have a situation upstairs."

Apep straightened the most imperceptible amount, his jaw ticking off to the side. "What's the situation?"

The guard cleared his throat, while the ones holding me paused mid-pull, dangling me by my armpits up in the air.

Delightful.

"The fairies at the ball, they're…well, fighting."

"Fighting?" Apep asked, dismayed.

"Yes, Your Majesty." He confirmed.

"Why is there fighting?" Apep's voice dropped low into an almost growl as he slithered out the words.

The guard gulped audibly. The movement and sound almost comically ridiculous. "The…the, uh, Princess, Your Majesty. Sh-she made a speech."

"A speech that turned everyone against each other?" Apep asked, incensed at the news.

"Yes, my King."

Apep sucked a deep breath in through his nose and paused, closing his eyes.

"You've only been deluding yourself into thinking you could control her." Liam's deep voice broke through the silence, resonating deep in his chest.

Apep looked down his nose at Liam's cell. "I sought to give her a fresh beginning."

"Ha!" Liam guffawed. "Is that what you tell yourself?"

I secretly loved that Liam was taunting Apep in such a way.

"You are a far bigger fool than I thought," Liam continued, "Apparently being able to read minds does not make you wise."

"You are the fool to antagonize me in such a way. That shield won't last forever," Apep's words dripped with warning. "And don't forget that your brother and friend have no such protections." Apep's dark wings flared out behind him in clear irritation. "Throw him back in his cell. He's not going anywhere. Then come with me."

Unceremoniously, I was tossed back into my cage. Bracing for the impact, I only allowed myself a small grunt of discomfort as my brittle flesh hit the hard surface and the door slammed shut behind me.

"Remember, if you try to leave," the guard swiveled his head toward the burning torch on the wall, "you'll get burned." He cackled his way out from the dungeon, the other guard joining merrily along with him.

With all of them gone, the silence was overwhelming.

I could hear the crackling of the fiery torch as if it were laughing at me now too. The pathetic king who couldn't leave his prison.

"Ryk?" Liam's tone was timid, concerned. "Are you okay?"

I couldn't answer.

He knew now.

Rafe knew too, if the lack of groaning was an indication he was actually awake now.

"Can you move?" Liam asked. His question was hesitant, searching. He wanted to know if the reason I wasn't leaving was because I was physically unable.

My heart ached at the thought of Liam being right next to me, having him listen to the abuse I'd received since I was first thrown in here that dreadful night. However many nights ago that was now.

Night.

Panic raced down my spine. My fairy would probably be visiting soon. A flare of red-hot jealousy pierced my overworked lungs. I realized in that moment I didn't want to share her. She'd been here for me, something I could have that was all my own while I wasted away in this darkness.

But that was the old Ryker talking again. The selfish Prince who wanted everything for himself.

"I will do whatever it takes to get you out of here." I hated hearing his strong voice so choked up. "I swear I will see an end to this nightmare. I'm so…I'm so sorry, Ryk." A gasping sob reflected sharply off the rugged slab walls that made up our dismal chambers.

"It's my fault." Rafe's voice was quiet. I think it was the first time I'd ever heard him speak so softly. "I should've been there that night, I should've…"

Still, I couldn't respond. Both of these men, the closest to me besides my father, blamed themselves. But it wasn't their doing, it was Apep's. Camilla's, even, for her betrayal that night.

I didn't want to talk about that night. I didn't want to even think about it.

"I finally understand." I spoke into the silence.

"What?" Liam's voice was gravelly with grief and confusion.

"Why you were so upset," I offered.

The heavy sound of his silence weighed upon the air.

"You were always there for me."

"You're my brother." He responded so fast it made my heart ache even more.

"And you're mine." I paused thoughtfully. "But I should've listened. I should've backed down."

Liam let out a harsh breath, but didn't deny it.

"Do you think she'll ever forgive me?"

"Ryk…" His voice was choked again.

Rafe jumped in then. "As much as I love the heartfelt brotherly talk, we need to get out of here. Any ideas?"

"I hope you leave me here." When I spoke the words, they sounded like a sullen little brat.

Pathetic.

"Well, that's obviously not happening," Rafe responded just as Liam said, "Don't start talking like that."

"Start?" A maniacal laugh escaped my lungs. "How long have I been here? Don't answer that. I don't want to know."

Liam's next huff was angrier. "I'll make him pay, Ryker. I'll make sure he can never hurt you or anyone else again."

I let out a humorless laugh through my nose. "It doesn't matter. I'm not a king anymore." I tightened my arms around my knees. "And you're not a prince."

"You are still the King." He spoke with such confidence.

How can he have such confidence in me after all this? I asked.

Because he hasn't seen you yet, I answered.

Soft, slippered feet shuffled steadily toward us.

"He's right, you know."

I closed my eyes, allowing her sultry voice to echo inside of my mind.

"You are King, and you're getting out of here tonight." She spoke much quieter the second time around, slipping me my water first and then each individual item afterward.

Turning away from my cell, she faced Liam's bars, still handing items of food to me. I felt that twinge of jealousy pop up again. Already I was having to share her, and already I hated it.

"I can't believe you boys got yourselves caught like this," she softly chastised.

"Nice to see you too, Camilla," Rafe drawled.

Her hand froze between the bars, holding half a loaf of bread out to me.

Camilla? Evelyn's step-sister Camilla? The one who...

"No," I whispered.

She dropped the bread then and snatched her hand back quickly when I moved to grab her. Scuttling towards the bars, I allowed my eyes to see her for the first time.

"You?"

The question fell from my lips as I stared at her, slack-jawed in disbelief.

But there she was.

Her long dark hair, nearly black in this darkness, had been untucked from the bun I was used to seeing her in as a maid. The severe, straight cut of hair across her forehead had grown out longer now. It was softer, framing her face with gentle edges.

Her dark eyes glimmered in the firelight, swimming with fearful regret. Her flawless pale skin practically glowed in the dim light. The wings behind her, gone.

Another lie.

I hated her.

I hated her perfect mouth, stuck in a fearful shock.

I hated her desperate eyes searching mine.

I hated her eerie beauty in this darkness.

I could feel it then.

The anger.

That fiery savagery that had me accosting my very own bedroom. Smashing everything in sight, including my own face.

That burning rage I'd felt when I saw Evelyn's blank stare and Apep's hand on her that fateful night.

That blazing wrath when I'd realized we'd been betrayed, when I'd heard Camilla's voice in the background.

You promised you wouldn't hurt him.

The voice was finally clear in my mind.

"You dared to come visit me?" I seethed. "You thought you could bring me hope? Bring my food like some divine paragon? You lying, traitorous—"

"It's not like that, brother," Liam jumped in.

"She betrayed us!" I yelled, swinging the door open so I could see her more fully. "You were in the room. You handed me over to him." I stood up then, stepping out of my cage to tower over her, allowing her to see all that she had done and caused.

"It is by the mercy of Evelyn alone that this wretch is still alive." I spoke to Liam, but my focus remained on her.

She winced. I didn't care.

"How dare you come to visit me here! How dare you pretend to befriend me!" I raged. "Do you report back to him? Do you tell him what excellent work he's done bringing the infamous rogue prince low? Making him grovel at your feet for scraps?"

"No," she whispered as tears gathered in her eyes, making them glimmer in the firelight. "I didn't know…he promised you wouldn't be—"

"Disfigured? Tortured? Used against the one woman you claimed to care about?" My new permanently rasping tone rose in volume every time I spoke to her, making the grating, guttural sound of my ruined vocal chords even more evident.

Her chin trembled slightly. "I didn't mean for any of this to—"

"Does she even know you're here?" I interrupted her again. "She did her best to save you from certain death, and you insult her by showing up again—and not only that, but you brought them with you, didn't you?" I pointed at Liam's cell.

"Ryker," Liam rebuked, but I ignored him entirely.

"My *own* brother?" I was teeming with anger now that it had finally been unleashed again. "How do you think he'll use him against her? Use *us* against each other?" I paused before adding, "You see now what he's done to me. What do you think he'll do to the man Evelyn truly loves? To the man who is *my* brother?"

"I swear to you, I'm only trying to help." Tears flowed down her beautiful cheeks. I hated her for her contriteness, her stupidity for coming back here, her hauntingly beautiful face.

I scoffed. "Help? It should be *you* in there instead." I pointed at my cell as she drew in a harsh breath.

"Enough, Ryker. You're drawing attention." Liam's firm words effectively calming my overwrought senses, I looked up. Sure enough, a guard was coming our way.

I had no way to stop him, no way to—

Water suddenly careened around his body, floating and twisting through the air like a transparent snake until it choked the guard, sending him to an odd watery grave as the liquid filled his lungs.

I wanted to laugh.

It was quite obviously the wrong emotion, but watching the terror and recognition of death light up that guard's face was remarkably satisfying.

After everything they'd done to me, I found the disturbing scene to be oddly cathartic.

There is something truly wrong with me.

As the guard fell, a man stood behind him. His eyes darted to Camilla first and then hardened before they looked back at me. "She's here to help ye, ye dolt. She risked her life to make sure she could get to ye, to get ye food, to make sure ye were looked after until we could get ye out. The least ye could do now is be grateful."

He stood in front of me, not even flinching at the sight of my face as he offered to help Camilla up off the floor. Maybe it was because he hadn't seen me before. Or maybe he was just used to looking at hideous creatures.

After he helped Camilla up, he turned back to the stairs and whisper-hollered, "Coast is clear!"

Rage still rushed through my veins, gifting me with an exhilarated energy I hadn't felt in weeks.

I liked it, this temper.

I liked spitting out wrath with my words.

I liked the small amount of power that flushed through my body when I acted on impulse.

I liked looking down on someone who had wronged me.

Looking down...

I froze.

To have gotten that close to Camilla, no bars between us...

That was when I realized I was standing outside my cell.

I was *standing outside* of my cell.

Before I could reckon much with that, Evelyn and Becca came barreling down the stairs.

"Be quick about it, lass. We haven't much time." The stranger spoke to Evelyn like they knew each other.

"Rafe!" Becca cried, racing toward his cell, her arms reaching through the bars.

"I'm here. I'm okay." He reached out his hands to grip her wrists.

Evelyn didn't miss a beat. I had to blink several times, because she looked like a queen. Her shoulders were back, her head was high, and her expression was determined.

The turquoise gown she wore swayed around her on phantom breezes. Even without wings, she looked as though she was flying through the air.

"Let me get him out of there, and then you can check each other for injuries." She smirked slightly, but it didn't really reach her eyes. "Rafe, move away from the bars to the far side." She waited. She looked exhausted, but energized. Not a physical exhaustion; more like the weight of the world was on her shoulders.

As soon as Becca backed away, her hands were in front of Rafe's lock, her eyes focused as she directed a small stream of magic straight through the lock. The magic was breathtaking to watch, and blinding, as I rubbed away the spots dancing in my eyes.

She moved to Liam's cell next. He had already moved out of the way, and though I couldn't see his expression, I imagined it mirrored my awe. The minute the hole was there, Liam was out, gripping Evelyn in his arms.

Then they both turned to me.

I stiffened as Liam's limbs froze. His eyes glued to my face. I self-consciously reached up to cover my burn scars. For some reason, having him see them was far harder than anyone else.

"Ryk…"

Tears shone in his eyes ,and mine smarted in return. In less than a step, he was on me. His arms wrapped around me, clutching me so tightly I could hardly breathe. But I couldn't even mind it as I clutched him back. Gripping at his clothes as if holding onto them would somehow keep him with me.

"I never thought I'd see you again," I whispered.

His body shuddered. "Please forgive me."

I let out a half-sob. It still didn't feel real. "Only if you forgive me."

His sad chuckle reverberated through my chest. "Done."

"Done," I repeated back, squeezing him a little tighter.

Then my eyes landed on Camilla, whose beguiling dark eyes watched with glimmering tears edging along the surface. She watched as though she had the right to grieve or celebrate with us. I glared back at her and she balked, taking a step back. No one else noticed our little exchange, and I was glad of it.

Liam stepped away, clapping me on the shoulder and giving instructions on getting out of here. He squeezed my shoulder before letting go and leading our group out of the dungeons.

Evelyn reached for my hand hesitantly. There was fresh dirt under her fingernails, as though she'd just come straight here from digging in the ground. When I looked up, her bright green eyes were watchful and wary of my reaction.

She didn't deserve my ire. So I offered her an almost-smile with a nod, while internally I nursed the anger rising back up to the surface, giving it room to simmer as I took Evelyn's hand gently and stared daggers at Camilla's back.

Becca and Rafe followed behind Evelyn and I with Billy taking a lead alongside Liam. I realized in that moment that we were truly leaving. I was getting out of here. That for the first time in…well, I wasn't sure how long…I'd breathe fresh air again.

I trembled with the now-familiar fear every time we passed a torch, and Evelyn squeezed my hand each time.

She understood this kind of fear, the kind that kept tormenting you long after the original pain. Looking back at me, she offered me an encouraging smile as we wound our way up the stairs.

I didn't deserve that smile.

I didn't deserve to breathe fresh air, let alone walk outside among the living. I was barely a man now. Apep and his goons had succeeded in turning me into a broken creature of fear, but maybe, just maybe, I could instead become a creature to be feared instead of one cowering in the darkness.

I liked the sound of that.

My rage hungered for more of it.

I smirked to myself for the first time since the night Apep had tried to make me into a monster, but instead of fighting it, I decided to embrace it.

They wanted a monster? I'd give them a monster.

CHAPTER 39

Camilla

I sucked in sharp breaths as we rounded the hall that led outside. Liam signaled for us to wait, and Billy went ahead to make sure the coast was clear.

Leaning against the nearest wall, I allowed the cold stone to jolt my senses as I clutched my trembling hand to my chest, trying to breathe through the pain of it all. But Ryker's words kept echoing in my mind.

You lying, traitorous…

His anger was so much worse than I could've anticipated. I'd never seen those beautiful pale blue eyes hold so much fury.

You were in the room. You handed me over to him.

I sucked in the ragged sob that tried to escape my lungs. I'd betrayed him again. I knew I should've told him who I was. But I couldn't do it, I couldn't make everything worse for him just so I didn't have to endure his hatred later. He'd needed hope, so I gave him someone who could bring him hope.

But now I missed it. I missed our conversations, the way he'd slowly opened up to me, trusting me a little more each night. I missed that I could be honest back, that I could share with him my true opinions and thoughts without worry. I missed being the girl he looked forward to seeing, the one who brought him hope and joy. I didn't mean to be so selfish, but it had been so nice to have these special moments all to ourselves.

And now, he hated me.

The grief of the moment clung to me like a second skin. As much as I wanted to escape it, I deserved it. I deserved his wrath.

My head hung low as my chest still rose and fell rapidly, my stomach roiling with horror.

"Camilla?" Billy's voice sounded next to me. His warm hand tugged gently on my upper arm. "We have to hurry, lass, we can't risk bein' caught."

My head swiveled from side to side as I realized everyone else had already left. I'd been so lost in my thoughts, I hadn't even noticed.

Reluctantly pulling away from the wall, I silently followed behind Billy, grateful that he'd remembered me. I couldn't lose myself like that again, lest I get left behind entirely.

Billy sucked in fast breaths as we rushed outside before murmuring, mostly to himself, "Hopefully, we find Ian and Chrissy quickly."

"I'm so sorry Billy. All of this is my fault," I stated it quietly. "It's because of my betrayal…"

He stopped and looked me straight in the eye, his hands on my shoulders. His eyes with the deep laugh lines at the corners were so serious as he whispered into the quiet night: "What's done is done. Ye cannot control how people react or what they think of ye, all ye can do now is move forward."

I couldn't help but think he spoke from experience as I nodded reluctantly, my chin quivering slightly.

Why was he so nice to me?

His eyes searched mine, and it was as if he could tell exactly what I needed as he tugged me into a hug. "Ye have the heart of a storm, lass." Pulling away, he gave me a stern look. "Use it."

My heart stuttered in my chest as a flash of warmth slowly spread out from deep within my soul. No one had ever said something so kind about me. Did he really see me like that?

Just up ahead, the thud of flesh hitting flesh grabbed our attention, but before we could turn around I was yanked from Billy's hold with a hand around my throat.

"Don't even think about it." The hand on my neck gripped tighter, pulling me harshly against a solid, unforgiving body. "Come nice and easy now, and the girl won't get hurt."

Billy nodded as another guard came up behind him, pulling his hands behind his back as he locked iron cuffs around his wrists. Billy hissed through his teeth, and I tried to swallow, but it was impeded by the tight grasp around my throat.

We were led back into the palace, one hand clutching my arm pulling it taught against my back, the other still grasping my neck.

I hated myself for it, but I couldn't help the small whimper that escaped me.

"Thought you could fool us, Beauty?" The guard's hot breath whispered against my neck. "Apep told us who you really are, and you'll find we don't take kindly to deceptive humans." He paused, sniffing up the side of my neck in a way that made me shudder and attempt to pull away, but his hold remained firm, "No matter how pretty they are."

CHAPTER 40

Liam

We were just about to the hidden back gate that was mostly used for deliveries, outside of the palace, when I stopped to listen for the footsteps of patrolling guards.

Tilting my head to the side, I rotated my head back and forth listening carefully, but all I heard was the light wind fluttering through the branches.

Relieved, I looked behind me to check on our group. Evy's eyes were worried; she clung to Ryker's hand with white knuckles, though he didn't even seem to notice. I gave her an encouraging nod before scanning Ryker from head to toe.

His light blue eyes nearly glowed in the darkness—they were so much paler than when I'd seen him last. No doubt having adjusted to the near-complete darkness that had been his living nightmare for the past month. More than a month. I grimaced and ground my teeth. His entire countenance was beyond terrified; his body trembled, his limbs were taut, and his head swung back and forth, constantly looking for a threat.

Apep had truly tormented him. He'd tormented my brother and best friend and the woman I loved. Lightning-fast fury zipped down my spine, settling deep in my stomach like a raging inferno. After I got them out of here, I would figure out a way to avenge them both. Apep would die by my hand. I wouldn't settle for anything less.

Rafe had his arm wrapped around Becca, holding her so close I wondered how they were able to move. Both of them looked at me expectantly, waiting for the go-ahead. Billy and Camilla were a ways behind still, seemingly having a moment.

We didn't have time to waste, but I trusted Billy to know that.

Turning back, I peered around the gate, checking one way and then...a thud, followed by a force that moved my head. Before I could fully register what was happening, my arms were wrenched behind me, followed by the cool clink of metal shackles.

I felt none of it, with Evy's shield still surrounding me, but at least I'd finally figured out what was happening. Without a second thought, I jerked my head back and tried to head-butt the figure behind me.

"Don't even try it, human," the male hissed.

Evy's startled scream froze my body before I could even attempt to turn around and see her. More thuds and grunts of fists hitting flesh followed by clanging metal rang out behind me.

"Come with us nice and easy now, or we'll have to do worse," the voice behind me threatened.

I obeyed, huffing out a frustrated breath, knowing I would be of next to no help if I wasted all my energy now. It was strange having my arms restrained behind me but not being able to feel the actual restraints.

We were marched back inside, and I had to suffer watching my friends and family be manhandled by these bastards without being able to do a thing about it. Every trip, smack, push and falter grated slowly at my insides, stirring the inferno already raging inside me.

Evy remained untouched, but four guards surrounded her effectively blocked her off from our group.

Ryker could barely move, so caught up in his fear his limbs had locked down. I wanted so badly to help him, to lift him up and to kill the fairy who kept shoving him forward. If given the chance, that one would die first.

After a few more turns, I realized quickly our destination was the throne room. I watched Evy's shoulders rise and seize up when she realized the same thing. I could only imagine the horror she was reliving.

Surveying the rest of our group, I gritted my teeth as Rafe's blood dribbled down the side of his face from his temple. His arms were wrenched back behind his back just like mine, but his eyes were trained on Becca. He kept speaking to her, but she was slung over a shoulder, head bouncing as the guard walked her unconscious body down the white halls.

They must've put up a fight.

Billy's shoulders were folded forward, and his brow dripped with sweat as if every step exhausted him to his core. I couldn't understand what would cause him to be so tired. Perhaps he put up too good of a fight and wore out all his energy trying to protect Camilla.

Camilla was being roughened up by a guard with a sick look in his eyes, one that gave far too much away. Apep really did know how to pick them.

Entering the sweeping circular throne room was far less appealing when Apep sat on the throne. Many guards—perhaps all of them—and several additional fairies were all gathered inside, awaiting our arrival. I looked beyond them all, glaring hard at the usurper who'd made this all happen. I hoped that even though he couldn't tune into my violent thoughts, he would know them by the look in my eyes. But his eyes were widened in a state of shock as they rested on Evy and Evy alone.

Our group was brought to the front of the dais.

Apep sat on the throne, mere steps away up on the dais. His lips tipped up in disgust as he surveyed the line of us.

"Kneel," he called out, and when none of us moved, the guards behind us made sure to help us down, painfully.

Except I couldn't feel any of it, and…

"Not her."

Apep's voice rang out, and immediately the guard's arm behind Evy dropped away and he jerkily stepped back. Clearly not of his own accord.

"Princess Evelyn, take your seat." Apep gestured to the throne next to his. The gilded seats, framed by tall pillars and a rounded ceiling, made for an incredibly imposing scene from this lowered viewpoint.

I officially understood now how intimidating this position was. "You shall judge with me tonight."

Evy jutted out her jaw in defiance, refusing to move.

"If that is the case, then I speak for all of these kneeling in front of you now and declare them innocent of all charges," she declared.

Apep shook his head. "You think it's that easy?" He smiled, but it was a cruel look, one full of arrogance and certainty.

In the next moment, agonized cries sounded next to me. I watched on in horror as all my friends, including Ryker, collapsed to the floor, writhing in pain.

"No!" I screamed, but I couldn't tell if any sound had come out or not. My throat felt raw and my limbs spasmed as they tried to move, but I could do nothing. I could do nothing but hope and pray that it would be over soon.

I opened my mouth to scream at Apep again, but the words were cut as short as the screams surrounding me.

Turning my head, I saw Rafe moving just as slowly as I was, his worried stare on Becca, who was just now beginning to stir again. His nose dripped crimson alongside the wound on the side of his head from earlier, and Billy was no better. Camilla's nose dripped blood too, but she didn't even seem to notice; her eyes were glued entirely to Ryker's rocking body. His eyes were clenched tight and his face was tucked between his knees as he rocked back and forth in silent torment.

Looking back up the steps, I searched out Apep's gaze to try and assess what was next for us, but his swirling black and white eyes were locked on the one standing next to me.

From my kneeling position at the foot of the dais, I saw the mud stains on her slippers and the hem of her beautiful turquoise gown as it moved of its own accord on a phantom breeze. But more importantly, I saw Evy's hand. It was held out in front of her as tears streamed down her stunning face. Her eyes were red and puffy, but there was an anger there I'd never witnessed before.

She was the fiercest warrior I'd ever seen.

A hazy, iridescent glimmer surrounded us. Beautiful and startling all at the same time.

"You cannot protect them forever, Evelyn." Apep's frustrated voice reverberated against the walls.

"Then I will die trying." Evy's words were a dark promise. She meant what she said as she held Apep's gaze, steady and controlled.

A true Queen.

She had found her hill to die upon, and she wouldn't withdraw, no matter what happened to her.

"Enough!" A familiar feminine voice rang out from behind the wall of people. I slowly turned to see wild white and grey hair float in on pearlescent wings. Her green eyes were fierce, but purpled half-moons still framed her bright gaze.

Ian floated in behind her, carrying with him two swords. One that I knew like the back of my hand.

A startled choke came from behind as I watched Apep's expression pale and slacken into one of utter bewilderment. The entire room held a palpable silence as we all waited to see what we were obviously missing.

"How could it…" Apep trailed off, "but you…"

Swinging my head back around, I watched Chrissy's face falter as it trembled slightly, but she steeled herself before she said, "Hello, son."

CHAPTER 41

Evelyn

Stunned, my shield faltered as I turned to look back at my grandmother.

Son?

The word reverberated around in my mind until it felt foreign.

What? How?

"You died." Apep's voice was so low and quiet I could barely hear him speak. "I watched you die."

"Nearly." Chrissy's broken voice sounded again. "Ian found me."

Apep's eyes darted to the man standing beside her. I didn't recognize his face, in fact nothing about him was particularly familiar, but the intense look in his eye as he beheld Apep was nothing short of menacing. It was obvious that if Apep so much as flinched toward Chrissy, he would retaliate.

Did this male love my Grandmother? Who was he to her? To Apep? And did that mean that Apep and I truly were related?

My mind swirled with so many questions I couldn't keep asking or trying to understand. If I did, I'd lose the shield protecting the people I loved most, and I couldn't let that happen.

Apep didn't say another word. He stumbled backward to sit on his throne in stunned silence.

The fairies littering the throne room were equally as shocked and confused. Apep's guards had been moving in to intercept Chrissy when she entered the fray, but with this new revelation, it was clear they didn't know how to proceed.

Neither did I.

"Grandmother?" I questioned. Shock and confusion furrowed my brow.

The male next to her, Ian, looked at me then, his eyes instantaneously softening. He knew who I was, then. I shouldn't have been surprised, but I couldn't wrap my mind around...

"I'm so sorry, dearie. I couldn't tell you." Her green eyes glazed over with fresh tears as she looked at me. The deeply grooved lines framing her eyes were shadowed and more pronounced, as was the exhaustion that mired her face.

"Couldn't tell her?" Apep rose from his throne again, his shock wearing away to incensed rage. Stalking toward the edge of the elevated dais, he cut his finger toward her in accusation. "What about me? Why did you never come to me? Why did you not tell me you were still alive?" His voice choked at the end, and my heart broke.

For the first time since I'd met Apep, I saw the lost little boy that he was. Forever fighting an endless battle to bring his family back, to protect them where he'd failed so long ago.

"I couldn't come to you. It was part of the agreement I made." Chrissy's wings slowly lowered her feet to the ground and then tucked behind her.

Apep shook his head back and forth in total bewilderment, questions and confusion darkening his eyes.

Chrissy swallowed, sucking in a deep breath. "I made a deal to spare your life," she began. "A deal with...the Penvarden king."

Apep's entire body sharpened. Ragged breaths sawed in and out of his lungs.

Chrissy continued, "You were just a boy. *My* boy..." Her breaths stuttered. "And I'd already lost your sister and father."

Apep shook his head violently back and forth, his rage and disillusionment coiling up his magic into a palpable force you could feel hanging in the air.

"I wanted to keep you safe and alive, so I…"

"You did this to me." Each word was spoken like a dagger being thrown. Every syllable held accusation.

Chrissy shuddered. "I did what I had to."

"You were my mother." Apep's voice pinched.

"I still am," she whispered, emotion choking her own voice.

Apep frowned harshly, the lines around his mouth deepening as his eyes glowed in a swirl of light and dark.

"You sided with the humans," he seethed. The current of his barely controlled magic had several of the fairies in attendance cowering away. "You supported those who tortured and murdered your own daughter, your husband, me!"

Chrissy steadied her jaw as Ian reached out to grasp her hand, intertwining his fingers with hers. "I did what I felt was necessary to help the good of everyone."

"*You betrayed me!*"

Apep's voice resounded in my mind as if he'd yelled directly into my ear. I clutched at my ears, falling to the ground in the same way everyone else in the entire throne room fell to the ground, grasping their heads.

My shields all shattered, including the one I always kept around my mind, as a warm sticky substance coated the palm of my hand.

"Evy?" Liam scooted awkwardly on his knees toward me with his hands bound behind his back. "Evy, look at me," he demanded.

I blinked my eyes open, not having realized that I'd closed them.

"Can you hear me?" he questioned quietly.

I nodded, fearing that if I spoke now, nothing would come out anyway.

"I made a choice, Apep. The hardest one I ever had to make," Chrissy whispered. Sorrow etched through every syllable. "You were out of control, but you were still my son. I gave you a chance to start fresh. I gave you the chance to live!" Chrissy's despair broke her voice.

"So you helped the human tyrants gain their throne. You helped them use me all of these years? You cursed me!" Apep yelled, his eyes livid with resentful rage.

"Do you take none of the blame?" Chrissy challenged. "You started the war. You forced the humans to rise up against us. You killed indiscriminately, taking even the youngest of children from their futures."

"Because they don't deserve to live!" Apep shouted. Most of the crowd had regained their footing, standing once again, but they'd also distanced themselves significantly from Chrissy and Ian, creating a small semi-circle around the pair.

And that was when I saw them. Tiny jasmine flowers pinned to tunics and cloaks. Scattered across the room. Jasmine flowers, like Jada had signed her letter with.

Princess Jada's symbol.

I made eye contact with a man who gave me the subtlest nod in return. They were here. They'd come after all! They...

Suddenly a shadow loomed over me, I had yet to get to my feet as Apep crouched before me, brushing something away from underneath my ear. His eyes searched mine, taking stock as he contemplated this revelation. "I didn't think it possible. I thought your eyes were a sign, but I never imagined..." He smiled, but the expression froze me in place. There was no love there, no joy, no compassion. The look in his eye was pure possession. As if officially being related had given him some kind of ownership over me. "Looks like you're family after all."

Apep stood, still towering above me as he faced Chrissy again. "You shouldn't have come here and revealed yourself to me." His voice was back to his elongated, menacing tone. Ian moved protectively in front of Chrissy. "My mother died long ago."

The gleam in his eye was filled with violence.

I started to stand, dread filling my stomach with bile.

"Apep, no." I reached out for him, but he didn't acknowledge me as his eyes whirled in furious intensity.

My head swung back to see Ian trying to pull Chrissy, but she stood her ground, staring Apep down.

"I loved you. I've always loved you." She spoke softly, but the look in her eye told me what was coming. She knew. She'd always known what Apep's reaction was going to be, and I couldn't bear it. I couldn't let it happen.

Her eyes darted to me. "I love you, my sweet Evelyn. I'm sorry for all I've kept from you." Tears ran down her face. Sorrow filling every wrinkle, every breath, every heartbeat.

I couldn't say goodbye, because that was what this was. Her goodbye. I'd only just found her. I'd only been given the chance to know her for such a short amount of time. I pivoted, facing Apep again, this time speaking with more force. "Apep, no. You can't."

Apep's eyes flashed with something like regret. Whatever it was, I knew I'd run out of time, and there was nothing left to lose anyway. The moment his face stilled with resolve, I removed my shield.

His body reacted violently, immediately seeking out Ryker and Liam as he screamed in significant pain, clearly fighting the curse this time instead of giving into it.

Wasting no time, I helped Liam stand, holding the iron chain that tied his cuffs together as I sent a small burst of magic through it, severing the chain entirely in half.

He jumped into action, finding Ian with his next breath and grabbing the sword in his hand. I moved down the line as Apep wailed in the background, pain and fury lacing his every cry.

Snapping Rafe and then Becca and then Billy's chains next, I tried to move on, but Billy didn't move. His chest beat in and out in rapid succession.

"Billy, what's wrong, what's happened?" I looked him over, searching for an injury.

"It's the iron." The fairy named Ian crouched next to me. Chrissy was hovering nearby, but there wasn't time to ask questions. Billy looked as if he was dying. "It poisons full-blooded fairies." The shocking revelation made me cringe.

"I don't know how to get them off," I said in a panic, and Ian looked at me as if I'd just said the stupidest thing. "I mean, I've never used my magic so close to a limb or even skin like that. I'm afraid I'll just injure him more."

Liam bellowed in agony as he clutched his head, and I realized I hadn't put a shield around him again. Turning from Ian and Billy, my eyes caught on the blood dripping from Apep's nose. His eyes were alight with a swirling rage as he focused all of his energy on Liam. Fighting suddenly broke out around us as the Terreno soldiers I'd seen hidden in the crowd quickly began cutting down Apep's guards. Confusion and turmoil cluttered the room as Liam fell to his knees in sheer agony.

With hardly a thought, I sent my shield around him, conforming to all of his edges and curves with ease. He sat back on his heels, breathing heavily as he looked over at me with worried eyes.

"Behind you!" I cried out and pointed to the guard swinging his sword at Liam's neck. I knew it wouldn't reach his skin, but the action still terrified me.

"Evelyn." Ian's voice was strong and calm, bringing my back to Billy. "Please try." He gave a pointed look down at Billy before standing and brandishing his own sword.

Chrissy took his place, momentarily guiding me through the process. "Remember to focus on the intention with your magic. Let it know exactly what you want." She reached out to cup my cheek. "You are so brave and strong. I love you, and I'm sorry."

With that, she leapt back up, and I realized pure chaos had erupted in the throne room. Grunts and cries echoed throughout the space, and I struggled to focus as I looked back down at Billy. "I'm so sorry if I hurt you. I promise I will do my best." I tried to encourage him, but my hands shook as I grasped one of his shackles in my hand, channeling my magic only into the metal itself. Such a fine, thin target. It terrified me.

Taking in a deep breath, I exhaled and let the smallest burst of magic through. The cut through the cuff was clean, as was the skin underneath it.

I sighed in relief and turned the cuff to complete the action on the opposite side, relishing the clanging sound of metal hitting marble.

Eagerly, I reached for his next cuff just as the swing of a blade barely missed our necks, and Billy rolled us to the side. One of the Terreno soldiers headed our way, but Liam was there, his sword and strength the barrier between the offending blade and our skin.

Trusting in Liam's strength, I gripped the second cuff, completing the same actions in no time at all. The minute Billy was free, color returned to his cheeks and his breaths slowed. He raised his arms up and began wielding his own magic.

I looked up to find Chrissy in celebration, but I couldn't see her in the mess of colliding bodies and magic.

Fire flew overhead and Ryker cried out next to me, clutching the marble stone as if it was his lifeline. Camilla flung her body over his in a show of protection I'd never seen from her before, and I instantly threw up a shield guarding us from the sweeping blast of heat.

I moved to Camilla's shackles first, breaking them apart as I heard her whisper in Ryker's ear, "You're not alone anymore."

She moved enough for me to gain access to Ryker's cuffs next, and I repeated the actions, completely removing them without even an inch of skin being tarnished.

This was what Chrissy had been trying to teach me for so long. My magic would do as I intended, but I had to control its output.

It was a liberating feeling.

Keeping my new shield around the three of us, I saw Rafe doing his best to fend off one of Apep's guards, but he was also trying to shield a helpless Becca in the process, and that just wasn't working.

I called out to them, and the minute Rafe's eyes connected with mine, he shoved Becca toward me. I made sure she was behind me, next to Camilla and Ryker as I watched Rafe swing his borrowed sword, slashing at whatever stood in his path until he made his way to Liam's side.

Searching the crowd for Chrissy and Ian, I found them in the middle of the mayhem. Chrissy's eyes met mine, and I waved for her and Ian to make their way to me.

I couldn't shield everyone individually, but I could make a big enough shield to protect them if they got close enough. The magic flaring around us and anguished cries punctuated the madness of the moment.

I couldn't believe what I was witnessing.

My eyes had darted away from Chrissy's for only a moment. One single breath of time. But when I looked back again, Chrissy's eyes were flared wide, and a horrifying scream rent from her lungs as though it had been brutally pulled from her. Her limbs buckled and her body collapsed; Ian only barely caught her before she hit the ground.

I swung my eyes back behind me to the dais, where Apep stood on shaky legs. His nose was bleeding profusely, his face was sunken in, and his limbs shook as though they were physically unable to move. But still, I saw the gleam of triumph in his eyes.

His focus was solely on Chrissy. My grandmother, his mother.

"Apep, no!" I screamed, but he didn't seem to hear me.

My head pounded and the dizzying fatigue I'd felt earlier came back with a vengeance, but I sent a bubbled shield around Chrissy and Ian. Rafe cried out as fire scalded his side, and my limbs shook as the fire-wielding fairy took aim at him again.

A wall of water doused his second attempt, but he'd been ready. His molten eyes locked onto something behind me, and I looked back to see Ryker's pale face. Camilla held him to her, whispering whatever encouragement she could as he shook and shivered in her embrace.

Turning back, I realized...this was the fairy who'd hurt him. This was the monster who'd burned and tortured Ryker.

A bitter wrath welled up, blistering my insides as it traveled up from my stomach, scorching my throat as I released the shield in front of me and instead gathered all of my magic into the palm of my hands.

His hateful eyes latched onto mine as he grew a ball of fire in his palm. Billy's water soaked him from the side, but his focus remained on me and then darted to Ryker again, a sinister smile forming on his face.

That look would be forever frozen in time as I clapped my hands together, sending my sharp, raw magic vertically towards him.

In one instant, one second of time, he'd been whole, his eyes gleaming with a look of sheer satisfaction clouding his features.

The next, he was split open, two halves of one whole cut entirely apart.

The room fell silent again as I realized what I'd done.

I felt nothing. No magic. No emotion. No...

"Evy?" Liam's voice was what hit me next. He was standing in front of me. His hands on my shoulders. "It's okay, Evy. Just breathe. It's okay."

Was I not breathing?

Well done, Evelyn.

The slithering voice snaked through my mind.

Apep? I spoke inside my mind.

I'm here.

What did I just do? How could I...I-I'm so...

It was beautiful vengeance, my young Evelyn. Come. The command was clear and final. *Come join me. I'm here, Evelyn. We're family.*

My legs moved of their own accord. Liam tried to hold on, but I couldn't stand there anymore. I had to move. I had to…

That's it, my girl. Come to me. Let us finish this.

Apep's hand reached out, and mine sank into his. He pulled me close and wrapped his arms around me, holding me to him.

Let me shield you now.

A gentle numbing sensation flooded my brain, making everything feel woozy and disoriented. Panicked cries sounded in the distance, but I paid them no mind. My eyes focused instead on Apep, who looked back at me with all the love and care I would ever need.

Use your shield now, Evelyn. Guard us from harm.

Instantly my shield went up just as a sword arched through the air. I glanced ahead of me to see Liam swinging wildly at my shield. His frightened and angry eyes bored into me, his voice screaming words I couldn't comprehend.

I am sorry for what I must do next, young Evelyn. You may watch or cover your eyes.

Not entirely understanding, I looked back at him, then followed his gaze outward.

Grandmother Chrissy stood there, her horrified expression alerted me that something was terribly wrong, but it was like wading through tree sap to try and figure out what was happening now.

I watched as her mouth opened in a silent scream.

No.

I watched as her beautiful green eyes that matched mine bulged unnaturally.

No.

I watched as her knees slammed against the stained white marble floor.

NO.

I watched as her eyes darted from Apep to me, and a lone tear ran down her cheek.

NO!

Magic burst through me, white and blinding, sending everyone to the ground with its force as I wrenched my hand from Apep's and rushed through the sea of prone bodies to my grandmother, gathering her slim form in my arms and bringing her to my lap.

"Grandmother?" I cried. "Grandmother, please!" I cried harder. "Grandmother Chrissy!" I shook her body, willing her to somehow still be there. To just look up at me. *Please look at me.*

She could've been sleeping.

Her face was no longer agonized, but instead there was a sereneness to it. Her eyes were closed and calm. Her skin was still warm.

Gentle arms wrapped around my shoulder. Hands tried to pull her away.

"No!"

Warm, tender eyes met mine. They were bloodshot and swollen. "We need to go, Evelyn. Your friends are still in danger, lass."

"But my grandmother…" My voice trailed as my jaw quivered.

"She's gone."

"No." My arms shook, and my head couldn't accept it. More hands reached for me. Sympathetic glances and tearful eyes.

"We need to go now, love. Let her go."

"I can't." I whispered.

His calloused hands wrapped around mine, gently prying my fingers from Chrissy's slack body. "I've got ye, lass. We'll do this together."

Reluctantly, I let him gather up my hands and pull me away.

CHAPTER 42

Apep

Evelyn's power never ceased to amaze me. She had leveled the entire throne room with her powerful magic. Magic my own mother passed down to her.

Those were my first thoughts as I blinked my eyes back open and stared up at Liam's furious face, the tip of his sword aimed directly at my chest. He had entertained me endlessly with his threatening thoughts, but out of the many ways he'd thought to kill me, this was the least inventive of them all, albeit the most predictable.

I did always love that righteous anger that poured out from him. His fury tasted delicious to my mind.

My wind guard blew him across the dais, landing with a thud as I righted myself. Unamused that the throne room was once again in chaos, I could hardly offer it another glance, because Evelyn was trying to escape. Her hands were stretched out protectively, forming a lovely glimmering wall of magic between me and her.

Her entrancing green eyes glowed softly, but her nose bled from the powerful magic overloading her fragile human body. The magic would eat her up sooner than it would continue to help. Her gaze snagged on mine, and the thrill of seeing her fire so present sent a thrill of delight through my limbs. She was so much like Sera. So much like…my mother.

Behind her, Ryker and Camilla disappeared into the secret tunnel. I sneered at the coward pulling Evelyn's stepsister behind him. That boy was never fit to rule a kingdom. His mother and father had spoiled him rotten, making him as selfish and self-seeking as his forefathers. It was only fitting that he snuck off now, leaving the rest to fight his battles for him. I would miss his peppery rage and anguish. Torturing him was like drinking a fine wine; his immense emotions calmed my own, giving them some much-needed rest.

My eyes drifted over the fallen bodies littering the throne room. Terreno would be quite upset to lose so many soldiers. Clever though they were, dressing up as my guards. I wondered how many they killed without my knowing. I'd gotten sloppy, ignoring the thoughts around me as they'd all become the same. Eager for my approval and terrified of what I would do next.

I shook my head at the few fairy nobles who had wanted to witness this evening's punishments. A shame to lose so many fae this night.

But I'd make them pay. I would make them all pay with this second war I was creating. This time, with Evelyn by my side, I'd be unstoppable.

The fire wielder remained in pieces on the now red-stained floor. I chuckled to myself at the macabre scene. These floors would never be white again. *How deliciously intimidating.*

And then, there *she* was.

My mother.

Lying motionless in the middle of the floor with her wild hair fanned about her head. The white and grey colors were unrecognizable, I'd known her in her youth with her beautiful chestnut hair, much like Evelyn's. The wrinkles and lines that marred her face, showing her age, were strange. I knew that using too much magic aged you, but most fae didn't toe that line.

My mother had been strange in that way.

A stranger to me in every way.

But for the first time in decades, I was free of my curse. Free of the humans who'd used me, abused my kind, killed my family.

Closing my eyes, I sucked in a long breath. The woman lying on the ground wasn't my mother. My mother died long ago, by the hands of humans who started the original war. Now it was my job to bring that war back on their shoulders. They'd become far too comfortable.

Swerving my head back to the hidden exit behind the thrones, I called out to Evelyn, "I never wanted to cause you more pain."

Liam's eyes met mine, and I tilted my head, wondering if he'd ever realized what I'd done to him.

He'd allowed me to trap him so easily, never even suspecting that I was the one who placed into his mind the notion to whisk Evelyn away for a stolen kiss at the ball and then flee up the stairs. That it was I who told Rafe to bring himself to us when I'd caught the little lovebirds in their attempted escape. Providing me the willing and easy leverage I needed to make Evelyn heel to my side.

I would truly hate to kill Liam, especially since Evelyn loved him so dearly. But he was still a coward, at least not as much as his brother. Liam fought his own battles, and faced his own mistakes. I could admire that, to a degree...but he still would never be good enough for my Evelyn.

"If you leave now, young Evelyn, you will not get far," I called out again. Her friends all stood around her, encouraging her to leave, but she held her ground. Clinging to my stare with her own fierce expression.

My little fairy warrior.

I allowed the threat to hang in the air as I turned to the fighting behind me, unleashing my power on the Terreno soldiers. They didn't stand a chance as my mind tasted their bittersweet screams of agony; each individual its own unique flavor.

The fairies who had been fighting earlier were all currently locked in the ballroom with iron and a bit of persuasion; after this mess was dealt with, I'd take care of the rest. The bloodlust in my veins looked forward to making a few examples so the rest would heel easily.

I loved the taste of fear in the air. There was power in fear, and I refused to ever be on the other side of that power again. This had been my vow long ago, and now I was fulfilling it.

"Stop!" Evelyn's bell-like voice rang out behind me.

I hated to bring her magic to its limit—she wasn't ready for that—but this was war, and extreme measures had to be taken. I knew her;

she wouldn't let them all suffer. They were innocent and had come to her aid. She would never allow them to die so easily.

Slowly, I turned back to look at her, arching a brow. "Some lessons have to be learned the hard way."

As I started to turn back around, her pointed words echoed inside my mind, leaving a horrible aftertaste. "My father said something very similar to me after he whipped me with his cane until I collapsed on the floor."

I faltered briefly. It was not the first time she'd compared me to her father, but after I'd seen what he'd done to her, the hurt he'd caused over the years...I'd tasted her ever-present anguish, and I could not stand to be compared to that abominable human. He represented the worst of them all, and his death still felt far too easy. But my Evelyn's mind had been too fragile to handle more than what I'd delivered.

Justice. Mercy. A fresh beginning.

"You're no better than him." Her voice was nearer now.

"I am nothing like that vile scum," I seethed through my teeth.

"You are." Her words were clear, sharp and steady. "You are just as corrupted as he was, hiding behind your pious pursuit of fairy sovereignty. You've deluded yourself into thinking you're doing the right thing, when in reality you're just selfish and self-serving as he was."

I turned to see her standing tall before the throne, her shoulders thrown back, her hands poised to act. She was the epitome of formidable loveliness.

"You see others as beneath you simply because they believe in something different...something far more equal and loving. You thought me weak because my heart bleeds for those I care about." Her words meant next to nothing to me, but I loved that they seemed to bolster her. "You saw me as something that needed to be fixed. To be guided, corrected into your own image."

It was in that moment that I realized my power was hitting a wall, and it took me several heartbeats to understand what was happening.

An iridescent wall glimmered around me. I reached out, touching it with my hand, in complete awe.

Instead of shielding me, she'd put me in a cage. *Ingenious.*

I turned back to her again, my sheer delight slipping away

as I watched in growing horror and rage as my guards became outnumbered. Liam, Rafe, Ian, and the other fairy with them ran into action, overpowering my guards until the cowardly ones fled for their lives.

"You were wrong about me, Apep," she stated, drawing my attention back to her.

No, I was never wrong about you.

I'd known she would be impressive if given the right opportunities. I'd known she would rise to the occasion, because she was strong and resilient. In these ways, she was the exact opposite of my Sera. My little sister never stood up for herself. She was timid and trembled away from confrontation.

Evelyn could've gone down that same path, but I wouldn't let her. I couldn't. She would be stronger than Sera—I would make sure of it.

"I am who I am regardless of who you wanted me to be, and today I defy you, Apep. I defy what you stand for. I defy your leadership, and I will do everything in my power to never let you hurt another soul again."

I smiled at her, genuinely beaming. She was a masterpiece, my perfect creation come to life. I had called her Princess when I took the throne, but now she stood before the throne, claiming it as a queen.

Did she see it?

Could she see how incredible she was?

"You are even more than I imagined you would be," I whispered, awe spun into every vowel.

Her eyes went molten, incandescently glowing the brightest, boldest shade of green, and I was enraptured by the movement of magic in her.

But then she cried out in pain.

I boiled over with rage as I watched her fall to the ground. *Who would dare to hurt her?* I smacked the wall of my cage, baring my teeth in frustration to get out. Becca was there with her, easing her collapse. The cage flickered as I kept striking at the magic, looking for a way to break free.

"Evy!" Liam's voice reverberated across the room.

"Ev? What's happening?" Becca's hands and eyes searched for a wound, a cause, anything. "Talk to me. Please!"

Becca was indeed a good friend to my Evelyn; that was why I couldn't truly hurt her. She might not be a fairy, but she didn't judge us like the others. Her heart was that of the bravest warriors. Tasting her mind had been like drinking the most refreshing water. She'd surprised me with her sincerity, and even now she hadn't left Evelyn's side even when the opportunity had been presented.

Evelyn's eyes squeezed tight and her mouth clenched, gritting her teeth. She rolled onto her stomach, and that was when I relaxed.

"It's all right, my Evelyn," I called out, using dulcet tones to help reassure her. "The pain will pass soon. Breathe through it."

"What's happening to her?" Becca's panicked eyes met mine. I smiled, but didn't answer.

Two small protrusions arched in her back next to her spine. I remembered watching my Sera go through this. I was still young and scared, but Mother had encouraged us both. She'd said ...

"It's a beautiful thing to witness." I repeated those words now.

The cage surrounding me flickered and collapsed. Eagerly, I took a step toward her—

My steps faltered. Red-hot, ripping pain burst through my core, lacerating my insides.

As if my mind had lost all control, my legs slumped, knees cracking against the stained stone floor.

Becca's face stilled in shock, but it was Evelyn's eyes I couldn't bear. Red tinged around the rims, so many different levels of pain embedded there, but the worst of it was over. Her back would ache for a few days, but just like every other time, she would grow stronger each day.

And she would.

The truth of those words brought me solace. My eyes welled with tears. She was perfect. They were perfect. Dark and light shimmering together in exceptional contrast, an exquisite blend of her heritage.

I squeezed my eyes shut, allowing the tears to roll down my face. It was the first time I'd cried since learning of Sera's death.

"So beautiful." I spoke softly, reaching out a hand as if I could touch her even from this distance. That was when I saw the tip of a blade. Drips of red splattered to the floor beneath me. It took a moment to register. But it all became clear when the blade pulled back out, tearing through tissue, muscle, and bone. I'd never experienced such a wrenching sensation.

Evelyn's wings fluttered behind her. Glowing, glimmering, bright and hopeful, like a luminescent dawn. She hadn't realized they were there yet.

She couldn't see herself like I could see her.

Pain etched into every crevice of her face, fresh tears raining down in fine rivulets. Heavy awareness gripped my mind as the world went quiet. Those tears were *for* me and *because* of me. I'd done this to her. I'd caused this pain.

She would never know how much I loved her. That I loved her the only way I could. That I loved her with what little was left of me.

"I'm sorry," I whispered.

The world tilted to the side, but I kept my eyes fixed on hers.

I hoped I would see my sister soon.

CHAPTER 43

Liam

There was a jarring finality to the motion of pulling my sword out of Apep's chest. It was like waking from a nightmare that you couldn't be certain was over yet.

It was done.

Evy's eyes followed his until his body became perfectly still. I watched her brand-new wings flutter awkwardly behind her, much like how a newborn learns to walk for the first time. I noted the stunning and perfectly unique coloring of her wings; stark black against stark white. I'd never seen wings like that before; all the fairies I'd seen so far had either lighter or darker wings. Different colors and textures of course, but never such contrasting, stark shades.

She was breathtaking.

Becca helped her stand, and her beautiful turquoise gown flowed effortlessly around her in varying shades of blues and greens mixed with disturbing splatters of mud and blood. Her hair was wild and untamed with strands and pieces falling every which way on phantom breezes. She stood on the dais, surveying the room with the two thrones and two regal columns framing her in the background. She looked powerful.

She looked like a queen.

"Liam." My heart stumbled. Her voice. Her concerned and exhausted voice still carried a slight musical lilt to it. She hadn't been beaten. She'd risen from the shadows, and she called my name first.

"Evy."

That was all it took as she barreled down the stairs of the dais, tripping over her own feet that were trying to adjust to the new weight on her back. I wondered suddenly if she even knew they were there yet.

But then she was in my arms. I held her around her outstretched wings, making sure not to crush them.

As she pulled away, her wings bristled, giving away her emotions at the morbid sight that surrounded us. I kept my arm tucked low around her waist, unable and unwilling to let her go. I needed the reassurance that she was okay. I needed the feel of her warmth under my fingertips.

She whipped wildly about, checking everyone left standing. "Is everyone all right?"

"We're okay," Becca's voice reassured. Rafe's arm was locked around her, much the same way mine was around Evy.

"Billy?" Ian called out.

"I'm here, but I can't find the lass." He looked frenzied. "Camilla?" His eyes were wild as he scanned each body for hers.

"She and Ryker escaped through the hidden exit just as everything went mad." I looked to Rafe. "Will you go with Billy to find them?"

Rafe looked down at Becca. "I'll go with you," she said, clearly recognizing he wouldn't leave without her. She wound her way through the bodies to hug Evy tightly before she walked back up the dais, past the thrones and out through the hidden secret passageway, following behind Billy, Rafe taking up the rear. Both Billy and Rafe looked worse for the wear, bloody and bone-weary. We'd all seen a lot this night.

Too much.

Evy turned back to Ian, who had walked up to us, and a few of the leftover Terreno soldiers made their way toward us as well. No one else was left standing.

"Is it over?" she asked hesitantly.

"More are locked in the ballroom." A Terreno soldier spoke up; he looked like the captain of this crew, if I wasn't mistaken. I recognized the responsibility in his gaze as if it were my own. "That's where the rest of our people were."

She looked at the ground littered with bodies again and swallowed. "I'm so sorry for your losses today." Her voice choked. "I didn't think it would…"

The Terreno soldier walked closer, carefully stepping between bodies. Once he came close enough, he bowed respectfully, eyeing both of us. "Apep was just as much a threat to our people as he was to yours. We volunteered to be here today, and I am honored we were able to assist." He motioned to the other guards. "If you will permit us, we will help you secure the ballroom and then begin gathering our dead."

Evy looked a little lost as to what to do next, so I nodded, acknowledging the next steps, "Of course." Then I looked to Ian. "Are you…"

I hesitated before finishing the question. Asking if Ian was all right was useless. There was nothing to be all right about. Chrissy's loss was not one easily spoken about, and it was obvious by their relationship that his grief would be immense.

"Aye, I'll be fine, lad. Let's deal with what's left in the ballroom and be done with this nightmare," he answered anyway.

I nodded in agreement, not trusting my voice as I saw Evy's face crumple again. I followed her gaze to see her eyes glued on her grandmother's fallen form.

Ian walked up, carefully extracting Evy from my arms and holding her in his embrace. "There's much to be said." He pulled back, his eyes full of far too much knowledge. "Did ye even notice?"

Evy's brow furrowed. "Notice what?"

A ghost of a smile crossed his lips. "Ye got yer wings, lass."

Evy gasped and immediately looked over her shoulder, turning to try and see more of them. "They're…"

"Beautiful," Ian offered. Then he stepped away and wound through the bodies, heading straight for the grand double doors of the throne room.

I couldn't help but chuckle and grin as Evy kept looking back, trying to catch a fresh glimpse of her new wings. While one side would stretch out, the other would always go the opposite way. "You'll get the hang of them in no time," I jested.

Her exhausted eyes stared back at mine in awe. "I didn't realize what was happening."

"I didn't either." I kissed her on the head, winding my arm effortlessly back around her middle. "But they're perfect. I know you're exhausted, but let's go finish this."

She sucked in a long breath, pushed back her shoulders, making her wings flare out, and then nodded.

***

The ballroom wasn't the chaotic mess I expected, but I also hadn't expected to see Silas sitting on the throne.

When we opened the doors, the relief was as palpable as the tension.

I squeezed Evy's waist and stood beside her as she surveyed the crowd below.

"I don't know what to say," she whispered.

But before I could respond, an overly diplomatic silver-tongued voice broke the silence first. "Princess. You've returned at last." Silas didn't move from the throne of the dais. In fact, he sat upon it in with overinflated confidence.

I pulled away from Evy, I hated to do it, but my instincts screamed that we had yet one more obstacle in our path to claim full victory.

Pulling aside the Terreno captain, I spoke quietly with him about the situation. He nodded in understanding as the sounds of the crowd suddenly turned to awe.

I looked back at Evy and saw her dark and light wings outspread behind her. She might've been a mess, emotionally and physically, but you couldn't miss her magnificence.

"I am here to inform you all that Apep is dead." Evy's clear tone rang out over the waiting crowd.

Gasps echoed, reverberating off the gilded walls of the ballroom.

The guard standing next to me quickly asked, "And who are the men standing beside the throne?"

"Apep's guards. Hopefully all that's left of them," I whispered. "They followed his dogma to the point of cruelty."

The guard nodded, and we both moved to Evy's sides.

Her shoulders relaxed slightly when my fingers reached out to lightly brush her white knuckles gripping the balustrade.

"I know many of you here may disagree, but as your...Princess," she hesitated, "I hereby reinstate the Penvarden line to rule this land."

Cries of dismay and angry yells broke out amongst the crowd. The Terreno guard standing on the other side of Evy signaled his people and then made his way down the stairs while the crowd was agitated and distracted.

Ian swooped in to take his place standing beside Evy, and I watched as she stood just a little taller with the both of us at her sides.

Silas's voice sounded again as he stood on the dais in front of the throne, his face bewildered. "Apep is dead?"

The Terreno soldiers must've gotten the word. I watched their lithe forms, dressed in the black uniforms of Apep's guards, carefully sweep through the crowd toward the dais. Their targets were clear.

"Yes," Evy responded simply to the posed question. "It is no secret that I did not agree with Apep..."

"Did you kill him?" someone called out.

Evy bristled, but I squeezed her hand as I answered, "No. I did."

The crowd grew agitated again at my confession, so I continued. "Apep was a tyrant, and the treatment of humans under his rule was no better than what my forefathers did to the fairies." Evy glanced over to me, and I met her gaze, a ghost of a smile brushing against my face. "But I can promise you that it will never happen again."

I cleared my throat, the skin of my neck turning warm as I realized how many eyes were truly on us.

"I am both fairy and human," Evy spoke again. "Which gives me a unique perspective, one I hope you'll all come to share with me. When Ryker reclaims the throne—" more groans and angry cries resonated from the large number of faces below, "—I will work closely with him to make sure *all* fairies in Alstonia are treated with equality."

"Will you still marry him?"

"You're standing next to his brother!"

"Will you be our Queen?"

Questions upon questions rang out, and Evy's limbs began to shake from exhaustion or overwhelm—more than likely both. To be honest, my body felt much similar, but I wrapped an arm around her again, helping to keep her steady.

"We will answer more questions soon," I called out, using my captain's voice to my advantage. "For now, the party is over. Spread the word that Apep is no more, and that cruelty to any citizen of this kingdom, be them fairy or human, will no longer be tolerated. You will allow humans to reclaim their homes, and we will begin a rebuilding process as soon as we're able. If you find yourself homeless, come to the palace, where we will find you accommodations in the meantime."

Evy turned to look at me, her face shining with complete wonder and awe as though I'd just saved her life from certain peril. I could relish that look on her face for the rest of my life and never tire of it.

The rest of our lives…

My hands instantly clammed up and my throat swelled.

Would she still accept me as her husband?

Perhaps the question of whether she should marry Ryker and truly rule should still be debated. I realized I had just assumed she would still want to marry me, but I hadn't asked again. Not like I'd had the time to, and—

Her soft lips reached up to touch mine, silencing my every thought except for the one focused on her small mouth, her warm breath and her soft body pressed into me.

"You're brilliant," she whispered against my lips, before slowly pulling away.

A startled cry ripped through the room, and we all turned to see Silas darting for the back door behind the dais as Apep's guards struggled in a brief fight against the Terreno soldiers before quickly falling back to follow him.

The door behind them slammed shut and locked from the other side, leaving the ballroom silently shocked.

I pulled away from Evy, giving her a chaste kiss on the forehead before turning to Ian, "Can you get her out of here?" I asked. After a dip of his head in reply, I turned back to Evy. "Go back to your old room and I'll join you there soon."

Evy shook her head. "But…"

I looked her straight in the eye. "Enough has happened tonight, and we can let it be over for now." I allowed my eyes to plead with her and reassure her at the same time. "I'll take care of this lot. Go get cleaned up, and I'll be with you as soon as I can."

Ian gently guided her away from the grand staircase balcony toward the ballroom doors, and I made sure they were gone before directing everyone to exit.

I knew many of those left behind didn't agree with what Evy and I had just said, but there were just as many who did agree, and I knew they'd help spread the word about what happened here tonight. It seemed no one was willing to risk further violence, not with so many already dead.

Our next phase of recovery would be the restoration process, which I imagined could take years to truly complete, but just like I always said…one step at a time.

Enlisting the Terreno soldiers, I had them help me gather the dead from the throne room.

Rafe, Becca, and Billy all popped their heads in not long after we'd begun to clean up, but as soon as Becca found out where Evy was, she was gone in a flash.

Rafe sidled up next to me. "No sign of them, Cap."

I rubbed the sweat off my forehead with the back of my forearm, the effects of extreme exhaustion beginning to cloud my comprehension. "What do you mean, no sign of them?"

"Ryker and Camilla are simply gone." Rafe shook out his dark curly hair and rubbed the back of his neck. There was still red staining under his nose and on the side of his temple, but it was his haunted and weary eyes that gave his ragged depletion away. "A horse has been taken from the stables, but only one. The trail wound through the forest, but with it being so dark outside, it was impossible to track."

I couldn't understand it. Why would Ryker leave? Why would he take Camilla with him? Where had they even gone?

"It doesn't make sense." My entire body trembled with fatigue now.

Rafe's strong hand gripped my shoulder. "Ryker was in such a state, I wouldn't be surprised if he panicked and rode off. Or maybe

Camilla took him to the estate to wait out the fighting. Hopefully they'll come back tonight, and if not, we'll go looking again in the morning. There's not much we can do in this darkness, nor in this state of exhaustion. Until we get more royal guards back…"

I wiped a weary hand down my face. "I know." My eyes met his gaze as my hand clapped onto his shoulder. "Thank you for everything."

We needed rest. It would be fruitless to continue looking for them in our conditions, but Ryker disappearing like that…despite what Rafe said about responses in a moment of panic, this somehow seemed intentional, and that was what worried me the most. Ryker was prone to rash decision-making, especially when it came to women, but to leave now? In the middle of this whole mess? Right when he was being rescued after all his torment? It didn't sit right with me. At least if he left intentionally, then it had been his decision, but what if someone else had found them first? Apep's cowardly guards who ran from our fight in the throne room, and now Silas' followers from the ballroom…they were all still running amok. What if they found Ryker and Camilla first? What if they…

"Liam?" Rafe's worried face came back into view as I blinked several times. "I think we need to get you to bed."

I waved him off. "No, no. I can still do a bit more."

Rafe pursed his lips, but didn't argue further. Tomorrow I'd speak with Evy and see if she might better understand Ryker's current state of mind. Maybe she'd even have an idea as to where they might've gone or what he was thinking.

We stacked the bodies of Apep's guards in a frozen field on the back side of the palace. There was no reason to prolong the process, so we burned the bodies that night, sending their ashes back to Nature, as Billy had put it.

Chrissy and Apep we held aside for a proper funeral. For as much as I wanted to chuck Apep's body into the burning mass with all the others, or maybe in with the horse refuse from the stables, I had a feeling Evy would want it this way.

We ventured back inside the palace, and I found Ian pacing outside of Evy's old room.

"You need to get some sleep." I offered, my throat hoarse from exhaustion and smoke. We'd set up the Terreno soldiers in a guest wing just moments prior, but there were a few more rooms open still. "I'll sleep on the couch," he replied, his gaze locked on Billy as soon as he rounded the corner. Billy walked directly into Ian, throwing his arms around the older fairy, and the pair embraced each other silently. When he released Ian, Billy led him straight into the sitting room, taking over from there. They'd known each other so long, I knew it was what they both needed to process Chrissy's death.

Rafe and I ventured into Evy's bedroom and found the two girls curled up on the bed, as if they'd fallen asleep while talking.

"Should we wake them?" Rafe asked.

I shook my head and made my way to Evy's side, crawling up on the bed behind her. I draped my arm over her middle, conforming my larger body to her smaller one. Rafe across the way did the same. We were all too exhausted to attempt anything more this night, and for as much as I wish I had my guards to put on patrol or that I myself could keep watch, there was no point. Exhaustion pulled me under like the closing of heavy drape.

CHAPTER 44

Camilla

Ryker's hand was firmly set over my mouth as he quietly pulled me down the tunnel. I didn't try to struggle against him or call out for help. There was no point anyway; fighting had just broken out, and everyone was too distracted and busy fighting for their lives. My life wasn't in danger…at least, I hoped not.

Regardless, Ryker had been right. I had done this to him. I had betrayed him, my sister, Liam, and the entire kingdom out of petty jealousy and misplaced anger. I deserved whatever punishment he saw fit for me.

Plus, *I cared*. I didn't want to, but I couldn't help it.

The last few nights visiting Ryker in the dungeon, talking with him, pulling him out of his misery one conversation at a time…

I felt close to him.

As he dragged me quietly, his hand dropped from my mouth and instead pulled at my arm, quietly leading me away from the violent throne room and all of our friends. Well, his friends, anyway.

I wasn't sure where we were headed, and I wondered what he planned on doing with me. If he even had a plan.

"We don't belong here, you and I." He spoke quietly into my hair as we rounded the back of the palace, heading towards the stables. "A traitor and a fallen king." He snorted darkly.

"They'll miss us if we're gone," I whispered.

He scoffed. "They won't miss you. They barely tolerated you."

I hated that I bristled at his words. I hated that they stung, but mostly I hated that they were far too close to the truth. Only Billy had really seemed to care, and that was because he hadn't known me *before*.

The woman I was *before* kept everyone at arm's length. She played the perfect little seductress so she could snag a wealthy husband. She was cruel and shrewd in her actions...she even turned a blind eye to her own sister's abuse and mistreatment, because then at least her mother praised her.

That was the woman I was *before*.

Ryker tightened his hold around my arm as we dashed from shadow to shadow, making our way slowly to the stables. I couldn't tell if he held on because he was afraid I'd leave, or because I had become some sort of lifeline and comfort to him.

I scoffed at myself. *Wishful thinking, Camilla. He's literally kidnapping you.*

A tremor tore through Ryker's body when he heard footsteps. He stopped abruptly, sinking us back into the shadows as his arm tightly wrapped around my waist, and his warm breath heaved in frantic spurts on the back of my neck.

I wanted to ease his worry, to tell him nothing would ever hurt him again. But I couldn't guarantee any safety; the only thing I could promise was if we were caught, he'd probably get his wish, because Apep would certainly kill me this time around.

The footsteps ran right past us, paying no mind to the crowded shadow along their path.

Once the footsteps faded into the background, Ryker gripped my neck. It didn't hurt, but it gave him unique leverage to pull me in even closer. His warm breath whispered quietly in my ear, "Since no one will miss you, and this kingdom deserves better than some weak and deformed former king, that, my dear, is why we can be gone as long as I *want* us to be gone."

Unable to stop the unforgivable shiver that ran through my body, a frisson of warmth shot straight through my stomach, even lower, and my eyes fluttered closed. All this time talking with him, we had barely touched, except for the occasional comfort of his hand over mine. This dominating sensation was entirely new and a bit alarming.

With an abrupt shove, he pushed me away from him and then grabbed at my hands so that he could pull me along behind him as we approached the stables.

Aiming for an empty stall, he carefully unlatched it and then pressed me inside.

Grabbing a loose rope hanging just outside the stall, he bound my hands in front of me all the while whispering. "Tell me, Camilla. What were you thinking as they roughly pulled me from my bed and bound my hands, like this, behind my back?" His words were harsh, but his touch was still shockingly gentle. "What were your thoughts as the rope scraped my skin away and you watched me struggle?" With one yank, he tightened my binding, the rope scratching. "Did you enjoy seeing your king brought low? Were you satisfied with the performance?" He raised the eyebrow on the good side of his face. The other brow had been completely burned off, but his slate-blue eyes still bored into mine with an intensity that couldn't be ignored.

"Ryker, I—"

Placing his finger in front of my mouth, he shushed me softly. "None of that now. I can't have you using my name like we're friends." He grabbed a linen towel off the side of the stall. It looked clean enough, but I still bristled when he brought it to my mouth. "Did you ask them to tie me up and gag me in your revenge plot against Evelyn, or was I just an added bonus?"

I tried to protest, but he wouldn't let me answer as he knotted the linen behind my head, then moved back down to grab the loose end of the rope tied around my wrists. He led me by the rope to the next stall with a horse in it and had me sit directly in front of the steed while he moved to saddle it.

"Don't move," he whispered.

Saddling the beast that towered above me, I watched him move with difficulty. His limbs quivered, atrophied from disuse. His entire body was filthy, simply covered in dirt, scrapes and bruises. His honey blonde hair was mangled with grease and who knew what else...

Guilt sat heavily in my stomach as I watched him slowly work. Even bedraggled as he was, there was something so arresting about the way his body moved. He carried himself with a confidence that couldn't be feigned, and I was grateful that even if he couldn't see it himself, Apep hadn't won. He hadn't succeeded in completely breaking Ryker, for Ryker was still there. Still confident. Still handsome, regardless of the burn scars on his face.

His charged pale blue gaze suddenly crashed into mine, as though catching me in the act of perusing his body. I stared back, admiring the determination in his brow and the fire in his eyes. If taking me like this, punishing me in a similar fashion as he had been treated gave him back that spark, or at least gave him something to focus on and work toward, then that's what I would give him.

Just like I'd promised in the dungeon, I wouldn't rest until I helped see him through this.

Once the horse was saddled, he brought me up to standing again. "Up you go. We've got a journey ahead of us."

I wondered quietly, as he helped me mount, fitting my legs all the way around the steed instead of attempting side saddle as I'd been taught. Did he have a destination in mind, or would we simply be wandering about the kingdom aimlessly until he found something to satisfy his vengeance?

He swung up behind me, wrapping his arm tightly around my waist again and pulling me back into him as he backed the horse out of the stall. We quickly trotted out of the stables and toward the forest ahead. The barren tree limbs mixed with the full evergreens made the copse dense, but manageable to navigate through.

After slowing to a walk, he spoke confidently from behind me. "I know they'll try to search for us, but I'm going to find someplace where we won't be found."

Picking back up into a trot thoroughly scrambled my brain as my body bounced mercilessly in the saddle. I tried searching for any clues as to where we were headed and gripped the saddle to steady my seat from all the incessant bouncing this ridiculous beast seemed stuck in. The sheer discomfort of the two of us squished into this one saddle while trotting on uneven ground was enough to convince me I was forming permanent bruises on my lower region.

Evelyn was the rider, not me. And why anyone found riding an enjoyable pastime was far beyond me.

When he kicked the horse and took off at a canter, my already stiff and bruised body jarred roughly back against his. I shifted to the side and looked back behind us just in case Liam, Evy, or one of our other friends was pursuing us, but no one was there.

With everything going on, they probably didn't even realize we were gone yet.

Turning back around, my body deflated into Ryker's rigid posture. He rocked and swayed with the horse's movements as if they moved as one, while I on the other hand jostled about painfully.

His arm loosened around my waist as we slowed to a walk through another thick copse of trees.

"Relax your body," he whispered, "Sway with the horse's movements. Let him lead you." His fingers spread out slowly, resting on my stomach and half up my ribs as he helped move my body with his and the horse beneath us. "Don't fight his natural stride, and the ride will be much better for it."

Heat flared, hot and unexpected in my stomach. Did he have any idea how suggestive those words...of course he did. Before Evy, he had been the *Rogue Prince*, after all.

I wanted to roll my eyes, because my imagination was running away with me again. There was no possible way he would ever set his sights on me like that. He *hated* me. He was *kidnapping* me to punish me for the role I played in betraying him.

"Ready to try again?" Ryker asked as we entered another small meadow.

My heart sped up in my chest as he kicked the horse into action. His hand rolled down my ribs, past my waist, and gripped my hips as he helped me move in time with the horse.

I wondered why he should want me to be comfortable at all. And yet, his touch was calming. It helped ease my ride, showing me how to move with a horse instead of against it.

Slowing to a walk again, my heart didn't slow, and his hand didn't move.

We moved slowly, carefully, methodically through the trees, the horse navigating our every step as a nearly complete darkness formed around us. My body quivered at the thought that Ryker was used to this kind of darkness, that it had been his every waking moment for far too long.

What had that kind of isolation and gloom truly done to him?

For now, it was obvious that Ryker needed his revenge, and I hoped that by going with him, this could be my penance.

He leaned in one last time, allowing his whispered words to brush softly against my ear: "All clear. You're mine now, Camilla."

CHAPTER 45

Evelyn

"Want to know what they look like?" Liam's deep, familiar voice made a delicious heat unfurl in my chest. I buried my face into his warm neck, not ready to face the day yet, soaking in his comforting cedar wood and musky scent that was so perfectly him. He smelled like home. Felt like home. And I never wanted to leave this position, curled up into his embrace. I wanted my every day to be filled with this and never end.

"Mmm. What *what* looks like?" My voice sounded tired and muffled against his skin.

"Your wings." His hot breath whispered along the exposed side of my neck before his lips gently kissed there. Delightful warmth swam to the pit of my stomach and then back up my neck at the brief touch, and I was suddenly desperate for more.

What did he say? There was no focusing on anything but the feel of his lips on my quickly escalating pulse.

"Mhmm," I hummed. The throaty sound was lazy and wanton.

He chuckled, softly kissing my neck again before shifting my body just so. More of his weight leaned into me as he kissed up and down my neck.

"Do you even have any clue," *Kiss*, "what I'm," *kiss*, "talking about," *kiss*, "my sleepy girl?"

"If you keep doing that, I fear I will lose every thought entirely." The husky tone that whispered those words was completely foreign to me, but Liam seemed to enjoy the sound as he kissed up my jaw, moving to my lips.

"And if you keep talking like that," his own voice was gruff and strained, "I'm afraid I'll be forced to stay right here in this bed, unable to leave your side."

"That sounds perfect." I replied.

He kissed my nose. "They're beautiful."

"What are?" I still hadn't opened my eyes and instead relished every touch, even breath, every...

"Your wings," he whispered again.

Wings. Wings! My eyes flew open wide, staring at Liam's darkened but amused expression.

I had wings now.

"There you are." He smirked, revealing that deliciously shy dimple in his cheek. "I think I like waking you up this way."

I smiled carefully back. "I think I like being awoken this way."

Liam pulled me closer, taking a steadying breath. "They're the most beautiful wings I've ever seen." He described them in detail, how they moved from dark black to opalescent white, a perfect contradiction.

Opalescent, just like Grandmother Chrissy's wings. I loved watching her wings move, catching every color in the light, and...

Grandmother Chrissy.

I clenched my jaw, my eyes and nose stinging as the images from last night ripped through in my mind.

"Evy?" Liam's concerned tone had me swallowing down the tears building in my throat.

I took in a deep breath, a fresh pang of guilt and grief squeezed my heart.

"Is Chrissy..." My words faded off, as I already knew the answer to my question. Closing my eyes, warm tears slid down my side cheek. "Was her body...?" I choked on the word.

"We recovered her body last night. I knew you'd want to hold a proper goodbye for her..." He hesitated a breath. "And Apep."

I sucked in a surprised gasp before nodding into his neck. "She would've wanted that."

He nuzzled the top of my head with his nose. "That's what I thought as well."

"Thank you."

Kissing the crown of my head, I pulled back, blinking open my lashes to focus on his weary dark eyes.

"You are the most incredible woman I have ever known, and I still can't believe that you love me." He spoke so softly, so carefully, as if somehow his words could be stolen if not treated with the utmost caution.

"Liam…" I studied his wearied face. Exhaustion tugged at his features and weighed down his expression. That single dark stray hair that loved to irritate his eyes hung forward, just begging to be played with. "Always you." I leaned forward, twisting it around my finger, whispering the words over his lips.

"Always you," he whispered back.

When our lips met again, we lingered as if it were the most natural thing in the world. There was no heat in this kiss as there had been when I first woke up. Instead this kiss was one of comfort. A bond that couldn't be broken. A way for us to communicate without words.

I loved Liam with my entire heart. My soul called out to his as if we were forever connected. It had always been this way, ever since we were children running through the fields all those years ago.

He pulled away, gently giving me two more pecks: one on the nose and then one on the forehead. "Ready to go find the others?"

I shook my head, and he laughed. "When did you get here anyway?" I puzzled. "I swear the last person I saw was Becca."

"Becca was here. Rafe and I joined you both very early this morning. They're already up, but none of us had the heart to wake you, so they left to give us some time alone."

"Ryker and Camilla?" I questioned next.

Liam gave a small shake of his head. "They couldn't find them last night. Followed their trail into the woods, but lost it from there in the darkness. We're trying again today with some decent light." He paused. "Billy and Rafe are already on it."

I worried my bottom lip, "I'm worried about them. Ryker…" I

trailed off.

Liam propped his head up on his arm, looking down at me with so much adoration in his eyes I felt it all the way to my soul. He brushed aside some of my hair over my shoulder, but the lines around his eyes were still laced with worry. I imagined that both of us would have that look until we found Camilla and Ryker safe and sound.

"Is there anything you can tell me about Ryker?" Liam asked. "Anything you think might help us look for them? Where they went?"

I sucked in a ragged breath, "He wasn't well, Liam. I'd never seen a person so broken. So angry." I shuddered at the memory of him smashing the mirror. I'd never imagined so much fury could be balled up in one person.

Liam winced as his breath stuttered in his chest.

"If he took Camilla with him," I started thinking out loud, "I can't imagine that would be good, but he's still Ryker at his core, you know? I don't think he could ever truly hurt her."

"I don't either, but you didn't see how angry he was with her right before you rescued us." Liam paused. "I'd never seen him like that. Ever."

I nodded in understanding.

Ryker had changed, and how could he not? For as much as Apep put me through, it was nothing compared to the darkness he forced upon Ryker.

After a long silence, Liam leaned down to nuzzle my nose. "Come on then, let's see if we can find our friends and get some food. Plus, you need some time with Nature."

He started to roll out of bed, and I was floored by how natural and normal this felt. Was this truly our new reality? Because if so, I never wanted it to end.

***

I hadn't wanted to enter the royal suite where Apep had made me stay with him, but Liam found me a fresh change of clothes while changing his own in his old room. We both did what we could to clean ourselves up a bit from the night before, but no matter what, we remained looking haggard and as though we'd been through war.

Which, I suppose we had. Though I tried not to focus on that as I stared at my wings in the mirror.

I couldn't believe how pretty but entirely foreign they looked on my back.

This is going to take some getting used to.

We found everyone setting out platters of food in the dining hall, inviting all to eat. Aster walked around healing leftover wounds, and Ian joined her; luckily there wasn't anything too serious. Those who had been seriously injured unfortunately hadn't made it.

The whole room of beings looked a little worse for wear, but Liam and I did what we could to thank everyone and apologize for any losses, especially to the Terreno soldiers who planned on starting their journey back today. I'd told them to convey my every appreciation to Princess Jada and King Jai for their help and made them carry our promise that we'd come visit as soon as things were settled again here.

"I found as many as I could this morning and set them to work," Becca informed me.

"You need rest, too," I gently chided.

She scoffed, flourishing her hand casually at me. "Not in the way you did. We need to make sure you get some time with Nature today, too." She looked over at Rafe's tired features, "Rafe could've used a little more sleep as well, but he insisted on being up early to search for Camilla and Ryker."

"Anything?" I asked.

She shook her head. "No one can find them." My whole body felt like caving in. Ryker wasn't in any condition to be lost out in the woods, and Camilla was clever, but she definitely lacked survival skills.

Had someone taken them? Had they gotten lost? Were they out there on their own now?

Becca continued, "Rafe, Billy, and Ian all went searching for them this morning. They said all the signs pointed to them taking off on their own. But they lost their tracks in the woods behind the stables."

I shook my head back and forth. "I just don't understand why they would leave."

I knew Ryker's mind had been altered, and I wondered at the damage we couldn't see versus the physical representation. I knew from experience that the internal damage was always far worse.

"None of us do. Now, you need to sit and eat," Becca demanded, "or I'll have to force feed you like an infant."

I snorted through my nose, but did as I was told, allowing Becca to fill an overflowing plate of food for me.

Ian eyes met mine across the hall, and he parted from speaking quietly with Rafe, Billy, and Liam. Billy's face was pinched with concern as he spoke with Liam, no doubt giving him the latest update on Ryker and Camilla just as Becca had informed me.

As Ian made his way over, my throat immediately choked up. I didn't know anything about him, except that he'd been the one to arrive with Grandmother Chrissy last night. He'd tried to protect her. I assumed him to be the person who'd known my grandmother the best, and for some reason, seeing him made me miss her all the more.

He stood before me, bowing slightly as his eyes glazed over. "May I have a moment, lass?"

Becca looked at me and back at Ian, then nodded to him. "Just let me gather my plate and I'll go join the boys."

She kissed me on the head as Ian sat down next to me, his gaze studious, taking in every facet of my face. I watched as his eyes reddened with fresh tears, and felt my own stinging in response.

"I know ye don't know me," he started, clearing his throat, "but there are some things I must tell ye. Things I'm assuming yer Grandmother never told ye."

I nodded to show I was listening, though I didn't trust my voice at the moment.

He took in a long steadying inhale, his breath wavering with what I assumed were nerves. "I'm yer grandfather."

Shock tore through my entire body as I processed his words, losing my voice entirely.

"I was not Apep's father," he clarified quickly. "That was my brother."

I blinked rapidly, attempting to process this fresh revelation.

"I was the one who found Chrissy the night of the attack. She was still hanging onto life by a thread, and I was able to heal the worst of her wounds, allowing her to recover slowly in my care. My brother... he asked me to watch over his family if anything ever happened to him." He sucked in another shaky breath. "Chrissy and I never officially mated. Our coupling was brief, one time really, but I took my duty to her seriously. She never wanted another mate. And I never wanted to push her..."

"But you loved her?" I asked, my voice gruff with emotion.

"Aye," he confessed. "She never really let him go. The loss of her mate and children damn near killed her." He sighed, brushing a hand down his eyes and over his bearded chin to catch a few stray tears that escaped. "We fought constantly about Apep and her agreement with the Penvardens, but she'd arranged a place for us to live in peace in that sleepy little town that they conveniently left off all their official maps. It gave us the privacy and space we needed to thrive as a community." A wry smile pulled at his lips, and his eyes danced over to Liam. "Except for the odd traveler who stumbled upon our existence."

"Did you help raise my mother?" I asked.

He nodded. "She stayed with us in that town until she decided to branch off on her own and explore the world of the humans. Since she never got her wings, I always knew she felt more human than fairy... she asked us to let her forge her own path, and Chrissy respected her wishes to raise ye human. I..." He stumbled over his words. "I struggled with that decision. Ye were my granddaughter ,and I wanted to know ye, but I was overruled." A ghost of a smile crossed his lips. "Yer grandmother was a force to be reckoned with, ye know."

I half-smiled back, chuckling softly. "I caught onto that."

His eyes darted behind me briefly before he continued. "Yer wings are as unique as she was. I've never seen such a perfect blend of light and dark. Though it makes sense, being that yer Grandmother was a light fairy and I am a dark fairy." His eyes glittered as he spoke about her and their fairy heritage, and I found that I instantly loved him. His deep brogue and warm hazel eyes were kind, gentle, and observant. His long light brown hair was trained at the sides as though he wiped his hands through it frequently. I liked that it was peppered with a mix of brown, grey and white strands. And now that I knew...I could see some of my mother in him. That kindness belonged to her.

As he spoke, the thick wiry forest of hair he wore proudly on his face moved with his reactions, adding a sort of coziness to his features and covering the fine lines on his face. Just like Chrissy, he seemed to laugh a lot, and that made the ache in my heart compress even further. I furrowed my brows at his last words. "Does that make me a *grey* fairy?"

He laughed, and the hearty sound was warm and joyful. "I suppose ye are, lass. A perfect combination. Rare, because our kind never really got the chance to unite, though we certainly tried before the humans invaded our lands." He sighed. "Usually fairies come out one or the other." He smiled genuinely then. "Seems yer the best of both."

Ian and I continued talking late into the morning. He told me things I'd never known or understood before, like how fairies used to be divided by two kingdoms, light and dark. How one had the power of Nature's magic, and the other had the power of the body, mind, and soul. In the early times they'd separated themselves, each kingdom thinking themselves better than the other, but then the humans invaded. *A sad tale*, he'd said.

As we talked, more and more people stopped by, both human and fairy. Many were looking for work, or more specifically to get their jobs back; several were Liam's guards who'd stayed as close to the palace as possible in case they could jump in to help. Liam naturally set them back to work immediately.

The day went by much the same, with people pitching in to help clean and pick up the pieces, allowing the palace to run a little more smoothly.

Ryker and Camilla never showed. I'd hoped all day that they would just miraculously reappear, but no such luck. Their absence weighed heavily on my mind. I made Liam promise as soon as we were able to send out a major search party, but even I knew we didn't have enough people to spare yet. The threat to the palace and the kingdom was still great, especially when we had no idea how many of Apep's followers were still at large.

Ian had told me the funeral for Chrissy and Apep would be held in the evening, and I felt like I'd moved through the day almost mindlessly, waiting for my moment to get to finally say goodbye.

Once the sun went down, just before dusk, we held a proper funeral.

"How does a fairy funeral go?" I asked Ian, who stood next to me, Liam on my other side. His fingers intertwined with my own.

"We honor Nature by placing fairies back into the earth. A growth fairy usually presides, using their magic to help the deceased back into the ground. They grow a tree over their bodies. It's to honor Nature's cycle of life."

Aster had found a willing growth-gifted fairy to oversee the funeral, and I witnessed my first fairy burial.

Billy and Rafe brought Chrissy's body out first, followed by Apep's, laying them side by side on the ground in front of us. I'd chosen the woods, since Chrissy seemed to love them so, and Liam had found us a small clearing to hold the ceremony.

"A mother next to her son," the fairy officiating had said, and hot tears gathered in my eyes. These two were family. I might not have known them long, but the impressions they'd left on me would both be significant.

No matter how much evil Apep had wrought, I still wished for his death to be peaceful, and I was glad he no longer had to live in the world that had taken his family, his sister, from him.

The solemn tone of the event was expected, but I was most grateful that no one protested against a proper burial for Apep. It was though we all knew this was for Chrissy far more than it was for him, though I still felt he deserved it too, despite everything.

I held in my cries as I witnessed and mourned the woman who'd helped us all accomplish the impossible. The wild female who couldn't be tamed no matter what life had thrown at her. The tenacious being who persevered no matter her experiences. The complex fairy who'd held many secrets, even unto her grave. And the grandmother who'd loved me instantly and believed that I was capable of so much more than I'd ever thought possible for myself.

I would miss her every day.

CHAPTER 46

Liam

The next few days were incredibly demanding. Word of Apep's death was slowly circulating, and people were cautiously trickling back into their towns and homes, but fights were breaking out every day in response.

Winter was officially upon us, and there were far too many people without shelter and warmth, so we'd opened up the palace to anyone who needed it. Ian had the idea of converting the ballroom into a makeshift shelter, and we enlisted a few growth fairies to help us create a system of hammocks and cots made of vines, branches, and flora to give people places to rest.

It was exhausting work, and it hadn't even been a week yet.

Evy and I settled squabbles on the daily, holding our hearings directly in the Hoddleston town square, as that was one of the most public and centralized locations. We wanted all citizens, both fairy and human, to see we were committed to the equality we'd promised for Alstonia. But to say it was a challenge to pick up the broken pieces of our kingdom was an understatement. The amount of damage Apep had caused in just a couple of short months would take years to repair.

I stared down at the rings on my fingers, thinking of Ryker.

Missing him.

I'd happily pried each and every one of them off Apep's lifeless fingers, quite possibly breaking bones as I did it simply out of spite. They belonged back on Ryker's hands, but I would wear them every day until he came back. They stood as my physical reminder that this wouldn't truly be finished until he returned. Until he took his rightful place as king. I would stand in his stead and hold his place, readying it for his return.

Because he would come back.

He had to come back.

It hadn't even been a week since that fateful night, but we'd searched for them as far and wide as we could. Billy had been out every day, before the sun even rose. I wanted to go with him, but the responsibility of the kingdom had fallen on Evy's and my shoulders for the time being. Ian and Rafe both reminded me I didn't have the luxury to leave every day, no matter how much it killed me to not be the one searching for them myself.

The latest update was that their trail had been picked up again in the forest, but lost quickly once they passed through a creek.

There had been no word, no sign, no clues as to where they'd gone.

Thankfully, there was also no evidence they'd been taken by force, no indications of a struggle or that anyone had intercepted them.

There were so many questions in my mind, but the most prevalent one was, *why?*

Why would he just up and leave with Camilla like that? What was he thinking? He'd been so angry with her…

Evy was just as confused as I was, though she'd shared more insight on his current mental state and what he'd experienced. All of it was horrifying. I hated every detail and struggled to not blame myself. But no matter what insight she shared, we still couldn't piece together his reasoning for this.

With everything going on, Evy and I had hardly had time together. We both knew the kingdom needed us to step up in Ryker's absence, but what she truly wanted was to go back to the estate and see Jimmy, Cook, and Daisy. I smiled at the thought of them seeing her with her new wings. I could already see Jimmy's beaming expression and the tears in Cook's eyes.

"Is it just me, or did she step into the role of Queen like it was made for her?" Rafe nudged me with his shoulder as we watched Evy interacting with a few children in front of us.

Today, we were in Hoddleston, cleaning up a residential section of the town, or at least starting to. A few children had appeared slowly from behind walls and alleyways looking worse for the wear. They hadn't been able to find their parents yet, and Evy was starting to worry that this would become an issue as the status of so many humans was still unknown after Apep's guards took over.

"I think that every day when I watch her," I said back to Rafe, my eyes glued to the woman I loved crouched down before the children, fluttering her wings back and forth, much to their delight.

Rafe nudged me again. "Someone else has taken to the role of King like he was meant for it, too."

My stomach sank.

This was never supposed to be my job. I was never meant to be in this role.

I turned to Rafe, who smirked back at me, his expression faltering at the look on my face. "It was never meant to be me," I croaked.

Rafe's hand clapped on my shoulder. "I know you think that, but regardless of what *should* or *shouldn't* be, you've taken to it well, and the people love you. The fairies love you, too." His eyes danced from Evy back to me, glittering with his hidden meaning.

My head and shoulders sank. "He should be here."

Rafe's features grew solemn. "But he's not. And I'm not sure—"

"Don't say it," I stopped him. "Please don't say it."

I played with the rings on my fingers, twisting them in the winter sunlight. They felt foreign on my hands, but familiar at the same time. A strange comfort and a constant reminder.

Rafe nodded, walking away from me as he went back to picking up the rubble from a collapsed building.

Each day we slowly did our best to rebuild. With the help of several fairies, including one who could move objects with his magic, we were able to restore several residences at record speeds. Though, it was still nowhere near the amount needed, especially for these last cold winter months.

Each of us had stepped into roles we'd never expected. Becca had been essential in helping direct and manage the staff. Rafe took it upon himself to be my personal guard and, of course, Captain of the guard. He rarely left my side now.

"Miss! Miss Queen!" A child ran out from the woods, his eyes locked on Evy as he waved around a white square in his hand. "Miss Queen, this is for you!"

I immediately dropped what I was doing and headed toward Evy, refusing to ignore the niggling suspicion nudging my gut.

"What is it?" I asked her as she reached out her hand to the child. Pulling the envelope toward her, she turned it over, searching it for clues.

"Where did this come from, young man?" she asked.

The boy shrugged his shoulders. "A man handed it to me, told me to give it to you."

"Open it, Evy, let us see if it's signed," I encouraged her. *Maybe it's Ryker.*

She pulled out the letter, and my eyes narrowed in on the signature at the bottom: *Silas.*

Disgust–and disappointment—immediately weighed my heart down. I called out to Rafe, "Take the boy and follow the lead. Grab a group to go with you, both fairy and human."

He immediately jumped into action, gathering the boy with him to ask more questions.

Evy's green eyes met mine, her lips thinned with disapproval. "Is that really necessary?"

"It is if we want to catch them any time soon." I raised a brow at her, and she sighed before turning back to the letter:

> *My dearest Evelyn,*
>
> *I know you think me the cad who betrayed you, but I need to explain that I ran that night out of fear you wouldn't listen to my side of the story. I know it makes me look even guiltier than I already am. I regret not telling you about Apep's requests of me. I was only trying to help, and that is still my intention.*

The truth you must know now is that those who followed Apep now follow me. I admit leading such a group like a king does give me quite a thrill, but alas, I don't hold the cruelty in my bones like they hunger for. Which is why I send you this warning now...

This fairy faction already misses what we had when fairies were in charge and humans cowered at their toes. They love the power and the fear, and they plan to wreak havoc across the land, even as you attempt to restore peace.

Now, I'm sure you're wishing for me to tell you where we'll strike first, but that would only succeed in outing me to my brethren. Even now they question me far too much, and in order to be of true assistance, I must play my role as a merciless leader.

As much as I wish to disrupt their bloodlust, don't expect me to forfeit my life for this cause. (Which is what would happen if I were to be found as a fraud.) Each of us must do what we have to in order to survive in this world.

Whether you choose to believe this letter or not, please know I hold you in the highest esteem. It was an honor getting to know you, even if briefly. I stand in awe at your strength of character and courage in your convictions, and I can only hope that one day you might forgive me for deceiving you even in the slightest of ways. If I am lucky enough for us to have a conversation face-to-face, I will relish the opportunity and grovel at your feet.

Until then,

Silas

P.S. I believe you will make this world better by being a great queen.

I rolled my eyes. "What rubbish," I said, dismissing every lying word on the page. The entire letter sounded like a mixture between an unrequited love letter and a two-faced spy.

"It's not rubbish," Evy chided as she folded the letter back up. "Strangely, I have the feeling he's seen extreme hardship and that this letter, even with all its pretense, is sincere."

I scoffed. "His life doesn't seem that hard to me."

She shrugged and turned to walk back toward our horses, tucking the letter inside the saddlebag. "He mentioned once that he'd had to hide who he loves, and that sounds like suffering to me." She shot me a look. "Trying to hide how I felt about you for even just a week was like torture. Besides, he *did* help us with that whole closet debacle."

I smirked then, moving in closer to box her in between the horse and I. "And how is it that you feel about me?" I narrowed my eyes, even as I lowered my voice suggestively, delighting in the pink dusting her cheeks.

She smacked me playfully on the pec. "You know very well how I feel about you…" Her eyes darted behind me and grew wide with disbelief. "Jimmy! Cook!"

My eyebrows shot up to my hairline, my ears ringing from the squeal that had been loud enough to burst my eardrum for all I knew, but when she barreled past me, I smiled as I turned around.

Tears and cries of joy were followed closely by the squeals and snorts of Daisy. I watched as Evy moved from Jimmy to Cook and then to Daisy, whom she tried to pick up, but couldn't manage. She collapsed onto her knees, hugging Daisy to her instead, already crying over how big she'd gotten.

Reaching out for Jimmy next, I pulled him into an embrace. "I see you got my message. Will you be staying at the palace with us for a little while?"

Jimmy patted me on the back. "We'll stay as long as she needs us."

Moving to Cook, I gave her a soft peck on the cheek, and she pulled me into a bear hug. "You did it, my boy! You saved our girl."

I pulled back, smiling softly at her. "It's more like she saved all of us."

Evy sobbed into Daisy's neck until Jimmy knelt next to her, pulling her into his lap. "There, there, Little Miss. I've missed you so."

Cook and I joined them on the frozen ground, everyone crying and hugging. I loved how greatly Evy loved others, especially these two. The tenderness and warmth she always exuded could bring anyone to tears.

"You five are going to make me cry if you keep this up." Becca's voice was choked with emotion as she walked up to our group and knelt on the ground, petting Daisy's head.

Evy peeled away from Jimmy, who stood up then, helping Cook stand up next before dusting off his clothes. "Any sign of your folks, Becca?" He asked.

She shook her head. "None yet." Evy and Becca stood together, and they each leaned in for a hug.

"Now, as much as I love the family reunion, we got work to do, folks!" Becca put on a determined and smiling face, but we all knew better. She was throwing herself into work because she worried. We all were.

***

Cook had made herself right at home in the palace kitchens, and that night we had a beyond delicious meal. It was good to have everyone together again, but Evy and I still decided to retire early to bed. The demands of each day weighed us both down to the point of exhaustion every night.

We'd taken over her old room and had no plans on leaving it. Even though we weren't married yet, I had made it clear I didn't want to leave her side, and Evy had made it clear she didn't want me to leave.

Closing the bedroom door behind us, I wrapped my arms around her from behind.

"I don't know how to feel." She shivered slightly inside my hold and I nuzzled her neck.

"Today Rafe commented on how natural you are at stepping into being Queen." I kissed her on the temple, and she sank back into me.

"I feel like I'm stealing the role from who it's supposed to be."

I kissed down the side of her face and over the shell of her ear before softly saying, "That's exactly how I feel."

Helping her into the bed, I followed closely after, opening the sheets wide as an invitation for her to curl up into me. Her head rested on my chest. "I love you, Liam." Her soft breath brushed a brief warmth across my skin, causing it to pebble up.

"And I love you." I burrowed my head into her hair, breathing in her comforting vanilla and wild jasmine scent. Her muscles softened in my hold, and her breath deepened.

How long I had waited for this, *wanted* this, with every fiber of my being. After years of praying and hoping for this as my future, it was strangely bittersweet.

Ryker was gone, the kingdom was a mess, fear was rampant, chaos still consumed every day, and Evy was barely beginning to process many of the events that had happened here, as was I.

A shimmer of gold gleamed faintly in the darkness as my hands wrapped around her, making the backs of my eyes prick with fresh tears.

I missed him.

I missed my brother, my best friend, the rightful king of this kingdom.

The hard truth was that this was likely exactly how he'd felt when I'd left him.

And maybe that was the answer to him leaving. Maybe it was as simple as it had been for me: he just couldn't handle it, and he had to go.

If that was the case, then I hoped he would come to his senses, like I did, and come back soon.

Evy's sleepy nuzzle made my next breath feel too tight. A tremor coursed through me as I attempted to pull her even closer.

"Evelyn?"

"You never call me by my full name." Her voice muffled against my chest.

I cleared my throat, as it suddenly felt too tight. "No, but I mean to ask you a serious question."

She pulled away, only enough for her bright green gaze to find mine in the dim light.

"Will you still have me?" I cleared my throat again. "As in, marry me? Will you still marry me?" The words stumbled clumsily out of my mouth, but my eyes never left hers.

Her entire being tensed in my arms, and she shuddered, her eyes glistening in the near darkness. "I will love you until there is no breath left in me, Liam Penvarden. Nothing would make me happier than to call you my husband."

Instead of responding with words, I kissed her. Not the kind of chaste kiss I'd intended, because once our lips met, it was like lighting a match. There was no taming the hungry flames between us. There was just us and all the pent-up longing we'd both tried to suffocate while we attempted to pick up the pieces around us.

My body shifted to settle more into hers as my tongue plundered her mouth, pulling a deep and heavy groan from my lungs.

This. This was right. We'd spent too much time apart. I'd run from her, hurting and afraid, and she loved me even still. I was hers, and she was mine. And that was how it was meant to be.

A knock on the door had us both pulling away from each other, but I kept my body smothered against hers, unwilling to move.

"You two still up?" Becca's amused voice carried through the door. I groaned into Evy's bare and perfectly tempting shoulder.

"I can hear you in there," she mock whispered, "so I'll just be waiting right here. Directly outside this door. Until you both come out. Preferably with clothes."

Evy giggled softly beneath me.

"We'll need a minute," I called out, looking back down at Evy, who flashed me a very mischievous smirk. "Do you have any idea what this is all about?" I asked her.

She shook her head, but her eyes were wide with mischief. "None, what-so-ever."

I sighed. "Well, I suppose we shouldn't keep them waiting…" I raised my voice a little more, "as it's *already so late!*"

"Don't you take that tone with me!" Becca called back, full of sass as ever.

"I'm your *Prince.*" Perhaps the first and only time I'd wield that title somewhat willingly.

"And *I'm* the Queen's best friend, who's going to kick you in the rear if you don't *hurry up.*"

Evy giggled again and then kissed me on the neck.

I dropped my head again, groaning into her tempting shoulder, kissing her bare skin where my head rested.

"You keep that up," my voice was low and gruff, "and I won't be able to leave without everyone getting more of a show than they bargained for."

"Don't think I can't hear you," Becca's voice reverberated through the door again. "I did tell you I was waiting *right here.*"

"Okay, okay!" Liam called out. "We're getting up."

"Sounds like someone already is," a masculine voice mumbled in the near background.

"Rafe!" Becca scolded, followed by a boyish yelp.

I shook my head, rolling off of Evelyn's warm and perfect body, cursing whatever our friends were up to. Though I tried not to show my excessive annoyance at the interruption, Evy's smirk told me she already knew.

We dressed quickly, throwing on some robes to help us cover ourselves, and then marched into the sitting room where Rafe, Becca, Ian, Billy, Jimmy, and Cook all waited.

I could feel the heat radiating off my face.

It wasn't awkward at all having Evy's basically adopted father and grandfather staring at us coming out of the bedroom together, especially after Becca and Rafe's teasing.

But everyone's smiles were playful and mischievous as they all stepped aside to reveal a cake.

"Happy Birthday, Cap." Rafe came up and ruffled my hair, narrowly dodging my retaliating smack.

I looked over at him in surprise, and then down at Evy, whose hand squeezed my own. "You definitely knew."

She chuckled. "Well, I wasn't about to forget your birthday."

I leaned down to kiss her. "Even *I* didn't remember."

The group laughed and then pulled me over into hugs and pats on the back. Cook shoved a huge piece of cake on a plate into my hand, and we all enjoyed the small treat before *officially* retiring to sleep.

Though Evy had already given me the best gift just moments before when she said yes again, my heart was still far too heavy.

Evy bumped my shoulder with her own as we said goodnight to everyone. "What's wrong?"

"He should be here." The words were quiet as my throat closed up and my eyes stung with unshed tears.

Evy laced her fingers through mine, staring down at the rings with me. "We'll find them," she reassured.

I clutched at her hand, bringing it up to my lips, kissing her knuckles softly. "I know this isn't the life you wanted…"

"But it's the life we have," she finished for me. "And as long as I'm with you, any life is worth it." She clutched at the necklace I gave her as her words whispered gently against my skin, penetrating through muscle and bone, filling up every part of me.

How had I gotten so lucky?

EPILOGUE

Evelyn

Four months later

Spring had arrived. And just like the fresh start of the season, Alstonia was finally beginning to heal and grow as well.

Trust didn't come easily, not that any of us had expected that, but slowly and surely more and more people were intermixing with the fairies. We'd done our best to hold open banquets for all to attend in order to help increase and encourage camaraderie throughout the kingdom.

Acceptance was a slow process.

Without any word from Ryker or Camilla, my hope of their return had begun to wither. We still had search parties looking for them, but there was only so much we could do without any leads or clues as to where they were.

I hoped every day that we'd hear from them soon, or better yet see them, but I was beginning to accept I might be waiting a long time before that happened.

The skirmishes that had been breaking out in the direct aftermath of Apep's death had significantly lessened, and everyone was beginning to find their place and ways to thrive in this new community.

Our biggest difficulty now was knowing what was happening in the towns further out and communicating properly with them when we couldn't yet leave to visit them ourselves.

We knew that Apep's followers were still out there. Silas had been honest when he warned us of their intended violence. We'd seen their handiwork in the burning of a freshly rebuilt home or the occasional assault, but no arrests had been made yet.

For those leftover from Apep's rule, most of them had come to terms with our new laws and expectations, but it was still difficult to know who could be trusted and who might secretly be helping the radical fairy faction.

At the very least, Liam had an uncanny sense about people that helped us weed out a few bad apples already.

"Stop your worrying and get over here." Becca waved her arms out in front of her, smiling wide. "It's time to get you into your dress!"

Bouncing up and down, she clapped her hands as the girls, Brigitta, Feleen and Anna, brought over the silky white gown.

All of their eyes were already glazed over with emotion, and I smiled wide at the group, never once taking for granted how much they had done for me and this kingdom. Risking their lives to get word to Terreno, they were some of the bravest and truest friends I could ever ask for, and I told them that every day.

"You girls are going to make me cry, you know," I sniffled.

"No crying until you at least have the dress on," Becca proclaimed, clapping her hands in my face.

I laughed, but my nose still stung from my building tears. For as beautiful as it was, this dress would never even hold a candle to the perfect gown Chrissy had made for me.

I ran my fingers along the sumptuous silk. "She would've insisted on making it herself."

I realized I'd spoken out loud when Becca's arm wrapped around my middle, her head leaning on my shoulder. "But she would've loved to see you in anything as long as you walked down that aisle to Liam." She poked me gently in the middle with her other hand while we both giggled sadly.

"Ready?" Feleen asked quietly as the other girls fussed over invisible wrinkles.

I smiled softly at her. "Yes."

The gown fit like a glove. Creamy silk and supple tulle flowed over the top of my body like a second skin. The back was long and open, perfectly accommodating my wings, which the girls gently pulled over the fabric, allowing them to stand out exquisitely on display in stark iridescent black and white.

My straps were topped with grand swaths of tulle pouring down my sides like tiny waterfalls covered in small crystals that mirrored the ones cascading down my bodice to just below my waist.

The shimmering effect rivaled magic itself.

"I told you Fairy Queens existed," Becca whispered in my ear as she placed a stunning white flower crown on my head. I giggled softly, admiring the crown in the mirror. All the flowers had been taken from Ryker's garden—that was what I called it now. I made sure to visit it every day, caring for it so it would be healthy upon his return. And I wanted something of him to be a part of today.

Liam and I had waited these several months, hoping they'd come back before making the ultimate decision that we were ready for this next step in our lives…*more than ready*. But I so desperately wished they were both here. My adopted sisters were helping me get ready, but Camilla's commanding presence was acutely absent.

Was she okay? Was she hurt? Were they caring for each other? Or ripping each other apart?

There was no way to know.

Jimmy popped his head in the door, knocking as an afterthought. "Just wanted to check in," he said, eyes gleaming with undiluted joy as he took me in and immediately crumpled into a fit of precious weeping.

I ran over to him, wrapping my arms around him without hesitation.

He tapped my back gently, huffing out a weepy laugh. "Don't mind an old man letting his emotions get the best of him." He drew back and cupped my cheeks. "You're the most beautiful bride I ever did see, Little Miss." Pulling me back into a crushing hug, he whispered into my ear, "And I love you so."

Now I was the one weeping into his shoulder. "I love you too, Jimmy."

"Stop all that blubbering, you two, or you're going to make me start." Cook stepped up next, taking over his hug already in tears, despite her playful chiding.

A clearing of a throat, and all of our eyes darted up to see Ian standing awkwardly in the doorway. "If I may…" He coughed into his fist. "Have a moment alone with the bride?"

"Of course, of course." Cook brushed the tears out from under her eyes. "Look at us," she wiped at Jimmy's eyes next, "a bunch of whimpering old ninnies, we are."

Jimmy's face both softened and brightened as he looked down at her. "You, my dear, are the furthest thing from an old ninny." He snuck a quick peck in on her lips. Cook blushed furiously, ducking her head, and Jimmy turned to the both of us, absolutely beaming. "I love it when she does that."

"Oh, you!" Cook playfully hit him in the chest before grabbing his hand and pulling him out of the room.

Becca and the girls followed behind, all chattering and gushing over me still. I was beyond grateful for them, and having them here with me, even after all we'd been through. After all they'd seen and done. Their tales of the desert and their handsome fairy companions never ceased to entertain.

Ian stepped forward then, gripping his hands tightly in front of him. He cleared his throat again before speaking. "I know I've not been around or in yer life before these last few months, and I don't expect ye to forgive my absence any time soon."

I opened my mouth to speak, but he continued on in a rush before I could say a word. "I just want ye to know that I care about ye, very much, and I wish ye and Liam a happy life together."

"Thank you, Ian." I smiled. "Having you here feels like having a piece of her still with me." I paused before adding, "Liam and I have been talking, and…" I hesitated. "We were planning to ask you together…but, since you're here now…" I took in a deep breath so I could just spit out the question. "We were hoping that you might stay on here at the palace as our advisor."

For some reason I was terrified of getting those words out. I'd been so worried about him leaving and heading back up to his mountain community where I'd never see him again that I'd struggled to open up to him. But his advice for us had been vital in trying to communicate better with the fairies, and we'd both been beyond grateful for all of his help and assistance.

"We could really use your continued guidance and help bridging the gap between humans and fairies," I continued, stumbling slightly over my words. "That is, if you'd even consider taking on the role? You don't have to, of course, I don't want you to feel pressure or—"

A soft smirk pulled at his lips. "I'd love nothing more."

Relief poured from my sigh, and I followed it up with a burst of joy that propelled me to wrap my arms around him with a fierceness that would rival one of Becca's bear hugs. "Thank you, Ian."

His arms wrapped around me in response as he spoke softly. "I'm honored, Evy."

We pulled apart, and he fidgeted slightly with his shirt. "Well, I guess I'd better get back out there for the ceremony."

"Let Liam know we talked and that you accepted." I smiled. "You'll make his day."

Ian chuckled and then winked playfully. "I'm pretty sure I've got nothin' to do with it."

My cheeks warmed, but I couldn't stop smiling as Becca came barreling back into the room. "It's time to go! We need to make sure you're ready."

Ian carefully angled himself back out the door, offering me one more smile before escaping the chaos of the girls flowing in after Becca, dragging a growth fairy after them who giggled with delight.

"Last finishing touches." Becca said, handing the fairy a few freshly picked lilacs. She took them and artfully placed them around my waist encouraging them to grow and sprout down my gown. The scent alone was lovely, but the look of fresh flowers adorning my wedding dress was exquisite. It made me think of growing flowers with my mother as a child.

"And last but not least…" Becca placed my mother's old comb in my hair, one of the few things I had left of her.

"Thank you," I beamed, "it's absolutely perfect."

All the girls gushed, and then Becca shooed everyone out of the room to go ready for the ceremony.

"One last thing." Becca went behind me, clasping Liam's necklace around my neck, then smiling at me in the mirror. "Ready?"

I straightened my spine and smiled so wide I could scarcely believe it was my face staring back at me in the mirror. "Ready."

"I'll see you out there." With a quick peck on the cheek, Becca left too, and then it was just me. Just how I'd wanted it, a moment alone to gather my thoughts before I married the man I loved more than any other.

Fresh tears smarted my eyes again as I thought about Grandmother Chrissy and my mother. This day was so special, so important, and so incredibly hard without them.

I let myself cry. I needed it. I missed them far too much to keep the emotions in.

Drying my eyes with a beautifully embroidered blue handkerchief that Cook had given me that morning, I sucked down a deep breath and marched outside, excited anticipation guiding every step.

Thankfully, the ceremony was held at the estate, specifically out in the field of wildflowers that were currently in full bloom. We'd decided to wait until spring so that we could marry among the wildflowers I loved so dearly.

The actual wedding was to be a small affair; only our nearest and dearest stood around in two small half-circles, leaving me a path down the middle directly to Liam.

We'd asked Jimmy to marry us, and seeing those two men waiting for me at the end of my small path was enough to start my tears up all over again. I'd promised myself I wouldn't cry, and yet here I was, weeping the whole way.

Becca stood next to her parents with Rafe's arm firmly tucked around her from the opposite side. They'd appeared a couple months ago, coming back with a large group of people from Hoddleston. The group had fled together hiding in the surrounding forests and word had taken longer to reach them, but I rejoiced at seeing them reunited. Becca deserved all the happiness in the world.

I would've had her standing with us today, but Liam and I had decided that if Ryker wasn't there, then we would have no one stand with us while we married. It was our small way of both honoring him and mourning his absence.

The girls tittered and smiled and swooned when they saw me.

Cook blubbered, keeping her handkerchief right next to her eyes the whole time. Ian stood stoically next to a beaming Billy, who winked and instantly made me smile through my tears.

I missed Camilla.

Our relationship was rough and rocky, but she was still my family, and I had wished so desperately that she and Ryker would've come back before this date.

The announcement of our wedding had been advertised far and wide months in advance in the hopes that somehow Camilla and Ryker would hear about it and make their way back to us.

I knew this would've been hard for Ryker, though. I wasn't sure how he still felt, after everything, but I knew he loved Liam, and I knew he'd still want to know. Camilla, too.

When my eyes landed on Liam, everything else slipped away.

He held out his hand to me, and the minute our palms touched, a sob raked its way out of my throat.

Somehow that touch alone made me feel like I had finally, truly, come home.

That after everything we'd gone through to get here, *it was worth it.*

Liam's dark and bloodshot eyes were no better than my own. Tears streamed down his face as he held both my hands in his and leaned in. His scent of musky cedarwood and sweet grass, mixed with the heady florals of the wildflowers surrounding us, reminded me of what I'd felt like as a child.

Free and happy.

It was as if my best and brightest years had simply been stopped in time and now, with just one touch, they were free to continue on.

He smiled and the shy little dimple at the side of mouth winked at me. His dark hair had been styled and slicked back, but his pesky little rebel strand still fell forward into his eyes. I reached up and twisted it on my finger, smiling wide.

The mere sight of him made me deliciously giddy. This man…my best friend, my first love, my second chance, my forever. He looked at me the way I imagined I was looking at him, full of awe and wonder and love.

"How did I get so lucky?" he asked quietly.

I grinned back at him. "I was wondering the same thing."

He leaned his forehead against mine, "Always you, Evy," he whispered.

I let the tears fall as I closed my eyes, simply breathing him in. "Always you, Liam."

.

.

.

.

.

"No kissing yet you two, you still have to say I do!" Becca's voice rang out from the crowd, and everyone laughed.

It was the best day of my life.

The end.

THANK YOU

for reading A Luminescent Dawn!

Please take a moment to leave a review on Amazon.

Indie authors (like me) make their living based on reviews. The more reviews my books receive, the more readers will be able to find and enjoy my stories. If you liked this book, and even if you didn't, please take a moment to let people know your thoughts.

Reviews don't need to be long, a simple star rating and an "I loved it!" or "Not really my thing..." is perfect.

Thank you so much for taking the time to help me spread the word about my books. Your support (and shoutouts on Social Media) mean the world to me.

AFTERWORD

If you're like me, you may be feeling a touch emotional after that ending. I love these characters so much and I want you to know that I absolutely cried while writing this book (so if you cried too, you're not alone). Between Ryker's debilitating depression and grief, Evelyn's bravery in the face of new trauma and Liam learning to forgive himself, I also introduced complicated Camilla who's just beginning to discover who she truly is and wants to be.

This book was by far the most challenging to write, simply because each individual journey was so unique and different from the others. But I absolutely loved getting to tell every single one of these stories and I hoped you loved and related to at least one of them, maybe multiple.

I know some of you may now be wondering,
what happened to Ryker and Camilla?

Well…good news! I'm officially writing their book, due Fall 2023, and I can't WAIT for you to read their story. Please note, Ryker and Camilla's book will be 18+ spicy. If this isn't your thing, don't even worry, there will be more books down the road that have less spice, including a special tale about a favorite foreign princess…(Princess Jada). But if you're a huge Ryker (and Camilla) fan, you are going to LOVE their steamy story.

Speaking of spice, for those of you wishing you could have a little more time with Liam and Evy… I have a treat for you!

I've written a bonus wedding night scene that can only be read if you're subscribed to my mailing list. (*This scene contains adult content. Recommended for ages 18+*).

Go here for your bonus scene:
www.briannewik.com/bonus

Thank you from the bottom of my heart for reading and supporting this series. If you haven't already, please leave a review on Amazon and/or Goodreads. It's the best possible thing you could do to support my writing, spread the word, and help me write more books in the future.

ACKNOWLEDGEMENTS

"Your strength may be too quiet for many to see, but I've seen it.
I see it in the way you approach life with so much love.
I see it in the way you adapt to your surroundings.
I see it in the way you persevere no matter your circumstances."

This book was an incredible challenge for me to write. I struggled, doubted, wrote and rewrote this book trying to capture the story as accurately as I could so you could experience it the same way it plays in my head. There's one particular that I can't even read without crying every single time and as morbid as it sounds, I hope you cried with me so I'm not alone. (ha!)

Thank you.

Thank you from the bottom of my heart for reading this story and supporting this series. Be sure to leave a review on Amazon, tell your friends, share on social media and get the word out about this book so that I can write more for you. *wink*

Thank you to the North Carolina Arts Council. This project was supported by the North Carolina Arts Council, a division of the Department of Natural and Cultural Resources; the Arts & Science Council with funding from Mecklenburg County and the City of Charlotte; and the arts councils in Cabarrus, Cleveland, Gaston, Lincoln, and Rowan counties.

The biggest and brightest thank you to my Mom for helping in so many ways I can't even begin to list them all. Thank you for being my constant and helping ground me even when I'm unmoored. Your support and love are the greatest gift God has ever given me and I thank God everyday for you.

A HUGE thank you to Cassidy for being so beyond talented and helping my books not only look and sound good, but also helping me become a better writer. Your support and encouragement mean the world to me (as do YOU - you wonderful woman you.)

To my incredible critique partner: Katie, you are truly one of the greatest supporters in my life and I am so beyond grateful for your friendship.

To my beta readers for this book: Rachel and Vickey. Thank you for not only taking the time to read an unfinished draft, but also for giving me fantastic feedback, excellent ideas and sharing your excitement with me.

Thank you to the wonderful Karri at www.artbykarri.com for creating this amazing cover art and helping bring my vision to life.

Thank you to every single bookstagrammer, booktoker, blogger and author who's shared this book and helped me get the word out.

My biggest thanks of all goes to *you*. Thank you for reading this story. For leaving a review, for sharing, supporting and encouraging me online. Your eagerness to read more from me and your love for my characters is the best encouragement ever.

I can't wait for you to see what's next in this world. If you haven't already, be sure to hop on my email list for exclusive details, deleted scenes, and more! https://bit.ly/briannenewsletter

THANK YOU!

ABOUT THE AUTHOR

Brianne Wik writes swoony, romantic, and magical tales that explore emotional trauma and the self-acceptance journey, while also giving you just the right amount of stomach fluttering moments to make your toes curl.

She loves happy endings that require a lot of hope and perseverance to achieve, and believes that all morally grey characters deserve at least one chance to right their wrongs, *maybe two or three*.

She believes there's something special about mixing the sappy and sweet with the dark and dangerous and that there's always room for humor, no matter the circumstance.

She wants to recognize bravery in all its forms, from the quietest acts to the most outlandish displays.

She shares the constant hope of a better outcome and believes in the power of stories to change not only ourselves, but the world around us.

When she's not writing, you can find her curled up in front of the TV with her precious kitty binging Bridgerton episodes or singing along to Disney classic movies.

Visit her website for signed books, character art prints, and special bonuses only available to her mailing list.

Books by Brianne Wik

(read them all!)

The Iridescent Series:

One Iridescent Night
An Evanescent Shadow
A Luminescent Dawn

Arranged Marriages of the Fae Series:

Married by Dusk
(set in the same world as The Iridescent Series)

Available on Amazon

You can connect with Brianne personally at:
BrianneWik.com

Made in the USA
Columbia, SC
23 August 2022

65435824R00221